Feels Like Rain

Feels Like Rain

"Little matches make big fires"

The fiction and true crime reportage of

Edward Anderson

Bruin Books
The Emerald Empire
Eugene, Oregon

Published by
Bruin Books, LLC
April, 2013

Special thanks to Rob Preston, who contributed some rare material from his personal collection. If it wasn't for this book, and my relentless search for anything Anderson, I would have never have discovered that Rob's impressive library of vintage magazines and rare books was only a mile from my house. A very happy turn of events indeed.

My ongoing gratitude to Mr. Tran Việt Húng for the cover art provided by Việthúng Gallery, 90 Nguyen Hue Street, Ho Chi Minh City, Viet Nam.

Cover design by Michelle Policicchio.

The illustrations in this book originally appeared in *American Stuff* © 1937 by The Guild's Committee for Federal Writer's Publications, Inc. The illustration on page originally appeared in Underworld, April 1933.

Printed in the United States of America
ISBN 978-0-9883062-1-9
Bruin Books, LLC
Eugene, Oregon, USA

Visit the scene of the crime at www.bruinbookstore.com

Feels Like Rain

Introduction:

A Brief Appreciation of

Edward Anderson

Feels Like Rain

A brief appreciation of Edward Anderson

Edward Anderson is a wooden match struck in a hay-strewn box car. Sputtering flame lights the shadows of the men rocking against the walls within, putting color in their eyes, reflecting the road-dust in their hair, drawing out their voices—their stories. As the fire crawls down the square stem of the match, close to the fingers that hold it, warming the tips, lighting the palm, we feel something real, and we also know that the dying wooden match is still capable of burning the place down.

His voice was a proletariat spark, an igniter for the masses. Anderson presumed to speak for his generation, the Starvation Army whose faces were gaunt as skulls and whose ribcages, when stripped of their tattered coverings, looked like xylophones hung from boney rails. Just as he found his voice, his narrative, his landscape and the people who would populate it, his artistic output inexplicably fizzled. The match burnt out. It was as if all the creative juices had been squeezed out of him. Most of the work he left behind can be found in this single volume.

For a period of about three years Anderson's writing garnered the attention of the highest literary circles. He quickly moved from pulp fiction to literature with a natural sort of ease, a self-assurance that can only be called brilliant. His authentic stories of dustbowl drifters captured the times in perfect pitch. He was the inheritor of London, brethren to Steinbeck. His work appeared side by side with Faulkner, Wolfe and Katherine Ann Porter. He was compared to Hemmingway by literary critics of the day and was lured by Hollywood like so many other hot talents . . . . but his light burned out so damned quickly. Ultimately he was shunned and left to measure out his days reporting for small town newspapers. He lived long beyond his fame and had to bear witness to his own impotent promise, like the parent who survives his child. Edward Anderson was the great American writer that never quite happened, but what he did leave behind, that teasing muse of the have-not's, should be cherished. He earned a place in our literature.

Edward Anderson left high school in his senior year to become a crime reporter. His first stories appeared in local newspapers, but he soon made a national splash in the exploitive crime tabloids, such as *True Detective* and *Daring Detective*. This early publishing experience is cleverly woven into his most famous novel, *Thieves Like Us*. The narrative picks up as the bandit trio of T-Dub, Chicamaw and Bowie breakout of prison and set out on a crime spree across Oklahoma and Texas. Ducking in and out of hiding only long enough to knock-off their next bank, the bandits follow their own exploits in the newspapers and crime tabloids (but oddly enough they only seem to use the radio to listen to football games and Mexican orchestras). At one point they are confronted by their own photos emblazoned in a national magazine:

> *"You're drunk, man, but you better start quieting down," T-Dub said.*
> *"Old Foxy T-Dub," Chicamaw said. "Old Foxy."*
> *Mattie came in, holding out a magazine. "Maybe this will sober him up some," she said.*
> *It was a True Detective magazine and on the opened page were all their pictures: Oklahoma Fugitives. $100 Reward.*
> *Bowie brushed back. "He don't care about seeing that thing. Go burn that damned thing up."*

Most of Anderson's crime writing centered around New Orleans, his home base at the time. There was plenty of crime to report. He entered the prisons, interviewed the inmates and guards, and took dictation from the District Attorneys and Police Detectives who were hungry for a little tabloid fame. The unexpurgated, gory details of their stories made for fascinating reading. It was a dose of reality that people couldn't get from the cinemas or radio dramas. The cruelty of the human species was on full display, and despite the mythology developed around some of the larger than life criminals—Dillinger, Pretty Boy Floyd, and of course Bonnie and Clyde of the Barrow Gang—these desperadoes were shown for what they were: public enemies.

The story of Henry the Hangman is the chilling profile of a pathological killer. It offers a disquieting twist on the run-of-the-mill crime story. The fact that Meyer was working for the State of Louisiana as its court appointed Executioner is truly unnerving. Anderson's encounter with Meyer occurs in the very twilight of Meyer's career as a professional hangman. We meet Henry just as the rumor of his dying rips through the local community. Henry is seventy-something, bent over by hard drinking, addled and bedraggled, but he is still a willing and able rope-man for the State. Clearly he has an ongoing need to take lives. The image of him lovingly greasing the ropes as he prepares for a hanging, and then slipping on a battered Mardi Gras mask as he climbs the scaffold, is a grotesque reflection of the American judicial system of the 1930's. The article follows both Henry "Tricksy" Meyer and the man he is about to hang, Kenneth Neu, a music-loving, affable young man who was sentenced to death for bludgeoning a hardware store owner. (A gentler take on Neu's character is later seen in Acel Stecker, the protagonist of *Hungry Men*.) By the end of the article it is Neu who evokes our sympathy and Henry who fills us with dread. Anderson's true crime reporting laid the foundation for what was to come later when he channeled all of this nastiness for a higher purpose.

Thieves Like Us is dedicated to his wife, Anne, and a mysterious second honoree named Roy. It is clear to us the supportive effect a wife can have on her aspiring writer-husband, and so there is no mystery in her mentioning, but who was this Roy, and why did he share the dedication with Anne? Although he is never referred to again, Roy was Anderson's cousin and he contributed a significant amount of background to Anderson's novel. Roy gave Anderson the sense of authenticity he desperately needed to lay down his first words. Roy was the McCoy, a hardened criminal serving a life sentence for armed robbery, and best of all, he was kin and more than willing to share his exploits with Edward.

With notepad in hand and a letter of permission from his former employer and current Texas Attorney General, William McGraw, Anderson entered the Civil War era Texas State Penitentiary at Huntsville. After repeated visits with Roy, sometimes with Anne in tow to take notes, Anderson pieced together the fictitious bandit trio of T-Dub, Chicamaw and Bowie. The resulting novel is not just another hardboiled crime story. It has an element of sadness and despair that pushes it into the higher realms of American Noir. Very possibly, it was Anne's presence during the fact-gathering and the actual writing of the story that steered the novel into a different direction, a more tragic and sensitive direction. Grit and reckless desperation are interwoven with tenderness, longing and loss. After all the thieving, drinking and gunplay is over it boils down to plain folk wanting a better life. *Thieves Like Us* is a love story about people who never could love the right way, a grease-fire retelling of Romeo and Juliet. It is a novel with heart, and the sadness it evokes is hard felt. Raymond Chandler declared it the best bandit novel ever written.

The first story in this collection, "The Little Spick," was Anderson's first published story. It is pure pulp, and anyone reading it would have trouble picking it out of the hundreds of other crime stories appearing in the pulps that year. It is the work of a talented novice. The writing is respectable and engaging, but it is an imitation of sorts, something Anderson knew pulp fans would want to read. The story's location, a nameless Mexican border town, would later become an obsession of Bowie Bowers, the ill-fated protagonist of *Thieves Like Us*, who dreams of disappearing into the sanctuary of an imagined Mexico. The two hobo stories that followed "The Little Spick," both appearing in STORY in 1934 and 1935, were something altogether different. They mark Anderson's leap into a higher plane and caught the interest of the more discerning readers of the literary magazines. Based on the strength of those stories, Anderson was invited enter a first novel contest hosted by the New York Publisher, Doran, Doran and Company; a contest he won with his novel *Hungry Men*.

Episodic in nature, *Hungry Men* captures a particular point in American history with beautiful clarity. The writing is authentic, gritty—these are Real People who haunt the wharves and flophouses up and down the east coast. We know that Anderson spent some time of the road "highwaying," and this experience doubtless gives the novel its grist. The ending of the novel is a bit odd, though, and one wonders whether there had been an alternate ending that was tossed into the round file. The oddness comes in the fact that it ends so . . . . upbeat and patriotic. After two-hundred pages of delicious despair our rail-sea Odysseus is lifted up by a random lucky break. Perhaps the ending was warped by Anderson's own new found good fortune. The struggling writer was making good. Regardless of the reason, this was to be last happy ending he ever wrote.

Thieves Like Us, published in 1937, is the culmination of Anderson's artist development. It is his best work. He was never again able to duplicate its success in the remaining 34 years of his life. "Drafted" by Warner Brothers Studio in 1938 on the strength of *Thieves Like Us*, he was not able to make the transition as a screenwriter or idea guy and spent his studio days with his feet propped up on his desk. After leaving Hollywood, he continued to earn a paycheck as a writer but was never to be anything more consequential than a crime-beat journalist, bouncing from paper to paper, 72 in all by some count. His personal life was heading down some dark, twisty paths, too, and it is at this point that we are left with more questions than answers.

Many parallels can be drawn between Anderson and fellow crime writer Jim Thompson (see Appendix B,) but it was Knut Hamsun (Norwegian writer and winner of the 1920 Nobel Prize for literature) who most influenced Anderson's work. Anderson's interest in Hamsun went beyond an appreciation of his writing. Some of Hamsun's unpopular political beliefs began rubbing off on him. Anderson somehow got off-track politically, supporting (as Hamsun did) the emergence of the Nazi Party. Little is known how deeply Anderson became involved in the American Nazi Party, but any inferred connection could only have tarnished his reputation. It is not the purpose of this this Introduction to expose Anderson's personal affiliations, but rather offer it as a possible reason for his 30-year writer's block. It's only a clue. It indicates an unsettling of ideals that may have corrupted the creative process. Most likely it was something else that knocked him off the rails, though, something that plagued many writers in the 20th century: booze.

According to Patrick Bennett, Edward Anderson's biographer, Anderson never drank and wrote; he always worked sober. Admirable as that was, defying the odds of what it took to be a successful writer in America in the 20's and 30's, it may have also limited him, for Anderson's drinking increased as his time in the limelight faded. The more he drank, the less he wrote. As the years passed, his interests drifted further and further from the writer's craft and strayed into peculiar regions, such as the study of Swedenborgism.

Swedenborg was an influential 17th century spiritualist and philosopher who remains controversial today. In defense of Anderson, many famous persons before him shared an interest in Swedenborg's ideas: William Blake, Jorge Luis Borges, Ralph Waldo Emerson, Carl Jung, Immanuel Kant, Honoré de Balzac, Helen Keller, and W. B. Yeats. The association with Swedenborg did not detract from their legacies. Even so, the ideas of a 17th century spiritual loon are far removed from the dirt-poor towns and simple people that formed Anderson's roots. Swedenborg, alcohol and radical politics were dead-ends for Anderson, but they were more a reflection of his diminished talent than the cause of it. We would have to summon his spirit to find the truth. And if such a thing were possible, some séance held in the cobwebby abandons of a backroom speakeasy, I would ask him why he never wrote a novel about Henry "Tricksy" Meyer.

The reasons behind Anderson's decline in literary output are locked in the past. Perhaps his rootless ways, so profound and inspiring in youth, became something more like despair in his later years. His serial job-hopping indicates some possible struggles with social skills. Meeting the grind of a daily newspaper could have sapped his creative energy, just as the plumber's wife has the leakiest faucets in town. I thought about Anderson a great deal while preparing this volume, and my conclusion in this mystery, as banal as it may sound, is that all Edward Anderson needed was a handler, a reliable and relentless literary agent who wasn't afraid to slap the whiskey out of Anderson's hand and see that this talented Young Turk bore down and did the work at hand. Maybe my view will change next week or next year, but it is time to move on and make my view a matter of history.

When you, Dear Reader, think of Edward Anderson, remember this: we can be thankful for those few short years when this self-educated, red-dirt Okie was muse-possessed and produced a compact cannon of sad, gutsy and genuine American writing.

—JE
February, 2013

Stories

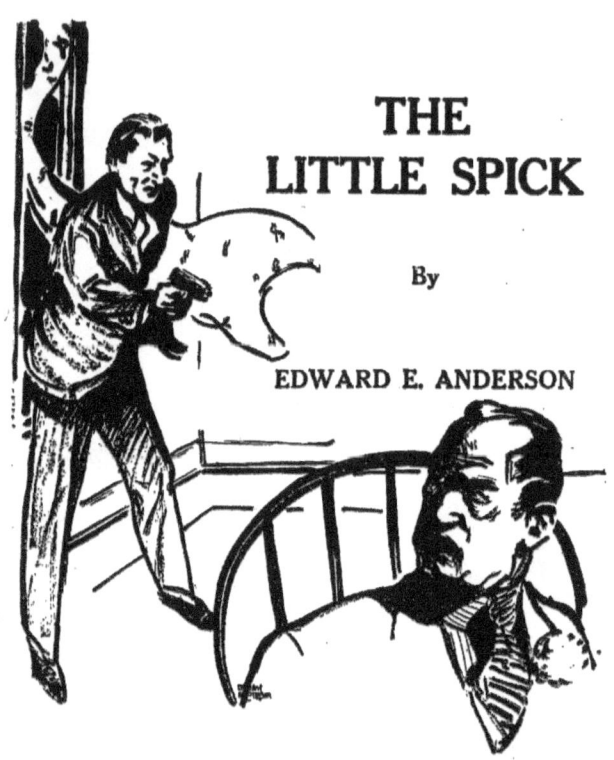

THE
LITTLE SPICK

By

EDWARD E. ANDERSON

A Newshound plays a Hot String

THE LITTLE SPICK

Don Kirkland of *The Border Blade* touched his snapped hat brim in casual salute to the fiscal guards stationed at the end of the International Bridge and sent his small coupé rattling into the broad, resort-lined *avenida* of the Mexican border city of Chavez. The sight of this notorious thoroughfare, its glittering cabaret fronts and revelry-intent throngs, always made something glow inside the American. Stimulated by the colorful atmosphere and the thought of the man he was going to see in a few minutes, shivery, but not unpleasant things happened to his spine. It was not every day that you got a break like this—a scheduled interview with *"The Little Spick,"* secret king pin of the Mexican border underworld!

There was a parking place in front of the small corner bar, *El Gato Negro*, and Kirkland applied the brakes of his machine and began working into parallel position. From here it would only be a block's hike to *El Tivoli*, Chavez' biggest liquor resort and its owner, *The Little Spick*. He climbed out, turned and inserted the key into the door lock. Twisting the key, he became aware of someone behind. He turned quickly, defensively. The small, razor-featured man who blocked the American's way peered up through squinted, insolent eyes. He swayed slightly on his feet and when he spoke his breath was liquor-laden:

"I thought it was you. You're Kirkland, yes?"

The big, blond newspaperman relaxed a little and nodded. He shifted on his feet slightly, watched the other guardedly. Out of the corner of his eye he saw two men standing in front of the bar, peon-looking Mexicans in blue denims and floppy sombreros. They were watching intently.

"Yeah," said the American. "I am Kirkland."

"I am Joe Causiere." There was a significant, sinister edge in the announcement of the smaller man.

"Frenchy, they call me here in Chavez. Frenchy Causiere."

Kirkland's mouth tightened impatiently. "Well, Frenchy, what you got on your mind?"

"Killer!"

Coming from the twisted mouth of Frenchy Causiere it was like the hiss of a cat. The reporter stepped back.

"You even had the guts to write about it," added Causiere, edging toward the other. "Henri. He was my brother. You helped those damned patrolmen kill him!"

Kirkland was edging back slowly and cautiously. The Frenchman was coiling. The American understood now. Two weeks before, United States border patrolmen killed two liquor smugglers in a river battle. Kirkland had been along as a newspaperman, but had been forced to take part in the battle to save his own life. One of the slain smugglers was named Causiere. Kirkland had written an eye-witness account of the fight for The Blade. And now this . . . . this brother here whose face was a network of swelling veins . . . .

"*Ps-s-st!*"

The spit struck Kirkland squarely in the face. Caught unawares by this Latin gesture of contempt and challenge, the American floundered back against his car. Causiere sprang. Kirkland was prepared for physical assault. Longer of reach, he beat the sweep of the Frenchman's knife. His fist drove solidly, expertly, against the other's face. Causiere dropped to the sidewalk like an emptied sack; his knife clattering on the walk.

Kirkland, the knuckles of his right hand tingling, looked guardedly about. The fight had drawn a circle of spectators. Two drunken Americans were counting for the fallen Causiere. Over the heads of the circle, Kirkland could see the two Mexicans in front of the bar. They stood there, staring stupidly, like leaderless sheep.

Abruptly, the reporter parted way through the circle and set out toward *El Tivoli*. Once he paused and looked back. The limp Causiere was being helped to his feet. Kirkland, scowling, wheeled and went on toward his destination.

~§~

The long bar of El Tivoli was jammed with patrons three men deep. Sweating bartenders worked like beefy prize fighters throwing brimming glasses instead of blows. There was no jingle of cash registers, no exchange of money.

Kirkland worked his way through the crush to the rear and into the cabaret. It was packed too. The music, because of the jam of dancers, sounded muffled and distant. He stopped the headwaiter and with the directing nod turned and made it to the short stairway that led up to a palm-screened Italian balcony.

Before the heavy door of the balcony office, Kirkland paused and rapped. The door was opened instantly.

The eyes of the man into which Kirkland looked for the first time at dose range gave him a sudden, poise-shaken feeling. They were not the sort of eyes he had expected in this man. Why, they . . . . they somehow reminded him of the eyes of that revolutionist he had seen, not so long ago, preparing to die before a firing squad. To conceal his surprise, Kirkland blustered:

"I'm Kirkland of The Blade. Are Chris Ricardo?"

The owner of El Tivoli nodded. Then he beckoned for the newspaperman to enter. "It is a pleasure to receive you, Mr. Kirkland."

The office was small and its furnishings suggested a studio rather business room of the biggest owner on the border. With the closed, the office seemed oddly and isolated. Seated, Kirkland deliberately studied his host. Chris Ricardo was a slender, middle-aged Spaniard of less than medium height. *The Little Spick*, he was called on the border. There were little baggy pouches under his eyes. His skin, astonishingly smooth, suggested cream-colored cellophane

"*The Blade* is a good newspaper," said Chris Ricardo as if prompting the visitor to conversation.

"Thanks," said Kirkland. He was taking his time. He was feeling resentful somehow toward this Spaniard who looked as respectable as a church usher. "I came over here," he began at last, "to find out the reason for the big party you're throwing in this place tonight. Giving away your liquor free? It has never happened before on this border. What are you celebrating?"

Ricardo smiled. "I am going out of business."

The reporter lifted his eyebrows in surprise. "Going out of business? Well, I guess the other cabaret owners here will be glad to know that." Secretly, Kirkland was scorning the other's announcement. This celebration tonight was not for anything so ordinary. The words of his city editor, not an hour old, repeated themselves in his memory:

"Now Kirk, you needn't expect *The Little Spick* to tell you the truth. But I'll bet my last dollar that this gesture of his tonight has something to do with those Sand Dune murders. That was the sixth body they found out there this morning. All of 'em were cabaret owners. Ricardo's celebrating because he's got it all his own way over there now. Well, trot along, kid, and see what the old cutthroat will . . . ."

"Yes, I'm getting out of the business," Ricardo interrupted the American's secret mockery. "For twenty years I've been in the game here on this border. It's about time, *verdad?*"

Kirkland cleared his throat jerkily. "What are you going to do? Sell out and go back to Spain or something?"

The Spaniard shook his head slowly. "No, I am going to give it away." A faint, queer smile touched the corner of his mouth. "Then, my friend, I am . . . . am going to die."

Kirkland started. "Die?" he echoed.

Ricardo nodded.

The American laughed, an uneasy, mirthless laugh. "I don't get you, Ricardo?"

The cabaret owner looked at his visitor for several moments intently. When he spoke it was with emphasis on each word:

"The day of the independent resort keeper on this border has ended, Mr. Kirkland. I am an independent and I must leave Mexico or . . . . or end up like those others they found in the dunes."

Despite himself, Kirkland was impressed. "You are talking now about this . . . . this monopoly that we know is working here in Chavez, aren't you? This Mexican form of racketeering, yes?"

Ricardo nodded grimly.

The newspaperman's eyes narrowed and he leaned toward the other in a don't-try-and-hand-me-that-stuff attitude:

"But what's this dope we hear, Ricardo, on our side of the river? That you're ramroddin' this monopoly?"

The owner of *El Tivoli* threw back his head in soundless laughter. Sobering abruptly, he shook his head. "That is what the guides whisper to tourists when they come into my place. It is simply color talk and nothing more."

Kirkland was unconvinced. "Those six they found out there in the dunes weren't *color talk* or suicides either, Ricardo."

"And neither will I be a suicide when they find me

out there."

The reporter was growing puzzled. "Are you telling me that you're . . . . you're on the wrong side of the fence? That you're liable to get it in the neck too?"

"Exactly."

Kirkland exhaled contemptuously. "If you're not the big boy over here, then who is?"

The Spaniard shrugged. "I can only suspect."

"Whom do you suspect?"

Ricardo took his time. Again he studied the American thoughtfully. He leaned a little now toward the other with the intensity of his words:

"Hasn't it ever occurred to you that the deaths of these Chavez cabaret owners have gone entirely uninvestigated by the *policia* here?"

Kirkland's eyes widened. "Are you intimating that the . . . . the police in this town are behind these Sand Dune Murders?"

"They are at least covering them up."

Kirkland's hand went to his blond head in an impressed gesture. He looked at Ricardo closely:

"And you are expecting to get it too?"

"Eventually."

"Well, what do you want to stay here for if you are without protection? Why don't you give Chavez the air and beat it for Spain? You've made enough dough here, haven't you?"

The Spaniard shook his head. "It is impossible now for me to leave Chavez."

"Why? What's to keep you from coming over to our side? You won't be bothered in an American town."

"A passport is necessary to cross your bridge. I am an alien to you country."

Kirkland frowned as if it were his own problem defying solution. "You don't mean to tell me that you can't get out of this town—*you?*"

"I have tried, my friend. Tried with every resource I had. Every move of mine is watched now. In the Chavez railroad station two weeks ago though disguised as a *peon*, I was seized and returned to my ranch. Twice, when I tried to escape by horse over the Chihuahua Trail toward Mexico City I was fired on as a warning. All my efforts to buy or beg my way across the Rio Grande into your country have been frustrated. You see, my life is not desired immediately. My enemies wish to torture me to a point of desperation. There is more at stake than this business. But I choose to die at least with the satisfaction of denying them that."

Kirkland's face was a puzzled scowl. He studied Ricardo. Sincerity and resignation were in every gesture and inflection of the other's voice. Kirkland's jaw thrust out resolutely:

"Are you on the level?"

The Spaniard's eyebrows went up questioningly.

"I mean, do you want to get out of Chavez?"

"We all wish to preserve our lives, my friend."

"I can get you across."

Ricardo started.

"I can put you in my hoopie and in fifteen minutes have you smuggled across that bridge. Those twelve o'clock bridge guards know me. They won't search my car or suspect. Do you want to go?"

The Spaniard had gotten to his feet. His voice trembled:

"Would you do it?"

"If your life depends on you getting out of Mexico, I can dern sure fix that. Passport or no passport!"

Ricardo swallowed. "But if . . . . if the patrolmen on your side should stop us? Will it not be . . . . be difficult for you?"

Kirkland gestured grandly. "Forget that."

Ricardo's eyes shone now with the light of a condemned man who has secured a miraculous reprieve.

"And if we make it," he said in a breathless, excited voice, "perhaps I can get to Galveston. And then a ship. My old home. Spain!"

"Sure," grinned the American. He looked at his wrist watch, frowning. "Let's get some action. It's a quarter to twelve. The bridge closes at midnight!"

~§~

The tall, big-shouldered Kirkland and the little owner of El Tivoli came out of the cabaret and paused on the sidewalk.

Ricardo was bareheaded and coatless. He took his companion's arm and pointed up to the heavens as if indicating a constellation.

"We will pretend we are getting a bit of night air. I am sure we are being watched. We will stroll to your car. We will shake hands as if saying goodnight. You get in and start away from the curb. Then I'll jump in."

Kirkland nodded. "We'll make tracks then for the bridge."

They moved down the street toward the corner of *El Gato Negro* bar in a leisurely stroll. The sidewalks had thinned of revelers. All the traffic was hurrying toward the bridge. Kirkland had the feeling of walking a tight wire. He chuckled grimly. Now what if that wreck of his wouldn't start or something? He'd set a match to it right there!

"I'll have to unlock the door, see?" he explained out of the corner of his mouth. "It'll just take a . . . ." He almost stopped, his voice trailing.

"What is the matter?" Ricardo had stiffened.

"Just a . . . . a friend of mine there on the corner. Name's Causiere. Ran into him tonight."

"You . . . . you talk as if he were dangerous ?"

"Well, I . . . . I don't know."

"You mean the white man there with the two Mexicans? The one watching us?"

"Yeah." The American's lips were compressed. "Don't pay any attention. Here . . . . here's the car."

Kirkland's hand trembled slightly as he inserted the key into the lock and then pulled open the door. He turned after that and extended his hand to the Spaniard, smiling:

"Well, *buenos noche*."

"*Buenos noche, mi amigo*," returned Ricardo. After that Kirkland turned and climbed into his machine. He switched the ignition, stepped on the starter. The car moved a little backwards in reverse and then the American turned the wheels toward the street. He started off, suddenly twisted and pushed out the door. The sweep of his eyes took in the corner. Causiere and his companions had vanished. Ricardo leaped in. Kirkland gave the coupé the gas and it bounded away from the curb.

~§~

Disregarding traffic rules, so alertly enforced in Chavez, the reporter turned his car to the right and started in bumping speed down an alley-like thoroughfare of darkened adobe houses and corner cantinas.

"If I go this way," he explained tersely to his companion, "we'll avoid the crush on the *avenida* and can cut right back into the bridge."

Ricardo, sitting tensely on the edge of the seat, nodded.

The machine bounced and rattled over the poorly paved, narrow street. Kirkland grumbled through clenched teeth at the necessity of slowing down for torn paving stones. His feet were working frantically on brake and clutch like a pilot setting a plane down. Suddenly, the lights of a car behind flashed in the mirror on the windshield.

"Who's that?" Kirkland dared not turn to look. The street ahead was like a shadowed path.

"It's a small car," reported Ricardo.

Kirkland pressed the accelerator farther. Two more blocks now and a turn and he'd be right on the bridge. Then . . . .

The hulk of a parked, unlighted truck reared up

before his straining vision. Desperately, he jammed in brake and clutch and whipped the wheel. The car swerved and then reared like a pitching horse. There was a muffled crunch of wheel spokes and the sharp report of bursting tire. The machine sagged.

Both men struggled now with the door handles trying to get out of the car. A distant, screaming siren sounded in Kirkland's ear. It gave him an eerie, fugitive feeling and he grunted with spurred efforts to push out the sprung door. He paused, breathing heavily and leaned back to kick. Again he heard the siren, nearer . . . . and running, approaching feet.

The door gave with his violent kick. He slid out, feet foremost. There was a rush of shadows about him; rough hands clutched him. The blow at the back of the neck seemed to paralyze his muscles. The shadows, he saw now, were human forms. He heard clearly Causiere's excited command:

"Not here, you two fools! Get him to the car. Not here!"

Kirkland was being dragged away from his car. He had the sensation of trying to swim in heavy seas . . . . seas that roared around him, swirled him off his feet, pulled him down . . . .

The siren, screaming suddenly up on them, was like a torrent of ice-cold water to Kirkland. The lights of a powerful automobile flooded the darkened street.

"*El Capitan!*"

It was the cry of a panic-stricken Mexican. The imprisoning hands left Kirkland as if he has suddenly caught fire. Causiere, wrenching away, growled like an animal robbed of its prey.

The released American swayed groggily on his feet. His would-be abductors had fled. He shook his head like a prize fighter trying to collect his scattered senses. He heard a voice, authoritative and confident:

"I am Captain Burger of Mexico City. It is lucky for you that I saw them after you. I am at your service, *señor*."

~§~

Kirkland turned toward the coupé, a dozen paces away. The voice of the rescuer was directed to Ricardo. The Spaniard sat on the running board of the wrecked coupé, limp and exhausted. Above him stood a man, a herculean figure in military cape and glittering boots. In his hand was a drawn automatic. He bent down now and touched the shoulder of the Spaniard solicitously.

"You are unharmed, señor?"

Ricardo's voice was toneless. "I am unhurt."

"Good," said the officer relieved. "That is good."

Kirkland moved now toward the two, reeling like a drunken man. Captain Burger wheeled.

"Many thanks, Captain," said Kirkland.

The officer seemed to ignore the American's gratitude. He turned back to the Spaniard. "May I help you to my car," he said and offered his hand.

Captain Burger, his arm about the Spaniard, moved toward the heavy, curtained touring car. On its side gleamed the brass horn of a siren.

Ricardo paused at the side of the big machine and turned back to the staring Kirkland.

"Come," he beckoned.

Kirkland, walking steadier now, responded quickly. He climbed into the rear as Burger and Ricardo got in front. As they rolled back over the street over which he had raced so desperately a few moments before Kirkland began to puzzle. He looked at the broad, muscular neck of Captain Burger, the closely cropped Teutonic head. It was odd how this German happened along so opportunely? And Ricardo's hopes? The little Spaniard sat with sagged, beaten shoulders. The American swallowed guiltily.

Captain Burger broke the silence of Kirkland's questioning. "You wish go to your place of business?" he asked Ricardo.

The Spaniard lifted his head with jerk as if stirred out of distant thought. "That will do."

"It might be best if I take you to our home," suggested the officer. Ricardo nodded. "*Esta bien.*"

"And you?" The German was almost challenging as he twisted his head slightly to indicate Kirkland.

"Any hotel will do for me, Captain," replied Kirkland. "The bridge is closed now."

Ricardo turned around. "Perhaps you would like to spend the night at my place? It is near town."

The reporter hesitated. "Well . . . . All right."

Captain Burger threw a reprimanding glance at Ricardo. "It is a bit dangerous, Ricardo, to go about with American newspapermen. Hasn't tonight convinced you?"

The Spaniard made no reply.

Kirkland chuckled in an effort at humor. "But thanks to the Captain here it isn't fatal, eh, Ricardo?"

Neither Burger nor Ricardo answered.

The *hacienda* of Chris Ricardo was situated about a half mile from the outskirts of Chavez. It was a modest, bachelor dwelling place of adobe brick and Spanish architecture. Gnarled and twisted mesquites grew in profusion on its level grounds. Up a narrow, gravelled drive Captain Burger sent the car and stopped before a doorless, stable-like structure at the rear of the house. In the building which served as a garage Kirkland saw a small, cheap truck.

Silently, the trio climbed from the car and moved toward the house, a stone's throw away. Ricardo led the way across the patio and into a long, low-ceilinged living room. The room had a cold, uninviting atmosphere and Ricardo set fire to a tiny heap of kindling in the big fireplace. Burger and the newspaperman edged up to it and held out their hands to catch its warmth.

All three moved about stiffly and unnaturally and presently Kirkland stretched in pretended sleepiness. "Think I'll hit the hay, Ricardo. I have to be away from here by daybreak to get to the other side by seven. Where do you want me to flop?"

Ricardo escorted the American back across the stone-paved patio and then upon a small porch which led into a cell-like sleeping room.

"I will call you early," said the Spaniard. "Do not fear you will oversleep."

Alone now, Kirkland sat on the edge of the blanketed cot, wide awake and thoughtful. Somehow he was regretting that he had accepted Ricardo's invitation to spend the night here. The menace of Causiere, he reminded himself grimly, had something to do with it. It might have been unsafe to spend the night downtown. And this Captain Burger who had rescued them tonight? He was an odd chap. What was he doing here from Mexico City?

Kirkland extinguished the oil lamp. He bent over and began unlacing his shoes. In a few moments he was undressed and between the rough Indian blankets.

Stealthy footsteps on the porch made him sit erect. He watched with taut muscles as the door opened. He relaxed as he recognized the form of Ricardo.

"You must leave," whispered Ricardo. "Burger is going to stay all night. He has framed you."

"Burger?" The reporter slid off the cot to his feet. "Framed me? What do you mean?"

"*Sh-sh,*" the Spaniard hushed the astonished American. "I heard him on the telephone. He is getting word to Causiere. They plan to have you ambushed at daybreak when you start to Chavez."

Kirkland's brow was a network of perplexed lines. "Say, what's Burger got it in for me a . . . ."

"Quiet, quiet," insisted Ricardo. "Burger knows you tried to get me across tonight. Don't you see? Burger is the man I am trying to escape from."

Kirkland was still at a loss. "Why, that guy saved my life tonight."

"Only in order to save mine."

"But why should he save yours? I thought that they wanted your life over here. Why didn't he . . . ?"

"Money," said Ricardo tensely. "Three hundred thousand dollars. The money is why I was not killed weeks ago. They know I withdrew that amount from the bank in Chihuahua. They know I have it concealed. Until they know where it is my life is fairly safe."

"Who in the devil is this Burger anyway?"

"He is an ex-officer of the German army. He was sent here out of Mexico City to investigate the narcotic situation. But he is working on his own . . . . for the monopoly. The police here are afraid of him, protect him. He is the monopoly's killer. The Mexicans here call that touring car of his the *curtained machine of death*."

Kirkland had slipped into his clothes. He felt a key slipped into his hand.

"This is for the truck," explained Ricardo. "Somehow you must get across that bridge tonight. Prevail on your border patrol friends. Take the truck on across with you. And when you are safe let me know. And here . . . . here take this gun."

"But you?" The reporter did not move. "What about you? Here with Burger alone?"

"Do not concern yourself about me now. Burger will not act until he has satisfied himself about the money."

The newspaperman frowned stubbornly. "Say, I hate to go off and leave you like this. You and me were getting to be pretty good pals in a . . . ."

"Go on," interrupted the Spaniard pushing the American toward the door. "Get on."

Kirkland balked again. "Listen, I'm gonna get you across that river if it's the last thing I do. I'm gonna ask Red Phelps to help me. He's a flyer. There's no bridges to cross up there in the air. Just as soon as I get across I'm gonna get in touch with Red. Let's make a date now. Let's set ten o'clock tonight at the airport here. You can make it out there, can't you?"

Ricardo pushed. "Hurry, my friend."

"I'm serious, Ricardo. Promise me. Will you be waiting at the airport at ten o'clock tonight?"

"Yes. Go!"

~§~

Kirkland made sure the mechanism of the truck was set before he stepped on the starter. It was a light vehicle, the cabless kind commonly seen on the border in the carrying of produce. In its rear was a pile of burlap sacks and hung on the picketed sides were several hoops of bailing wire. The response to the starter was instantaneous and in a moment Kirkland had shifted gears and was bumping down the drive and into the road that led to Chavez.

It was a moonless night. A quarter of a mile from the *hacienda*, Kirkland slowed the truck down for a dip and a small wooden bridge. On both sides of the bridge a profusion of mesquite and sage grew. The American sped past it with a relieved shake of his head. It was a swell place for ambush.

Jolting up and down on the truck's precarious seat, Kirkland turned at last onto the now darkened *avenida* toward the International Bridge. Only one resort, he observed, seemed to be open—Big Boy's Bar, just across the street from *El Tivoli*.

Before the closed wire gate of the International Bridge, Kirkland stopped his truck. He jumped down and ran to the gate and shook it. An olive-drabbed figure emerged from the sentry house, peered questioningly toward the other and then approached in an unhurried walk.

"Say, buddy," the reporter greeted the guard, "I'm Kirkland of *The Blade*. I got held up over here tonight and it's important as the dickens that I get across now. You boys all know me around here."

The guard shifted the chew of tobacco in his mouth. He surveyed the reporter from head to toe in a slow, deliberate manner.

"Nuthin' stirrin'."

"C'mon, Cap. Call Chief Ewell. He'll tell you who I am and that it's okeh to let me across at this hour. I got to see a fellow on the other side before seven o'clock. He's liable to be gone if I don't get to him pretty soon."

"If you was the president himself I couldn't let you across." There was finality in the guard's voice.

"Now, listen, buddy. This is a matter of . . . ."

"It's not so long until seven. The bridge will be open then. Sorry." The patrolman turned and moved back toward his sentry box.

For several minutes Kirkland stared after the guard in speechless frustration. Suddenly, his teeth snapped angrily. He wheeled and retraced his steps to the truck. He set off in it with a savage meshing of gears. Smart guy, that patrolman. He had to get hold of Red Phelps. No telling where Red would be if he didn't get him before he got up. And it was certain he couldn't bump around on top of this truck all night.

The light in Big Boy's Bar shone suggestively. Why couldn't he phone Red? There was a telephone in Big Boy's, a private booth. But call Red Phelps from there? The American's tongue went to his cheek with the coupling of Big Boy Kraft and Red Phelps. If Red had a single enemy on the border it was the big Dutch saloon keeper, Big Boy Kraft. And they had been big pals once, Red and Kraft. It was common knowledge that Red had flown many loads of contraband liquor across the Rio Grande for Kraft. And then Red had been arrested. Instead of helping, Kraft had called his employee a fool and a bungler. Red Phelps turned bitter. He made no bones about his intentions. When he went to trial he was going to spill all the lowdown on border smuggling. And Kraft, in reply, had said Red's life in Chavez was not worth a *centavo*.

"Aw, raspberries," Kirkland shouted his fears aloud. Kraft wouldn't be around his place at this hour of the morning. Besides, even if he was, he'd never suspect that Kirkland was calling Red Phelps and asking him to bring a plane to Chavez!

The newspaperman parked the truck parallel with the curb in front of Big Boy's Bar. He seemed to be the only one astir on the whole thoroughfare. He walked up to the saloon's swinging doors and pushed in.

Big Boy Kraft looked up from the pack of cards with which he was toying idly. He was a massive-headed man, beefy in build. He sat alone at a table to the left of the bar.

"Hi, Big Boy." Kirkland struggled for an everyday air and touched his forehead in an airy salute. Kraft's bushy, black eyebrows beetled. "Hi."

Besides Kraft there was another in the bar, a square-featured Mexican bartender who had paused in his work of polishing liquor glasses. He stared now at the early morning visitor.

"Wanta use your telephone a minute," said Kirkland, smiling.

Kraft jerked his head toward the upright telephone on the bar. "There's one."

Kirkland frowned.

"There's the booth if you want it private," added the Dutchman.

The reporter went to the booth. Kirkland was more annoyed than alarmed. What was that squarehead doing in his joint at this hour? He closed the booth door carefully, lifted the receiver. In a few moments he had connection with the American operator on the other side of the river. He gave Red's hotel number and then looked through the glass of the booth. The bartender was busy with the polishing cloth again; Kraft was toying with the cards.

"Ye-ah?" The high-pitched, boyish voice of Red Phelps burst in Kirkland's ear. He turned back to the mouthpiece:

"Hey, Red. This is Kirk."

"Ye-ah. What the hell you want?"

"I got some flying for you to do."

"How much dough is in it?"

"Don't worry about that, kid. I got a pal over here, see? He's got to get across. No passport. I want you to air over here in that Thunderbird tonight. Set down at ten o'clock. At the Mex airport. It's a matter of . . . ."

"Can't do it," cut in Red. "It just can't be done."

"What's the matter?"

"I'm gonna be in jail then."

"Jail?" Kirkland's lips went closer to the mouthpiece.

"Ye-ah, don't you remember? My trial. Starts this morning at nine. My bond ends then. It'll be bars for me at least until the trial's over." The flyer laughed mirthlessly. "Maybe a helluva lot longer than that."

Kirkland grimaced. "Well, that puts me in a nice fix."

"It's just that way, Kirk, old boy," said Red regretfully.

"You was our only hope, Red."

"Well, you know me, Kirk. If there was any way in the world to help I'd . . . ."

"Say, Red!" Kirk was griping the receiver in fresh emotion.

"Ye-ah?"

"How about right now? I think I can do it. Can you get out to the field and get your ship over here by daybreak. We got about an hour and a half. Can you?" Kirkland had spoken as if he was using his last lungful of air.

"Well, I . . . . I . . . ."

"C'mon, Red. For crying out loud!"

"Good Gosh, Kirk. This is smuggling. I'm already in it up to my neck. If I got into another jam they'd put me so deep in the stout house my whiskers would turn white."

"This is to save a man's life."

"But, Kirk . . . ."

"What do you say, Red?"

"Okeh. I'll shoot the wad!"

"The Mex airport at daybreak?"

"There with bells on!"

"'Atta boy, Red."

"S'long, Kirk."

Kirkland threw the receiver on its hook; wiped the sweat from his dripping brow. He turned quickly and shoved out of the booth. What he saw then made him stiffen, made the color start ebbing from his face . . . .

Kraft still held the bar telephone in his hands. A mocking leer curved his heavy lips.

The reporter swallowed. "You . . . . listened ?"

With a slow, tantalizing movement Kraft returned the telephone to the bar. Facing Kirkland again he leaned back against the bar's edge, crossed his legs confidently:

"You are indiscreet, Kirkland, for a would-be smuggler."

The American's lips compressed. "You cut in on me." There was a steely edge in his voice.

The saloon keeper grunted. "Red Phelps has guts. Does he think he can come over here and live to testify against me in that trial today?" Kraft's fists began to close.

Kirkland's heart had given a sickening lurch at the sound of his friend's name, but when he spoke his voice was controlled:

"I'm going to use your telephone again, Kraft. The one on the bar this time." The American took a step toward the other. Kraft stiffened. The Mexican bartender stood directly behind his employer, watching the newspaperman intently. "Just move over," continued Kirkland in a low, level voice, "while I . . . ."

Big Boy Kraft acted exactly as had anticipated. His right hand moved toward his hip in an easy confident sweep. The lightning draw of the American took him unawares. His gun hand halted as if stricken by paralysis. The Mexican's had dived under the counter. It up . . . . flaming . . . .

Kirkland's gun exploded once . . . . thrice. Firing at the bartender, it seemed to that the other's face flickered as if on a misty screen. There a crashing of glass; the thump of a collapsing body behind the bar.

Kraft stood in stunned terror, his right hand still in that crooked, paralyzed position.

"Out that door, Kraft!" Kirkland's command had the ring of steel. He stepped to the other, prodded him savagely with the gun. *"Pronto!"*

With Kirkland at his back Kraft made it to the door and out into the street. The *avenida* was still deserted. The American jabbed the saloon keeper again:

"Get to that truck. Behind the wheel. You're gonna drive."

Kraft heaved his huge bulk up into the driver's seat. Kirkland was beside him in a bound.

"Shove off!"

The truck moved away from the curb.

"Turn to the right there. Yeah. You know where Chris Ricardo's place is. That's where we're going!"

~§~

Captain Burger grunted with irritated gusto and pushed his chair back from the chess table. The stiff collar of his military jacket was opened and revealed a black, bushy mat of hair. He twisted his head now to look at the small ivory clock on the mantel of Ricardo's sleeping room:

"Four o'clock," he observed fretfully.

"We've almost made a night of it," nodded Ricardo. He was gathering the chessmen. "I'm afraid I have you bested in chess, Captain."

The officer scowled. "I'll grant you that." He rose to his feet and began working his shoulders as if to ease the stiffness.

The Spaniard went on removing the chessmen, placing them in neat rows in a lacquered box. The German was studying the bowed head of the other now with thoughtful, intent gaze. At last he cleared his throat:

"I want to ask you something."

Ricardo lifted his head, his eyes widening in mild expectancy.

"Why did Kirkland leave so suddenly tonight? Why did he not wait until morning like he planned?"

The Spaniard shrugged. "Who knows?"

"You mean you let him have that truck of yours and don't know for what reason he left so suddenly?"

"I do not question my friends, Captain."

The scowl deepened on the officer's forehead. When he spoke it was with blunt challenge:

"Did you know that I used your telephone tonight?"

Ricardo rose to his feet. He looked directly into the other's eyes. "Yes."

There was a flicker in Burger's eyes like light across the blade of a knife.

"You heard me then?"

"Yes."

Tiny lines snaked from the corners of Burger's mouth in an ironical smile. "It looks like we're getting to the point where we can throw pretense aside and get down to business."

"It is well, Captain, that the American left. Harm to him would not have gone uninvestigated on this border. The *policia* could not cover that up."

The officer smiled mockingly. "If anything had happened to Kirkland it would not have gone uninvestigated. His murderer would have been arrested at once by Captain Burger of the Mexico City Secret Service."

Ricardo's mockery matched the other's. "Alas, the clever captain has been foiled."

"In that perhaps, Ricardo, but not in the main purpose of my being here."

"No?" The Spaniard was almost exultant.

"No!" The officer took a menacing step toward the other. "No, Ricardo. I've beat about the bush long enough here tonight. I'm telling you pointblank what I want. Three hundred thousand dollars!"

The Spaniard shook his head in mocking triumph. "You have been cheated in that too."

The officer's eyebrows beetled. "Cheated?"

"Like Frenchy Causiere, you have been cheated."

"What do you mean?"

"Causiere was cheated of the American's life tonight, you of three-hundred thousand dollars."

"What are you telling me?"

"When the American left here tonight, Captain, he took with him what you seek . . . . the money."

Captain Burger's face suddenly became a vicious mask. "You toss that very casually. As if it . . . . means nothing to you."

"It means something to me. It gives me decided satisfaction."

"But your life, Ricardo?"

"Is the captain ready now to . . . ."

Burger lunged. The hastily drawn automatic in the Spaniard's hand spat. The older man had not been swift enough. The German, unharmed, was upon him. The weapon was shaken from Ricardo's grasp. Like a wrestler hunting for a fatal hold, Burger's python-like arms enveloped the other. There was a popping sound as the Spaniard's neck muscles protested the killing pressure of a headlock. The veins of his white forehead began to swell, stood out now like purple, crawling worms . . . .

The barking exhaust of a laboring machine made Burger release the other. He jackknifed erect, ears straining. It was the truck . . . . coming up the drive!

Ricardo lay on the floor, gasping.

Burger looked quickly about. On the mantel was a silver pitcher. From his pocket the officer took a handkerchief. He stepped to the mantel and plunged it into the pitcher. With the dripping wet cloth he bent down the Spaniard and began soaking the death-white face.

~§~

The fingers of Kirkland's right hand had grown numb with the vigilant grip on his gun. He shifted it to his left as Kraft stopped the truck in the gloom of the *hacienda* garage. Lights and motor were cut.

"Now, Kraft," warned Kirkland, "I don't want to hear a word. I'm going to tie you up. That's all." The reporter edged to the corner of the seat, thrust out his foot to feel for the running board . . . .

The world seemed to heave to Kirkland. Kraft, with a desperate intake of breath, had taken a chance. The reporter found himself hurtling headlong to the ground. His gun went flying. He broke the fall with his hands. The other was upon him like a smothering blanket, a blanket that kicked and stomped in a violent assault. Kirkland rolled and twisted up to a half-sitting position. He clutched frantically at the booted, punishing feet. The Dutchman's knee caught him under the chin and sent him sprawling back. Again the American rolled and he came up this time on his elbows. Spinning on his elbows he made a rigid sweep with his legs. The blow cut Kraft down like a scythe. The saloon keeper struggled to rise.

The more agile Kirkland was on his knees, fists cocked, seeking to distinguish Kraft's jaw in the wavering shadow. He made it out and drove with his left. It missed. All his strength was in the following right. It collided. Kraft collapsed with a grunt, knocked cold!

Kirkland lost no time. From the truck's sides he yanked

down coils of bailing wire. Clumsily, but effectively he bound the legs and arms of the unconscious Kraft. After that he stuffed his handkerchief in the other's mouth and bound it.

The American looked toward the house. Still no one seemed to be aroused. He grasped Kraft's arms and pulled him to a sitting position. He bent down, placed his shoulders under the Dutchman's midsection and heaved. In a few moments he had Kraft in the rear of the truck, covered with burlap sacks.

Kirkland set toward the house in a run. In the patio he halted. There was a light in Ricardo's room and toward this the American moved cautiously.

At the door, Kirkland hesitated. Then his jaw set determinedly and his hand moved toward the knob . . . .

The light released by the room's suddenly opened door splashed about him. He drew back instinctively. In the doorway stood Captain Burger. For moments the two men stared at each other in startled surprise.

"Where is Ricardo?" asked Kirkland at last.

"In here," replied Burger.

Again they studied each other. Suddenly, Kirkland stepped forward and brushed past the officer. At sight of Ricardo he stiffened. The Spaniard lay back in a chair, his feet out-stretched lifelessly. His eyes, looking up at the American, were two sunken pools of despair.

Kirkland wheeled on Burger. The officer stood stiffly, his hands clasped behind him.

"Heart attack," he explained.

Kirkland's eyes returned to the Spaniard. On the floor he spied the automatic. Outside, a cock lifted its heralding cry of nearing dawn. Ricardo stirred and when he spoke his voice was like a melancholy rise of wind:

"I was not expecting you back tonight, Kirkland."

"I could not get across the bridge," replied Kirkland.

Burger's hands fell to his sides. "You have not been on the other side tonight?"

"Of course he has," cried out Ricardo struggling to a sitting position. "Of course he . . . ."

The officer's harsh laughter cut the Spaniard short. "I don't think so."

Kirkland stared bewilderedly at first one and then the other of the men. He jerked violently with Burger's sudden movements. The officer had sprung to Ricardo's chair, bent down and then jackknifed erect with the automatic in his hand. He leveled the weapon on the reporter:

"Pretty tough isn't it, Kirkland, to be on this side of the river with three hundred thousand dollars."

The reporter stared at Burger as if he saw an insane man.

"Don't look innocent, my friend," the officer shook his head derisively. "Ricardo talked too soon. His little joke hasn't turned out right." He looked toward the Spaniard. "Cheated did you say, Ricardo?"

"I am at a loss, Captain," protested Kirkland. "You are talking of something that I know nothing about."

"If you left here tonight with this man's money," said Burger in a level voice, "and never reached the other side it seems to me that the money would still be in Mexico."

Kirkland shook his head, confused.

"Now let's not haggle, Kirkland. You left here with

three hundred thousand dollars. Ricardo told me. I want to know where it is?"

Kirkland shook his head in a gesture of helplessness. "I repeat, Burger, that I . . . ."

"I am not a patient man!" Burger's neck seemed to swell.

Ricardo raised his head. "I thought we had agreed, Burger, that harm to an American is not a trivial affair. Even if he did not get across tonight it is certain that friends of his have been informed."

The officer smiled contemptuously: "You are warning me with three hundred thousand dollars at stake?"

"Kirkland here does not know where that money is any more than you," said Ricardo.

"No?" It was Burger's last mocking word. His mouth set grimly. He held the gun now in a steady bead on the American's chest. "It is too bad then, Kirkland," he said in a hissing, murderous voice. "It is . . . . just . . . . too . . . . damned . . . ."

"Burger!"

Ricardo was on his feet in frantic appeal. "Burger, listen. I will tell. You may have it. It is in the truck. Under the seat!"

Burger relaxed slowly. To Kirkland that slow diminution of threat was like the recoiling of a giant snake that had struck once and missed and was now . . . .

"Lead the way to the truck, Ricardo," commanded Burger abruptly. "You too, Kirkland. Follow him!"

Outside, the darkness of night was receding. Kirkland walked stiff-legged behind Ricardo. Burger breathed heavily in the rear.

"Show me," rapped Burger as Ricardo halted beside the truck. The Spaniard stepped upon the running board and began to pull and tug with the seat. He breathed raspingly with his efforts and in a moment had the cushion lifted. He pushed it aside and reached down into the opening underneath. Presently, he raised erect and in his hands was a metal box. With this he turned.

"Put it back," commanded Burger.

Ricardo obeyed.

"Start the motor," ordered the officer. The motor was soon running. "Get down," yelled Burger. Excitement was in the officer's voice and movements now. "Get back you two. To the house."

Brandishing his gun, the officer leaped into the truck.

Kirkland and Ricardo moved backwards toward the house. The truck was going down the drive toward the Chavez road.

Ricardo stared after the truck in stunned defeat. Kirkland suddenly clutched his arm.

"Let's get," he cried. "Red Phelps is going to sit down out there at the port in a half hour. There's Burger's car. We can get away in it!"

Ricardo did not move.

"C'mon," cried the American desperately. "C'mon. We can't lose time. Kraft is in that truck. Burger mustn't find him. Hurry, man!"

The Spaniard shook his head. "Escape means nothing to me now. I could not stand to be a penniless refugee in your country. I am an old man."

"But Red is going to be there!"

"And you had better not leave at this hour, my friend. Causiere was to wait for you at daybreak down there...."

The clap of gunfire made them both jump. It came from the road .... the little wooden bridge. There was a crashing sound; then bloodcurdling Apache-like yells of triumph. The shouts ceased abruptly. Kirkland and Ricardo listened with straining ears. Moments passed. Then the coughing motor of a starting car; the swift meshing of gears. The machine was moving toward Chavez. It was the truck!

Kirkland spun on Ricardo.

"Causiere," said the Spaniard. "It was planned for you. Maybe . . . ." Ricardo was suddenly in action. He bolted for Burger's machine. Kirkland pounded behind.

The truck lay on its side where it had plunged off the bridge. One of wheels was still turning in a dying spin. Kirkland and Ricardo leaped into their car and ran onto the bridge.

"Burger," cried Ricardo in discovery. He pointed to the body lying off to the left, partially concealed by the gully brush. The head was twisted grotesquely. The Spaniard scurried to the truck's seat. Kirkland was investigating the truck's rear. Ricardo shouted exultantly with the treasure box in his hands. The American muttered. Kraft was gone!

Ricardo took the wheel. In a moment they were speeding in the wake of the assassin's machine. Kirkland's heart churned in rhythm with the motor that was hurtling them toward the flying field. He spoke aloud his ears to the grim-featured Ricardo:

"Causiere found Kraft. They're going to the airport."

His companion was too busy driving to reply.

"It's Red that Kraft wants bad,'" continued Kirkland. He made a mirthless, chuckling sound. "And he wouldn't mind having me now as second choice."

"It was Kraft that Burger phoned tonight," said Ricardo. "Burger was working for Kraft. It is Kraft who has corrupted the police here."

Kirkland swallowed as if his throat was sore. "But maybe Kraft was back there in the brush, thrown where we couldn't see him? We didn't look very close."

"Possibly," helped Ricardo.

~§~

The Chavez flying field stretched before them on a far-reaching, wind-swept mesa. Kirkland's eyes swept the field which was being revealed in the light of breaking dawn. He nudged his companion's attention. At the far north end of the field near the darkened airport hangar was parked a small sedan.

"Go to the south end of the field," directed Kirkland. "Red would come in that way to set down."

Skirting the field's rim, Ricardo sent the heavy machine skimming toward the south. At its end he turned and followed the edge to the middle. Here he stopped. Kirkland leaped out and threw his eyes upward. There was only gray, veiled skies and low, tumbling clouds.

Ricardo cried out in warning. Kirkland followed his

pointing hand. Away from the airport buildings the sedan was moving . . . . toward them!

The American and his companion watched the approaching sedan, fascinated. The car was moving slowly forward in low gear. Its occupants seemed to be uncertain. It stopped. A figure climbed from it, a short, slender man; another, a beefy bulk. They stood at the side of the car, waiting.

"It's Causiere and Kraft," said Kirkland and turned to the Spaniard for confirmation.

It was not Ricardo's confirming nod that made Kirkland's heart suddenly begin to pound like an overheated motor. It was a drone . . . . a drone in the skies!

The American looked upward. The drone grew louder . . . . louder. Abruptly, it faded . . . . roared again . . . . faded. Kirkland gulped.

"Red! He's gettin' ready to set down!"

Motor throttled, a two-seated bi-plane had dropped out of the early morning mist and was diving for a landing at the southern end of the field.

"Kraft and Causiere!" Ricardo's fresh warning made Kirkland turn his eyes toward the sedan. The sedan was advancing again.

The wheels of the biplane were bumping on the field in landing. Kirkland raced toward it.

"Go on, Red. Don't set down, Kraft. Go on!" Kirkland had the sensation of trying to cry out under water.

It was all lost to the flyer. With despair Kirkland saw the ship halt, the helmeted Red Phelps slide from the rear cockpit. The reporter threw a look back. The sedan was less than a stone's throw away. And Ricardo? Ricardo was leaving . . . . in the touring car!

Red was at the side of the stricken Kirkland.

"Where's the passenger? Let's air!"

Rooted, Kirkland stared at the two automobiles. Ricardo had turned the big car around . . . . heading toward the sedan.

"Say," cried Red. "What we hanging around . . . . Gosh! Those cars. They're going to . . . !"

"Crash!"

The noise was like the thundering clap of a sea storm's spray against the broad amidships of a vessel. Panic-stricken screams of imprisoned men were cut short in a rending, terrific collision. Chris Ricardo had driven the powerful touring car headlong into the light sedan!

The two Americans, still rooted in amazement, stared toward the debris. Escaping steam from torn radiator gave the wreck a slight smoke screen.

Kirkland gulped. "Ricardo got 'em," he said in an awed voice.

"Was he the guy we were going to hop?"

The reporter nodded reverently.

"The guy in the big car may not be bad hurt." Red Phelps' hopeful observation set Kirkland in action. "C'mon Red," he cried and broke into a run for the wreck. Red was at his heels.

The two machines lay twisted two strange animals in a fatal struggle. The nose of the larger car had ploughed into the other and then topped it. The sedan was a prison for its crushed occupants. There was no movement of life about the wreckage, only the hissing of the radiators.

They found Ricardo crumpled in the bottom of the

seat. The two Americans worked swiftly. In a moment they had the unconscious Spaniard extricated. Making a pack saddle of their hands they started with him toward the plane.

Suddenly, Kirkland halted. "Take him on to the ship, Red. I gotta go back. Get on with him!"

Kirkland raced back to the touring car as Red made it on to the plane with Ricardo. From the automobile the newspaperman retrieved the almost forgotten treasure box. In another moment he was speeding back toward the plane like a football player with a clear field ahead.

The biplane skimmed the like a pursued quail and rose into air with scarcely a waver. In the forward cockpit sat Kirkland with Ricardo in his arms.

The drive of the wind felt good in his face. He shifted slightly to ease the burden in his lap and arms. Ricardo stirred, opened his eyes. Kirkland bent over and shouted exultantly into the other's ear:

"Everything's okeh, Rick. Everything."

—Underworld, April, 1933

THE GUY IN THE BLUE OVERCOAT

When the brakeman's heavy feet thumped on top of the boxcar, the Kid and the guy in the blue overcoat down in the refrigerator hole stood up fearfully. The clumping stopped and then the brakeman's bristly face was framed in the crack. "Aw right, you punks, up outa there."

The brakeman stood on the gray gravel of the roadbed and waited for them to get down the rungs. He had a club in his hand. When they were on the gravel, the brakeman said: "Now don't you try to get back on this train. Both of you. I don't mean maybe."

The Kid and the guy walked at the edge of the roadbed down the train toward the town. The gravel was loose and their feet would slip. The sides of the right of way ditches were covered with wild berry vines. The Kid looked, but there were no berries on the vines.

The Kid thought about the guy walking along with him. If you hadn't stuck your head up out a there that brakie wouldn't have seen us. You've balled things up for me now good. Kicked off in this place and no tellin' when a man can get a train outa here again. I'd of been in St. Louis in the morning like I was planning on if you hadn't of stuck your head up.

They passed the caboose. "That's that," the Kid said.

"I wish we hadn't got put off," the guy said. "I wanted

to hurry and get on."

"I didn't ask to be put off myself," the Kid said. "You shouldn't have stuck your head up."

The guy did not say anything.

The face of the guy in the blue overcoat was dry and gray like school tablet paper. His eyes were red-veined and deep in their sockets as if they had been pushed in. He had climbed into the reefer with the Kid back in Little Rock in the night. At first the Kid had welcomed the guy for company because he had been riding all night by himself. The other had talked a lot. He said he was twenty-three and it was the first time he ever rode freight trains; that he had driven a car for a man out to California and the man was supposed to pay his transportation back to Cleveland, but he didn't. The guy was getting back to Cleveland the best he could.

"Looks like a pretty good-sized town up there," the Kid said.

"I don't like to go into towns," the guy said.

The Kid decided he would not say anything more to the other.

I don't want this kind of a guy for a buddy, he thought. Afraid of his own shadow. When you meet up with a real fellow on the road its O.K. to have a buddy and split fifty-fifty with him, but not a guy like this. Him twenty-three, too. When I'm twenty-three I'm not even going to be on the bum. If I don't have a good job then I ought to be on the bum.

They neared the depot. Long fruit express cars were lined up alongside the loading platforms. The wooden platforms were the color of washed-out mops. Workmen stood on top of the fruit cars and packed ice into the holes. Their voices carried far and clear in the morning air.

The Kid felt at his watch pocket. The quarter was still there all right. He was saving the quarter until he got to St. Louis. When he got to St. Louis he was going to find one of those places where you got hot cakes and syrup for a dime and spend the other fifteen cents besides. All night when he was not sleeping he had thought about how he would spend the quarter. I don't care if I am stuck here, even if it's a week, I'm not going to break this money until I get to St. Louis, he thought.

Of concrete blocks, the depot was the color of rust. A baggage-man was rolling a truck down the platform and when he stopped the Kid asked him when the next train was leaving. The baggage-man said a manifest was going out at four in the afternoon. It stopped to pick up a string of fruit cars. It was a hot shot to St. Louis.

The Kid felt good about that information and went ahead and held the depot door open for the guy to catch up with him. They went through the station and stopped on the outside and looked across the street up into the town. The paralleling street was like the hump of an ant bed and into Main Street people were pouring. It looked like Saturday, but in this Arkansas town the strawberry season was on.

The Kid moved across the street and the guy followed him. A girl in a white sailor blouse and black cotton hose was preaching on the corner. She had a heavy Bible in her hand and when she slapped it she almost dropped the book.

Looking at the girl, the Kid thought she didn't have much build on her. He started to say this to the guy, but then he remembered he was through with him. He left the group of spectators and went over and stood in a cleared space on the sidewalk next to the hardware store. The guy came on over.

"Well, I guess we'll start digging up something to eat," the Kid said. "You can take one side of this Main Street and I'll take the other. That side over there looks good to me. There's a bakery right up there. You can have that side. It don't make any difference to me though. You can have this side."

"It doesn't make any difference to me," the guy said. "I can just go along with you and wait outside."

"Naw, that's no way to do. A man ought to bum by himself. When they see two of you together you can't get nothing. You just go in and tell them you're broke and hungry and they'll put out something. Which side do you want?"

"It doesn't make any difference to me. Where am I going to see you after while?"

"I'll be around here somewhere," the Kid said.

Up the Main Street the Kid went, and he did not look back. He was not going to do any bumming. When he had money in his pocket he could not bum. I just can't do it when I got money on me, he thought. I'll bum the dickens out of them when I'm busted, but I don't feel right going in a place and bumming when I got money on me.

At the next corner the Kid turned to the left and went down an unpaved street. Just beyond the vacant lot on which were wagons and unhitched teams was a white frame cafe that looked like a big box. In the window was lettered a sign: STRAWBERRIES AND MILK, 5¢.

The Kid's eyes lingered on the sign, but he went on. No sir, I'm holding onto this dough. I'm gonna hold onto it until I get to St. Louis just like I planned. I don't care if I'm here a week.

At the end of the street which was crossed by a road like a T was a wood of pine trees. It was a free tourist camp. He entered the grove. The carpet of leaves were springy to his feet and he had the sensation that the ground might give way and he would go up to his knees in the carpet. He went on through the woods and crossed the cement highway which split the camp like a bright ribbon. On the other side of the highway were a half dozen parked automobiles with tents at their sides. In front of one automobile, which had a house built on the back, sat a girl in a red dress and an older woman. The Kid went on a little beyond them and sat down at the foot of a tree. He sat there and looked toward the highway because he did not want the girl in the red dress to think he had just sat down there on account of her.

The girl was bare-legged and had on boy's oxfords. She was eating peanuts. She would let the hulls fall into her lap and after a while stand up and brush them off and then sit back down and start eating again. The older woman had on a man's rope sweater.

The Kid thought about how he would like to get acquainted with the girl. It would pass the time away until four o'clock when the manifest left. If the old lady got her hat and went off to town and the girl stayed behind? I'd go over there. I'd go over and say: "I see you're from Texas. I noticed your license plate. I've been all over Texas. I've been in Fort Worth and Houston and El Paso."

He thought about what would happen if the old lady left and he went over to the girl. The girl smiled and told him to sit down. She reached out and filled his hand with peanuts.

"Mama and me are traveling by ourselves and we sure do need a man. We need somebody to drive this car and get up the firewood and do things like that."

"It don't make any difference to me where I go. I'm just running around."

"I wish you would come with us. When mama comes back I'll tell her that you are going with us. We sure need a man."

"I'm just running around and I'd be glad to."

The girl got up and smiled. "Would you like to see how we got it fixed up inside the car?"

"I'd like to."

The girl led him back to the rear of the car and he followed her up into it. It had a bed and everything. The girl closed the door and they sat down on the bed. His hand went out and lay on her bare leg and then he kissed her.

"I've been wanting somebody," she said. "I've been so lonesome and I saw you over there and I wished you would come over. I was wishing I had some . . . ."

The guy in the blue overcoat stood there. "I found you," he said. "I been looking everywhere for you. It's lucky I found you."

"What's on your mind?"

The guy was excited as if he had seen something happen down in town. "I found a place where we can eat. I mean it won't cost us anything. I was walking around and come right up on it. I know right where it is. It's a mission and they got signs all over the windows telling you to come in and eat. I can go right straight to it."

"Why didn't you go on in?"

"I wanted to get you. I wanted somebody to go in with me and I started looking for you."

"You can go on."

"When you see it though you'll want to go in. There are signs all over the windows. I looked for you just especially."

The Kid looked back toward the car. The girl was gone. Just the old lady sat there. "You will be glad you come," the guy said. "Just wait until you see it."

What if I jumped up and took a poke at you, guy, the Kid thought. You're just messing things up for me right and left. Here I was about to meet that girl and you come along and now she's gone. I'm warning you, guy, that I can take just so much.

"You will be glad when I show it to you," the guy said.

The Kid got up and the other started off like a dog eager to lead the way. He fell back in a moment, though, to walk at the Kid's side. "I want to tell you something," he said. "I know you won't believe it, but I want to tell you something. I haven't eaten nothing since I left Dallas. In Dallas I ate in the Salvation Army, but I haven't had nothing since I left Dallas."

"Godamighty," the Kid said. "That's a thousand miles

from here. That takes a man three or four days."

"I knew you wouldn't believe it, but that's the truth. The funny thing is I'm not hungry. That's the funny thing. Of course I can tell I haven't eaten anything, but I'm not hungry. Just hot inside. If it was not for just being hot inside I couldn't tell it."

"I wouldn't go that long without eatin'. It's not good for a man."

The guy pointed ahead down the street. "It's just right down yonder. Right around that corner. It's not far."

The glass front of the building was painted white and lettered with signs: YOU ARE WELCOME . . . . STEP IN . . . . WE FEED DAILY.

"I told you," the guy said and he went up and grasped the knob. But it did not turn. He turned stiffly and looked at the Kid.

"Rattle it," the Kid said.

The door opened and a man stood there. He had a long face. It looked like a big capsule. He looked them up and down and then said: "You fellers come back tonight. Maybe we'll have something then."

"That sign there says you give something to eat," the guy said. "It says on the signs there."

"Come back tonight."

"Look there, mister, at the signs. What's the idea of having signs? It says there."

"C'mon," the Kid said. "Let's go."

"I told you to come back tonight," the capsule head said.

"What did you leave home for? I can't help it if you're

running around the country."

"What's that sign there for," the guy said. "You son of a bitch. What you got signs for? You bastard."

Capsule Head looked scared. "I'm gonna have the law down here on you in just a minute. You can't talk that way . . . ." He closed the door.

The Kid was going up the street fast, but the guy trotted and caught up. "It was there on the signs," the guy said. "I don't care. They ought not to have signs if they don't mean it."

"You've played hell," the Kid said. "You can't go around cussing people. That guy is calling the law. You can bet on that. I'm gettin' out of this town myself and I'm not waiting for a train. I'm hittin' the highway. The law is going to be after us, you can bet on that."

The guy did not say anything.

"We better split up," the Kid said. "You better go one way and me the other. They'll spot us quicker if we're together this way. You can bet the law is after us. I wouldn't be a bit surprised if I was in the can tonight. It wouldn't surprise me one bit."

"I don't care," the guy said. "I'd just as soon be in jail as not."

"Well, I care," the Kid said. "You get that straight. I care."

The guy was silent.

The Kid walked faster and faster. It'd be just my luck to land up in jail in a dump like this, he thought. It'd have a jail just about like that one in Shawnee. Stink like that one and have a plank for a bed with bugs on it. They'd feed you a sandwich of fat bacon at ten o'clock and soup

at six. I got this quarter, though. I could get a chocolate
bar every other day. It'd be just my luck for them to have
a smart jailer here and he wouldn't get the chocolate bars
for me.

Down the street the highway glistened. The guy
panted behind the Kid.

Oh, you don't have much to say now, the Kid
thought. Oh, no. Now that you're getting us in jail, you
don't have much to say. What do you keep hanging
around me for? You're twenty-three and can't take care
of yourself.

They reached the highway and went down it about a
half mile and then the Kid stopped at the Ozark Trail
marker. There was no traffic on the road. The Kid sat
down in the shade of the marker and then the guy sat
down.

Diagonally across the highway, a half block down,
was a lumber yard and a grocery. The side of the grocery
had been papered with circus posters and they were
broken and hanging. The lumber yard was the color of
goldenrod and its windows were trimmed in white. In the
yard two men were loading small lumber on a wagon.

I'd like to be working in a lumber yard, the Kid
thought. I'd go to the show twice a week and buy me at
least two detective story magazines a week.

The guy was sitting there in his overcoat with his
knees under his chin and staring across the road.

"Why don't you take that overcoat off?" the Kid said.
"I'd smother to death."

The guy took the overcoat off.

The Kid looked across the highway toward the lumber yard. I'm not his buddy, he thought. If I was his buddy, it'd be different and a man has a right to pick out who he wants to be on the road with. I never did go that long without eatin'. Godamighty, that's a long time. If I was working in that lumber yard over there I'd have money in my pocket on Saturday night and I'd go and get that girl in the red dress and we would go to the circus. But I'm not his buddy. Oh, Christ, I guess I might as well do it. I guess I might as well . . . .

The Kid held up the quarter. "Look, what I found."

The guy looked.

"That's what I call lucky," the Kid said. "Just looking down and picking up a quarter. That's what I call lucky. That means we eat. You know what it means, don't you? That means you and me are going to get something on our stomachs besides air."

"You are lucky," the guy said.

"I can stand to eat now myself," the Kid said. "That's what I call lucky. I tell you what, you go get the grub. I'll give you this quarter and you go over to that grocery store yonder and get the grub. I could eat a snake's head. I'll wait here and you go get the grub. How does that sound to you?"

"I don't mind."

"I'll bet you're pretty good bargainer, aren't you? I tell you what, when you get the beans and the bread you tell the guy to throw in a couple of onions. I'll bet he will do it all right if you ask him. All you have to do is ask him. He'll do it all right."

The guy nodded.

The Kid watched the guy cross the street. The guy

carried the coin in his clenched right fist. That guy hasn't got no guts, the Kid thought. I'll betcha he won't get nothing but just the beans and bread. He won't ask for onions. I'll feel good after I eat. I always feel good when I go a pretty good while and then eat. When we eat I'll say to him: "Well, bud, I'm going on up the highway and you can stay here. Or you can go up the highway and I'll stay here. We never will get a ride together. You can . . . ."

The touring car with the flapping curtains drove up alongside the Kid. There was a man at the wheel in a cowboy hat. "C'mere boy," the man said.

The Kid hurried to the car. The man was a bull all right. He had a gold badge on his blue serge vest.

"Where you going?" Gold Badge said.

"St. Louis."

"Where did you come from?"

"Well, I was in Little Rock last . . . ."

"I didn't ask you that."

"Oh, you mean where my home is. It's in Bovina City, Texas. That's where I was raised. I see now what you mean."

"What were you doing up town while ago cussing a man? What do you mean by doing that?"

"No sir, Mister. I wasn't cussin' nobody. You got the wrong feller, Mister. Honest to God, I wasn't cussin' nobody. That's something I won't do."

"You're lying like a dog."

"Honest to God, Mister. All I'm doing is trying to get to St. Louis. I think I'm gonna get a job there and go to work and that's all I'm trying to do. Honest to God, Mister."

Gold Badge grinned. "All right, boy. You got a good face on you. I'm going to let you go this time." The Kid grinned.

A whistle came from across the highway and Gold Badge turned in his seat and he and the Kid looked toward the grocery. On the porch a man in a white apron was beckoning excitedly. Gold Badge started his car and turned in the middle of the highway and headed for the store.

The Kid stood there and looked toward the grocery. Something has happened over there, he thought. I'll betcha I've lost that quarter. I'll betcha a hundred million dollars I've lost that quarter.

The Kid started across the highway toward the store. I don't have no business going over there. I'm lucky that that bull let me go and here I am going over there and sticking my nose into something else. Something has happened though . . . .

The guy in the blue overcoat was lying on his back on the floor with his eyes closed. There was blood on his mouth and chin. His beard looked dark against the bloodless skin.

The bulky man in the white apron looked like he had been stuffed into his shirt and breeches. "No man can call me a son of a bitch and get away with it," he said. "I don't take that off no man."

"This your buddy?" Gold Badge said to the Kid.

"No, sir, he's not my buddy."

"Don't you know him?"

"I just picked up with him this morning. No sir, I don't know him."

White Apron got a wet towel and Gold Badge began to wipe the guy's face. There was a loaf of bread and a can on the floor near the guy's out flung hand.

"I'd hit Godamighty hisself if he called me that," White Apron said. "I don't want customers like that kind. Put this quarter back in his pocket. He's off or something, that fellow is. He must be off."

Gold Badge opened the guy's shirt and put the wet cloth on his chest. "This must be the one I got a call on. He must be off. I guess he oughta be watched in jail awhile."

"No man can call me that," White Apron said. "I was just kidding him and he just puffed up right now. Why, I was going to give him the onions. But he just got puffed up right now. I'd hit Godamighty hisself if he called me that."

"I'll take him to jail," Gold Badge said.

The kid cleared his throat. "I know what's the matter with him, Mister. What he . . . ."

The guy on the floor opened his eyes. For a moment he looked like he was tired and wanted to go back to sleep again, but then his eyes saw the Kid and they fastened.

Oh God, the Kid thought. He'll be getting up and wanting to go with me. He'll get up and start wanting to go with me.

White Apron went over and started helping the guy to his feet. The Kid went out the door. He jumped off the porch and started walking up the highway fast. He felt like somebody was reaching out to grab him in the seat of his pants. He went on past the highway sign and broke into a trot. He's got the quarter. A man can buy a lot with a quarter. He can buy some candy. I wouldn't mind going to jail if I knew I was going (to have some money to spend. You're not having such tough luck, guy. I wouldn't mind it myself.

Along the highway the heat glimmered up from the paving. It's like there was a fire underneath the paving up there, the Kid thought, and the heat is coming right up through it. It might blow up just as I get up there. I'd sail up hanging onto a hunk of the paving and when it got up as far as it was going I'd let go. I wouldn't come back down as hard if I let go. No guy, you got that quarter. You're not having such bad luck.

—Story Magazine, October 1934; later selected by Robert Penn Warren for A Southern Harvest, 1937, an anthology of contemporary southern fiction.

BARE LEGS

Hooker thought about what happened to the six Negro hoboes down South. Two women got into a boxcar and now the Hot Seat was coming up for that bunch.

It was chilly and still dark, but Hooker raised up from his bed and covers of packing paper. The boxcar door had been closed during the night. There was a crack and it was coming daybreak.

He looked toward the corner where the woman and the man had bedded down last night. It was pitch black.

The track bed was smooth and the car swayed rhythmically over the gnawing trucks and wheels. Hooker lay down again. This won't last long though, he thought. Pretty soon it will start bouncing like hell . . . .

Yessir, if I was taking a woman on the road with me, I'd pack a blackjack. Something. He's lucky I'm the only one in this car. There could be a dozen bums in here. I wouldn't want no woman of mine sleeping in a car with a bunch of bums.

Nossir, you can't expect no private boxcar, Bud. Not on the road. You got in here after I did. Yessir, I'd pack a piece of lead pipe or something and the first bindle stiff that even looked like he wanted to, I'd let him have it.

When Hooker awoke again it was daylight and the wheels were grinding and clashing as if they were going to tear up through the flooring. He sat up. The boxcar door was open and the woman, standing near the edge, was a silhouette in the gray morning light. Hooker jerked his head. The man was sitting in the end of the car where they had slept. His back was against the car's side, his eyes on the woman.

Hooker fumbled in his breast pocket for tobacco. The woman had on a brown beret and a man's double-breasted gray coat. The skirt was of red plaid flannel and it was short. Her legs were bare, the calves straining in the spiked-heeled shoes.

Hooker's fingers were numb and stiff. The inhaled smoke seared his lungs, burned his empty stomach.

The woman turned, smiled and touched her mouth with two stiff fingers and blew imaginary smoke. Hooker nodded and got up.

Her mouth was lush and soft like an overripe tomato. It worked in another smile as he handed her the sack. There were hollows under her eyes. The buttoned coat strained over her breast.

Hooker held the match for her and then, suddenly, he turned and looked toward the man. He went toward him with the sack extended.

The man shook his head. He was smaller than the woman. His face was the color of wet, packed ashes and pitted with stubble. He had on new, blue coveralls.

"We made plenty of miles last night," Hooker said.

"They told me in that division she was a hot shot and she sure is."

Ash Face nodded. He was looking at the woman again.

The din of the moving car heightened and Hooker shouted: "I'm ready for it to stop myself. I could take on something to eat."

Ash Face nodded and drew his knees closer under his chin. There were two suitcases beside him, new and cardboard-looking.

Hooker went back to his place and sat down. The damned hillbilly, he thought. The damned little hick. If you don't want to talk, that's O. K. with me. If you don't want your woman bumming smokes, get them for her yourself. You're a hell of a man anyway. Letting your woman ride a freight.

The woman sat on the door's edge, her legs dangling. The thighs moved under the flannel.

The train moved slowly up the grade. It seemed to be plowing through the high, moist embankment.

I'm looking out this door, see, Hooker thought. If I was in this Car by myself I'd be looking out the door and I can't help it if your woman is sitting there. And she isn't so bad, if you want to know it, Old Boy. I don't blame you, Baby. I'd burn smokes too and work that mouth. That hillbilly sitting over there like a I-don't-know-what.

Hooker started rolling another cigarette. He studied his shoes. They were good kicks. Ten dollars. The corduroy trousers. The leather jacket. That's one thing about me. I never look like a bindle stiff. I keep up a front and I don't burn tobacco from hoboes.

The embankment disappeared as if it had been hacked away with an axe and now the train was paralleling a highway that raced smooth and sharp like a knife blade.

Road signs popped up, vanished. We're getting into a town, Hooker thought. He got up and started toward the door. To hell with him. I always go to the door when a town is coming up.

He stood above the woman, grasping the door's edge and peering ahead. It was a good sized town. A division point . . . . The hairs on her legs were black and coarse.

Hooker sat down beside Bare Legs. She leaned toward him:

"You know the name of this town?"

"Must be Raton."

"Raton."

"Don't take my word for it, though."

"I've heard of this town."

"First time out this way, uh?"

Bare Legs nodded.

"Towns don't make no difference to me. One is just as good as another."

"They do to me. The sooner we'll be in California."

The speed of the train suddenly slackened. "She's going to bump," Hooker said. "Watch it, Kid."

He got up after the cars bumped. They were entering the railroad yards, passing strings of sided cars.

"So long, Kid," Hooker said. He jumped from the car.

The train crawled on. Hooker kept his eyes on his feet and the chalky rock of the road bed. She liked me.

The train stopped and Hooker halted too. The air brakes under the cars began hissing as if in exhaustion after the long run. Let them get out and get on way to hell ahead of me. I got off, you hillbilly, like I'd get off any train and don't get any ideas in your head that I'm following you. I'm staying right here until you get way on ahead.

Feet crunched in the gravel and Hooker looked up. They were coming toward him—Ash Face, carrying the two grips; Bare Legs and the Railroad Bull.

"Down that way," the Bull said. He pointed with his stick toward a weedy path that ran into a ditch and under a fence to the highway.

Bare legs started down the path with Ash Face behind.

"I got a printer's card, Mr. Officer," Hooker said. "Would you mind telling me when the next train leaves West?"

"Four o'clock," the Bull said. "But I don't want to catch you in these yards. If you catch any trains, catch 'em outside the yards."

Bare Legs and Ash Face were standing under a locust tree near the highway.

"I heard you ask him," Bare Legs said. "When is the next train?"

"Four o'clock," Hooker said. "That Bull was O. K. The thing I'm going to do now is hoof it over to the other side of town and catch it when she leaves the yards."

"I hope we can catch it," Bare Legs said.

"All you gotta do is get on," Hooker said.

Ash Face sat down.

"Well, good luck, you folks," Hooker said. "I'm going to town and see what I can stir up to eat."

"Goodbye," Bare Legs said.

Hooker did not look back. To hell with them. I would have given them my tobacco and helped them get a feed. That damned hillbilly. That guy's neck. I could snap it between my thumb and finger. Just like that . . . . I'll swear to God I could. Just like that . . . .

After fifteen minutes in the Quality Print Shop, Hooker emerged with two half dollars. One of the printers in there and he knew a couple of the boys in Little Rock, they found out.

At the newspaper office, the superintendent told Hooker it might be a good idea if he showed up for the morning paper that evening and put his name on the extra board. A special edition was coming up and a good ad man might pick up a few days' work. Hooker said he would show up and the superintendent gave him a dollar to get something under his ribs.

Hooker spent one of the dollars in a grocery. Beside the groceries, he got two sacks of Bull and a pack of tailor-mades.

Just off the railroad property on the west side of the town was a small stream and along its tree-shadowed banks were the blackened cans and flattened ashes of old hobo jungles. Bare Legs and Ash Face were alone.

"You folks found the right place all right," Hooker said.

"I just hope we catch the train," Bare Legs said.

"I got a break uptown," Hooker said. "I got more grub here than I know what to do with. I was wondering what I was going to do with it."

"You look like Santa Claus," Bare Legs said.

Hooker placed the sack on the ground and ripped it open. "Did I bum that town or did I bum it?"

"Bacon," Bare Legs said.

"You folks are welcome," Hooker said. "I'll stir up some firewood."

Bare Legs looked at Ash Face. "Don't sit there like a bump on a log."

Hooker got a dead branch and came dragging it back. "I knew there would be something," he said. "I forgot bread. I just happened to think. And no salt either. That's the kind of guy I am."

"That's all right," Bare Legs said.

"I won't hold up the deal long," Hooker said. "We got plenty of time. There's a store about a half mile up there and I'll get it."

"No, you won't," Bare legs said. "You rest." She looked at Ash Face. The Sunlight made the veins in his thin nose look like tiny, live wires. "I'm going to cook this and you're going to go and get the bread and salt too."

"It's all my fault," Hooker said. "Won't take me a half hour."

"He's going," Bare legs said.

Ash Face started down the road.

"Listen, Lady," Hooker said. "This is no business of mine, but that man didn't like that."

"He makes me sick."

"I guess he's got some change on him?"

"I don't know whether he has or not."

"How's he going to get that stuff?"

"Let him worry about that."

Hooker looked after the figure growing smaller down the road.

"How long you two been married?"

"I didn't have no sense. I was just a kid."

"You haven't been doing this long. Traveling this way?"

"He's got some folks out in California. Run a dairy. That's what we were doing in Berwyn. On a dairy. Two miles outside of Berwyn. I was sick of that place."

"He's crazy about you."

"I can't help it. I've told him a thousand times if he didn't like it he could lump it."

Hooker sat down. "Cal's a good place."

Bare Legs sat down. She brought her knees up under her chin and pressed the flannel down and clasped her hands under her thighs.

"I don't guess you ever trifled on him?" Hooker said.

Her lips parted and she smiled loosely. "I've had a boyfriend or two."

"I'll bet you have too."

"That's what he thinks I want to go to California for. There was a kid back in Berwyn who's in California now. As if I would see him in California."

Hooker picked up a small, dry stick and began to tap it on his leg. "I guess you were crazy about that boy all right?"

"I wouldn't say so much as that. He was all right."

"I'll bet he was plenty crazy about you."

"What makes you say that?"

"I'll bet any boyfriend you ever had is still crazy about you."

"Don't kid yourself."

Hooker watched her take off the coat. The breasts moved and swelled under the green jersey.

"Jesus," Hooker said.

She eased back, planting her hands palm down on the grass.

"What's the matter?"

"You'll never know."

"You're just a kid," she said. "I'll bet I am older than you are."

"Don't kid yourself."

She looked toward the road. Her lower lip hung.

"You're sweet," he said.

She kept her eyes on the road.

He edged toward her. "Sweet."

"He'll be back," she said.

"It's a mile. I'm telling you. It'll be an hour."

"You better be careful."

"Sweet," he said.

"You better be careful."

"Sweet . . . ."

~§~

Hooker snatched wood near the road's edge. I got to have a fire going, he thought. I got to at least have the fire going.

Bare Legs lay lazily on the grass and watched him break the sticks and I arrange them into a heap. "What's your hurry?" she said.

"We got to have coffee," he said. "Christ, I don't even have a can. Now I got to go look for a can."

"Where you going?" Bare Legs said.

"I got to find a can."

He looked for the can. Why in the hell doesn't she get up and do something. Laying around there.

Sitting up now, she watched him approach with the can of water. You better be looking the other way, Hooker thought. You better be letting that old man of yours see you looking for him.

"Hello," Bare Legs said.

"Hello," Hooker said. He knelt down and held a match to the twigs. The smoke came up and dug into his nostrils. "Goddamn it," Hooker said.

"I'll bet you've said that to a hundred girls," Bare Legs said. "Sweet."

"No, I don't," Hooker said.

"I was just thinking."

Hooker stood up and looked toward the road. "Your husband ought to be getting back."

"He'll be back."

"I should have given him a piece of change."

"Don't worry about him."

"It's not so easy. Bummin'. I got a racket and it's easy for me. I should have given him a piece of change."

"Maybe I'll see you in California," Bare Legs said. "Maybe we'll run into each other out there."

"Sure," Hooker said. He looked down at her. The bare ankle looked tough and wrinkled under the cake of dirt. "This water never will boil," he said.

"It'll boil."

"What would he do?" Hooker said. "I mean if he had come back a while ago?"

"I don't know."

"You mean to say you have lived with him as long as you have and don't know what he would do?"

"I don't know."

Hooker heaped more wood about the fire and steadied the can. I'd have popped his neck, he thought. I wouldn't have given him a chance. I would have beat him to it.

"Yonder he comes," Bare Legs said.

Hooker looked. It was Ash Face all right. "For God's sake," Hooker said, "don't start fussing with him or anything."

"He's got something to drink," Bare Legs said.

Ash Face was smoking a cigar. He dumped the sack on the ground.

"Where did you get it?" Bare Legs said.

"Town," Ash Face said.

"A drink never hurt no man," Hooker said. "That's a fact."

Ash Face pulled a can out of his bosom. "Wanta drink?"

"Hell, yes," Hooker said.

"Old woman?" Ash Face said.

"You go to hell," Bare Legs said.

Ash Face squatted on the ground. He started spreading a soiled, moist handkerchief on the grass.

"Wait a minute," Hooker said. He extended a clean handkerchief.

"Dirt never hurt nobody," Ash Face said. He dug his

fingers into the waxy substance.

"God," Bare Legs said.

"Dirt never hurt nobody," Ash Face said.

"Let's dig into this grub," Hooker said. "That's what it's here for. Ain't that right, Bud? Liquor is to drink and food is to eat."

"Eat," Ash Face said. The alcohol dripped as he squeezed the handkerchief.

Hooker looked at Ash Face's bent head. "I'm going to town," he said.

"What for?" Bare Legs said.

"There's not enough here to go around. I feel like I'm crashing the party not having my own liquor. I'm going to town and get a armload."

"What for?" Bare Legs said.

"When I decide I need a drink I need it," Hooker said. "They ain't no stopping me. That's the way I am about it."

"You're going to miss that train is what you're going to do," Bare Legs said. "It's' after one now."

"Don't think I'll miss that train."

"You're going to fool around and miss it."

"I'll be on that train. I'll catch it in town if I have to. I can snag a train like a brakie. I'll grab it and I'll have a arm full of heat. When she rolls by I'll be on her and don't nobody think I won't."

Bare Legs got up.

"So long," Hooker said. "I'll be seeing you folks pretty soon."

He walked briskly. When he was down the road a good piece and the trees hid him, his head went up and down and he made laughing sounds. Yeah, I'll be on that train. Just like President Roosevelt will be on it. Yeah, just like hell I will. Yeah, everybody watch me get it.

The overhanging trees of the residential street made a cool tunnel. At the intersections, the sun was penetrating and warm. What I need is a bath. There ought to be a two-bit barber shop bath in this town. I got a buck. That would leave me six-bits.

After the bath, Hooker went and sat on a bench on the courthouse lawn. There was a box-like cafe across the street and on its windows were lettered short orders: *Chili, 15¢. Soup, 10¢. Two eggs, any style, 15¢.*

The face of the young waitress was as clean and smooth as the whites of Hooker's eggs. She had on a heavy, gold wedding ring. There was a man in the kitchen.

I would like this, Hooker thought. He's lucky. A wife and a little eating place and a few dollars a week to spend.

Hooker sat on the courthouse bench again. The clock in the tower indicated: *3:30.* Two men in soiled overalls lay in the shade of the building with newspapers over their faces.

I will go up to that newspaper office around six, Hooker thought. "Glad you showed up, Hooker. Pull off your coat. Forty-two bucks a week and it's steady."

I'd drop dead if he said that. I'd drop dead if I got a job again.

Down the street two blocks the railroad tracks glittered like thin wires. There was an edge of the Spanish stucco station. That was where the freight would pass at four.

Hooker started rolling a cigarette and one of the men who had been sleeping in the shade came over. He was a bum all right.

Hooker handed him the sack. "When did you get in?"

"Last night." The bum's eyes were rimmed with coal soot. "And the only reason I'm not out of this town is because there's just one freight going west a day."

"There's going to be one right down there in just a little while."

"I know. Me and my pardner's been waiting."

Hooker watched them. A little way down and the one who had the cigarette gave it to the other.

She will be on that train, Hooker thought. Don't think I don't know she didn't fall for me. I could have had her as long as I wanted. Don't think I don't know it.

The two bums paused and the cigarette exchanged fingers again.

That *derail* with her. I ought to get a load of canned heat and keep him stewed up until he don't know which end is which. Keep him canned-up all the way to Cal, by God.

One of the two bums stopped an old man with a cane. The old man handed out a tobacco pouch and the other bum went over and they began rolling cigarettes.

She was O. K., Hooker thought. I got to hand it to that kid. She'll be looking for me. It's a shame to disappoint the kid like that. I got to hand it to her. That mouth . . . .

The courthouse clock gonged. Hooker stood up. It was four.

You haven't got no sense, Hooker thought. Not one lick. He was walking rapidly toward the crossing.

The locomotive whistle sounded. You have lost your mind, Hooker thought.

The engine lunged from behind the stucco depot. Hooker ran. The cars were rattling across the intersection.

He reached for the rungs, clung and the jerk shocked his bone socket. Up the rungs he climbed. On top he lay flat down, head buried in his arms. Cinders spattered on his head. I got you. I got you. She was going like a bat, Bud, but I reached out and grabbed me an arm full and hung on. It was in a jerkwater town over in New Mexico—

He peered through slitted eyelids ahead. No one on top toward the engine. He looked behind. There was a sitting figure on the next car. He had on goggles.

Why don't you lay down, Hooker thought. That's the way to get us thrown off.

Goggles got up and jumped the cars and came spraddle-legged toward Hooker. You damned punk. You're going to get us thrown off. Walking the tops like you owned the train.

Goggles sat down. He was a kid. "You got a match?" he shouted.

Hooker handed him a match. "Lay down," he said. "That's the way to get us thrown off."

Goggles lay down.

Ahead, the locomotive whistle whined. There was a country crossing and a small trestle clicked underneath.

Goggles shouted: "You didn't see it happen back there in the yards?"

"See what?" Hooker said.

"You caught it up town, that's right," Goggles said.

"Yeah," Hooker said.

The speed of the train lessened. The first stop and I'll climb down, Hooker thought. I'll run back and find an empty. If they're in it, I'll just say hello. If there's anybody else in the car I'll buddy up with them. She'll bum me for a cigarette. I'll let her make the first step.

The train was stopping.

Hooker looked at Goggles. "What she doing, stopping?" His voice sounded flat in the quiet.

"Holes up here for a passenger," Goggles said.

"Did you notice any empties?" Hooker said. "I'm gonna get off and get me one."

"A gondola. I saw a guy throw a woman out of it back yonder. She went right under the wheels."

"Threw what?" Hooker said.

"Just before you got on. She come running for the train and this guy was right behind her. She climbed up in the gondola with us and that guy threw a hunk of coal at her and then she tried to get out of the car at the end and he pushed her off. I saw it every bit happen. One of her shoes come off before she went under and she didn't have no stockings on."

"That happened," Hooker said.

"I got out of that gondola myself. Most of them stayed. That guy pushed her off. I'd swear that to God. They stopped the train and a bull came and took that guy and a couple of the bums. That guy was crazy. She just went right down under."

The train stopped.

Goggles moved toward the rungs. "You wanta look for an empty?"

"I think I'll just stay here," Hooker said.

—*June, 1935, Story Magazine*

Novels

Hungry Men

1: THE STARVATION ARMY

The weak bubble of the mission's water fountain and its flat, swimming-hole taste washed away the dull satisfaction that had been Acel Stecker's on reaching the free shelter.

He straightened slowly, wiping his mouth on the shoulder of his corduroy jacket, and looked around him with a smoldering hostility.

The afternoon shade was lengthening into the baking side street. Bums sat on the curb, their backbones arched like drawn bows; squatted against the mission's scaly walls, dragged aimlessly around in that calloused weariness that men of the road know. Some of them had that faded clean lines that the dark washrooms of flop houses give, but there were others, like Acel Stecker, with lusterless, blood veined eyes to which the cinders and dirt of freight-train travel still clung.

The eyes of the man approaching the fountain were watery, as if overflowing with the soup he had consumed, and his face was dry and brown like a crust of begged bread.

Acel moved aside for him and, watching, saw the

shoulder blades push up the sweat-streaked denim shirt in two sharp ridges. Flabby lips hid the bubble and made animal noises in drinking. Acel turned away . . . .

The damned lice, he thought. There's no getting away from them. They're the same everywhere. In Denver and El Paso, Pittsburgh, Los Angeles, Atlanta . . . .

A man with a raw, shaven face came up and squinted at Acel uncertainly. "Ain't you the guy I saw on the *Bullet* outa Portland about two weeks ago?" he said.

Acel nodded. "I came out of Portland. I remember you now. You're the A. B. I was talking to."

The seaman brought out a Prince Albert tobacco can and shook two cigarette butts out of it into the palm of his hand. "You didn't stay over in Baltimore, uh?" He extended his palm, and Acel took the shorter of the butts.

"I didn't have a chance gettin' out of Baltimore. Those tankers were just taking on company men, and their discharges couldn't be more than six months old."

"Well, you've hit a no-good bastard now," the seaman said.

"Washington?"

"The bonusers put this town on the bum."

"I heard this was a good town."

They went over and sat down on the curb. The seaman had a naked woman tattooed on his forearm. He began to clench and unclench his hand, and they watched, abstractedly, the suggestive wriggling of the tattoo's belly.

"So this town's no good?" Acel said.

The seaman let his arm drop. He said that yesterday he had lost his buddy. The buddy had put the bing on a plainclothesman on the capitol grounds and was in jail now for panhandling.

"I just hoofed it out to the end of Pennsylvania Avenue and put the bum on a priest out there," Acel said.

"Didn't you have any luck?"

"Not the sweat under his arms."

They watched the peanut vendor work his cart against the curb across the street. The vendor took three bags and arranged them on the cart's top.

The seaman said he had been staying in the mission for a week. He was trying to get a pair of shoes. "You got to do a nose dive," he said. "You know what I mean. Go up in front while they're singing and kneel down and let 'em pray over you. I haven't done it yet, but I think I'll do it tonight. There's a Jew here that's got shoes and breeches, and he come here the same day I did."

A line began forming at the entrance, and the seaman told Acel they were registering the new transients and he'd better get up there.

The man at the registration desk had a bleached, womanish face. He wrote with a stub of a pencil and screwed up his mouth when he crossed letters.

There were eight men ahead of Acel in the line leading to the desk. I don't mind this registering business so much, he thought. I gripe out on the road about having to go through all this red tape for a bowl of soup, but I don't mind this so much. I guess it's because I like to have somebody ask me questions. It's an illusion that somebody is interested in me personally. Who is interested in me? The government. That's because I am a social menace. That's being something, anyway. But that old belch there doesn't care who I am or where I slept last night. Maybe that's why I lie like I do. I'll tell this old boy I'm a prize fighter. I was a dishwasher in Columbus.

"What is your name?" the registrar said.

"Acel Stecker."

"How old are you?"

"Twenty-five."

"Religion?"

"I don't have any."

The registrar looked up, and his lips tightened. "You have to have one to stay here."

"Make it Protestant, then."

~§~

Dusk veiled the mission street. It shadowed the road-seared faces and blurred their shabbiness. Men moved closer together and talked more boldly and laughed. Down on the corner the portable organ was groaning in a street service preliminary to the services that were to be held in a few minutes in the mission.

Acel was directed to a bench on the left of the altar, a place designated for the transients spending their first night in the shelter. He sat there and held the soiled hymn book in both hands.

The preacher was a tall man with long jaws on a bony neck. The hollows under his jaws could pocket golf balls. He smiled now and patted the hymn book in his hand. "It is good to sing, brothers. Let's turn now to that old favorite, '*He Lifted Me.*'"

A boy in a torn white shirt sat next to Acel. He nudged Acel now and exhibited the hymn title to which he had scrawled: *into a Mission.* Acel winked in mock gravity and looked back up at the preacher.

On the platform in a wide half-circle of yellow, cane-bottomed chairs sat a dozen men. They were men of middle ages and with coats and trousers that matched, and some of them had watch chains across their vests. After the first song the collection plate was passed, and these men were the only ones who dropped coins.

The boy next to Acel sang in a falsetto tenor and then in a croaking bass. He would look up to Acel from time to time for approval. The man on Acel's left held the last note of each verse as if he wanted to convince everyone he was singing.

After the singing the preacher read from the Bible: "And he would fain have filled his belly with the husks that the swine did eat; and no man gave unto him."

I ought to listen to this sermon on the prodigal son, Acel thought. Time would pass by quicker. But I've heard this sermon a hundred times.

"I know, brothers," the preacher said, "that some of you out there may think that you do not have much to be thankful for, because you do not have jobs or money—at least I don't have any money; but what I want to tell you is that you do have something to be thankful for. You do have something to be thankful for. You have the chance to accept Him."

The man with the yellow shoes and white cotton socks seated at this end of the half-circle said, "Amen."

"No man in this world can ask for more than the opportunity of accepting Him," the preacher said. "He will provide, brothers, and all you have to do is place yourself in His hands and He will take care of you."

I wonder what kind of husks the prodigal son wanted to eat, Acel thought. Were they the kind of husks that tamales are wrapped in? I don't see how a man could eat them . . . .

With the sermon's conclusion the preacher invited member of the gathering desiring special prayer to come for war while the gathering sang, and kneel down before the altar. "I want you to come down and feel Him in your heart," he said. "Don't be ashamed in the presence of God. You must stand before Him some day, and then you must be able to say, 'I accepted You on earth, Lord.' Come forward brothers, while we sing, and get down on your knees before Him."

Men got up and lurched noisily forward. They bumped into one another in their haste to take kneeling places before the altar. Acel looked for the seaman, but he was not among the nose divers.

After the special prayer the kneeling men were told to rise, and then they were directed to sit on a bench at the mess-room entrance.

The preacher was less solemn now. He moved lightly about on the platform and smiled again. "We have some visitors with us tonight," he said, "some men who have honored our little house of worship with their presence."

The men in the cane-bottomed chairs sat more erect. Yellow Shoes blew his nose.

"These men, I am proud to say," the preacher said, "are Christly men, men who walk in His footsteps. I am going to call upon them to say a few words to you, and let me tell you out there, brothers, that you are in for a treat, because these men here can tell you out of their own experiences just what He means to you."

Yellow Shoes came forward. He had the poise of a man who had talked to many gatherings like this and pretty soon was gesturing like the preacher.

"Brothers, I want to tell you that I'm a man forty-eight years of age and a happy man, and what I want to tell you is that for forty years of my life I lived in the darkness," Yellow Shoes said. "Now you wouldn't do that, would you? Live forty years in the darkness like a blind man? But that's what I did, and all the time, brothers, I could have lived in the light. I don't mind confessing to you out there that I was a drinker of whisky once. I caroused around, and I thought I was having a good time, and all the time I was living in the darkness. I didn't know what it meant to be happy, but, brothers, I finally saw the light. It was eight years ago the fourteenth of last month and, brothers, I want you to know that He can show you the light, too."

"Ah-men," the preacher said.

"Glory to God," the man in the chair next to that vacated by Yellow Shoes shouted.

"And I don't want you to miss forty years of your life like I did," Yellow Shoes said. "Don't live in the darkness. Don't deny yourself the great good He can give."

"Ah-men."

"Glory to God!"

Acel stared at the floor, his arms folded across his chest. The kid was sharpening his knife on his shoe again. It's after ten o'clock now, Acel thought. Now there goes another up there to spout off glory-to-god stuff. The bastards. Do they think anybody here wants to hear that stuff? Can't they find anybody else to tell it to, besides a bunch of bums who came in here to get something to eat and a place to flop? A little singing is all right, and a little preaching don't hurt, but this is carrying it into the ground. Now there's another one gettin' up. The bastard. There ought to be a law against this. Gentlemen of the jury, is this right? Look at this, gentlemen of the jury. This is the case of Hungry Men against Men Who Live in the Light. See yonder gentlemen, the closed front door. That means no bum is going to enter this place now because he hasn't paid the price of listening to these holy men. Observe the holy nose divers there. Why did they trot up there and get down on their knees? Don't bull me. It wasn't for salvation, but to be first in the soup line and maybe get a pair of shoes. What do you call this? Isn't this forcing religion down throats that want soup? Religion is for full bellies and for men who can drop coins in a plate—

It ended at last, like night rides in the Rockies; like tunnel and searing cinders; as all hardships of the road end.

They were handed bowls of navy-bean soup and three slices of bread. They ate standing at long, plank tables, swiftly and ravenously, and lifted tin bowls to their mouths to get the last half-spoonful. Then they bolted, like fugitives into the street.

The youth in the white shirt and black bow tie announced to the cluster of first nighters in front of the mission: "We're taking you first nighters to another place tonight. Aw right, you guys, follow me, single file."

He set off in a fast walk, and some of the men had to trot to catch up. He led them across the courthouse park, down the street and past another park. Idlers in front of drugstores stared.

Anybody could have come up, Acel thought, and told this bunch to fall in line and we'd have fell in. Anybody in a clean shirt and slicked hair. All he would have had to say was, "Fall in" and we would follow him the rest of the night, to Alexandria even. It was a big, empty building with a clean, fresh-paint smell. In its cool bareness the voices of the first nighters sounded deep and free. The washroom was on the fourth floor, and the men, after undressing on the second floor, walked naked up the tickling cement stairway. After the shower they returned to the dormitory of cots.

Acel lay on his cot and ran his hand slowly through his damp hair. The bare feet of men returning from the showers padded on the cement floor.

"Somebody strike a match so I can find the light in this place," a voice said, and there was laughter.

Men sat on the edges of their cots, picked their toes and talked to men around them. Acel listened to the voices:

"Bulls are sure gettin' tough in Pittsburgh. I saw one gun-whip the hell out of a guy. They weren't so tough about a year ago when I was through there. I was there when those four boys in that gondola were killed."

"I got a real sit-down this morning in Richmond. Ham and eggs and pie. The old woman told me she had a boy on the road."

"The guy who says you can't blind the Twentieth Century is crazy as hell 'cause I sure held it down . . . . Water on the fly . . . . last winter . . . . four of 'em . . . . chopped 'em out with an axe . . . ."

"Texas Slim ain't so tough . . . . Denver Bob . . . . One-armed Kelly . . . . The Gila Monster . . . . Did you hear about? . . . They was waitin' for him in the car, and when he stuck his head in the door they slammed it on him. Drove spikes in his hands and through his feet and one up his backside."

Acel had impulses to sit up and join in the road gossip. He could tell them about that Negro bull some bums had dropped a coupling on. The Kid, lying on the next cot, turned over again restlessly, and Acel opened his eyes and half sat up: "Well, good-night, Kid."

The Kid raised up on his stomach and looked at Acel. "I just couldn't keep from thinking about it all the time he was preaching. Why in the hell didn't that prodigal son kill them hogs and eat?"

2: THE WINDOW BUSTER

The morning shade of the park trees covered Acel like a cool sheet. Curled on the thin grass, he watched, with screwed-up eyes, the tiny ant struggling through the hairy forest of his forearm. Whitey, the Californian, had left him to rummage for newspapers in the park waste cans. It was a relief for Whitey to be gone awhile. The

Californian had two rigid creases between his eyes, as if he were continually trying to work out a mathematical problem.

I wonder what the name of this park is, Acel thought. I've been in a lot of parks I don't know the name of. I've been in Central Park and Boston Common and Grant Park and the Plaza in El Paso and Lafayette Square and Pershing Square. I've been in a lot of parks. Is that what I can boast about now? That I've been in a lot of parks? Is that a bum's treasure?

How long have I been running around the country now? Two years. Damn near two years. It has been two years since I played in that Juarez cabaret. Godamighty. Two years I been on the bum. I thought I was too good for that Spick's orchestra in Juarez, and that's why he fired me. I was a lot better than the rest of them. I'd played in a lot better bands. It would have scared me to death then if somebody had said: "You won't even have a job two years from now." I didn't have any guts then, though . . . .

Whitey, the Californian, dropped the newspapers on the grass and then, his bony knees popping, bumped into a cross-legged sitting position. His scalp was pink and slick-looking underneath his straw-colored hair. He began flipping the sheets of the spread newspaper, as if he expected something concealed in the folds to jump out at him.

"I just decided to go back to New York," Acel said.

"Whatchu going to do up there?"

"I'm going to get a job. There's a fellow up there from my home town who's a pretty big shot in the music game. I'm going to look him up and tell him I need a job."

"When you thinking about going?"

"In the morning. I'm thinking about highwaying it."

"That town's too big for me. There's nothing up there for me."

They watched the man in the pearl flannel suit and rib-boned panama hat go by on the walk.

"You know when I was a kid," Acel said, "I used to think hunger was something like the toothache, only worse. I mean when you went a long time. But now I know there isn't much to it."

"All hunger is, is your belly muscles drawing up."

"Yeah, a man could starve to death and not know it."

"You'd flop over before you starved to death. I saw one do it yesterday around at the Sally. I thought he was drunk for a minute, the way he was staggerin' around. He hit the floor like a ton of bricks, but he was all right after they fed him. Goddamit, though, that's not right. I'm going to bust me a window yet. Work you six hours a day in the woodyard and feed you twice, and what they feed you there isn't any nutrition in it. I'm always hungry as hell an hour after breakfast."

"The thing that bothers you, Whitey, is you havin' to stick here for that mail. I know how it is. I sure get ants when I have to stay in a spot long."

"That bud of mine is a horse's behind. Been on that fire department for ten years and never been out of Southern California. He don't know what it is to be out of a job. He may not even answer my letter."

The boy in white duck trousers with the ice-cream box slung across his shoulder looked at them but did not pause.

"That's what makes you so sore, waitin' on that mail," Acel said. "When a man is on the move it isn't so bad. I know that that's a fact. A man on the road has something to look forward to even if it's just the next town. And you're so busy going that you don't have time to think about how tough things are. No man thinks about dying much, and that's because he's too busy worrying about keeping alive."

"What I'd like to do," Whitey said, "is find that son of a bitch that stole my drawers last night. I watched everybody dress this morning, but I didn't see 'em. I'm gonna watch again tonight."

"A man that would steal a bum's drawers would spit on a church altar," Acel said. "That makes me think about that suit of mine I got in New York in the Seafarers'. I got to raise a couple of bucks some place to get them cleaned up. I got to get a shirt, too, somehow. If I'm going to look up Red Gholson I got to have a front. I can't look like a bum."

A rain-heralding draft swept across the park and stirred the spread newspaper. Whitey slapped the sheets back down and tapped the big photograph on the society page with a firm forefinger. "Look at this bunch of women," he said.

Acel got up and looked over his shoulder. The débutante looked like movie actresses with their curving hips and firm breasts and poised smiles.

Whitey tapped the photograph again. "They may be dressed up and lookin' fine, but their armpits stink the same as mine."

Acel got up, loosened his belt, and began stuffing in his shirt tail.

"Where you going?" Whitey said.

"C'mon, let's go bum us something to eat. I'm not hittin' that penny joint this time, though. They worked me two hours in that joint yesterday, and they didn't give me a dime's worth to eat. I'm going to hit a hotel."

"It's only about two hours now until the Sally feeds."

"I got to eat good today. I'm going to do a bunch of walking gettin' out of this town in the morning, and I want to feel pretty good."

3: UP FROM THE STOCKYARDS

Acel trudged in that heel-dragging walk of the hitch hiker who has miles to go and is in no particular hurry to get there. The hot morning sun tingled in the roots of his bare head, and he held his eyes down, watching the toes of his scarred shoes.

He asked the man standing at the corner bus station: "Am I going right, mister, to hit the Baltimore highway?" The stranger gave the directions in detail—the boulevard, the stop lights, the school—but Acel only half listened to the latter part. It was easier to ask someone else later on than remember all the directions. Sometimes he would walk miles out of his way for not remembering, but it was a nuisance watching for direction marks.

He moved on, down the sidewalks of a long, wide street. There were young trees in the parkways and smooth, green lawns. There were white frame houses with green shutters and compact brick houses with bright deck chairs on the porches. The houses and the lawns moved past him as if he were standing still, so insensible was he to physical effort.

Just ahead of him a youth in a blue turtle-neck sweater ran across the walk and bounded onto the running board of a new roadster. He was tanned like saddle leather. A girl sat behind the wheel of the mirrory car smoking a cigarette.

A good bum, Acel thought, would approach the fellow and put the bing on him. A fellow with a girl makes a good touch. He could go up and say: "Bud, could you help a man who hasn't had anything to eat today?"

The roadster shot off with a quick shifting of gears.

How long have I been walking now? Acel thought. Two . . . . three hours? It is the wear on shoes and the fuel it takes that matters in hiking. It's going to be noon before I even get to the highway. If there should be a revolution, on whose side would the fellow in the hot sweater be? Would the revolution be between fellows in cotton pants like myself and fellows in sweaters with girls in shiny roadsters? Would the revolutionists say that all men who lived in houses that cost more than ten thousand dollars were their enemies? But men in ten-thousand-dollar houses needn't worry about bums revolting. They don't have guts. Look at me. If somebody came along and picked me up, I'd think the world was level. If I was a revolutionary leader, though, I'd like to have one of these rich bastards come before me. I'd say: "Did you ever give a bum a lift? No. Take him out. Off with his head!"

Hunger seized him almost without warning and with a vicious, shaking grip. It was as if a draining needle had been plunged into him and now his strength-emptied body trembled in outraged protest. He was a little awed. "Now this is hunger, real, sure-enough hunger," he said half aloud.

Across the street was a beauty shop with an orchid front. A woman with her hair plastered down and in a net came out and got into a sedan. At the fountain of the drugstore a man on a stool sipped through a straw. The screen doors of the grocery store slammed as a man smoking a cigar came out.

Acel lifted his hand and watched it tremble. There was oatmeal left in that bowl in the Sally this morning and he should have eaten it all. He had told himself so at the time.

This was hunger, all right. It wasn't illness, because he was thinking about oatmeal. That truck driver who picked him up last summer: "When I pick one up and they begin to talk about how long it is since they've eaten, I say to 'em, 'I got a nickel here, Mac, and I'll get us a loaf of bread and we'll split it.' And then I gets the bread, and if they eat that, then I know they're hungry, and at the next diner I buy 'em a real feed."

I'm trembling like I did when I come down out of the capitol dome yesterday. There's no use of me standing here like this. I'll go in that grocery yonder.

Acel entered the store, and when he reached its center he stopped and looked around at the clerks. A little man in billowy sleeves approached in a little lope.

"Do you have some old bread, mister?"

The little man turned quickly, but his movements after that were unhurried, and he went to the screen door at the back and spoke to someone above. "Bread," Acel heard him say.

Acel watched the little man. I'm going to rate something all right, because I heard him say, "Bread." I heard him say that.

The man brought out a roll of lunch meat from the icebox and cut three slices. He left the icebox and went up front, but Acel kept looking at the icebox.

The little man handed Acel the paper sack. "Thank you," Acel said. The man did not say anything, and Acel twisted his head. "Many thanks to you, sir."

He was outside of the store now with the paper sack in his hand. He walked toward the highway, and it was as if something were prodding him in the back and if he walked fast he might escape its pressure.

There was a tree on the left of the highway, and it curved out at the trunk. It was shady, and the curve fitted his back. Everything is working fine now. Right here on the highway and a good tree and a sack of something to eat. One . . . . two . . . . three sandwiches: Tomatoes! By god, the old boy put in some bananas!

After he had eaten, Acel got up and stood at the edge of the highway. He felt strength in the breadth of his chest and the slope of his shoulders, in the steadiness of his legs and the firmness of his stomach. He stood there on the highway that curled northward like a long greyribbon and thumbed with rhythmic boldness.

The big moving truck approached slowly, but when Acel thumbed, the driver shook his head and spread his hands apologetically. Acel, nodded and saluted under-standingly. He watched the truck lumber on up the high-way. I know, bud, it isn't you. It's the insurance com-panies, and you'd lose your job if they caught you picking somebody up.

The tires of the long sedan sung on the pavement. A girl in the rear looked back through the glass and smiled. Acel waved. He double-shuffled and hooked a left and crossed a right.

Machines came in rushes: a Lincoln with a Negro chauffeur and two toady women in floppy straw hats. A driver with a cigar, clinging stiffly to the wheel. A farmer in a Model T, and two machines with running boards loaded and California licenses.

There were lulls with the highway emptied and silent, and Acel stirred the gravel with his toe or tossed pebbles at the telephone pole on the other side.

A hitchhiker with a canvas bag came up and set his bag down. He had on a tan flannel suit with patch pockets. "How long you been holding this spot down?" he said.

"About an hour, I guess," Acel said. "You have a smoke on you?"

The other produced a cellophane pack.

"Tailor-mades," Acel said. "Been a long time since I smoked a good cigarette."

"I was six hours on a spot yesterday," the newcomer said. "I was thumbing everything that passed me, too, women and everything. I hope I get out of this place pretty soon."

Acel exhaled with a quick upward jerk of his head. "I ride trains mostly when I'm traveling, but I'm only trying to make Baltimore today, and I thought I'd highway it. I don't like this thumbing myself."

"I may get a bus when I get to Baltimore. I've been three days now from Richmond, and at this rate I'm not going to save very much gettin' to Boston. I may just get a bus."

"If you got a few bucks you might as well hang onto them. A ride might come along here and take you clear into Boston. I wouldn't spend any bus money."

There was a rush of cars, and Acel thumbed half heartedly. "The trouble with them," the hitchhiker said, "is that they're afraid of getting hijacked. That's just their excuse. They just don't want to stop and fool with you."

"That's it."

"If it wasn't that I wouldn't have a cent when I got to Boston I would get a bus and say to hell with them, but I just have a few dollars, and I need them when I get there."

"If a man will just be patient a ride will come along. I a get sore as hell sometimes and wish one of them would turn over down the road after he passed and then yell for somebody to come and pull the car off of him. I guess he'd let you do that, all right."

"Women never do pick you up. You ever had a woman pick you up?"

"Once or twice. I never do thumb women. They're afraid they'll get, raped, I guess."

The hitchhiker picked up his bag. "I guess I'll go on down the road. Two of us together won't do any good. This hiking is like sticking your tail out and every time somebody passes they kick it."

In just a few minutes the black sedan stopped, and for several moments Acel did not think the driver was stopping for him. He had been made foolish a lot of times by drivers who were simply going to turn around. But this driver was opening the door!

The driver had on pinch-nose glasses, and his middle-aged face had a barber-shop freshness. When they settled in high gear he said:

"Where you going, young man?"

"I'm going to New York."

"You are not a New Yorker, are you?"

"No, sir." Acel reached out and waved at the hitch hiker in the flannel suit. "No, sir, but I'm going to be if I get this job I'm planning on."

"You are from the South, aren't you?"

"Well, Oklahoma. I was born in Oklahoma."

Acel shook his head when the other offered cigarettes. They rode in silence. Acel extended his feet a little and slid down on the cushions.

The driver made a sweeping gesture with his hand.

"Yonder across that water there is going to be a bridge soon, and it will be a vision fulfilled. That span will connect two communities, and it will be a dream realized. It is to be a reality, too, because the government has appropriated the money, just about, and construction will start soon. One man dreamed that bridge and planned it for a long time, and soon he will see his vision take form."

Acel looked at the driver a little furtively. The other spoke as if he were addressing an audience and with a careful selection of words. Acel cleared his throat.

"Who is the man?"

"I am the man." The driver rapped on the steering wheel with the palm of his hand. "I am the man."

"You are going to build a bridge over there?"

"I visioned that bridge five years ago."

"Oh, I see. You're an engineer."

"No, I am chairman of the Chamber of Commerce bridge committee."

"Oh, I see."

"You can do the same, young man. Don't think there is not opportunity in this world. I started out working when I was twelve years old in the old Kansas City stock-yards. I worked in the stockyards for a mere pittance when I was a boy and on top of that was practically an invalid. I had an operation, and for two years I had a hose running out of my belly. And I worked right in those stockyards with that hose in my belly until the boss saw that I wasn't physically able to do that kind of work and put me in the office. I couldn't add two and two, but I tackled it and began studying nights . . . ."

Acel slid farther down in the seat and folded his arms. A mushed cat lay on the pavement ahead, and he flinched as he felt the car's wheels bump on the carcass.

"I worked very hard in that office. I didn't know what hours were. They made me a clerk, and I worked at that about a year and then had to have a new operation. I had my eye on a salesman's job all the time, though, and when I got that, the first month I made more sales than any other young man on the force."

Acel recrossed his legs. I ought to pay more attention to what this man is saying, because he might ask me a question in a minute. He must be somebody, all right.

".... sent to Fort Worth .... man for the job .... big interests .... merger .... opportunity .... St. Louis .... sweet little girl .... married .... Oklahoma City .... apartment .... five hundred dollars saved .... hard row .... while I was gone the man that lived in the apartment across the hall tried to make my wife .... business picked up ...."

I'll say to Gholson: "I'm Acel Stecker, Mr. Gholson, from Bovina City. I just got in New York and I'd like to see you."

He'll let me come up, I'll bet, telling him I'm from Bovina City. I should have looked him up before. I don't see why I didn't think of that before.

".... Kansas City .... office in shape .... fifty-percent increase .... Philadelphia .... merger .... vice-president .... Packers' Association .... you can do the same, young man."

".... It was like this, Mr. Gholson, I didn't know times were going to be so hard, so I quit the Apaches and with a few hundred I'd saved worked my way to Europe. I knew your dad pretty well, Mr. Gholson. If you will give me a tip on a job, I sure will appreciate it. If you will suggest somewhere I could try, I'd appreciate it a whole lot. If I could just get a couple of nights a week, I'd certainly appreciate it."

A coupé approached, and the driver suddenly stiffened and leaned out of his car and waved wildly.

"That was old Jock Early," he said to Acel.

"Insurance man. Fine a fellow as ever lived."

Acel nodded.

"I have a boy about your age in Columbia. Have a girl, too. She's in California now. I say let them do what they want to . . . . Insurance . . . . Rotarian . . . . Chamber of Commerce . . . . Well, I'll let you out here, young man."

Acel stirred up with the alertness of a man who has been caught napping. They were at the outskirts of the city.

"I turn this way here," the driver said. He reached across and twisted the door out. "Sorry I can't take you any farther."

Acel slid out. "Many thanks, mister, for the lift."

"That's perfectly all right, son. Remember, now, you can a do the same."

4: "BOATS"

With the roll of tabloid newspapers under his arm, Acel stood there on the walk looking across darkened Battery Park at the still forms which lay scattered on the grass like corpses on a battlefield. A train crashed around the elevated curve toward South Ferry. Ship horns groaned on the East River, on the Hudson, and in the Bay. The traffic of lower Broadway ground on like a giant unoiled machine.

He stepped over the strand of wire separating the walk from the grass and moved across the black carpet. He chose can a spot distant from the other sleepers and spread the newspapers. After removing his shoes and tying the laces, he covered them with his jacket for a pillow. He lay on his back and looked up at the swirling heavens.

The girl's laugh, excited and repressed, made him stir up on his elbow and look about. Just a few yards away a couple was spreading newspapers. The youth was bareheaded and the sleeves of his white shirt were rolled high on his biceps. The girl, lifting her dress a little, went to her knees and then fell around to sit beside him. Acel turned on his side in order to watch them.

The couple lay on the papers now, but presently the girl sat up, her chin on her knees. The youth chuckled and then, grasping her, pulled her down to him. Their mouths met, the girl with teasing pecks. Suddenly the youth grasped her fiercely, and then they clung in possessive embrace . . . .

The draft blowing over the bay and across Battery Park was moist and chilling. Acel awoke with the back of his hand lying in the wet grass. He placed it between his legs and hunched tighter, but it was no use. He sat up, shivering, and fumbled with shaking fingers for cigarette papers. When he had the cigarette burning he put on his shoes and jacket and moved toward South Ferry.

Bums slept on all the benches, some of them wrapped in newspapers. He peered into the bandstand, but its floor was covered with human bundles.

On the illuminated walk near the ferry buildings

there was a bench of men. They were talking and laughing. Acel sat down on an adjoining bench, and presently a short, stocky youth in wide-bottomed, blue denim trousers came over. "Spare another smoke, mate?"

Acel handed him the sack.

The youth had gold teeth. "Been sleeping in the park?"

Acel nodded. "It's too cold. I couldn't sleep."

The other handed him the sack. "If you get on a bench and wrap up with papers it isn't so bad."

"Try and find a bench, though."

"I'm going to turn in pretty soon, and if you want to I'll show you where you can flop. It's warm, anyway."

Gold Teeth returned to the other bench. "They can kidnap them all if they want to," he said. "What are those rich guys to me? They wouldn't spit on me if my guts were on fire."

Acel went over and stood at the end of the bench of men.

"None of these rich bastards ever did anything, for me," Gold Teeth said. "They can kidnap every damned one of 'em."

The man at the end of the bench made room for Acel. He had on clean, khaki work clothing. His clean-shaven face had a rich, healthy coloring. "I haven't seen you around here before," he said.

"No, I just got off the road this afternoon. I been in this town before, though."

"Well, a man won't starve here." He got up and picked his up a cigarette butt off the walk. He was short and built like a fire plug.

Acel brought out his tobacco sack. "I got tobacco here, buddy."

"Save your tobacco." The man pulled out a pipe and crammed the broken butt into it.

Gold Teeth kept talking. He said he had quit looking for work. The field was too overcrowded. He looked at the man beside Acel. "Ain't I right, Boats?"

"Stay in there," Boats said. Aside he said to Acel: "That fellow is a character. Gorki or London could have used him. Tully, too."

Acel nodded.

"That is the type that will furnish the drive and power for the revolution. They don't think, but they have the guts."

"Why, do you think there is going to be a revolution?"

"Of a certainty. Just as soon as the men on this bench and the men on benches all over the country realize why they're jobless. Then the revolution will come. But the masses haven't been aroused yet. They feel that something is wrong, but they are too stupid to understand why."

"I don't see much chance for a revolution myself," Acel said.

Boats looked at Acel. "Why don't you think there is much chance?"

"Oh, I don't know, I haven't thought about it so much, to tell the truth."

"That's it, then, comrade. The average man doesn't think about it. The average man is just an alimentary canal with a billiard ball for a head."

"You know what it's all about, then, uh?" Acel spat scornfully between his teeth.

"At least I think about it, comrade. I don't sit around and pick my nose and say, 'This country is all right. I'll get mine some day.'"

"Well, friend, I'm not shouting hurrah for the kidnappers, and neither do I intend to be like this the rest of my life."

Gold Teeth beckoned. "C'mon, you two, let's go."

Boats waved him back. "We'll go in a minute." He looked at Acel again. "No, you won't be a bum all the time. All this is temporary to you, I suppose. I guess you're having a pretty good time."

"Nope, this isn't my idea of a good time."

"I can't see how a man can live this sort of life and fail of to see the injustice of the governmental system that spawns it. Now you—"

"Forget it, bud. You don't know anything about me."

"I'm going, you guys," Gold Teeth said. "If you're going now, let's go."

Boats and Acel followed Gold Teeth. They crossed lower Broadway. Out of the cigar store at the corner came a youth in white linen trousers and a yellow silk polo shirt. Gold Teeth stopped him. "How about a cigarette, Queenie?"

Queenie tossed his head. "Sorry, I'm trying to make a dollar myself tonight."

They walked on, and Boats winked at Acel. "You're too ugly, Goldie."

Gold Teeth laughed. "Yeah, I'm just too ugly."

Sleeping forms lay in building entrances and on the

slant in doors of coal chutes. "American seamen," Boats said and gestured with mock dramatics. "Galley slaves were at least taken care of when they weren't at sea, but a capitalistic slave when he isn't working sleeps in the street. And they talk about Russia."

"Well, what are you going to do about it?" Acel said.

"Little matches make big fires, comrade."

"What these guys ought to do is get 'em some six-shooters and get it," Gold Teeth said.

They turned into a darkened alley and moved up it single file. Halfway up the block, Gold Teeth stopped and then, agile as a monkey, climbed up and disappeared through a narrow opening in the boarded window of the big building.

"This is the Hoover Hotel," Boats said, and he followed Gold Teeth.

Acel pulled himself up to the ledge and then squeezed through the aperture. It was dark as a ship's hold inside, and for several moments he stood there like a man blind folded. The feet of his companions scraped ahead. He lowered himself to the gritty cement floor and then moved across it in the direction of their sounds. The place smelled of charred wood and human bodies.

Acel could see a little better now. He stood at the foot of a fire-razed, skeleton stairway. He no longer heard his companions. He started up the stairway, and once he touched a charred beam that had fallen across it, and its crust loosened.

He peered into rooms on the second floor. Light from a street lamp filtered through the boarded window cracks on the forms of sleeping men. There were no spots here.

Acel climbed on up to the next floor, but here too the newspaper-covered floors were strewn with sleeping hulks. On the fifth floor he found a spot and, carefully stepping between the sleepers, he made his way to it and lay down.

5: LUNGDREN

Jim Lungdren and Acel Stecker sat at a table in the seamen's eating place, "seventy-six." Their table was at a window overlooking the East River. At the dock lay a freighter flying the flag of Spain. The hull was streaked by red lead, and her shore lines gleamed in the morning spring sun like huge watch chains.

Lungdren and Acel had been shipmates. They had encountered each other in the recreation hall of the Seafarers' Home that morning.

Lungdren was a lean, bony-hipped man with a chin like a doorknob. It was covered with a pubescent fuzz. He chewed the sweet roll now with the fearful cautiousness of a man whose teeth are bad. "You don't have any business hanging around a waterfront," he said.

Acel stirred his coffee. "What I want to do is look up that fellow here. I just got a hunch that something might come out of it. He's from my hometown, see? If he wanted to he could steer me onto a job as easy as that."

"You're not going to get any place hanging around a

waterfront."

"I can't go and see him, looking like a bum."

"I got a couple of bucks if that's what it takes to get that suit out. Don't stand back on that."

"I don't want to take your money. You better hang onto that."

"It's going, anyway. I'll be carrying the banner myself in another week. There's old Boats. Hey, Boats!"

Boats came to their table and placed on it a cup of coffee and three sweet rolls.

"How's the revolution coming along?" Acel said.

"Hello," Boats said. "How did you like your bed last night?"

Lungdren pushed the tin of sugar toward Boats. "I hear you got a ship."

Boats nodded. "I'm shipping Monday. About a four weeks' trip, I guess."

Acel watched Boats's right hand stir the sugar. It was larger than his left and scarred.

"So you got a good sleep in the Hoover Hotel?" Boats said.

"It was okay. I been thinking about putting up in it by the week."

Boats laughed. He broke his sweet roll and then looked at Acel again. "Did you ever read Karl Marx?"

"Uh huh."

"Bernard Shaw?"

"Nope."

"Don't let him horse you," Lungdren said to Boats. "I was shipmates with this guy. He reads all the time. He's had some good jobs, and I been telling him that he—"

"Aw, can that stuff, Lungdren," Acel said.

"If I could play a ukulele I wouldn't be around this part of town," Lungdren said. "Ace is a musician."

"Seamen are not the only ones having a hard time," Boats said. "Say, you two, you want to go up on the Bowery at noon for something to eat? I raised a few nickels this morning."

"There's a joint up there that really feeds," Lungdren said. "Three hunks of ham that thick and enough potatoes for an army, and I don't mean a cup of coffee, but a bowl. And cake. By god, all the cake you can eat. And just for fifteen cents."

"Aren't you going to take him up on that feed on the Bowery?"

"You can go on with him if you want to. I'm not."

~§~

The man approaching the bench on which Acel and Lungdren sat walked with a stiff-kneed, painful gait. He had on a new, tight-fitting suit and brown army shoes. His face looked like a movie muscle man's. He lowered himself carefully to the bench.

"Looks you got a game leg on you," Acel said.

Muscle Man nodded. "Yeah, I just got out of the hospital." He had a growling voice. "Seven months I did. Busted both these legs right across there." He drew a forefinger across his knees.

"Good god, how did you do that?"

Muscle Man said he was standing on a corner, fog-bound over a girl, and some gangsters mistook him for an enemy and threw him in front of a truck.

"You look like a dick, all right," Acel said.

"Everybody takes me for a dick or a gangster."

Muscle Man eased off his shoes and exhibited a blood-soaked heel. He said he got it from walking that afternoon over to Jersey looking for a ship job.

"You want a ship bad enough," Acel said.

"I'll have one pretty soon."

"How do you ship?"

"Like I told that skipper today. I've shipped everything from deck boy to master."

"You been a skipper?"

Muscle Man said he had been the master of a three-sticker. He lost the ship in a fire on the Gulf, but it wasn't the loss of the ship that caused him to lose his officer's papers. It was a missing Filipino that was on the ship. Everybody on the ship was saved except the Filipino. The *goo goo* was the one who fired the ship, Muscle Man said.

"You mean they thought you wouldn't let the *goo goo* go?" Acel said.

"I ain't saying," Muscle Man said.

Lungdren sharpened a match and began cleaning his fingernails.

"Have you ever been in the Orient?" Acel said.

Muscle Man said he had lived in the Far East seven years and had captained a ship for a river pirate queen. He said he had been master of a treasure-hunt ship. There was a volcano lake in South America that was filled with the gold sacrifices of natives. He knew how to drain the lake, and as soon as he got on his feet he was going to raise the finances for another expedition.

Lungdren got up. "Let's go," he said.

Acel told Muscle Man goodbye, and he and Lungdren walked toward the Hoover Hotel.

"There's a man that's sure been around," Acel said.

"That guy was full of blow."

"Those knees weren't full of blow."

"There's plenty of men around here that's been farther than that guy. Boats has been ten times more places than that guy. Boats can talk Chinese."

"He might be bullin' some, but that man has been around. He's not any South Street bum."

They found spots under the boarded window on the fifth floor. Soon Lungdren was snoring, but Acel shifted restless and curled in vain in an effort to escape the warped floor board underneath the newspapers.

I turned in too soon, Acel thought. If a man is going to sleep in a place like this he ought to at least wait until he's played out. This time tomorrow I ought to know if I'm going to get any place with Gholson. It's a long shot, No use of kiddin' myself or expecting anything. But a man can't ever tell.

The only way a man ever gets a job is to ask for it. I've asked, haven't I? Yes, but a man has to keep asking. I'm due for a break. If I got a job I could get a girl. If I could get a job in a dance band . . . . It's a long shot, though, seeing Gholson.

I should have waited until I was tired. Old Lungdren there is a white man. I'll pay him back that two bucks if it's the last thing I do. That suit of mine won't look bad. These shoes are bad, but I'll get them shined. If I did get a job I'd sure see to it that old Lungdren got a break. I'll come down here dressed up sometime and visit around, and if I'm doing pretty good I'll stake Lungdren to a new suit. I'd like to be jellied out and staking Lungdren and run into Boats. "Well, you started that revolution yet, Boats?"

Muscle Man? Fogbound over a girl and thrown in front of a truck? If that had been me standing there on that corner I'd of jerked away from them. *The truck swerved around the corner and Ace Stecker leaped to safety. There was a jarring crash, and the truck turned over. The gangsters were pinned underneath. A black bag fell at the feet of Ace Stecker. A crowd was gathering. Ace picked up the black bag unobserved and stuffed it underneath his jacket. He walked away and went into the subway station. In the pay toilet he opened the bag. There were stacks of currency held by rubber bands . . . .*

The crackle of papers at the entrance of the room disrupted Acel's daydreaming, and he raised up and peered through the darkness. A big, compact figure moved painfully into the room and looked about, searching. Lungdren and me got the last spots, Acel thought.

Acel lay back down and listened to the slow, painful steps of Muscle Man fading on the gritty stairway.

6: GHOLSON

On the shawl-draped piano of Red Gholson's studio apartment was a photograph of the orchestra leader in a gold frame. The frame matched the golden rug. Acel, sitting on the piano bench and waiting for Gholson's appearance, decided again not to smoke.

I hope he doesn't smell the gasoline or whatever it is they cleaned this suit of mine with. That's the trouble with four-bit cleaning. At least I can say I met Red Gholson. I can say, "No, I've never met Ben Bernie, but I know Red Gholson. I met him in New York one time." I feel pretty cool waiting to see him. He talked over the telephone like he was a pretty good fellow . . . .

Gholson came in. He looked older than his photographs. He was a small man with red hair, and his face had a Turkish-bath flush. The hand he extended had the diamond on it. Acel had heard Gholson's daddy in Bovina City talk about that diamond. It cost five thousand dollars.

"I'm sorry I kept you waiting," Gholson said.

"That's all right," Acel said.

Gholson sat down in a blue-cushioned chair, and Acel lowered himself to the bench again.

"How is everything in Bovina?" Gholson said.

"Everything was okay when I left there. I haven't been there in a pretty good while myself."

"What's on your mind, Stecker? That is the name,

isn't it?"

"Yes. I tell you, Mr. Gholson, I just got in town and I'd like to find a job."

"Are you a musician?"

"Oh, yes. Ten years. I was Wymore's first trumpet for two years and a half, and I had the Apaches at school. You know some of those boys."

"Yes, I know some of those boys." Gholson twisted the diamond on his finger thoughtfully for several moments. "I tell you, Stecker, times are pretty hard here in New York now. Lot of boys out of work now."

Acel nodded. "Yes, I know. I tell you, just any sort of job would put me on my feet."

"You are not particular, then?"

"Oh, no. To tell you the truth, I hoboed it up here. Anything would look good to me."

"Lot of boys are out of work. Some very good boys are out of work now."

"I know things are tough, all right."

Gholson got up. "I tell you what, then. Where are you staying?"

"I'm staying at the Seafarers' Home. It's a pretty reasonable place"

"Well, I'll see if I can't dig you up something. If I hear of anything I'll let you know. You keep in touch with me."

"That sure is nice of you."

"I'll see if I can't dig you up something. You give me a ring in a week or so."

Acel walked down Park Avenue. By god, by god, by god . . . .

~§~

Lungdren, sitting with his feet over the edge of the pier, shook his head. "No, you don't have nothing to worry about now."

"It's a break, all right," Acel said. "Just a little pull, that's what it takes. A man like him can just put in a word for you, see? and you're sittin' jake. There's jobs, all right. Now you take these excursion-boat musicians. Those fellows get sixty-five bucks a week. I wouldn't know what to do with that much money coming in every week."

"Naw, you ain't got nothing to worry about now."

"I've made more than sixty-five bucks. Listen, when I was eighteen I made that. I had a band on a carnival, and I had a couple of concessions. Ball games. Had a couple of broads running them. One day I cleared forty bucks. I'll bet you think I'm bullin' you."

"I can tell a guy, all right."

"Gholson is really a big shot, see? When I shook hands with him I felt of that ring. I thought, Bud, you got a rock on you worth five thousand bucks and I got subway fare back to the Battery."

"You got a break all right."

"He says to me, 'Give me a ring and let me hear from you.' A big shot like him isn't saying a thing like that unless he means business. And he didn't ask me why I was out of a job or how come me to be in a seamen's place or anything like that."

Lungdren pointed up the pier. "Yonder's the Mad Wolf I was telling you about."

Acel looked at the figure going across the pier in a half-loping walk. His hanging shirt tail napped like a coolie coat, and his trousers bagged like the skin on an elephant's hind legs.

"So that's the Mad Wolf?"

"That's him."

"I wonder if he did lose two thousand dollars in a bank and it made him go crazy."

"That's what they say."

"Don't look to me like that would make a man go crazy."

"If you'd saved it all working below you'd think it was enough, I'll bet."

"I don't know about these loons running around here. I don't know whether they're so crazy or not. I was watching that guy they call Doc up in the Bowery the other day. That one they say went crazy after he operated on a caught girl and she died. I watched him. Every time anybody offered him any money he acted like he was insulted and run off. What does he go around looking like a bum for and mixing around with crowds unless he is a bum? I think he enjoys martyring himself."

"You can't tell me they're not crazy."

The excursion boat rounded the bend from Battery Landing. Holiday flags whipped in the breeze, and a black plume rolled from her high stack. The loaded decks were splashed with the bright-colored figures of women.

Acel and Lungdren stood up as the ship neared. It was so close that they knew now that the girl in the red jacket was waving at them. Another girl beside her focused a camera on them. Acel and then Lungdren waved. The girl in the red jacket waved until the vessel was almost around the bend.

They sat down. "If you'd say anything to one of them on the street they'd call a cop," Lungdren said.

Acel nodded. "I've thought about it when I was on a freight train and some girl would wave at you from a Packard. They'll flirt and wave at you like you were somebody they knew as long as there is plenty of distance between you."

"That's right, all right."

"I know one thing, if I get this job I'm gettin' me a girl the first thing. I'm fed up on this."

"That's what I got against the sea. All you meet is a bunch of whores rollin' you for your dough."

"The last girl I had put me on a wild-goose chase. I was up in Denver, and I got a letter from her. She said I had a good chance for a job in a band she was singing in. I lit out. That was the trip I saw that bum commit suicide on."

"What did he do it for?"

"I don't know. He just jumped out on his head. I'd been riding with him nearly all day. He never had said much, and then that night he just started hopping toward the door like a frog, and then out he went. The train was going like a bat out of hell."

"I wonder what he did it for."

"I don't know. When the train stopped at the next station, my buddy and me told the brakie about it, but they said they couldn't do anything about it. I sure had some tough luck on that trip. We got out of that car and was gettin' in a reefer and I busted this little finger. See the scar here? Damned near took it off. It made me sick as a dog, and my buddy wrapped it up in a handkerchief, and I rode all that night, and the next morning we got in Albuquerque. I put a Catholic hospital there on the bum to dress it up. I was afraid of lockjaw or something. They fixed me up, and I got a train out of there that night for El Paso."

"Where was you eatin'?"

"They fed me in the hospital. One of them sisters gave me a whole bunch of cakes. But I was telling you about gettin' to El Paso. I got booted off that train, and I don't mean just pushed off. The conductor that kicked me off had had a brother killed by a bum just about a week before. He kicked me off in the damnedest town you ever did see. Wasn't nothing but Mexicans there. Well, there was a school teacher and his wife. I hit those Mexicans up, and I couldn't even rate a cigarette. I found out there was a passenger train that stopped there for mail at three in the morning. I had to stay in that place all that afternoon and night until three o'clock next morning. I walked up a road about a mile where these school teachers lived and hallooed and hollered around. I'd waited like a damn fool until after dark. Finally some woman come to the door and said she couldn't do anything, so I started back up the road."

"She didn't give you a thing?"

"She was scared and afraid to open the door, I think. What was funny, though, was going back. The mosquetoes along the Rio Grande there make those in Galveston look like gnats. I decided I'd better make one of those smudges to keep them off of me. I started looking for cow chips in the road. It was dark, and I got down on my knees and started feeling around. I couldn't even find cow chips in that damned town."

7: THE CAKE LINE

Lungdren blew his nose again in the grey handkerchief and then folded it up and stuck it in his hip pocket.

"You ought to try and get some hospital relief, man," Acel said. "You've had that cold long enough."

"My eyes is what bothers me. It's my eyes."

"They'd fix you up with glasses. They would stop that burning."

"There's so much red tape to go through."

Acel got up from the bench and stretched, raising up on his toes. He turned around and placed his foot on the bench. "I think I'll see what I can get on that suit tomorrow. I ought to get three or four bucks. That suit cost me forty-five bucks new without extra pants, either. It's pretty old now, but it isn't worn through any place."

"You better not hock that suit. That Gholson guy might call you yet."

"I've checked that. If he was going to help me get a job he'd have done it long ago. What good does it do for me to phone except cost me a nickel? That stuff about him not being there is all bull."

"You can't expect a job in a couple of weeks."

"It's been four weeks. Man, you oughten to blow your nose that hard. That's the way mastoid trouble gets started."

Lungdren got up. "If we're going to make the Tubes tonight we might as well get started."

They crossed the park and at the corner stopped and watched a razor-blade demonstration. The vendor gesticulated and sprayed spittle like a Socialist in Union Square. He showed how the blue could be scraped off the steel.

They moved on. "That's what I need," Lungdren said. "The next piece of change I get hold of, that's the first thing I'm going to buy. Razor blades."

"I went three weeks one time without shaving at sea," Acel said. "I had a beard that long. I wish I was at sea tonight. I'm going to make the rounds tomorrow again."

"If you had four or five dollars to slip to one of these shipping masters you might could get out," Lungdren said.

"I wish I could get a ship. You know how I'd pass the watches away when I was at sea? I'd skip and shadow-box around the winches. It'd be blowing to beat the dickens some nights, and the lines and the waves hittin' 'midships, and it would all sound like a thousand kettledrums. I'd sing, too. Down the ventilator, every song I could think of."

"I'd rather have a good job ashore."

"I ought to get a ship if I keep on. I'd like to go to the Orient. Did you ever date a Chink girl?"

"Yeah." Lungdren pointed at the bright entrance of

the restaurant across the street. "That place is good. I've seen fellows hit it, and they never do get turned down."

"You take that place and I'll take the one right below it," Acel said.

Lungdren shook his head. "I just don't like to do that. You can go on and hit it. It's good."

"That's funny to me, why you won't hit cafés. And you'll stop anybody on the street and bum them for a smoke. I'd just as soon ask a man for a dime as a cigarette."

Acel went across the street and entered the restaurant. Pretty soon he came out and rejoined Lungdren leaning there against the lamppost. "You've seen one guy turned down, anyway. They told me the boss was out and they couldn't do it."

"That must be the reason, then, because I've seen plenty make it. Here, here's a tailor-made . . . . That's all right. I bummed a couple of them."

Acel entered the cafeteria on the corner. It was a glittering place of tile floor and porcelain cases trimmed in shining nickel. The bald cashier looked at him.

"Could I do a little work for something to eat?"

The cashier jerked his head toward the rear.

Acel walked down the bright floor past the long glass cases of food and approached the white-uniformed man behind the counter. "The man up at the desk sent me back," he said.

The counterman went to the kitchen slot and yelled: "A bowl."

The heavy soup was like liquor in Acel's stomach, and he grinned triumphantly as he approached Lungdren. "That was a white place, boy," he said. "You ought to go in there."

"We better be gettin' on down to the Tubes. It's gettin' close to midnight."

The crowds, were thinning in the great underground station of the Hudson Tunnels. Here and there in waiting huddles of twos and threes Acel and Lungdren recognized and spoke to the shabby figures of South Street acquaintances.

"They ought not to gang up like that," Lungdren said, "That's what makes the cops sore."

They moved about in the crowd, always hovering near the lunch stand where, at twelve o'clock, the left-over sandwiches and cakes of the day were distributed.

They paused to speak to a seaman called Hunky. He was a short, rotund man with small glassy eyes and a deep cleft in his chin. "We had a pretty good thing here," Hunky said, "until all the damned bums in New York started making this place. There's more here tonight than I ever have seen. Those old smoke belches from the Bowery are gumming it up. They'll make it so pretty soon that it's not worth a man's time to come here any more."

The white-capped counterman began dumping doughnuts and sweet rolls on the counter. Ragged men sifted quickly through the crowds of commuters, and soon a limp line of more than fifty bums had formed. The counterman began handing out two doughnuts to each man.

Commuters halted and stared at the dragging line. Lungdren, in front of Acel, turned and said out of the corner of his mouth: "The sons of bitches. That's what I hate, them standing there with their goddamned eyes stickin' out and watchin'."

The counterman handed Acel one doughnut, and Acel did not move.

The counterman made a shoving motion with his hand. "Not enough to go around now."

Acel had to hurry to catch up with Lungdren. The gaunt seaman, handed a cruller, had walked swiftly away. Acel found him panting in a shadowed aperture which led behind a big display case.

"I hate them bastards standing out there and looking at us," he said.

Acel sat down beside him. "That guy they call Hunky. I don't have any use for a man like him. Griping around as if this was his own private bumming place. Those Bowery bums are not walking clear over here for the exercise."

Lungdren bit cautiously on the cruller.

"No, those guys don't deserve anything," Acel said.

"There was one thing about Boats, he was willing to share what he had, I wonder where that bird is."

"I just can't eat these things." Lungdren's voice had broken, and he looked helplessly at the dry cake in his hand. "I just can't eat them. They turn to powder in my mouth."

He swallowed as if his throat were sore.

Acel extended his doughnut. "Maybe you can eat a doughnut. It's not the same kind of dough."

Lungdren shook his head. "I don't want to take that from you."

"Ferchrissakes. Go ahead. Here . . . I ate good in that

restaurant. You remember. I don't want it, anyway."

"You can have this cruller, then."

They ate silently. Acel listened to the roar of the great station. He brushed sugar off his trouser legs. I'll soak that suit tomorrow. I'll get two or three bucks for it. I'm going to hit every agency and every ship that comes in until I get a ship.

"Say, Lungdren, it'd be pretty nice if we could get a ship together."

Lungdren nodded. "It's funny, ain't it, how we don't work and yet we live?"

8: SHIPMASTER KLOTZ

There were not even pictures of women in corsets in the backs of these old magazines—*Farm & Fireside, American Boy, Editor & Publisher*—not even bathing suits. The hairs of Acel's moist forearm clung to the fly-paper varnish of the reading table as he pushed the magazines aside.

Acel looked across the hall. Lungdren was entering, and he stood now looking about searchingly. Acel stood up and waved. Lungdren leveled his finger at Acel like a pistol, jerking his thumb, and then came toward him. The man with him was Boats.

Boats had on a new blue serge suit and a gray felt hat and red tie. "Hello, Ace," he said. "How's the boy?"

"Okay. You look like you stepped out of a bandbox."

"I been working."

"He's going back tomorrow night," Lungdren said. "He's going to treat us to a spaghetti dinner uptown tonight."

"I wish to hell I had a job," Acel said.

"I can put you next to a mess punk's job," Boats said. "On the *Picfair* over in Jersey. It's an excursion boat that runs up the Sound and back every day."

"I never did work in the galleys," Acel said. "I'm not looking particularly for that kind of a job."

Lungdren exhibited two coupons. "I wouldn't have gotten these if I'd of known old Boats was coming in."

Acel frowned. "What did you do, go and get relief tickets? If you do make a trip, you're going to owe this place every thing before you get back."

"All you get around this place free is water," Boats said.

"They haven't charged me yet for sittin' in here," Acel said.

"I don't know whether you're getting that free or not, though, when you think about it," Boats said. "You don't get anything around here for nothing. This place is run to give big salaries to executives. You know how much Judge Ross gets? Seven thousand dollars a year to direct this place. And how much does that bird up there get that writes stuff about starving seamen? Five thousand bucks. Five thousand dollars a year he gets for writing to these stuffed shirts, getting them to jerk loose with endowments and contributions. They raise thousands of dollars every year, and they've had millions of dollars given them, and if a seaman comes around here and he doesn't have any money he's out of luck."

"If they can get away with it, they're pretty smart," Acel said.

"I know that a couple of dollars comes out of my pay every trip I make, and they say it goes to this place. I guess, though, that's why I can get credit here."

"Are you telling me, Ace," Boats said, "that you think it is just for these men that run this place to get big salaries and four hundred seamen sleeping every night over there in the Hoover Hotel?"

"You can't do anything about it, Boats."

"That isn't the question. It's okay, you say, for them to pay themselves seven thousand and five thousand dollars a year and hire cops around here who don't know a half-hitch from a chain locker. At least they could hire a few seamen around a place like this. The only seamen working around this place are in the galleys. Look, Lungdren, did you ever get anything around here for nothing? Did you ever sleep in this place and not pay for it? Did they ever give you a single meal? You've needed them, haven't you? So have I, but it would do me a helluva lot of good to ask for it. No, this place is to provide seven thousand dollars a year for Judge Ross and some of his women around here. Seven thousand dollars a year. Why, godamighty, the dictator of Russia only gets two hundred and fifty bucks a month, and he runs a nation of one hundred and sixty million people. And that old belch up there gets seven thousand a year, and there are three thousand seamen sleeping every night on the streets or in flop houses or half-burned buildings like the Hoover Hotel."

"Get you a soap box," Acel said.

"You're no seaman, though, I forget," Boats said. "You're just a vacuum-headed horn blower who got kicked out of his own racket and is hanging around a waterfront now."

Acel got up. "Listen, bud, you don't talk to me—"

"Don't take things too seriously, Ace," Boats said.

"You guys quit your damned arguing," Lungdren said. "You act like a couple of punk. Ferchrissakes."

"You're a long ways from not having a head on you, Ace. That's why you make me so mad. If we men down here struggling in this kind of life can't see the injustice of the capitalistic system, then even a god wouldn't help us."

"I don't see that you have any kick coming," Acel said. "You've got a job, and you got you a good suit and some money to spend. What do you have to gripe about?"

"Christ, man, don't you believe in social equality? Don't you think every man is entitled to food and clothing and shelter? Do you approve of a system that operates so one man can have enough to buy a billion meals and another can't raise the price of one?"

"Like I've told you before, this is a dog-eat-dog world, and if I don't get mine I'm not going to whine."

Boats knocked the ashes out of his pipe into the spittoon.

"I got to go see about some gear. I'll see you boys down in the lobby about six. You two need tobacco money?"

Acel shook his head.

They watched Boats walk across the hall and disappear on the stairway.

"Are we going around to any shipping agencies this afternoon?" Lungdren said.

"I'm tired of sittin' around those places."

"I heard below a while ago there was a couple of tankers in, and there might be something doing around at Klotz'."

~§~

Klotz was head of the Forecastle Shipping Agency. He stood now in the doorway of his office at the end of the long, bare hall. He was in his undershirt, and the belt around his fat stomach was loosened. Under his arm was a bright can.

The benches on the sides of the hall were sprinkled with men. There was a big blackboard on which were printed sea occupations, but the spaces for openings were blank.

There was one unoccupied bench, a broken plank, and Acel and Lungdren seated themselves carefully.

Klotz came over to them. His eyes were glassy with drink. He extended the can. "Have a drink," he said.

The beer was tepid and flat. "Thanks, Klotz," Acel said.

"Got any jobs around here today?"

Klotz did not answer. He turned and went across the room and stood before a long-jawed seaman in a straw hat.

"Hi, Lantern Jaw," Klotz said.

Lantern Jaw smiled uncertainly.

Klotz reached out and brought back the man's hat. He held it for a moment and then dropped it on the floor. The hat made a crackling sound as he stomped on it, and men in the room laughed.

Lantern Jaw's lips twisted vaguely.

Klotz returned to his office and closed the door. "Playful today, isn't he?" Acel said.

"The son of a bitch," Lungdren said.

"I don't see much use hanging around this place."

"They shipped a couple of wipers out of here yesterday after we left."

Lungdren got up, and Acel followed him. They descended the stairs and crossed the street and went out on the cement pier. Muscular youths in underwear were running around on the docks and diving into the river.

"Didn't you say you had some folks in Detroit?" Acel said.

"I got a dad and a sister and a brother. I guess they're still there."

"If I had a home I believe I'd go to it."

"I wouldn't go home now. I kept thinking I'd go back home some Christmas with some money, but I don't know, one thing and another come up. I wouldn't go back like I am now for nothing."

"If my aunt hadn't married I probably would be in Boviana now. My aunt raised me, see? She didn't marry until she was forty."

"If I could make a pretty good trip and get a hundred dollars together I wouldn't mind going home. I got a bud. He's twenty-two now. He was eighteen the last time I saw him."

"Don't you ever write to them?"

"Not any more."

"Postcards are about all I write. I haven't written one of them in a long time. When I go to a new place I usually send a few."

Across the river the flags on the two American freighters fluttered violently in the wind. The sounds of winches and booms came across the water.

"I wonder if Boats was on the level about that mess job over in Jersey," Acel said.

"Yeah. Boats wouldn't bull you."

"No, I don't guess he'd bull you about a thing like that."

"Naw, he wouldn't kid you about a thing like that."

9: A DOLLAR A DAY

Acel descended the steep companionway into the galleys of the S.S. *Picfair*. The heat came up around him like steam. A small, wizened man in silk undershirt and carpet slippers turned from a simmering pot he was stirring on the big army range. The tattooing on his soggy flesh was faded.

"I'm looking for the steward," Acel said.

"I'm him." The steward wiped the front and back of his hand on his soiled white trousers. "I'm the steward."

"I hear you need a messman."

The steward showed teeth like rusty nail heads in a

smile. "You get long hours on here."

"That's okay with me. I been on the beach so long that anything looks good to me."

A dark-skinned youth in white trousers and cotton undershirt came down the companionway with a hunk of ice in his hands. Sweat made his long, knotty muscles shine.

"Joe, here's a new messman. Show him around."

In the forward part of the galleys was the officers' mess with a heavy, oil-clothed table and twelve swivel chairs. A locker through which the steering gear ran from the pilot house above separated it from the crew's mess near the stove. The crew's table was bare and grey with the streaks of scrubbing brushes and rimmed by folding chairs. There were three portholes on both sides of the galleys, but only the two forward holes were open. Joe said this was because the wash of other ships sometimes flooded the forecastle.

The sink was at the left of the stove. Dishwater was heated by a steam pipe which made a deafening, terrifying noise when it was turned on. The water was pumped out by hand.

"This is where you'll get lots of work," Joe said. The sink was filled with pots. "But I get up first in the mornings and make the fires."

Acel stripped to his undershirt and started on the pots. After a while the gangplank thudded on the deck above, and pretty soon the ship began to quiver as the screw turned. Sweat slid off Acel's nose into the sink. He got the steel wool and rubbed vigorously the black-crusted bottom of the pot.

When Acel hung up the last pot and placed the rags over the hot steam pot, Joe came over. "How you like galley work?" he said.

Acel brought out his tobacco. "I don't mind. I always worked on deck, though. This is my first time in the galleys, between you and me. I've worked in kitchens, though."

"Deckhands get sixty a month on this boat," Joe said.

"One thing about working in the galleys, you get plenty to eat. That's something."

"This boat feeds good."

"The steward is a guiney, isn't he?"

Joe nodded. "He's a good fellow, that guy is. He'll give you the shirt off his back. He owes me about twenty dollars now I been lettin' him have along, but he'll pay it back. People are all the time taking advantage of him, especially women."

"Yeah?"

"He never has a cent after pay day. He'll pay me that, though."

"I'm going to save the money I make on here. I'm sure not going to spend any." Acel dropped his cigarette in the slop bucket.

Joe reached up and rearranged the cloths Acel had hung. "This wouldn't be such a bad job only the hours are pretty long. That's why a lot of these fellows quit."

"'Bout how long do you have to work on here?"

"I get up at five, but you don't have to get up until five-thirty. Then every other night one of us has to put out the night lunch for the crew."

"Night lunch on an excursion boat?"

"Yeah. We don't tie up until around nine o'clock at nights. I usually find time in the afternoons to get an hour or so sleep. If you ever want to go ashore to get something when we're at the battery, you can get off for ten or fifteen minutes."

"And every other night one of us has to work later than nine o'clock?"

"Not much to it. Just set out a lunch for the deck and black gangs. Just see to it that they don't get in the icebox."

"That's a helluva lot of work for a dollar a day, though."

"They don't care on here whether you stay or not. The steward will tell you himself he don't blame a man for quitting."

"Well, I got to save some money."

"I can't be independent like you fellows. I got a mother and sister I got to help. Say, you don't have to fool with the officers' mess. All you got to do is handle the crew's table, see?—but I split the tips with you off the officers. I got a dollar and a quarter last pay day."

The steward came back to the stove. "You fellows better get started on the tables," he said.

Acel started setting the crew's table. He placed the soup spoons alongside the forks, but Joe came and placed them in front of the bowls. He said he had been doing it that way.

There's one thing about long hours, Acel thought, I won't get to go ashore and blow any money. I'm saving my money. I'm going to keep on smoking Bull, too. I won't draw my pay. Just enough for tobacco, and I can get some razor blades. I'd like to get a hundred dollars. If I work the rest to of the summer I can do it. With a hundred bucks I could get a new suit and new shoes and have fifty bucks in my pocket. With a new suit and everything and money in my pocket I'd feel different. That is what has been the matter m with me. It's psychological. A man can't get a job looking like a bum or feeling like one. I'll see Gholson again. I should never have went to see him in those shoes . . . .

Acel looked around the mopped, shining galleys and then remembered he had not filled the coal scuttles. It was around eleven o'clock. He started filling the scuttles when Joe came in. Joe was dressed up in a brown suit with red stripes. He said the Ken Maynard picture he had seen was good. "You got to hack slivers out of those boxes over there for the fire in the morning, you remember. You'll get through quicker as soon as you get onto things around here a little better."

While Joe was changing clothes, Acel hacked up the box. He swept the splinters into a pan and brushed them in the stove. Joe came over and said the next time Acel should make the slivers smaller.

"How many men have had this job of mine since you been on here?" Acel said.

"I've been on here two months now, and you're the seventh. Naw, eighth, that's it."

"They just quit, uh?"

"Well, one of them was sent uptown by the purser with forty bucks to buy some stuff for the ship, and he just didn't come back."

"I don't much blame them for quittin' around here."

"I can't be independent like you fellows. Don't say anything about it, see? But the purser told me he was going to get me in the cafeteria the first opening. Don't say anything about that."

"Seven quit this job since you been here, uh?" Acel looked toward the thin bunks. "What I hate is the idea of sleeping down here in this sweat box. A man isn't going to rest very well in this."

"I take my mattress up on deck some nights . . . . Whatsamatter, you got a splinter in your hand?"

Acel quit squeezing his thumb. "By god, can you sleep up on deck? I didn't know they would let you do that. I'm going to stay on this boat until I save some dough. That's all there is to it."

10: NIGHT LUNCH

Mess periods rushed swiftly for Acel on the S.S. *Picfair*. When Joe went up the companionway to ring the bell, Acel gave the tables a last onceover to see that everything was in place: the catsup and mustard, the salt and pepper, the plates of butter chips at both ends of the table, and the can of condensed milk punched twice with an ice pick.

As the steward filled the soup bowls, Acel would carry them to the table. The crew made a great stomping as they came down the companionway. By the time the first man finished his soup, Acel would be waiting with the big platter of hot meat. He had to see to it that all the platters, the potatoes and gravy and greens, kept moving. There was the pitcher of iced tea that had to be kept filled, too; and, for the men who asked for it, coffee. It was a sort of game to keep someone from yelling for something. If somebody yelled, the steward would rush over: "Whatsamatter? . . . No potatoes. Goddam. They haven't got nothing else to do but wait tables, and I got to cook and wait both."

The steward never yelled directly at Acel. He would curse Joe, though. "Goddamit, you got lead in your pratt. If you can't do this work, say so and I'll get somebody that can."

The crew was discouraged from lingering at the table after dessert. Their dishes were jerked away as soon as they had eaten. This was because there were two other set-ups at the noon period, one for the relief gang and the other for the orchestra. After the three set-ups, Joe, Acel, and Steward ate.

Steward would be solicitous of his messmen when they were alone. "You boys are not eatin' much today. Maybe you want to cook yourself some eggs?"

Joe drank his milk out of a coffee mug.

"I couldn't drink milk that way," Acel said.

"It don't have much taste to it this way, but I drink it like this, see? Because they don't know but what I'm drinking coffee, and what they don't know don't hurt them."

"The boss wanted to know yesterday if you boys were feelin' bad," Steward said. "He saw you lying there on your bunks. I told him you boys were hard workers and I don't as blame you two for sittin' down whenever you get a chance, but you know how bosses are."

"Yeah, we better watch it, I guess," Joe said.

It was Acel's job, every evening after the supper dishes were washed, to go above and back aft to the cafeteria and get two pitchers of milk for the breakfast cereals. He would wet his hair under the sink faucet, comb it carefully by the cracked mirror over the steward's bunk, and put on clean white trousers and jacket.

If the countermen in the cafeteria were busy this gave Acel a chance to stay on deck awhile. At this time of day the boat would be nearing Hell Gate.

Acel leaned over the rail and watched the shore line and river crafts. The breeze tingled in the roots of his wet hair.

They passed another excursion boat, and passengers on both ships waved. A motor launch skimmed astern. Astraddle its bow was a tanned girl in a white bathing suit. She looked like a picture in a movie magazine. Convalescents of the County Hospital stood on the shore in bathrobes and waved. Acel waved at them.

The counterman yelled that the pitchers were filled, but Acel lingered to gaze at the solid masonry and human-specked streets of Manhattan's shoreline.

After the boat berthed at its Jersey dock, the black gang came down into the galleys for a night lunch of cold tongue and cheese and leftover cafeteria sandwiches. The black gang were pallid-skinned, and they did not eat as much as the deckhands, who were making a big clatter at this time stacking chairs and washing the decks above.

After the black gang cleared out, Acel wiped the crumbs off the table and put away the meats and butter in the icebox. Both the steward and Joe were ashore. The boy who came every evening selling Manhattan tabloids came in. Acel bought a tabloid and gave the boy a piece of cake. Feeding the boy made him think of Lungdren. He had left word for Lungdren on the bulletin board of the Seafarers' Home, but the other had never showed up.

Acel did not mind if the deckhands lingered at the table after the night lunch, particularly the Armenian deckhand, Kasha. The Armenian was a broad, wrestler-muscled seaman who could lift up one side of the gangplank singlehanded. He gave Acel a book on Socialism by Bernard Shaw. He said he had bought the book, but he had thrown his money away because he couldn't read it.

Tonight, after the other deckhands had gone above to play poker, Kasha said: "Did you read any of that book today?"

Acel shook his head. "No, I didn't find any time today."

"I was thinking about what you said yesterday," Kasha said. "About men who won't work ought to be killed whether he's a bum or a rich man with a million dollars. I believe in that."

"That book says that it takes nine men working hard to support a tenth man in wealth, and it's this tenth man who ought to get it in the neck. I guess it means that when times are hard the tenth man can't use but five or six men and the rest have to bum."

"And they do their bummin' off the five or six men

who are working for the rich men," Kasha said.

"That's right."

"And if these three or four men out of a job kick about it, the tenth man gets the five or six working for him to whip them."

Acel nodded. "You got it figured out right. That's the way it is. The police work, for the rich."

Joe came in with a shirt he had gotten at the Chinese laundry. "The steward is up the street drinking three two," he said.

"If he's drinking I'll bet you have a hard time gettin' him up in the morning again," Acel said.

"I saw a couple of bums have a fight up the street," Joe said. "The little bum threw a rock at the big one, and it hit a restaurant front and the glass fell down on the big guy. The side of his face hung down on his shoulder. It made me sick at my stomach."

"He must have been canned up," Kasha said.

"Yeah, he was. Both of them."

"Did y'all ever hear about those Chinks in that chain locker out on the West Coast? . . . That's the bloodiest thing I ever heard about. Some mate was smuggling Chinks over here, and he'd put them in the chain locker, and when everybody else went ashore he'd slip forward and let them out. He got a hundred dollars a head, I think. One time, though, the ship had to anchor out before they could tie up. He had about six Chinks in that hole, and he was sweating. If he went ahead and let them drop the anchor, those Chinks would come out of that hawser hole in chunks, and if he told the skipper, it meant prison for him."

"What did he do?" Joe said.

"The Chinks went out in chunks."

11: STEWARD

Acel's new suit was a tweed with patch pockets and broad, peaked lapels. It cost fourteen dollars and ninety-five cents. There was a new shirt, too, blue, and a dark blue tie and socks and underwear, all bought in the five, twenty-five, and one-dollar store. The canvas beach bag with a zipper and an orange-and-chocolate stripe around it was the bargain. It cost ninety-eight cents. A man could highway or grab a moving train with it. The extravagance was the shoes, black-and-white oxfords. A bum with white shoes? They weighed on his mind.

He kept the new clothes under the curtains by his bunk, and for a while he worried a good deal about the possibility of having them stolen. He would part the curtains several times a day and make sure they were still there. But it would be pretty hard for somebody to get them, because he was in the galleys nearly all the time, and if he went ashore he would wear them.

I have a good front now. Lungdren won't recognize me in that rig-out. I can have those shoes dyed black this fall, and if I stay on here thirty more days I'll have fifty bucks. I got twenty coming to me now, and when I get the fifty I'm ready to shove off. If a man can't get places with a good front and fifty bucks he might as well quit. I'll see Gholson, and this time I will ask him to suggest some men I can see. If I can go to them and mention that Gholson suggested it, I'll get places. I can do it with a good front and staying at a "Y" and not worrying about where I'm going to put the bing on somebody next. I can look like somebody now.

Joe was having a hard time getting the steward up this morning. It was seven o'clock, and Acel had the breakfast set-up on and the cereals ready.

Joe shook the steward again. "Aw right, Steward, you'd better get up. It's after seven o'clock, Steward. You better get up now."

The steward made a croaking sound and pretty soon was snoring again. Joe kept going back.

"Ferchrissakes, let him lay there," Acel said.

The steward finally got up. His face looked like a bacon rind, and his hangover breath was rancid. He went over to Joe. "Who told you to put that bacon in the stove?" he said.

"I just thought I'd do it."

"Am I the steward on here or you? You're meddlin' all the time. Meddlin'. *Meddlin'!*"

"I just thought I'd do it for you."

"Who told you to? You're not responsible for breakfast. If they don't like it on here, they can fire me. It's none of your goddamned business."

"Aw right, Steward."

"It's none of your goddamned business"

"Aw right, Steward. Aw right."

After breakfast they made turkey sandwiches. This was Sunday, and the excursion-boat crowds were big. It was Acel's job to smear melted butter on the slices of white bread and pass them to the steward, who sliced the turkey and patted the meat on the bread. Joe wrapped the sandwich in waxed papers.

Sweat dripped from their foreheads. Joe went out and tried to get some beer for the steward, but the Sunday-closing law made him return empty-handed. The steward muttered as he sliced the meat.

"Folks ought to like these four-bit sandwiches," Acel said.

"They're sweat-flavored."

The steward straightened. "We're clean down here."

"The hell we are!" Acel said.

After that they worked silently.

At noon the steward was solicitous of the crew as they ate. He waited on them himself. He stood at the table, a towel around his neck, and complained about Joe. "If they like him better than they do me, they can fire me, but I'm the steward on here now and he's just a smart guy. That's what he is, smart guy. I try to be a good guy, and in my heart I know I'm a good guy, but I'm not going to stand for any two-facin', and if they like him better than they do me, they can just tell me and I'll get out and they can have him."

Acel was washing dishes when the steward yelled at him. The steward pointed at Kasha. "Coffee for this man," he said.

Acel lifted another plate out of the hot water and placed it on the drain board. Then he dried his hands.

"I'm the steward on here, and it's none of his damned business whether this ship eats or not, and if he keeps on, either me or him is going. They can decide between us, because I'll fire him off of here if he don't snap out of it, and that goes for you, too, *big boy!*"

Acel lowered the cup of coffee on the table beside Kasha's plate. When he looked up, the steward was shaking his finger. "I mean *you,* too!"

"I quit this job," Acel said. He began undoing his apron.

"You betcha you quit. Tonight you're finished."

"I'm finished now."

"No, you're not finished now."

Acel went over and threw his apron on the bunk. He pulled a towel down off the pipe and began wiping his face.

The steward approached him. "You're not going to quit now."

"You go to hell, you goddamned guiney."

The steward jerked forward, stopped, and strained as if on a leash. Kasha looked at Acel and made a spiraling motion with his finger against his head and pointed at the steward. Acel's right hand hung loosely. The steward suddenly looked drained. Acel turned and began taking off his undershirt.

After he had arranged his new clothes on the bunk and crammed his working gear in the zipper bag, Acel filled the galvanized iron bucket and began to shave. The steward went over and began to help Joe wash the dishes.

~§~

"*I quit that job* down there," Acel announced to the purser.

The purser nodded.

"I'm going to stay up here on deck, and if you want to charge me like a passenger you can take it out of my pay tonight when we get back to Jersey."

"That's all right," the purser said.

Acel bought a package of tailor-mades in the cafeteria.

After that he went over to the saloon where a half-dozen couples were dancing to the ship's orchestra. After watching them awhile he went up on the top deck and walked forward and sat down on the lifeboat cradle behind the pilot house.

Twenty bucks I got coming. Twenty bucks and a half really, but I won't get paid for this morning. Twenty bucks? I can last a long time on that. I can carry the banner three or four nights a week and every weekend get a six-bit room at the Seafarers' and clean up. I can last a long time that way. Times are picking up. This N.R.A. Ships are coming out of the boneyards. Russia. Plenty of cotton freighters will move this fall.

Two girls sat on chairs next to the rail diagonally from Acel. The one with the orange scarf around her neck faced Acel. Her feet rested on the chair of the other, and her candy-striped skirt lay parted high on her slightly opened knees. Acel looked at Orange Scarfs knees. She brushed the skirt down a little.

The other girl had on a plaid gingham blouse. She said, "D.D.R.," and Orange Scarf put her finger to her forehead thoughtfully and in a moment said, "Dolores

Del Rio."

After a while Orange Scarf looked at Acel and smiled. "Would you like to play movies with us?" The girl in the blouse turned and looked at Acel.

Acel shook his head. "I'm afraid I wouldn't be much good at that game."

They went on playing the game.

I should have went over there, Acel thought. I had a good chance to get in with them. But what could I do with a couple of girls? Get stuck for sandwiches and beer. I see myself puttin' out for beer, and me with the beach staring me in the face again. I'd just be chump enough, though, to do it if I went over there. I don't have any money to blow on women.

Acel got up and walked toward the pilot house. Before he turned he looked back. Orange Scarf was watching, but she lowered her head. Acel walked on, and his heels clicked on the deck.

Kasha turned from the flag line he was tying. "I didn't know you in that rig-out. Well, what do you say?"

"Everything is okay with me."

"That steward is screwy," Kasha said.

"I got a bellyful of it. If I'd of stayed there much longer I would have had to take a punch at him or something."

"They told me in the cafeteria to tell you that if you got hungry they'd fix you up."

"That's white of them. Yeah, I just got a bellyful of it down there with that steward."

"What are you going to do now?" Kasha said. "You going to be around the Seafarers'?"

"I guess I'll go down there. I got a few bucks, though, and I'm not worrying. Maybe we can be shipmates again sometime."

Acel went back to the saloon and leaned through the window beside the orchestra. When the dance ended, the fat saxophone player got up and stood beside him.

"I used to play in bands," Acel said.

"That's what one of the boys was telling me."

"Y'all got a pretty nice band here."

"Thanks. Why don't you dance? There's plenty of good-looking women on this boat today. Why don't you tie into one?"

"I been thinking about it."

"The next number is a waltz."

"I been thinking about it, all right."

A girl in a white linen suit holding the hand of a child in a sailor's blouse came out of the saloon and took seats beside two older women. The girl was not much larger than the child. The light brown curls under her cocked beret looked soft and fresh.

Acel kept looking at Soft Curls. Now that's something. I could go for a girl like that. Baby, you're the prettiest thing on this boat. I could marry a girl like that. You are exquisite, baby. That's the word for you. *Exquisite.* Will you dance with me? May I have this dance with you? You're the prettiest thing on this boat . . . .

The waltz began. Acel went over and stood above Soft Curls. "Would you dance?"

Soft Curls smiled and got up. The two older women smiled. Acel's hand trembled on her back as they entered the saloon.

The floor was like cork, and the music seemed noisy. Acel winked at the fat saxophone player. "Do you live in New York?" Soft Curls said.

Acel lessened the pressure of his hand on her back. "No, I live in California."

"California. My, you are a long ways from home."

"It's a pretty good piece, all right. Do you like this step all right? I saw it first in Denver. I like waltz rhythm, don't you?"

"I don't dance much on account of my operation."

"Have you had an operation?"

"This is about the first time I have danced since I had my operation."

A couple bumped into them, and Acel apologized.

"You don't look like a girl that's been sick. I looked at you a long time before I asked you to dance. I was thinking that you're the prettiest thing on this boat."

"What did you say? I did not understand you."

"I say you don't look like you've been sick."

"Mama says I shouldn't dance at all, because it is too soon after my operation. That's my mother yonder and my aunt."

"How about the next dance? I'd like to sew it up, because there's more fellows on here with their eyes on you, and it's not safe to wait until the last moment."

"I don't think so. Mama will just have a fit now because I've only been out of the hospital five weeks. I can't dance too much."

Acel escorted her back to the older women and then went over and leaned through the window by the fat saxophone player.

"You know how to pick them, all right," the musician said.

"She wasn't so bad."

A slender girl with a grey tunic coat on her arm stood in the doorway on the other side of the saloon. A pancake hat tilted forward over her right eye. She had a long nose and a dark complexion. As soon as the music started, Acel approached her.

She shook her head.

"Why, don't you dance?" Acel said.

"Not very much."

"I'll bet you do. I wish you would."

"I don't dance very well."

"Come on, let's dance."

"But I have this coat here."

"You let me have that and I'll go check it. I'll go check it for you."

She handed him the coat.

Kasha was standing at the checkroom with the first officer He grinned. "Say, how do you do it?"

"Did you see me? You haven't seen this last one, though. I got one now."

"You got to let me in on how you do it," Kasha said.

"Boy, it's a secret."

After they danced they went up on the cool top deck, and Acel got folding chairs and arranged them on the port side distant from other passengers. The breeze ruffled the silk over her breasts.

"I told you I couldn't dance," she said.

"Shoot, you dance keen. That floor up there isn't so hot, and that band could be a lot better."

She touched her chin. "I wish I didn't have these hickeys on my face."

"You got one of those? I didn't even notice."

They looked across the waters. A horizon of sea crawled against a blue sky. Wind-driven white clouds raced before a smoky blob that seemed to pursue them.

After a while she said her name was Corinne and she had been up in Connecticut visiting an aunt.

"I thought you were turning me down flat, Corinne, when I asked you to dance. I was about to give up. I didn't feel so hot there for a moment."

"I thought you were being fresh when you said, 'Don't you dance?' I told myself I'll just show this fellow I can dance."

Kasha went by and winked.

"Everyone on this boat seems to know you," Corinne said.

"I've been working on this boat. I just quit at noon."

"What did you do on here?"

"I worked on deck."

"You're not going to work on here any more?"

"No, I quit. I took a poke at a fellow and quit."

"It must be fascinating to work on a boat."

"This isn't my line. I've just been doing this to get by for a while. It isn't so bad, though, if you're on a ship that is going some place like Europe, but this river stuff is no good."

"Have you been to Europe?"

"Sure. More than once. My game is music, though. I've played in some good bands. That's the racket I'm getting back into just as soon as things pick up."

"Maybe this N.R.A. is going to help us."

"I hope it does."

Corinne nodded. "I hope it does, too."

After a while Corinne opened her handbag and brought out some Kodak pictures. "These are some pictures we made up in Connecticut. Would you like to see them?"

"If you are in them I do."

There was a picture of Corinne in a bathing suit. Her hips curved voluptuously under the skirtless garment. A youth in slacks and sweat shirt stood there with his arm around her.

"That's a boy I ran around with some while I was up there."

"I don't like that part of the picture."

"I got a silly grin on my, face."

"I don't call that silly. If you want me to talk plain, that picture is hot. That suit kind of fits you. Looking at that makes me feel funny inside. Honey, I'm tellin' you."

"You are just saying that."

"Don't think I'm just sayin' it. Already I know meeting you isn't going to do me any good. No kiddin', that's a knockout. That suit kind of sets you off."

"He's just a boy I ran around with some up there."

"You're not sweet on him?"

"Lord, no. He's just a boy I knew up there."

"I'm glad to hear that. No kiddin', sweet, I'm beginning to feel sorry I met you. I was getting along pretty good without a girl, and then one like you comes along and makes me wish I had one. I'm sorry I met you, because now I'll think about you. That's the trouble with you, honey, you're too sweet."

"You are sweet yourself."

Corinne lived in Brooklyn with two unmarried aunts, she said. She was a typist, but she had not worked in more than a year now. Her aunts worked in a department store and threw it up to her at times that she did not act like she wanted to work. "They are awful narrow-minded," she said.

"Yeah, I know," Acel said.

"I hate to go back."

"You had much experience, honey?"

"Sure."

"I mean, you know the kind of experience I mean?"

"Sure."

"I mean sex experience."

"Sure."

Acel pulled out cigarettes, and Corinne took one. The match he held for her trembled. "That's what you are doing to me," he said. "I'm falling for you, honey."

"You certainly are different."

"I'll bet you got a kick out of me choking up the way I did when I asked you if you ever had any experience. I didn't know but what you taught a Sunday school somewhere. I'll bet you got a kick out of that."

"You are sweet."

"I'm gettin' fogbound over you, if you want to know."

"You are only saying that. I know that I am skinny."

"The only thing I don't like about this picture is this guy here. He looks like he thinks he's with Miss God or some body."

Acel flipped his cigarette high in the air and watched

its breeze-tossed spiral to the water. "I guess your aunts will be waiting for you at the Battery?"

"Lord, no. They don't know when I'm coming in for sure. I wrote and told them I would be home yesterday, but they don't know."

"They don't know when you'll be in, then, for sure?"

Corinne shook her head. "They'll complain whenever it is. I know them."

"Let's make it tomorrow then?"

"I don't know what you mean."

"I mean that tonight you and I will be together."

"Oh, I can't do that."

"What's to keep you from it?"

"Oh, I couldn't do that. I'm in bad enough at home now. Besides, where would we go?"

"Don't you worry about that. We'll find a place to go."

"No, I can't do that."

"Why not, honey? You can't let me down now. I'm too far gone on you. I don't want to tell you goodbye down at the Battery. C'mon, honey. Say yes. Say it."

"I can give you my address."

"Aw, we're together now, and why can't we just keep on? Aw, don't now. Say yes."

"I really shouldn't."

"Gee, honey, that's the way. That's a break. It's such a break I'm afraid there's a catch in it. Is there a catch in it, baby?"

"I really shouldn't be going with you."

12: CORINNE

Barefooted deckhands worked furiously, stripping the chair-littered decks of the darkened, tied-up S.S. *Picfair*. Acel, with the canvas bag at his feet, waited for the purser. Kasha, chairs under his arms and with his trousers rolled up on his muscular thighs, stopped.

"Where did the girlfriend go?"

"She's over in the Lackawanna station."

"She going to cost you much?"

"This is on the level, Kasha. She's nice."

"Oh. Well, I guess I'll see you around the Seafarers' this fall. I guess I'll stay on here until she ties up this fall."

"Sure, we'll see each other."

The purser called through the grilled window of his cabin. He spread the bills out and pushed them under the grill. "Twenty-one dollars. That is right?"

Acel nodded. "Thanks."

The steward, in his apron, leaned in the galleys companionway. When Acel started for the gangplank, he said, "Well, so long, Steward."

The steward approached eagerly. "I told them to pay you for today, a full day."

"That was white of you."

"I'm sorry we couldn't get along."

"I am too, Steward. So long."

Corinne was not in the railroad station. It was a big station, high-vaulted and full of deep-toned echoes. There were not many people on the long, glistening benches. Acel looked over all the benches twice and then went over to the ferry station.

The ferry ticket agent said he hadn't noticed a girl in a pancake hat carrying a weekend bag, but Acel could go in and look around.

She was not in the ferry station.

Acel came out and set his bag on the sidewalk close to the curb. He shook his head at the cab driver. Sweat dripped off his nose, and he wiped his face with his hand and threw off the sweat with a click of his two fingers. He took off his coat and rolled up his sleeves. I don't believe that girl ran out on me. That's the kind of breaks I get, though. A dollar on my pay I wasn't expecting, and now the damned girl gone. It's the best thing, though. I got twenty-one bucks, and it's going to have to last me a long time. I'm pretty good, thinking about blowing money in for hotel rooms with the beach staring me in the face. I would have spent it, too . . . .

He went back into the Lackawanna station.

There she was!

"God, I been lookin' everywhere for you. Where have you been?"

"I was in the rest room. I thought you would be a long time on the boat."

Acel sat down on the bench beside her. "I'm hot as hell."

"You sure are perspiring."

"I'm hot as hell if anybody wants to know."

They lighted cigarettes. "What do you think of us staying over on this side tonight and going on over to New York in the morning?" Acel said.

"If you want to."

He got up and picked up their bags. "Let's get in the saddle, then."

Shadowed fire escapes cobwebbed the rust-colored stone here of the waterfront hotel. Acel gave the cab driver a dime tip. They entered the hotel, and Corinne sat in a chair by the elevator, and Acel went up to the clerk with the black sleeve bands.

"How much?" Acel said.

"Five dollars for a double."

"You saw me coming, didn't you, mister?"

"I got one with shower. Four dollars."

Acel picked up the pen. "That's better."

They followed the clerk through narrow, carpeted passageways. Acel grasped Corinne's hand and pressed it. "You got to strike a match to see the light in this hall."

Corinne pressed his hand.

They were alone in the room now. Acel looked at the print of a ship at sea on the wall. "This isn't so bad," he said when he turned around.

Corinne sat on the edge of the bed. She shook her head.

"They tried to stick us five bucks for it, though."

"You can stay in uptown New York hotels for that," Corinne said.

"Four dollars isn't so bad, though." Acel slapped his hands.

"Can you hold the fort down while I go out and see

about a little drinking liquor?"

Corinne stood up and took off her coat. "If you won't be gone too long."

A man at the corner told Acel he could buy gin in three places in that block.

Acel bought a drink at the bar and then two bottles of gin. The gin was seventy-five cents a bottle. He bought two bottles of ginger ale and two lemons and a container of ice.

Corinne was in pajamas. They were blue silk and wrinkled. She sat on the bed with her back against arranged pillows. The humming fan on the wall made the damp curls on her forehead tremble.

Acel placed the sacks on the dresser. "The old man below gave me a lecture," he said. "He said young fellows didn't know when to stop drinking. I told him not to worry. I wasn't going to raise hell. Baby, you look mighty sweet and cool there."

"Did you stop at the drugstore?" Corinne asked.

"Drugstore?"

"You know."

"Dern, I forgot that. Well, I forgot to get cigarettes, anyway, and I got to bum old Sour Face below for another glass. Hold the joint down again, will you, honey?"

When he returned, Acel took a shower. He toweled himself until his skin glowed and came out of the bathroom, bare to the waist. He flexed his arm muscles. "How you like these, baby?"

The surface of the dresser was an untidy miscellany with the gin bottles and cigarettes and Corinne's opened handbag. There was her lipstick and her comb with hairs clinging to it.

Acel took the cork out of the bottle again. "You about ready for another shot?"

"I have been ready."

"We ought to be gettin' a buzz on this stuff pretty soon."

"I feel it some already," Corinne said. "Don't you a little?"

"I feel it a little, all right."

Corinne sat on the bed and made the ice tinkle in the glass. When she smiled, her lips unsheathed saliva-bright teeth. Acel sat down beside her on the edge of the bed. "I've just been thinking that girls like you ought to go to heaven. This is the best time I've had in a long time. I was lying in a park not so long ago, and I saw a couple pettin', and I wondered then how long it would be before I had someone. It's mighty nice sittin' here and looking at you and knowing that you are mine."

He bent over her, pressing his mouth on her lips and holding her tighter. She stroked his back.

Corinne came out of the bathroom and got a cigarette off the dresser. "I have an uncle who is a cashier in a restaurant over in Astoria, and he says this N.R.A. is going to put a lot of men to work in cafés. Maybe he could give you a job."

Acel got up off the bed. "You wouldn't want no bus boy for a sweetie, would you?"

"I had rather have you that than a sailor in Africa or some place."

"Don't you worry about me gettin' a job," Acel said.

He poured gin into the two glasses. "I'm liable to have a real one pretty soon. You've heard of Red Gholson, haven't you? Well, there's a man who's promised to give me a job. I mean Red Gholson, too. I'll show you some of my clippings in a minute."

They drank the liquor.

Acel brought the newspaper clippings out of the big soiled envelope and spread them on the dresser. Some of them were yellow and broken. He pointed out his name and identified himself in the photographs of orchestras. "I didn't know you could sing."

"Sure. 'Course I'm not any big shot, but I could do more in a band than double-tongue a trumpet. I can dance, too. I don't mean amateur stuff in that, either. If I ever get hold of a band, I've got some publicity ideas that will work. I'll have me a band some of these days."

"I hope you stay in New York."

"Don't you worry about that."

"What are you going to do tomorrow?"

"I don't know. I know this, though, I can get a lot drunker on you than I can on this stuff."

"I was thinking that you could come out to the house. I could tell my aunts that you drove me down from Connecticut, that I just waited and came with you. Don't you tell them, now, or say anything about being out of a job or working on a boat. I'll tell them you are a musician."

"Don't your aunts like old salts?"

"Sure enough now, don't you say anything, Ace. My aunts are funny."

"Here, honey, here's another drink."

"I don't want one this time."

"You going to be a sissy on me?"

"I don't want one this time."

Corinne showed Acel her memorandum book. In it were pasted a lot of poems, most of them by Dorothy Parker.

There was a letter from a boy in school, and she showed this. It was illustrated with pen sketches that depicted grief and loneliness and love.

"This guy must be sweet on you."

"Don't you think these drawings are cute?"

"That's what I got against you women. Now this fellow here probably thinks you're in church tonight."

"He's not thinking about me. This letter is three months old. He's got a girl, you can bet."

Acel poured another drink. "How many sweethearts you had?"

"Not very many. I've just had two, really sweethearts."

"Just two, uh?"

"Just two really."

"I've had a bunch of sweethearts."

They lay on the bed. Corinne said her first sweetheart was the brother of her best girlfriend. He worked in Wall Street and had a Cadillac. She never did get to drive the Cadillac, though. She had an abortion. He lost his job in the crash and was in California now. Once in a while she got a letter from him saying he was going to send for her.

"I guess you wish he would, don't you?" Acel said.

"Sometimes."

"I guess you're still pretty sweet on him?"

"I don't think about him much. My aunts throw it up to me, and sometimes I get tired of staying at home."

Acel cleared his throat. "How many affairs you had?"

Her head moved on the pillow toward him. "Not many."

"How many you had, like us here?"

"I don't make a habit of this."

"Nineteen? Twenty?"

"I am not as common as you think I am."

"A couple of hundred?"

Corinne got up. "You are getting smart now." She slid off the edge of the bed and stood above him. He stared at her sullenly. "You don't have any business talking to me that way," she said.

"You haven't answered me yet," he said.

Her navel showed through the damp, twisted pajamas.

"I knew I should not have come up here with you. I wouldn't have come up here with you if I had known you were going to act this way. It isn't too late for me to go home."

"Forget it," Acel said. "I'm just poppin' off. It's none of my business. I know that. Forget it." He got up and reached out to touch her, but she drew back against the dresser.

"Hell, honey, you're not going to get sore about it, are you? What are you so mad about? I didn't mean anything. I spoke out of turn, all right, but golly, don't get mad about it. Jesus Christ. You're not going to get mad about it, are you?"

Corinne began straightening the damp pajama jacket.

"C'mon, honey, I didn't mean anything. No use of gettin' this mad over nothing. Why, honey, I'm not good enough for you to wipe your . . . . your feet on. Don't be mad."

"You have no business talking to me that way."

"I know it, honey. You don't have to keep telling me. Here, honey, let me just hold your hand."

"I would not have come up here with you if I had known you were going to act this way."

"Aw, Jesus Christ. Let me kiss your hand, honey . . . . Just your hand . . . . That's a girl . . . . You're sweet . . . . I'm not going to be able to get along without you . . . . Let's take another drink, and then we got to get some sleep."

13: HANGOVER

Corinne would not take a drink. She was going home now, and she did not want it on her breath.

They stopped at a café near the ferry station, but they only drank the coffee and left the sweet rolls untouched.

They sat forward on the ferryboat and watched the Manhattan shore line push toward them like a mammoth postcard. "You will be out all right tonight?" Corinne said.

"You know how to get there now all right?"

Acel nodded.

They walked from the ferry station to the elevated railway and stood by the newsstand. "Maybe you would like a paper to read going home?" Acel suggested. "The *News?* . . . The *Mirror?*"

She shook her head.

"Don't you want to ride a taxi home?"

"No, the subway is just right up there. This is your L here."

"Which side of this L do I go up on to get to South Ferry? I'm always turned around in this damned town."

"This is the side."

"Well, I guess we might as well say goodbye?" Acel said.

"I will see you tonight?"

Acel nodded. "Be a good girl." He watched her cross the street and then turned and began the Elevated climb. His stomach burned.

~§~

The sun lay on South Street like a blistering plaster, glaring up from the sidewalk. The chowder smell from the curb lunch wagon nauseated Acel. A man in a sweat-discolored felt hat and with a finger missing on his left hand dragged ahead of him. Acel spurted by.

At the cigar stand in the lobby of the Seafarers' Home he bought a sack of Bull Durham. The tobacco smoke was like hot water on his lungs, and he dropped the cigarette.

Lungdren was not in the lobby. That guy may still be around here, Acel thought. He went up into the recreation hall, but Lungdren was not there, nor in the writing room, nor in the washrooms.

Acel came out of the Home and stood on the curb. A squat figure in a blue serge suit, smoking a pipe, came across the street toward him. It was Boats.

"You haven't seen Lungdren around, have you?" Acel said.

"Didn't you know about him?"

"What?"

"I thought you knew. He's dead. Two months."

"Lungdren is?"

"Didn't you know it?"

"I'll be goddamned."

"Let's go over to the Wobbly and get some coffee," Boats said.

"That's the damnedest thing I ever heard of. It makes me want to puke. That's the way it makes me feel."

The coffee burned in Acel's stomach like hot lead. He drew his forefinger across his forehead and flung the sweat on the floor. "How long you been ashore, Boats?"

"I been back two weeks. I'm shipping boatswain on the *Seagal* next month. It's going to be a long trip. How would you like to come along?"

"Naw, I don't know."

"We're going to Frisco, and I know I could get you signed on there."

"Naw, I think I'm going to hang around here. You know, I told Lundgren he ought to do something for that cold. I kept wondering why I never heard from him. Pneumonia, uh?"

"A man can't starve himself and expect to fight pneumonia."

"I guess so."

A man with a bowl of soup cupped in both hands worked cautiously past their table and lowered it carefully on the adjoining table.

"So you quit the *Picfair?*"

"Yeah."

"I don't blame you."

"Yeah. I'm planning on hanging around here in New York. I'm going to get a shore job. I got a girl I kind of like."

"You got a pretty nice front on you there. Where did you get that suit?"

"I got this, anyway. I got that much out of that boat anyway."

"So you got you a girl now?"

Acel nodded. "Pretty nice girl."

A counterman came and tacked up a placard on the wall above their heads: *Bread, beans & coffee, 10¢.*

"Where you stayin'?" Acel asked. "The Seafarers'?"

"No, I'm on their black list sure enough now. They won't hardly let me come in the lobby now. I'm staying in a two-bit place over on the Bowery. They're just stalls, but they'll give you a quarter for every bedbug you find."

"Chicago's a good place to get by in if you just got a few nickels. There's a place there they call the Legion Hotel. For two bits you get a flop and coffee and rolls for breakfast and soup in the afternoon."

"That's pretty good. Chicago's a pretty good town."

"I wish I had me a good job just for a couple of months," Acel said. "I don't mean this dollar-a-day business."

"You busted?"

"No, I got a few dollars. It won't last while you got a girl, though."

"Where does she live?"

"Over in Brooklyn about a million miles."

"We're having a little meeting tonight, some of the boys. We're going to get up petitions asking the Seafarers' to open up that fifth floor and make a dormitory of free beds out of it. We're going to ask them to start putting out a free meal every day, too."

"They won't give you nothing over there."

"How would you like to meet with us?"

"I'm going to see my girl tonight."

~§~

Acel found the house in Brooklyn at last. It was a three-story frame house with bay windows and a "Room for rent" sign. There was a sign, "Ice," over the basement entrance, and in the doorway stood a man in a black shirt smoking a cigar.

On the third story was Apartment 3-F. Acel knocked on the door, and then a tall woman in a black silk dress and lace collar stood there. Her face was shiny and porous.

"May I see Corinne?"

"She does not live here anymore."

"You mean she does not stay here?"

"She is not here," the woman said.

Acel descended the stairway and passed the ice man. He went on down to the corner and looked at the display of bottles in the grocery-store window. The ginger ale was three for a quarter. In Jersey he and Corinne paid two bits for two bottles. Things were cheaper here in Brooklyn.

"Nice weather," the ice man said.

Acel nodded and went up the stairway again to Apartment 3-F.

Steps approached the door firmly, and then the door opened and the woman in the black dress stood there again.

"Would you tell me where Corinne moved?"

"I could not."

Another woman came and stood in the doorway. She was plump, and her hair was plastered down as if she had been to the beauty parlor.

"I was to see her tonight, and that's why," Acel said. "She does not live here, and we do not know where she is," the plump woman said.

On the subway Acel thought he might just ride it the rest of the night. The papers said hundreds of fellows and girls rode the subways all night. The people in this car, though, didn't look like people who would ride the rest of the night. Those two fellows there with wrist watches, they're not all-night subway riders. And that girl there with the hatbox isn't. That old man there might. The girl with the hatbox got up and moved toward the center of the car. Under the diaphanous chiffon of her dress the curving outline of her tight undergarment moved on her thighs. Corinne's panties showed through her dress like that.

Acel got off at Fifth Avenue and walked up to Central Park. The band was playing in the Mall. He sat on a bench and watched skaters go by in churning streams.

A blonde, loose-breasted woman and a little boy sat on a bench next to Acel. The boy kept wandering off, and the woman would get up and call him until he returned. She looked like that blonde woman in the tabloids, the one they were trying upstate for poisoning her husband, Acel thought.

When the little boy unbuttoned his trousers, his mother laughed about it and looked at Acel and smiled. The child tottered over to Acel and stood before him with his hands held up and his elbows on his stomach.

"What have you got to say, big boy?" Acel said.

The child struck at Acel and then wobbled back to his mother.

14: ANN

With Corinne's letter, Acel waited in Battery Park for the fixed hour of their meeting. Three pleasure steamers lay alongside the landing, their decks aflame with holiday seekers Out of the flashing bells of the musicians' instruments at the rails came spurring gusts in Harlem tempo. Water-soaked boys swam underneath the passenger-lined rails begging for pitched nickels. Excursion barkers moved in the dock crowds with the airs of circus ringmasters.

"Mr. Stecker, I believe," Corinne said.

Acel jumped up. "Hello there, Corinne." She was wear in the grey tunic coat, and her lips looked brighter with paint.

"I begin to think you weren't going to show up," Acel said. "I begin to get worried."

"I am not late, am I?"

"I guess not. It's okay."

They sat on the bench.

"Why didn't you wait for me the other night?" Acel said.

"You could have waited on the corner or something."

"I did. I waited a long time. I just thought you were not coming. I thought I was stood up."

"I was a little late, but I got off at the wrong station and got all balled up, but you ought to have known I would have been there."

"I started to not even write you. I did not know how you felt about it."

The whistle on the stack of the largest steamer groaned in a little cloud of white steam, and the deck-hands attacked the gangplank as if their jobs depended on doing it in two minutes. She parted from the dock sluggishly, like a gorged sea mammal, and then, her screw kicking up a taffy spray, slid releasedly toward the East River.

"Damit, honey, I wish you and me were on that boat. You sure can have a good time on a boat, can't you?"

"I hate to see boats go. They always make me blue."

"We'll take a trip some of these days. Up to Bear Mountain."

Corinne nodded.

Acel's finger went into his watch pocket. "While I think about it, you better take this money here."

Corinne pushed his hand back. "No, I don't want to do that. You need that yourself."

"Now don't start any of that stuff. It's bad enough the dab it is."

"No, there is not any use of that. I don't want to."

"Why isn't there some use? This is enough to get you by for a few days. A lot can happen in a few days. I'm going to look up Gholson. I'm going to tell him this time that my wife is here and I have to have something to do."

A flake of a man in a shriveled seersucker suit went by with a yellow roll of paper under his arm.

"Are you my girl, or are you?" Acel said.

"Of course I am, darling."

"That's all I want to know."

"I did not know for sure whether you even thought about me or not after we left. I did not know whether to write you or not."

"You know now, and I want you to take this money. You got to have a place to stay until I kind of get on my feet."

"I have a place to stay for a while. You do not have to worry about that."

"Where are you stayin'?"

"With Ann."

"Who is Ann?"

"She's a good friend of mine. You'd like her. I can stay with her."

"Where does she live?"

"On Fifty-first."

"What does she do?"

"It's a sort of a little tearoom. She sells liquor."

"A joint, uh?"

"You can call it that if you want to."

"That's what it is. I thought so. You're stayin' in a whorehouse, uh?"

Corinne got up. "You're going to be reasonable now or I'm not going to stand here and talk to you. Ann is as square as she can be. I told her about you, and she understands."

"I guess you told her I was a bum."

"I most certainly did not. I know you are going to be somebody some day. The difference is that you can sleep on park benches and get by now. Ann says that a down-and-out man begs and a woman sells."

"So that's it. I thought so. I figured that." Acel got up.

"So that's what you're going to do?"

"Goodbye, Ace."

"Wait a minute. Sit back down here." Acel thumbed at the bench. Corinne returned and sat down.

"I can't pull money out of the air," Acel said. "I can't do that."

"I know it. But you don't have to say anything about Ann."

"So you're stayin' with a whore?"

Corinne got up again. "I am not going to stay here

another minute."

"That's okay with me.

Corinne looked at Acel sharply, and he reached out and grasped her hand. "Now wait a minute, let's figure this out."

Corinne looked toward the boats.

"Take this money and stay some place just for a couple of days. I don't want you going around that place, Corinne. I'm not going to be long about gettin' a job, and then everything will be okay. You just wait and see if you don't believe it. There's enough for you to get by on for a few days. I'm tellin' you, Corinne, I'll have a job pretty soon. Let's figure this out now. Corinne, I'll swear."

15: FIFTY BUCKS

The stirring leaves above Acel and Boats rattled like typewriters behind closed doors. Acel sat with his knees drawn under his chin, staring across the sloping grass of Central Park toward the shaft of Columbus Circle. Boats spat the blade of grass off his tongue. "Now you take you going around and trying to get a hashing job. You're equipped to entertain people with music. There's a lot of music-hungry people in this world. They are denied music, and you are denied the chance to entertain them. Any clodhopper can beat you washing dishes, and if I was a boss I had rather have him. You should be doing the thing you can do the best, and the reason you are not is

because under this system of government they call democracy one man can pay a crooner one thousand dollars
for one night and another man can't let his child give a
penny to a grind organ."

"I got to get something to get by on awhile."

"If you went on the *Seagal* you could get some
money ahead."

"I'd like to make a real trip like that, but I'd be just
like I am now when I got back. I can't get a job in an
orchestra on a freighter out in the middle of the ocean,
and there is no use of trying to have a girl if you go to
sea."

"I wish I could tell you what to do."

"Something is going to happen."

The approaching policeman was smacking the soles
of park sleepers. Acel and Boats got up and moved
toward Columbus Circle.

"What do you think about these girls that hustle for
a living?" Acel said.

"I have as much respect for a woman who sells her
body for pleasure as I do for these sweatshop slaves and
these girls in these cheap department stores. Take all
these women running back and forth from these offices.
They are prostituting their minds and their hands to
make some man richer. As long as a country is run to
make men rich there will be harlots and robbers. I can't
understand these men who claim to be Christians. Jesus
Christ was a Socialist, and damn near every preacher
crucifies him to this day. That's why I spit on the church."

Acel nodded. "I've thought that the difference
between a bank president and a bank bandit is that the

robbery of the banker is legal. The bandit has more guts. I think that's the reason bandits are made heroes by the public, because people sort of sense that there isn't much difference."

"You got it right there. When I see one of these rich women with a fistful of diamonds, I think that there goes a woman who represents a half-dozen bums, a bunch of whores, and a bunch of dead babies. I don't see how they can call a country like this civilized. What they mean is that they've civilized murder. Even a dog when he gets his guts filled will go off and let another dog have the carcass, but not man. He'll eat his fill and either put the carcass in cold storage or peddle it for thirty-three and a third per cent. Then they say there is a heaven for man and when a dog dies he's dead all over."

"I've always figured," Acel said, "I mean for a long time, that we don't know what it is all about. We're just a bunch of microbes living on a big body, the earth. Just a bunch of germs, and we know just about as much what it's all about as the germs do in our own bodies."

They stopped and looked at the display of silk socks in the Times Square shop window. They were fifteen cents a pair.

"I wouldn't mind having a job clerking in a store," Acel said.

"I despise these sentimentalists," Boats said. "Guys that drop a coin in a beggar's cup and consider it heaven insurance."

The sign in the stairway lobby, posted amid a photographic display of dancing girls, read: *Are you lonely in the Big City? One hundred beautiful hostesses.*

Ten cents a dance. No extra charge.

"I tried to get a job up there," Acel said. "They got a couple of bands."

The barker in front of the flaming canvas had long side burns "In the flesh, gentlemen, in the flesh. We do not appeal to the base in men. That is not our purpose with this exhibition. This is educational. But I'll tell you men that if you are red-blooded and virile, regular he-men, you will know that you are men when you see this. And just for today, gentlemen, in the flesh, mind you, fifteen cents. That's all. Fifteen cents. And you see everything, in the bare, naked flesh . . . ."

They walked on. "It's all in bottles," Acel said. "I've got hooked."

"Things like that are the eruptions of our moralists. What the moralists in this country need is a good physic. They are encouraging race suicide and perversion."

The young orator in front of the library flung out his hand. "Don't tell me I don't know what revolution is. My father died in Moscow. But how did the leaders of our Communist party go to Washington? How did they? In airplanes. How did me and my comrades go? In a Model T truck without brakes."

The Teutonic-headed man with his arms folded across his chest said: "Don't you think our leaders should go in style?"

"We should all go alike. We should all dress alike. Our Communist leaders dress like Jim Walker and have a different woman every night."

"Do you think our leaders should go like bums?" the Teuton said. "Do you think overalls should be the uniform of our party?"

"No, but they don't have to look like Lexington Avenue and ride in Packards."

Acel and Boats left the gathering around the young speaker and went over and leaned on the balustrade overlooking Fifth Avenue.

"I listened to a nigger over there one day," Acel said. "He said the black man would rule the world some day. He said everybody was black in the first place, but a bunch of humans have bleached out."

Boats laughed.

"I can't get interested in that sort of speaking, though," Acel said. "I mean that bunch over there. Some guy will say the world is round, and there'll be another dope who'll jump up and say it's a triangle and offer to go in the library and prove it. They argue over there like they were going to cut each other's throat."

"Some of them don't know what they're talking about, all right."

"This isn't gettin' me a job, standing here, spittin' on the sidewalk. Listen, Boats, I got to get some money."

Boats looked at Acel sharply.

"I'm going to tell you something, see? I've been thinking about it a whole lot. Now don't think I'm bullin'. I know a fellow here that's got plenty, and he's making plenty of money and I can see him. He's got a ring that's worth plenty. I can get it."

"What do you mean, stick him up?"

"Yeah."

"With your finger?"

"I can get a gun."

"You're talking like a crazy man now."

"I told you I was serious."

"You'd be about as good a hijacker as I am a horn blower. Don't think I'm getting righteous, but leave hijacking to the guys that know something about it. Why don't you take this girl and you two go get you a little dump some place and give yourself a chance? You could live on almost nothing."

"Not on nothing, though."

Boats spat over the balustrade. "I like to hit that bird going there."

"I'm either going to sleep in a jail or a house," Acel said.

"I'll be damned if I sleep in any more stalls."

"Listen, why don't you do like I said? You get this girl and you two get you a little place somewhere. I'm shipping out in a couple of weeks, see? And I got fifty bucks I'm not going to need. Don't worry, I'll get it back from you."

"Where you got fifty bucks?"

"I worked all summer. Don't worry about that."

16: MR. AND MRS. STECKER

Acel had lettered the slip above the brass mailbox himself: *Mr. and Mrs. Acel E. Stecker.* He looked at it now as he opened the empty box. Shifting the bundle and the small cardboard box back under his right arm, he went down the hallway and turned and started up the stairway.

The apartment of the Steckers overlooked the alley. There were two rooms, one which contained a cook range, a dining table, and a curtained kitchen table which concealed the bathtub; the other, a bed and a mirror. Clothing hung on the walls of the smaller room. In the larger, too, there was a small table on which some day they expected to place a radio. On it now lay the book by Bernard Shaw.

Acel unwrapped the bundle on the kitchen table. It was a bottle of gin. If she squawks about this, I'll tell her that she didn't say anything when I bought two bottles over in Jersey. It isn't going to hurt anything with Boats coming to eat with us tonight.

It was only a little after five o'clock, and Acel had an hour to wait for Corinne. She worked afternoons at the newspaper office, soliciting classified advertisements over the telephone. She got ten per cent commission.

Acel raised the window and looked down into the alley. A bunch of kids were playing with a rubber ball. A woman on the roof across the alley was taking clothes down from a line. A truck honked, and the children took their time getting out of its path.

Acel turned back and looked around the room. He could go out and get the steak, but Corinne had warned him about that. There was no icebox, and the thing to do was to wait until the last minute. He could peel the potatoes, though, and put them in cool water so they would stay crisp.

After he peeled the potatoes he went over and count-

ed the packets of razor blades in the cardboard box.
There were fourteen. That was what he had thought. That
made twenty-two packs he had sold that day. One dollar
and ten cents clear.

He looked out the window again. The kids were
gone. The trouble about living in the back of a joint was
that you couldn't see if anybody was coming. You didn't
know they were here until the knob turned in the door.
Seven flights of stairs was too much for a girl to have to
climb. It made a man puff.

Corinne came in with the meat and lettuce and a jar
of strawberry preserves. She showed Acel the runner in
her stocking. "Can you beat that?" she said.

Acel scraped the grease out of the can into the potato
pot. "I sold twenty-two packs today."

"That's good," Corinne said. "I did not do so bad
today.

"I sold twelve dollars' worth of ads."

"What I got to do is get a side line," Acel said. "Abe
was showing me some cards today I believe I can sell.
And some booklets. French stuff."

"Women?"

"Yeah."

"You don't want to start around with that kind of
thing now."

"What's the difference? It would just be a side line,
and you make four times more off of them than you do
razor blades."

"You don't have to sell those things."

"Why, did you ever see any?"

"Yes."

"Where did you ever see any?"

"I don't know, I forget. I don't know."

"At that damned Ann's, I'll bet." Acel dropped the potatoes in the boiling grease and jumped back with the splutter.

"I wish you didn't have to just sell around South Ferry,"

Corinne said. "Why do you have to just be around down there all the time?"

"I know a bunch of seamen, that's why."

"You could sell a lot more uptown. Why don't you stay around this part of town?"

"I couldn't sell snowballs in hell up around here."

"You and that Boats." Corinne went into the bedroom. "Hey, Corinne, I got us a little bottle of gin."

Corinne came to the door. She was in a slip and was running her hands up through the gingham house frock. "What did you get that for?"

"I thought we'd have a few drinks tonight."

Corinne lifted the dress and began pulling it down about her head. "So you and Boats can get drunk?"

"There you go. Boats doesn't even drink. What do you think about that? Now that's something else you got to hand him. Don't think I haven't noticed you digging him. I don't suppose I should have gotten it."

Corinne came over and took the fork out of Acel's hand and stirred up the potatoes.

"It just cost fifty cents," Acel said.

"Oh, I don't care, honey. I just don't like to see you around down there so much. It's just that Boats is always .... always ...."

"Always what?"

"Always preaching. You are not going to get any-where as long as you run around with him. You're not a sailor. What good is it doing you?"

"I'm not going to argue with you. What do you mean, not doing me any good? Because I'm not making fifty dollars a week?"

"No, that is not it. I mean what good is all this talking around about seamen going to do you?"

"You mean about the petitions? That's not talking, that's taking action. I've got two hundred names on my petition, and Kasha has almost that many. Boats has about four hundred, and there's some more out. That's not talking. They are going to do something about it down at the Seafarers' this time, I'll bet you. They can't look at a thousand names of seamen and then fail to do anything."

~§~

Acel washed the dishes and Boats dried them. Corinne, barelegged, mended the runner in the stocking. When the dishes were finished, the men seated themselves at the table, and Boats filled his pipe. Corinne went into the bedroom and put on her stockings.

"So you think we ought to present the petitions tomorrow?" Acel said.

Boats nodded. "Yes, because I can't wait much longer now, leaving Monday. We got enough names. I think they'll come across."

"You want Kasha to go in with us to see the Judge?"

"Yeah. Three is just enough."

Corinne came out. "What are you going to do to-morrow?"

"I told you, honey," Acel said.

"We are going to show Judge Ross the petitions," Boats said.

"You want to talk to him straight and plain," Acel said. "Just put them on his desk and say, 'Look here.'"

"I will tell him that these petitions represent the sentiment of eight hundred seamen against the manner in which the Home is being operated. I will tell him that these seamen feel that if the Home continues to raise money and get endowments on the grounds that it is providing homeless seamen with food and shelter, that it will have to start seeing to it that jobless seamen do get some benefit or we will hold demonstrations all over New York."

"They got it coming to them."

"I'll tell him that if the salaries of executives must be cut in order to help these seamen, then the salaries must come down. I'm going to put in, too, about the hiring around there of men who know nothing about the sea."

"They got it coming to them, all right."

"I want you and Kasha to be there just to sort of lend moral support. If they get on a high horse, we'll go out in the park and make some talks and get up a crowd. I think the Judge will listen to us, though. If we got any hotheads started down there, it would be just too bad. We don't want any trouble. Then they would have an excuse to yell Bolsheviks and Reds and call the city cops. Caution everybody to keep cool, see?"

After Boats left, Acel cleaned the saucer they had used for an ashtray at the sink and dried it. He looked at the picture of the radio crooner's wife in the tabloid who was suing for divorce, and then read the story. After that he turned off the light and went into the bedroom.

Corinne had on the blue pajamas tonight. She lay on her side and did not look up. Acel undressed, turned out the light, and then went over to the window on the fire escape and lifted the shade. It ran to the top.

"I'll be damned if I get that down now," he said.

Acel lay on the bed and listened to the clock ticking in the next room. An elevated train's roar drowned the ticking, and after it was gone Acel tried to pick up the ticking sound again, but a fog horn sounded on the river. He turned over again cautiously.

Corinne reached out and placed her hand on his breast.

"What are you thinking about?"

"Aren't you asleep? Aw, I don't know. I was thinking about tomorrow."

Corinne pressed closer, and Acel's arms went around her, and his lips found her mouth. Her fingernails cut into his flesh.

17: MUTINY

Mack Winters, chief of police in the Seafarers' Home, was a tall man with a crop of hair like steel wool. He sat now at his desk looking up at the three men, Boats, Acel, and Kasha.

"Judge Ross has refused to see us," Boats said. "I have come to you to tell you that we represent more than four hundred seamen and feel entitled to an audience." He placed the soiled petitions on the desk. "There are nearly eight hundred signatures on these petitions. I have the consent of these men and am urged by them to present them formally to Judge Ross. I believe the claims we have are just."

Winters stood up and took off his glasses. There were colorless dents on the bridge of his nose. "What claims do you have?"

"You may read the petition there. The details I will give the Judge. What I am asking you to do is tell the Judge we want to see him."

Winters looked at Acel. "Who are you? What are you doing here?"

"I'm a member of the committee."

"You're a Communist, aren't you?"

"He's an American seaman," Boats said.

Kasha blew his nose.

Winters looked at Boats. "How would you like to do

six months in jail?"

"You mean you think you can send me to jail? What's holding you? I'm no kid, Winters, don't pull that stuff on me. Are you going to arrange for us to give these petitions to the Judge or not?"

"I am going to do this for you. We have told you to stay out of this place. It is not a place for Reds or Anarchists or Fascists or anything else but Americans. Now if you ever come in this place again I am going to file charges against you myself."

"That's the way it is?" Boats said.

"I mean it, too." Winters lifted his finger. "And that goes for both of you, too. We don't want your kind around here."

The three men left the Home and crossed the street into the park. Men followed them, surrounded them when they stopped. The circle grew.

Boats got up on a bench and held up his hand, palm outward, and then with his left hand pointed across the street. "They've told us to kiss their ass!"

"Give 'em hell, Boats," a seaman in an oiler's cap shouted.

Acel and Kasha steadied the bench. Boats slapped his chest. "Are we American seamen going to stand here and allow ourselves to be prostituted by a politician they call a judge who sits up there in a three-room office and gets seven thousand dollars a year? Are we going to allow a man who used to walk a beat around and gets three thousand dollars a year now to see to it that we can't see this politician and tell him we need shelter and we need food?"

"Tell it to 'em!"

"Pour it on 'em!"

"Give 'em hell!"

Boats waved the petitions above his head. "They've told the eight hundred men whose names are on these sheets to go to hell. That's what it amounts to. What we ask is just and right. They raise money in our names, and why aren't we entitled to some of it when we need it? Are we seamen or are we men who paint our faces? How many of you men will go into that place with me?"

Acel got up on the bench. Kasha supported him. "I'll follow him," Acel shouted. "I'll follow him!"

Boats got down and, with Acel and Kasha at his sides and a crowd of fifty men following like a wedge, moved across the street.

The young policeman at the door turned and ran up the steps. The wedge entered.

Winters stood in the doorway of his office at the top of the broad stairway.

"Tell the Judge to come down and listen to us or we're going right on up to his offices," Boats said.

"Judge Ross is not in the building," Winters said.

"You're a damned liar," Boats said. "His Pierce is around the corner there. Get him down here or we're going up."

Winters withdrew into his office and closed the door.

The wedge surged into the already crowded lobby.

Boats clutched Acel's arm. "You tell this crowd here in the lobby what it is all about. Kasha and me and some of the rest will go on up to the Judge."

Acel climbed up on the water fountain. "Judge Ross

won't look at the petitions eight hundred seamen have signed," he shouted. "Jobless seamen should have free beds and food. Politicians have no business in a place like this . . . ."

The loud speaker on the shelf high on the column in the center of the lobby began to roar: *"All out of the building. Everybody out of the building. City Police are coming . . . . All out of the building . . . ."*

Acel pushed through the lobby crowds to the column. The seaman in the oiler's cap lifted him up, and he grasped the loud speaker and began wrenching at it. A glass, hurled from the lunch counter to the left of the lobby, shattered on the column. The seaman let Acel down. Acel's face was cut and bleeding. . . .

Sirens screamed outside . . . . policemen came like boats on waves of seamen, their clubs rising and falling like paddles. Pistol shots sounded above like the muffled collapse of a tin roof. *Everybody out of the building . . . . Everybody out . . . .*

~§~

It was a whirlpool of clubs and fists and escaping bodies. It became a torrent, and the lobby throng poured out of the building into the street.

The crowd was like a piano on Acel's back, and he strained to keep his feet, reach the park. The seaman with the wiper's cap clutched his arm and shook him. "You better wipe your face and get the hell out of here while the gettin' is good. Real hell has happened over there. Somebody is hurt."

Policemen were coming across the street into the park now. Acel ran.

18: CRIMINAL ASSAULT

Acel sat there on the chair looking at the jersey silk undergarment on the line above the stove. Corinne called them panties. When they were washed they were not much bigger than your hand. He listened for Corinne's steps in the hallway. She had gone out for gauze and iodine and newspapers.

The food on the table had not been touched. There was Swiss cheese and pickles and crackers. Acel looked at the coffee pot on the stove. I bought that the second day, he thought. It was twenty-five cents. It seemed like a long time ago, but it just seemed that way.

He had held the one-legged man up under the shower in that Columbus flop house. That was a long time ago. The man had a stomach that bobbed like jelly. The flop-house men had made them dip their feet in a bucket of something before they let them under the showers. It was to prevent toe itch. He had wanted to ask the one-legged man if he had got the leg cut off under a train. It's funny how I sit here and think of things like that.

He had argued with the war veteran in Philly. The veteran was a lunger, and when they cut his pension he had to leave Arizona. He put his wife and kid on the bus and started highwaying it out of Phoenix. He stood there all day, and nobody stopped, so he got a freight train. He was dumb, though. He said the bonus marchers made the President sore, and that was why the pensions were cut. I called him on that. I shouldn't have argued with a lunger, though.

Corinne came in. She placed the newspaper on the table and began unwrapping the gauze.

"Paper say anything?" Acel said. "It is in there, all right."

"What does it say?"

"He's dead, all right."

"Boats is?"

"Yes. Now hold your head up and I'll paint this."

After Corinne painted Acel's cuts with iodine, she lit the gas and put the coffee pot over the blaze. She stood there and watched the pot.

"A man has to die sometime," Acel said. "It won't make any difference a thousand years from now. Hand me the paper."

Footsteps sounded in the hallway, and Corinne looked toward the door. The steps faded, and a door opened and closed. The newspaper crackled as Acel turned the page.

Corinne poured the coffee into cups. She sat down and waited until Acel dropped the paper on the floor. He got up and dragged his chair to the table. When he sat down he winced and touched his shoulder. "I guess I must have got a lick or something."

"I guess you noticed it in the paper, Ace. I am sort of worried about it."

"I guess they'll get some sort of case against me."

"What is criminal assault, Ace?"

"It's when you hit somebody."

"Does anyone know down there where you live? Did you ever tell anybody down there where you lived?"

"Don't start bawlin' now, Corinne. It's bad enough as it is. They can find out easy enough. I don't care."

"I was just thinking that if they don't know where to look for you, why, you can just not go back down there anymore and maybe they'll forget about it."

Acel lifted the cup, but set it back down. "I've been sort of thinking I might just get out of town."

"If you just don't go back down there or anything they won't know where you are."

"They can find out easy enough. They had to call the city police in. That was dirty. That was dirty." Acel turned and looked at the panties on the line.

"You better drink your coffee while it is hot."

"I was thinking about Boats."

"Does he . . . . who are his people?"

Acel shook his head.

"Drink your coffee, Ace."

Acel turned and lifted the coffee and gulped. He placed it back down and looked at Corinne. "I've done you a helluva lot of good. If I go down South maybe I can find something to do. I'll send for you."

Corinne nodded.

"It's not that I'm afraid of jail or anything. I'd just as soon be in jail as any place. The only thing, I may get a job down South and then I can send for you.

Corinne nodded.

Acel got up and went over and looked out the window on the darkened alley. In the window across the way a man stood beside a bed in his underwear. Acel turned back. "I ought to go down there where he is or something. It didn't even say where they got him. I never thought they'd kill anybody. They shouldn't have done that. That's a lie. He didn't have no gun. I know he didn't lave no gun. Why didn't they fight with their fists? That's all he had. It doesn't even say where they got him now, does it? I guess it's the City Morgue. I ought to go down there."

"I'll go," Corinne said. "I'll see to it. I'll go. I'll see to it."

19: ON THE ROAD

The soft glow of a spent sun toned the harshness of the slag-crusted railroad yard. Acel, concealed behind the string of sided cars, watched the corralled company of hoboes move up the yards. The two detectives herding them had on dark suits and light, wide-brimmed hats.

A youth in a sweat shirt dropped down from the bumpers of the car ahead and paused at sight of Acel. Then he approached. "You got out of sight, too?" he said.

Acel nodded. "We'll get by if we just keep low. Those bulls are taking them out on that side of the yards."

The corralled hoboes and the detectives passed out of sight.

"I don't want to miss this *manifest*," Sweat Shirt said. "A man could be in Atlanta tomorrow. I'd like to be in Atlanta this time tomorrow night."

"Those bulls are going to have their hands full holding that bunch. We'll work down toward the end of the yards in a minute."

"I'm just hoping none of those bulls decided to ride it out," Sweat Shirt said.

Up in the yards by the roundhouse a locomotive whistled . . . . *twice!*

Acel and Sweat Shirt started up the string of cars, their feet crunching in the gravel, and pretty soon broke into a half-run.

The locomotive of the long freight puffed and labored as if held in a giant's leash. Acel and Sweat Shirt lay on their stomachs at the bottom of the high embankment outside the yards. The locomotive went by. On the rungs of the first oil car rode a dark-suited figure with a club in his hand.

Acel nudged Sweat Shirt. "Wait until ten or twelve cars get by."

Sweat Shirt nodded.

The cars lumbered by . . . . three . . . . four . . . . *faster.* Seven . . . . eight . . . . *faster.* The man with the club disappeared between the cars!

Acel went up the grassy incline on all fours. He crossed the track, ran alongside the rocking boxcar, clutched at the rung, and, swung up and in between the cars on the bumpers. The wheels below began clicking in heightened speed. He clung stiffly, throwing his head from side to side expectantly.

"Getoffathere, goddam . . . ."

The voice of the detective standing on the right-of-way was like an explosion smothered in the grinding of the trucks. Hurled rocks spattered on the car's sides. Acel went up the end of the car to the top. The train's surface was clear. This car was a refrigerator, but the reefer was sealed, and Acel started back on the train in a crouching, hand-extended run. He leaped to the next, and this reefer was unsealed. He squeezed backwards into the trapdoor opening clung for a moment, like a jack-in-the-box, and then dropped into the hole.

The hole was dark. An acrid fume choked his nostrils, and he turned and tried to peer through the wire mesh: *onions*. The floor was tin and dented like a big scrub board.

After a while Acel lowered himself to the floor. The car began to bounce with a staccato roll, and he gripped the sides to ease the punishment. Pretty soon the roll lessened, and he stretched out with guarded slowness, pillowing his head on his arm . . . .

The thing to do is not to think about her. When I get a job and can do something about it, then that will be the time to think about her. It doesn't do any good just to think. The thing to do is just put her out of my mind. I'm gettin' thirsty. I've never seen it fail. Every time I get a hot shot I start gettin' thirsty. Before I get out of the yards I want a drink.

No, the thing to do is just not think about her . . . .

The car began to bounce violently again, and Acel sat up, lifting himself on his hands until the bumping lessened, and then he lay down again . . . .

If I had a drink now, this wouldn't be bad at all. I'm going to hold this train down until she stops. A hobo in a refrigerator hole and his throat feeling gluey! It would make a short story, one of those short short stories they print in *Liberty*. Writers got one hundred dollars for those stories.

There wasn't nothing, though, to just a hobo riding in a reefer. Something had to happen. It would be something if I got off at the division to get a drink and a bull nabbed me? And I got thirty days? When the train stopped, the hobo in the story would crawl out and make a run for the hydrant in front of the shanty. The bull would jump out and grab him and say: "You got your guts, you son of a bitch."

You couldn't put "son of a bitch" in a magazine, though. "You got your guts, you punk. You're going to take a little ride."

Nothing to that, though, just a hobo gettin' run in for riding a freight train and caught because he got off the train to get a drink. Those stories had to have surprises at the end.

The jail where they take this guy would look like that one in Fort Worth. It would stink like that one. The sergeant would write down the guy's name and then the charge: *trespassing on r.r. prop.*

The cell would be like that one in Portsmouth, just a plank with bedbugs in the cracks. As soon as the hobo got in the cell he would start yelling: "Don't a man get a drink around here? I want a drink of water." He'd claw at his throat and make strangling sounds and yell: "Water! Water!" There would be a fellow in the next cell. He would say:

"What's the matter, Mac?"

"I haven't had a drink all day. I want a drink. Bring me it some water."

"What are you in for, Mac?"

"Train riding. Water! *Water!*"

The guy in the next cell would laugh. "You'll get it, all right, Mac. Don't worry. That's what you get in this man's town for riding freights. *Three days on water.*"

With a hundred dollars I could send for Corinne easy enough. She could come all way to New Orleans on that. She could do it on fifty dollars. Then I'd have fifty to get things ready. But there's no use of me thinking about it until I can do something about it . . . .

~§~

The sun pierced the hole of the still car like a knife blade. A green fly buzzed in attacking gyrations. Somewhere a power pump throbbed. Acel got up, rubbed his stiffened arm, and then climbed up the hole.

It was a jerkwater town. The highway ran alongside the track, a bright strip of pavement flanked by dust-filmed houses. Acel descended the rungs stiffly, and when he dropped to the gravel his numb feet ached with the jar.

The depot was a frame, scabby-green structure. Inside, it smelled of stale smoke and sawdust boxes. A telegraphic instrument clattered behind the closed ticket window. There was a padlock on the washroom.

Acel came out. His skin under the beard felt hot and sore. He moved across the tracks toward the filling station on the corner. There was a sign: *Hitchhikers keep hiking*. A man in overalls and with a forehead and long nose like a wire-haired terrier stood in the station door and watched Acel wash at the hose. The water slid off Acel's face like thin oil.

Acel combed his hair. "I went to sleep in a car set off here last night," he said. "I thought I'd be in Atlanta by now."

"There won't be any more freights through here until tonight," the man said.

"I thought I might blind a passenger. I guess a man can do it all right around here."

"I saw them pick one up with a shovel that tried it over there one day. The railroad had to bury him."

Acel recrossed the tracks and sat down on the low-railed lawn to the left of the depot. Below the filling station where he had washed was a two-story white house with a low white picket fence. A new Chevrolet was parked in front. Two men in shirt sleeves rocked in chairs on the porch. One of them was smoking a pipe.

Acel pinched off the burning end of the cigarette and, breaking the paper, poured the tobacco in the sack. For a little while longer he looked at the men on the porch and then, suddenly, got up and moved across the tracks toward them.

The men stopped rocking as Acel came through the gate and went up to them. "Could I do something around here for something to eat?" Acel said.

The fat one said, "You hungry, boy?"

"Yessir, I'd like to work for something to eat."

"Where you from, boy?"

"New York."

"You're a long ways from home, aren't you?"

"Yessir."

"You shouldn't have left home. I'll bet your folks would send for you if they knew you were out like this. Why don't you get them to send for you?"

"I don't have folks."

"You look like a boy that would work to me. You got a good face on you."

"I'll work, all right."

"I'm just boarding here myself, this fellow here and me, but the woman that runs this house is a good lady, and she will give you something to eat. I'll go in and tell her." The fat man got up and went into the house.

The other man was lean and wore suspenders. He did not look at Acel, but gazed across the tracks toward the depot.

The fat man came back. "She's fixing you up something."

He lowered himself back into the rocker and went back war and forward for a few moments. "I'm a traveling man myself, but I don't pick up men on the highway. I'd like to, but it's too dangerous. There's too many men going around the country hungry, and you just can't take chances."

Acel nodded.

"I'd like to pick fellows up, but I just can't afford to take the chance. There was a man killed picking a fellow up here not so long ago. Killed him and took his car after he had picked him up. When was that, Bob? . . . Was it that long ago? . . . Six years. I didn't know it was that long."

The woman came out with the food wrapped in bread paper. She had on a checkered apron. Acel went up the steps, and she handed the food to him. "I'll be glad to do any work around here, lady."

"That is all right."

"I sure do thank you." Acel backed down the steps and then looked at the fat man. "Many thanks to you all."

"Wait a minute, boy." The fat man stood up and put his hand into his pocket. "You got a good face on you, boy. You look like a good boy to me. Here, here, I'm going to give you a dime. You can buy yourself some tobacco or something."

Acel caught the flipped coin. "Thanks. Many thanks, sir."

Acel went down to the red, peeling water tank and sat down on the Bermuda grass. He unwrapped the bread paper: cold bacon, a biscuit with red jelly; dry, crumbly cake and two slices of light bread. After he ate he went over and began examining the writing on the legs of the water tank. There were some obscene drawings and rhymes.

The old man came up and lowered his pasteboard suitcase to the ground. His faded eyes looked out of cave-like sockets.

"Hello, Dad," Acel said.

"Hello." The old man began taking off his coat. Acel left the water tank and approached the other.

"How's the road treatin' you? Pretty good?"

"I ain't complainin'. Pretty good. Yessir, pretty good. I'm four days out of Daytona Beach. That's pretty good."

"You bet that's good. That's a lot better than I've been doing."

"It's pretty good for an old man."

"How old are you, Dad, anyway?"

"Seventy-four. Seventy-five this coming November."

"You sure don't look that old."

The old man pulled the suitcase toward him. "I got something in this bag here." He began undoing the rope around it. "I got something here."

It was a drawing of an airplane. Dad said it was a model of a humming-bird airplane and he was the inventor. He had showed it in Lindbergh's office in New York, he said, and now all he needed was twenty-five dollars to have a model made.

"Don't you have a family?" Acel said.

"Me? Yeah, I got a family." Dad returned the drawing to the suitcase and began fixing the rope around it. "Yeah, I got a family. Haven't seen none of them in twelve years, though. I've had family troubles, if you know what I mean."

"You had family troubles, uh?"

"Yeah, but I don't like to talk about it."

They watched the truck climb up to the crossing down the tracks, stop, go into low gear, and then labor over.

Dad said that before he started inventing and running around he had been a Baptist preacher.

"I've been thinking that if the preachers quit yelping about hell and prohibition and dancing," Acel said, "and took an interest in things that mattered, they would come a lot nearer emulating Jesus Christ. Why don't they drive out a few money lenders? They holler, 'Give to the poor,' but they don't realize that there is no need for the poor at all."

"I haven't preached in twelve years."

"I was in a jungle up the road night before last, and a bunch of us got to talking, and I told that bunch that we were just like a bunch of immigrants running around the country trying to find a place to dig in. In the old days they called us hordes and barbarians, but the men in those days had swords, and if the people who had plenty didn't share it, they took it. I told that bunch that every one of us should have a home and a wife and plenty to eat in a country like this, because there is plenty, and the trouble was that some men have more than they should. I asked if anyone there was a Socialist. One guy said something: 'I'm for better living,' he says. Godamighty. No wonder we're just scum. I'll bet you are a Socialist, aren't you, Dad?"

Dad nodded. "That's for young fellows, though. What I got to do is invent me some little something I can sell. There's a lot of money down in Florida, and I'm going back there this fall. I'm not going to sell pencils or anything like that, though. What I got to do is invent me some little something I can make myself."

A freight truck rumbled on the station platform, and Acel watched the station agent trundle it into place.

"So you've had family troubles, Dad?"

"Yeah, but I don't like to talk about them."

"I guess you busted up with your wife?"

"Yeah. But I don't like to talk about them. You know what I mean by family troubles. I don't like to talk about people that are dead. You know what I mean, though. She liked men too much. That woman just liked it too much. I saw it plain after it was pointed out to me that the kids were his."

"You mean your kids weren't yours?"

"The oldest was mine. I never did tell nobody but him. I saw it plain after it was pointed out to me."

"Did you know the man?"

"I reckon I did. He used to lead singing at my meetings. But I don't like to talk about family troubles."

20: CHAIN-GANG COUNTRY

The lights of a restaurant's front lay on the sidewalk ahead like a bright tear in the black mantle of the street. It was after midnight. Somewhere a trolley car screeched at a turn and then rumbled on to fade into a singing murmur.

Pushing himself erect from the lamppost, the youth in the slip-over sweat shirt and suspenders stopped Acel: "You got a match?" His breath stank of alcohol.

Acel handed him the pack. "You know where the Muny is around here?"

The cigarette clung to the moist lips of the other and bobbed as he spoke. "You want to go with me?"

"Go to hell."

Acel went on and around the corner stopped a Negro. "You know where the Muny is around here?"

"The what?"

"The place where a man can get a free flop."

"Oh, now I knows what you mean. Sometimes I sees a bunch hanging around the city auditorium. Yeah, that's the place you wants. Now I knows what you mean. You go right down this street foah blocks and then foah thataway. Now I knows what you mean."

The free shelter slept. Acel rattled on the door and shook the knob, but there was no answer.

The trays of fruit in front of the stand at the corner gleamed like metal under the street lamp. There was a policeman at the end in a white-billed cap and Sam Browne belt and a stand attendant in a soiled white apron. The policeman looked at Acel over the edge of a half-eaten slice of watermelon.

"Could you tell me, officer, where a man could get a bed this time of night who hasn't any money?"

The policeman took another bite of the melon and spat the seeds out with a quick twist of his head. "You're out of luck."

"I was just down to the municipal place, and they were closed up. I guess all the places are closed up now?"

The officer spat out another mouthful of seeds. "Yeah, they're closed."

"I guess it would be a good idea for me to go down to the police station and not hang around on the streets?"

"If you want to get locked up and spend the night with a bunch of drunks, you can."

"I wouldn't like that. Naw, I guess I can just sleep on

a park bench somewhere."

"You don't sleep in parks in this town unless you want to be vagged."

"This is kind of a tough town."

"Tough." The officer tossed the rind into the gutter and looked back at Acel. "That's the trouble with this country, birds like you running around."

The head of the standkeeper began to go up and down.

"Where you from?"

"Memphis."

"I thought so. What did you leave there for?"

"1 got a pretty good job prospect down in Jacksonville, and I didn't have any other way of getting there except beating my way. I got a pretty good chance to get a job, and I wanted to get there."

"You oughta stayed where you come from. That's the trouble with this country now, you bums running around and living off people."

The standkeeper's head bobbed.

"I'm paying taxes every year just to feed birds like you. That place right down there costs us a hundred thousand dollars a year just to keep birds that are here today and gone tomorrow. Have you been to the Salvation Army? I don't know whether you can get in there or not. Don't think you can this time of night. You can go try it, though. You birds don't have any business leaving where you come from. Go on down there and try to get in there."

Acel followed the policeman's directions. Learned man, he thought. Paying taxes to keep bums up. Who is paying his hundred bucks a month? And that old belch standing there with head going up and down and feeding him watermelon. The bastards.

This is fun, runnin' around looking for a place to flop. I don't want to work. Me, want to work? It's too much fun running around from town to town and seeing the country from nice freight trains. It's the bums' fault. A bum shouldn't be running around the country without money. He should make it a point to have two or three hundred dollars when he gets in a town. He should attend to things like that. The big bastard. And that old belch standing there with his head going up and down—

The second shelter was open.

~§~

The farmer-looking transient with the whittled cane and slow, painful gait said he was walking in the direction of the railroad yards himself and would show Acel the way. Acel did not mind the slow gait of the other. It was Sunday morning, and the streets were almost deserted. The sunshine was cool.

"That wasn't a bad breakfast we had this morning in that place," Acel said. "That's a new one on me. Fried bread with bacon in it."

"We got it on the farm," Whittled Cane said. "I just got out. A year and a day I did."

"Just got off a prison farm, uh?"

"Year and a day." Whittled Cane said he was sent up for firing some woods down in the southern part of the state, but he didn't no more do it than Acel did. He said he was ruptured and didn't do a lick of work all the time he was there. He whittled canes and sold them to prison visitors.

"Prisons are the cancers of the capitalistic system," Acel said. "And bums are its boils."

"I didn't do a lick of work while I was there."

They waited until the trolley car passed and then crossed the empty street.

"America is the richest country in the world and at the same time the most criminal. They can spend forty billion dollars for policemen and jails and put an electric chair in every town, and they won't stop it that way. They are going to have to open their eyes to more than that to stop it."

"You talk kind of like a feller I knew down there on the farm. He was one of them radicals, one of them Communists, like Jews and niggers. 'Course I don't mean to say you're like him."

"What was he in for?"

"Freight-train ridin'."

"You mean they got them on that farm for that?"

"They got a hundred out there for that."

"Hell, I didn't know that. I didn't know they were picking them up for that."

"Don't think they're not. There was a hundred of them in there."

Whittled Cane stopped and pushed the bright, coin-sized piece of metal with his stick. It was tin. "I'm headed for home myself," he said. "I haven't seen my old woman now for more than a year. The kids come down once, but the old woman stayed home."

"I guess you can stand to see her, all right, after a year in that place."

"The old woman's got pellagra pretty bad. She ain't much use to me that way any more. I was thinking about stopping at one of these hotels and seeing me a woman before I went on home."

"I got a wife back in New York," Acel said.

"The old woman's got pellagra pretty bad."

"So they had them in there for train riding?"

"Yeah."

"Might be a good idea if I highwayed it out of here like you are. Out of this state, by god. I sure didn't know that."

"Yeah, you make me think of that feller that was down there on the farm with us. There was one thing about that feller, he didn't take nothing off the guards. I'll bet they whipped his behind a thousand times. He was too thick with the niggers, though. He treated them like they was white."

21: BIG Boy

Rain cracked against the sided boxcar at the edge of the yards in wind-driven sheets. Acel, in the warm and dry car, rewrapped the sack of tobacco and matches in the waxed bread paper and put it back in the bosom of his shirt. He felt over his watch pocket. Yes, the twenty-five cents was still there.

The car shivered in a fresh gust. Two weeks now he had been out of New York, and not a single time had he been caught in the train. That was pretty good. The other time it rained he was in that little town in North Carolina. He had been run out of the depot, but he had found a window open in that church. The church smelled of fresh paint, and he had slept on a bench with hymnals for a pillow.

A face peered in the box-car door. It was a square, Scandinavian face with a flattened, scarred forehead.

"Come on in, Big Boy," Acel said. "It's pretty dry in here."

The man climbed in. He was big, with bulky shoulders and thick hands. He took off his soggy cap and shook it.

"Kind of wet outside."

"It's pretty wet, all right," Acel said.

Big Boy took off his coat and shook it and then hung it on a nail on the door. He came over then and sat down on the other side of the car facing Acel.

"Which way you headed?" Acel said.

"North."

"I'm headed west. New Orleans."

"I don't see what anybody wants to go there for. Ain't nothing in that town."

"It's pretty cheap there."

The door of the car rattled with the wind. Rain sprayed through it, and the two men moved deeper into the car.

"I ain't exactly decided where I will go," Big Boy said.

"It don't make no difference to me much."

"One place is about as good as another when you're on the bum, I guess."

Big Boy crossed his legs. "I'm over the hill myself. You know what I mean, I guess?"

"Army?"

"Naw, the bug house. They say I'm crazy. I got more sense, though, than some of those fellows working that hospital, though. One of 'em asked me to shine his shoes, and I told him to go to hell and walked out of the place and went over the hill."

"How do they feed in those places?"

"Aw, pretty good."

"How do you get along with people in those places?"

"Aw, those fellows that run it are no good. They operated on me while I was in there. See, right here? I got a plate right here in my head. See, right there, see?"

"Uh."

"I had another plate in there, but it was pressing on my head. I got hit there in a fight when I was in the navy. A guy hit me with a marlin spike."

"You got a lick there, all right."

Rain sprayed into the car again, and Big Boy got up and slid the door almost shut. He felt of his coat and then came back. "Lots of robbing going on over this country now," he said.

"Bums are not doing much of it," Acel said. "Take these box-car robberies. It's towners that are doing it. A bum doesn't have any way of carting the stuff off. Aw, they might get a couple of oranges once in a while, but it's the towners that are doing it, no matter if these bulls do lay it onto them."

"They can rob 'em all as far as I'm concerned."

"I'm not going to run and tell anybody if I see it happening. I was reading the other day about a poor bastard who got five years for robbin' a pay telephone of eighty-five cents, and right beside him was a picture of a banker that got one year after the bank he was president of went busted. Things like that is what burns me up."

"Me, too."

"We're going to have revolution," Acel said. "People are not going to stand for stuff like that always. I'll be glad when it comes. The first thing the revolutionists will have to do away with the tin soldiers and flat-feet."

Big Boy's hand came out of his blouse with a flour sack in it. He put his hand into the bag and looked at Acel with an odd quirk on his lips.

"What you got? Somethin' to eat?"

Big Boy nipped the roll at Acel's feet. The money looked like a green bullfrog lying there.

"That looks like whether I'm crazy or not," Big Boy said.

"Jesus Christ," Acel said. "Is that the real stuff?"

"That don't look like I'm crazy, does it?"

"I wouldn't mind having a sack like that myself."

Big Boy bent forward and picked up the roll and began to bounce it on his flattened palm. "I knew your eyes would pop out," he said.

"You ought to be pretty careful showing that around."

"If a man thinks he can get it, he's welcome to try. I'm not half as buggy as some people think. This don't look like I'm crazy, does it?"

"Naw, that looks pretty good."

"What do you call yourself, buddy?" Big Boy said.

"Ace."

"How would you like to go get us a little something to eat? Some pork and beans or something?"

"I wouldn't mind it."

"I mean as soon as it quits rainin' some."

"It's okay with me."

Big Boy unfastened the roll and tossed a bill at Acel's feet. It was ten dollars. "I'm hungry as a bitch wolf myself," he said. "I could eat the hindin off a skunk."

Acel picked up the bill. "What kind of grub do you want?"

"Don't make no difference to me just so it is grub. If you see any of them there little chocolate cakes, get some of them. It don't make no difference to me. And you can put the rest of that in your sock."

"This money is okay, all right, I guess?"

"You're not afraid of it, are you?"

"I don't care if it is hot. I just don't want to fool with it if it's phony."

"If you're afraid, it's okay with me."

"I'm not afraid. It looks good to me. I'm going to change clothes, and you watch this bag while I'm gone. I'm going to put on a pretty good front so they won't look at me too much when I bust this ten."

"Now you're talking. That's the trouble with me, I can't look like anything in nothing."

Big Boy watched Acel dress. "You heard anything about them going to stop this train riding?"

"You hear that all the time. Everywhere a man goes, somebody is going to tell him he can't get out on a train. But I been gettin' out pretty good everywhere. I come all the way from New York on trains except one jump. It's tough highwaying down here. The folks down here are afraid of their shadows."

"It was in the papers that they're going to put marines on the trains and shoot bums off."

"They've been riding trains in this country ever since there's been trains, and they always will."

"That's the way I look at it."

22: BILL

The freight train crawled guardedly across the high trestle, its trucks and beams grinding and swishing sluggishly. In the wide doorway lolled silent riders, silhouetted against the Gulf and a sky stained in smoky gold and orange.

The silhouettes, Acel thought, would be something for an artist to sketch. Maybe some day I'll see a sketch like this and I'll have money then and will buy it. Big Boy lay at Acel's side, his lips blubbering with his snoring. The newspaper he had held over his face had slipped onto his chest.

On Acel's left sat Bill, the newspaper reporter on the bum. Bill got up now and walked to the door. He was a short, trim man with a broad leather belt around his waist and a grey snapped-brim hat which had been trimmed with scissors. He leaned out over the silhouettes in the doorway, peered ahead, and then returned to Acel. "We'll be there in another half-hour, buddy," he said.

"Think it will be a good idea to get off before we get in the yards?" Acel said.

"This town isn't so hostile, but we'll get off anyway."

One of the silhouettes in the doorway pointed out to the Gulf, and pretty soon Acel saw it, too: the sails of a fishing boat, a tiny white thread on the horizon. He showed it to Bill, and the older man nodded.

"You needn't worry about eating in this town," Acel said. "I got a few nickels."

"That is all right. I got some change myself."

Acel shook Big Boy. "Hey, get up. We're gettin' in the yards. Get up."

Big Boy sat up and rubbed his mouth and chin and then began tying the laces on his shoes.

Acel looked through the doorway over the water again. A bum never lacks companionship, he thought. On every train there is a new buddy to pal up with, and in every jungle there's a bum going your way. A road buddy is someone to watch your bundle while you go get a drink or he dings the salt and bacon if you agree to get the pepper and bread. Maybe he has been over the route before, like Bill here, and knows whether the crews are tough or if there is a hard bull ahead. You can talk to a road buddy like you were talking to yourself. There were some good guys on the road. Take Bill here. Bill, had had some good jobs and had been somebody. You could tell that by looking at him and the way he talked.

When the train entered the yards, Acel, Bill, and Big Boy jumped from the door and then waded through the tall grass of the right-of-way to the street.

"Let's don't walk right up through town," Big Boy said.

"I heard a cop say one time it was the bums walking around out in the residential districts that they suspected and picked up," Acel said. "I always just go through town like I owned it."

"You can't ever tell," Big Boy said.

"It doesn't make any difference to me," Bill said.

On the sidewalk ahead a group of children were playing, and the three men turned into the street in order not to interrupt their game. A little girl broke from the group and ran up the path to the house. "Some old bums, Mama. Some old bums," she cried.

Acel laughed. "You two shouldn't scare kids thataway."

"I think I'll holler boo at the little dickenses," Big Boy said.

"And have their old men out with shotguns," Bill said.

~§~

The jungle was a clearing in a woods of scrub oaks within a stone's throw of the railroad. It was strewn with blackened cans and empty rubbing-alcohol bottles. At its edge was a steep gully at the bottom of which ran a thin stream.

A dozen hoboes occupied the clearing. One of them had a mirror fixed in the bark of a tree and was shaving. A hobo, naked to the waist, came up out of the gully with a can of water. Big Boy lay on a spread of newspapers with his head wrapped in his coat. Acel and Bill sat on the edge of the gully looking down into the trickle of water. "I'm getting fed up on this kind of life," Bill said.

Acel nodded. "It's pretty tough, all right."

"I'd rob a bank if I thought I could get away with it."

"You'll get a job, Bill. A man like you with those letters will get a job. I hate to see a guy like you on the bum. You're the first man, Bill, I've run across on the road in a long time that really thinks. They can call it what they want, Communism or Bolshevism or Socialism, but there is going to be a change. Men are not going to keep bumming or work in flop houses for ninety cents a week forever. Not when there are other men they can whip with their hands riding in Packards and giving twenty-dollar tips."

"I can sympathize with a man that steals. You must be a pretty good bum to keep in change like you do."

"Like I was telling you yesterday, Bill, if dividing the necessities of life up between men, food and shelter and clothing, is being red, then I am red as blood."

"The world galloped to Democracy and it may gallop to Communism some of these days. You can't ever tell. Everything dies. And that goes for countries and governments, too."

Two men in overalls and with cotton sacks on their shoulders came into the jungle. Acel lifted his hand in salute. The men sat down, and one of them opened a loaf of bread and split it into two parts.

"They don't know what it is all about, these bums," Acel said. "I talk to them, and all they can think about is where they're going to get their next lump or sack of tobacco. A revolution never will start among a bunch of bums. Sometimes I wonder if it's worth your time to talk to them about it all. Little matches make big fires, though. That's what a fellow I used to run around with would say. He's dead now. I thought a lot of that guy. But there's a million men in this country on the road, and if these men were organized or were prepared to follow some organization, it'd be something."

"I guess you have worked for some organization?"

"No, that's a funny thing, I never have. To tell the truth, Bill, I don't know what I am, except that I am a Socialist. That reminds me, I'll bet you could get a job on one of these Socialist papers. I wish I could write."

"I'm getting fed up on this, all right."

Acel pulled up his foot and examined the loosened sole of his shoe. "I'm going to have to get these fixed pretty soon. You got a good pair of shoes on you, Bill. These were white shoes I got on here, but I had them dyed."

"I may start north tonight to Birmingham," Bill said.

"I know some fellows up there."

"I'd hate to see you go. Say, Bill, don't worry now. If you don't have anything in sight particular, just stick around with old Big Boy there and me. I'll tell you something on the quiet. Big Boy's got some dough. I've been with him more than a week now, and he sure is a good old boy. You stick around, and I'll see to it that you eat. He likes company, and we are going to New Orleans in a few days. I sure want to get over there, because I'm expecting some mail. I got a girl, see? I sent her a few dollars the other day."

"That partner of yours is a funny-looking bird," Bill said.

"Old Big Boy is okay. Funny thing, he's been in the bug house. Did you notice that scar? He's got a silver plate under it."

"I wonder how he got hold of that dough."

"I don't know."

"He's a funny-looking bird, all right."

~§~

Embers of the jungle fire blinked through the scrub oaks and brush. Sound of the hoboes' voices came to Acel as he cut across by the stock pens, the bundle under his arm, and made for the clearing. It was pitch dark. There were more men in the jungle tonight than there had been that afternoon. There were three or four around the fire, but the rest lay scattered over the clearing, dark, unrecognizable, sleeping bundles.

"If one of you guys will get the water, I got coffee here," Acel said. The kid with the bandana handkerchief around his neck got up and picked up a can and disappeared in the gully.

"She'll come out on that third track," the hobo with the cotton sack around his shoulders said. "It'll be a 'levenhundred engine. You wanta catch her back toward the crumby, though, 'cause there's always a bunch of empties up forward, and they'll set them off the first fifty miles down the road."

Acel took the can of water out of the Kid's hands and placed it on the fire. There was no use waking up Bill or Big Boy for coffee, he decided. They were sleeping somewhere around.

"Have any of you guys ever had the syph?" Cotton Sack said.

"I've had the gon," the hobo with the black beard said.

"Soon as I get a few more dollars I'm going to Hot Springs," Cotton Sack said. "The government treats you there for nothing, I hear."

Acel placed more twigs around the can. Big Boy and Bill didn't drink much coffee, and there was no use waking them up. They had turned in awful early.

"I ran into a good place here about two months ago," Black Beard said. "I spots this house, and I says to myself, I'm going to ding this place if it's the last thing I do. It was a big white house, with flowers and things all over the yard. There was a big car out in front. I goes up to the front door, and a woman comes up. She was a good-lookin' woman and says, 'Come right in,' and I went in.

"She cooks me up a real feed, ham and eggs and two cups of coffee and some grape jelly. When I got through, she leads me to the bathroom and says for me to wash up and shave. There was a razor and everything in that bathroom, and I got all cleaned up and looking pretty good and come out, and she takes me to the bedroom, and there on the bed is a whole outfit, blue serge suit and shoes, and everything just fits me. I got all dressed up and went back in the parlor where she was, and she says to me, 'Did you see that car out in front?' and I said I did, and then she says I can drive it if I want to and stay there as long as I wanted to and have everything I wanted."

The Kid laughed. "Why didn't you stay?"

"I just didn't want to get tied down."

That guy is a big liar, Acel thought. He's just day-dreamed that and is telling it for the truth now.

"I ran into a funny case here about two weeks ago on the highway out of Dallas," Cotton Sack said. "I was walking along, and a woman in a car stops and tells me to get in. We get to riding along, and she tells me she is going to El Paso to see her husband and got to talking about how she was hating to make the trip by herself. Just before we gets in Fort Worth she stops at a pig stand and gets a couple of sandwiches and some soda pop, and I gets another cigarette offa her. We gets into Fort Worth, and she says she has to see some friends there, and if I wanted to I could go out on the highway and when she come along she would pick me up. She gives me a quarter, and I gets a plate lunch. I was going to Big Spring, and I just went on down and got me a train, and I found out later that Big Spring was right on the way to El Paso and I could have rode with her easy enough. I never have figured out that woman, but you know how women are."

The water in the can began to simmer. "It won't be long now," Acel said.

The Kid got up and squatted beside Acel. "I got some

coffee in my bundle if you need any."

"I got plenty," Acel said. "I got a whole lot in town."

"Which way you headed?" the Kid said.

"New Orleans, if I ever get there. I got a couple of partners sleeping over there, and I'm going to try and get them to go tomorrow."

"You can get it in New Orleans for a Poor Boy sandwich," Black Beard said. "That's how tough things are in that town."

"I had my first experience with a girl that had never been around this summer up in Idaho," the Kid said. "That's where I'm going now, back to Idaho."

"I guess you want to see her, all right," Acel said.

"I was working for her old man, and I kind of think he'll give me a job back. You know how they make fires at night up there in that country around the herd to keep the coyotes away? . . . Well, she would set those fires at nights for her old man, and I'd meet her out there. I'd take a couple of blankets, and we'd stay out there doggone near all night. I kind of hated it on account of her brother. Him and me run around together."

"I got a girl. I know how it is," Acel said.

"Have any of you fellers heard about them going to stop train riding on the first?" Black Beard said.

"I've heard about it," Acel said. "What they're going to do is put up more transient houses, and you're supposed to stay in one spot. There's nothing but decent jobs that will stop men from running around."

"I don't like the way the birds in these Sallies and Munies order you around," Black Beard said. "They're nothing but bums themselves. I stayed in a few, but I'm not any more. Nothing but guys new on the road stay in those joints."

"They're no good," Acel said. "They can't get away with it long, working men six hours a day for ninety cents a week and rotten grub. The only thing that would make us worth a little more now would be a war. If some of the rich guys in this country decided we had to whip Japan or Germany or Russia, they would see to it that the government paid us a dollar a day and call us heroes to boot. Cannon fodder is worth a little more. But now we're worth ninety cents a week or nothing. If they ever want any of you guys to go and fight to save the world for Democracy, you tell them, 'No, thanks, it was saved once, and a couple of thousand men got richer and thirty or forty million got poorer.' I think this coffee is about ready."

"I wonder what the cops did with that guy they took away from here this afternoon," the Kid said.

"Were the cops down here?" Acel said.

"I knew that bird with that trick hat on was a dick," Black Beard said. "I've seen him on this road before. I knew he was a dick, and I had my eye on him the minute I got in this jungle."

"What bird is that?" Acel said.

"They're talking about that bird that had that dinky hat on, the one with that big belt on," the Kid said. "It was just before dark, just before you got here. Some cops come down here and took them off, but they say the guy with that hat on was a dick."

"Who did they take off?" Acel said.

"Some big old boy with a scar on his head. They put

the bracelets on him. They searched us all, but they only took him. I thought we were all going to get run in, but they only took that big guy."

"The big guy, uh?" Acel said.

"That's the way they do now," Black Beard said. "I was up in New Mexico on a train one time and ridin' along with a guy, and he was telling me how he was a t.b. and everything, and damned if he didn't turn out to be a bull. He got a half-dozen guys on that train when they busted into a boxcar. I've seen that guy with that hat on before. I knew he was a dick. I had my eye on him the minute I hit this jungle."

23: WALKING PAPERS

There were four men in the small, L-shaped kitchen, three Negro workers and a white cook. The sweat on the dark skins of the Negroes stood out like blisters.

The cook had broad hips under the apron like a woman. "I don't know where we're going to put you," he said.

"We got more back here now than we need."

"The manager told me to come back," Acel said.

"All right. Go over to Sam, there. Sam, give this man something to do."

"Ah'll give you an easy job," Sam said. "You can just do the glasses."

The white busboys would bring the dirty dishes back and stack them on a table next to the swinging kitchen door. It was Acel's job to pick out the glasses and shake them in a pan of soapy, warm water. After that he stacked them on a tray and, when it was filled, carried it to the little window looking out over the dining room and tapped a bell for a busboy.

Sometimes plates came back with half-eaten pieces of pie or cake, and Sam, the head dish washer, would hold it up and offer them to one of the other Negroes.

On the big iron range simmered a dozen pots. There was a long oilclothed table laden with pans of salads and cold meats.

Sam and the cook were talking. "It's not that Ah minds the foahteen hours in heah or the five bucks a week Ah gets, but Ah'm not gettin' the five bucks, and that's what Ah think Ah got a right to kick about."

"We're going to have a new deal in here," the cook said.

"We'ah gonna have somethin' or Ah'm not gonna stay," Sam said. "Ah work in heah all day and Ah gotta bum the tobacco Ah smoke."

The cook indicated the others in the kitchen with a twist of his head. "There's plenty in here that'll take your job. Any of these men in here would be glad to have your job."

"Whatsamatter? Ain't Ah doin' my work okay?"

"Sure, it's okay."

"All Ah was doin' was just kickin' about not gettin' paid. A man's got a right to kick about that."

The cook came over to Acel and said, "Well, how are

you making it?"

"Okay. Say, chef, you know if they'll let you see a prisoner over in the county jail here?"

"You know 'em over there?"

"No, I don't. I don't guess they'd let me see anybody. No, I'm a stranger in town. Say, I wonder if I could work for my dinner tonight?"

"You oughten to be working for nothing. That's the trouble with things today, men working for nothing. This is a nigger's job, anyway."

Acel could see the clock in the dining room whenever the doors swung out, and now he saw that his two hours were up. There were two more glasses, and he washed these and arranged them on the tray. He folded the drying cloth carefully, hung it on the line, and then went over to the cook. "The manager said when I worked two hours I'd have a feed coming to me."

After he had eaten, Acel started for the courthouse across the street. It was a new, four-story building, with the windows of the fourth story barred.

There were two men in the sheriffs office. They had on wide-brimmed hats, and across their vests hung heavy gold chains. The one chewing the match came to the desk.

"I wonder if I could see a prisoner you got in here," Acel said.

"What's his name?"

"I don't know. You got him yesterday out at the edge of town. I'd like to know what you got him for."

"What is your name?" the officer asked.

"Stecker."

The officer spat out the match shred. "What are you doing hanging around this town for, anyway? I know about you."

"I been working across the street in that café. You can ask them. I worked over there for my breakfast."

"Now that you got your breakfast, the best thing for you to do is get on out of town. We don't want no Reds in this town. We got a pea farm for radicals like you. If you punks don't like this country, why don't you go back to New York, go back to Russia where you come from? Now you get out of here, and you keep going and don't you look back."

~§~

Mist played in the giant beam of the approaching locomotive. Acel, waiting on the steps of the sided caboose at the edge of the yards, shivered again. The engine puffed by, its fire boxes glowing, and Acel lowered himself to the ground. Then he moved across the tracks toward the mist and night-blurred train.

The dripping runs were slippery, and Acel went up them cautiously, clasping each rung firmly and planting his feet securely. He climbed up onto the top and lay down on his stomach. The train jerked violently and then seemed to stretch in a sudden pick-ups of speed. It began to rain.

This is pretty bad, Acel thought, riding in the rain like this, but you had to expect things like this when you were on the road. It was just six hours to New Orleans.

Six hours, that was all. This is pretty tough, but it isn't like that train I held down up in Minnesota that February. That was a cattle car, and it rocked like a ship, and it was cold, and his eyes got filled with hot cinders. This wasn't anything to compare with that. That was really bad, because he had asked himself then if he had ever gone through anything worse: when they cut out his tonsils? When he got his hand mashed? This ride wasn't anything.

Water trickled from his hair and smarted in his eyes. The wet from the car's surface penetrated his clothes and placed a damp hand on his stomach. That's all I could do, Big Boy. It was me. I know it. I know it, Big Boy. I don't blame you. I know I am. You are right. I know I am . . . .

The whistle of the locomotive whined back through the rain.

24: NEW ORLEANS

Acel came out of Jackson Square and stopped at the curb cart of colored bottles and ice. "Strawberry," he said, and the vendor shaved the ice, patted it into a paper cone, and sprinkled it with red flavoring. Acel handed him a penny.

On the pavement of darkened Chartres Street clung mirror puddles from the evening shower. I'm going to walk clear to the end of this street. I like this street. I like New Orleans. It's kind of like a girl you have met two or three times and didn't think so much of and then all of a sudden you see her again and you want to hold her.

The shutters on this house sagged in all the windows. A dark passageway looked into a dimly lighted courtyard where four figures sat at a table playing cards.

I like this street. It's a street for a guy like me. It doesn't matter how you look or who you are on a street like this. It wipes its mouth on the back of its hand.

An old Negro sat in a chair on the sidewalk in front of his lamp-lit parlor and dozed. At the corner three men in work clothes came out of a place lettered: *Three Joes.*

I'm not feeling so bad tonight. That part of it all was for the best, and I didn't have any business thinking about it. It's just one of those things you couldn't do anything about, and that's all there is to it.

The girl sat alone on the stoop, her knees pressed together and the skirt held tighter under her legs. She did not look up. The sign read: *Tony's Second-hand Store.*

I have walked down a lot of streets, just moseying around like this. In Frisco and Minneapolis. In Denver and St. Louis. In little towns like Paducah and Ranger and St. Augustine. I have kind of liked them all and sort of hated to leave them. Each new town makes me forget the other. They're like girls.

A woman in the window of the building that looked like a school was placing shining linen on a bed. *Beer, 5¢. Poor Boy Sandwiches, 10¢.*

I feel better like this, in cotton pants and this old jacket and with two bits in my pocket, than I do when I'm dressed up and with a couple of dollars. When I'm dressed up I want tailor-mades and I see people with things and it makes me feel bad, but like this I don't care. I can flop right over there in that doorway if I want to, and two bits seems like a lot to me.

From the lighted, unoccupied room with its bed of twisted clothes came the smell of marihuana. The trolley rails glimmered up Royal Street to vanish into a blaze that was Canal. *Fishermen's Exchange.*

Old Hewitt would have given mc a job if he had one. He was as nice as a man could be. A man can't give you a job unless he's got one to give, and he explained just how everything was and patted me on the back. If a man doesn't have a job to give, he certainly can't make one. *Hing Wo Long.* Just keep moving and you will always run into something. That was what that old bum in Omaha said. Just keep moving and something will turn up—a flop, a handout, a ride, a cigarette, a piece of change. All you had to do was keep moving.

The girl had blonde hair and a blue silk dress. The man looked like a Filipino. *The Golden Dragon.* It is kind of like Negro music, this night. It's like a trombone quivering something hot and sweet and then a muted trumpet harmonizing . . . .

The woman seated there on the shadowed steps looked up boldly and held his eyes. The rouge on her face was like brick dust.

"Hello," Acel said. "What are you doing here on this side street this time of night?"

"This isn't no side street. This is Royal."

"All these streets here on this side of New Orleans look like side streets to me," Acel said.

The woman moved a little to the side, and Acel

lowered himself beside her on the steps. She had on a man's coat, and her black straw hat was pulled down over her ears.

"Must be getting pretty late," Acel said.

The woman nodded. "It's getting late, all right."

Feet scraped on the sidewalk, and they watched the approaching figure. It was a Negro, and he lurched past, head down and muttering.

"That jig is worried about something," Acel said.

"Some wench rolled him for his dough, I guess," the woman said.

"What are you waiting here for, trying to pick up some change?" Acel said.

"Maybe. Not particularly."

"I'm going to have to mosey on to the flop in a minute."

"Where you staying, kid?"

"Down the street yonder at Mom's Place. I was headed for it when I saw you."

"You got a place to stay, then."

"Uh huh. Why, don't you?"

The woman nodded. "Yes, I got a place. Right across the street there, that light up there. I've been staying with an old man."

"Old man, uh? How old is he?"

"Oh, he's past seventy. What I'm doing is sitting here trying to make up my mind whether to go up there or not. That bed of his is full of bugs."

"I don't guess a man that old bothers you, does he?"

"Naw, he doesn't bother me thataway. But he don't think about anybody but himself. Spends all his money for drinking, and nobody else matters. Wine. He bought a gallon this morning."

Acel stroked the hairs on his forearm. "Uh," he sympathized.

"You're staying down at Mom's, you say? I know that old lady. She's a good old woman."

"Yeah, I moved in there this afternoon. It's pretty good for a buck and a half a week. This town sure is cheap. You can eat mighty cheap in this town, all right."

"I can't make up my mind whether to go up there to that old devil or not. That's what I've been sitting here for, trying to make up my mind."

"I wish I could help you."

"What kind of work you do for a living?"

"Christ, I'm not working. I'm on the bum. I looked up a fellow here this morning I used to play in a band with, and he put out a couple of bucks. I paid up my room and got a quarter left."

"Was he working?"

"The fellow I got the two bucks off of? . . . Sure. You know that circus that was here this afternoon? He was director of that band. I used to play in a dance band with him."

"Is that all you got off of him and him working? You oughta got more than that if he's working. You oughta got all you could have off of him."

"I guess I could have gotten more if I'd of asked him."

"They don't think about nobody, those people that's working and got money. That old man up there has some money, but he's the stingiest old devil that ever lived.

Wine!"

"It's pretty tough, all right." Acel ruffled the hairs on his forearm and began stroking them down again.

"So you're on the bum. Just go around from town to town, uh? How much money can y'all pick up a day?"

"Oh, I don't know. I'm not exactly a professional bum. Some of them, though, pick up around two or three dollars a day, I guess. He has to work pretty hard, though, and don't let them ever kid you about a bum being lazy. That fellow I got that money off of this morning, though, I knew him. I've loaned him money."

"What do you do for women?"

"Just do without."

"Just go around from town to town, uh?"

"Sort of. I haven't been out on the road very long this trip. I left a girl I was living with up in New York."

"What is she doing now, living with her folks or something?"

"I don't know. She and I are washed up. I got a letter from her yesterday, but she and me are all washed up. It's for the best. Just one of those things, you know."

"I guess it is pretty good, just going around from town to town and seeing different things."

"It isn't so bad.

The lights in the window across the street went out.

"The old devil's getting in bed, I guess," the woman said. "You got a cigarette on you, kid?"

"I sure haven't. I just rolled my last one before I saw you. I got a quarter here, though, and I can go get us some tobacco. Where would there be a place open around here this time of night?"

"You'd have to go clear over by Market. No use of doing that. I wish I could make up my mind whether to go on up to that old devil or not. Wine he was drinking, and he wouldn't even give me the money to get something to eat."

"Haven't you had anything to eat?"

"I haven't had anything to eat today, and all he does is swill and swill."

"Hell, I got two bits here. Listen, you wait here and I'll go get some tobacco and this two bits changed."

"You won't come back?"

"Sure I will. Good god."

"You'll be back, then?"

"Sure."

In the café across the street from the Market, Acel bought a pack of Bugle. He got two dimes in change, and one of these he placed in his watch pocket and the other he carried in his hand. The stalks of bananas across the street at the Market corner gleamed. Acel went over and bought five for a nickel.

I shouldn't have bought these bananas. She'll think I'm a cheap skate bringing these back. If she hasn't eaten anything though, they'll taste good. When I'm hungry a banana looks good to me, by god. I'll give her this dime, anyway. I'll keep the tobacco and the nickel and in the morning get eggs at Young China.

She was not there. This was the place, all right; this was the stoop. But it could be that next block up there?

No, that was the place back yonder. She was gone. That was all there was to it.

The window where the light had been was still dark.

Acel put the dime in the pocket with the nickel and then opened the sack.

25: CLOSED DOOR

When the Paul Whiteman program ended, Acel left the two young brothers, Lou and Wayne, at the radio in the parlor of Mom's Place and went out onto the gallery. Cook, the man who had a job coming up, was standing there looking across the street at the two girls on that balcony. The girls were fat, and every evening they sat on the gallery and rocked.

"Those gals are not going to give you any come-on," Acel said. "They know what kind of guys stay in this place."

Cook grunted. He was a man around thirty-five, with a body that bulged in the middle like a top.

Acel placed his elbows on the shaky balcony railing and looked down into the brick-paved street. A man in fuzzy white flannels and straw hat came around the corner, halted, and reached down and picked up a cigarette butt.

"I was around to the café again today, and he told me to come back," Cook said.

"He must mean business or he wouldn't be telling you to come back," Acel said.

"I got to hurry up and get something, because I can't wear these white pants in the winter."

"I look for you to get that job. He wouldn't be telling you to come back if he didn't mean business. I smell onions cooking somewhere, don't you? . . . That's one thing about you, Cook, is you've been looking for something to do in the line you know about. That's where I've messed myself up, fooling around with everything. That's what I've been telling the kids in there, a man ought to look for work in the thing he knows the best."

"This fellow has a pretty good joint. It's N.R.A."

"I hope you get on. Maybe you can work me in down there?"

"I'll do it if I can. I was reading in the paper over in the library this afternoon where the government is going to give a hundred thousand berries to this town to feed the bums on this winter. The government sure is going to help fellows. It's about time."

Acel shook the rail experimentally. "I saw that myself. Stabilizing transients, they call it. You're supposed to settle down in some place and quit riding around the country on freight trains. They're going to start vagging everybody they catch on the highways and around freight yards."

The mother of the two girls on the balcony came out with a platter of candy and handed it to each of them. A dog sniffed at the fire plug on the corner and trotted on.

"If they paid anything for cooking in one of those transient places, I wouldn't mind a job doing that," Cook said. "If they're allowing a dime a meal for each man, I can give them a lot better than I've seen. But hell, they expect you to work for nothing. You know how much those cooks over in Houston are getting? One dollar a week. And that's supposed to be the best place in the country."

Acel spat between his teeth over the railing and then looked to see if anybody was passing below. "It's tough, all right."

"I think I'm going to get a job, all right. He's got an N.R.A. sign up on his place, but of course you can't depend on that."

"Those girls over there never do look this way, do they?" Acel said.

"I could go for that one with the big bottom," Cook said. "Yeah, he was telling me today that the cooking was getting too much for his wife and he'd have to have a man pretty soon who was good on short orders."

Acel turned and faced Cook. "Well, I can't kick today. Mom sure did me a favor, putting me onto that nine bucks. I'd already borrowed four bits from her to get this suit out of the cleaner's. I sweated blood day before yesterday trying to raise a half-dollar to get this suit out. I went in one place right after another and offered to do anything. It's easier, by god, to bum four bits than it is to earn it."

"Nine dollars is a lot of money these days, all right."

"You don't need a buck, do you? I let the kids in there have a couple of bucks."

"No, I'm not busted yet. Did you know those kids in there before you got in New Orleans?"

"No, I just run into them like I did you. They used to play in some shows, and I know a few musicians they know. Dern nice kids."

Cook spat out a shred of fingernail. "Say, let's take a

walk over in the Quarter and see what the gals are doing tonight."

"I don't care nothing about going over there. I don't have no business over there."

"C'mon. We don't have anything else to do, and it's too early to turn in. Looking isn't going to cost us anything."

"It don't appeal to me tonight. I don't like to go over there without I'm going to spend some money, and I'm not going to spend any of this."

"It won't hurt anything. Leave your dough with the kids and we'll just walk through and look at them."

They combed their heads, came out of the rooming house, and stood for several moments looking up at the girls across the street and then set out toward the Quarter.

"I was thinking that if some cop had come along last night I'd been in a hell of a fix while I was watching that house," Acel said. "I'd of had a swell time explaining what I was doing out there in the weeds of that vacant lot at twelve o'clock at night. Mom, I guess, though, could have got me out of a bad jam. That was an easy nine bucks, just watching a house to see who was going into it."

"That girl wanted to know if her sweetie was going in that house, uh?"

"Yeah. That's the first time I ever did do any detectiving. I'd of looked good, though, if some cop had come along."

"How come Mom to put you onto that?"

"This girl knew her, see? I kind of hated to take the money from that girl. She works in a cleaning shop, and

you know good and well she doesn't make hardly anything."

"That wouldn't worry me none."

They split and let the woman in the black dress and
carrying a paper satchel go through.

"I could have had a job today," Acel said. "I'll bet you
would have grabbed it up."

"What was that?"

"Posing. Dollar an hour."

"What kind of posing?"

"Naked posing. You know I thought about doing it
there for a little while, but then I got to thinking. There
was to be women there, too."

"You're not bulling, are you?"

"No, sir. That's a good racket here in the winter time
when all the art schools are running. Mom was telling me
she used to have three or four boys staying at her place
who picked up four and five dollars a day posing. That
was another thing about this job they called Mom up
about. It was just for an hour. If it had been regular or
something, I might have taken them up."

Three children stood around the penny-snowball
cart waiting for the vendor to fill cones.

"If I'd been posin' and there was women there, it
would have been too bad," Cook said. "I could have made
them a Nero. I'd pose naked before anybody for a dollar
an hour."

"Mom was telling me they used to get fellows for the
hospitals here. Doctors would use them for sterility tests.
They gave them fifty cents for every test."

"If they furnished women it wouldn't be bad," Cook

said.

They turned up a street of the Quarter. Women sat behind shuttered windows or stood in the cracks of partly opened doors and called and beckoned.

"Come here, darling."

"Sugah, come heah to me."

"I know you. I know you now. Come here!"

It was like flipping the leaves of a book, passing the crib-like brothels, escaping from the hawking voices.

A woman in a red silk dress reached out of her door and motioned. "Wait a minute, boys."

Cook shook his head and laughed. "Too late, sister. You're just a little too late."

They passed the old graveyard, leaving the Quarter behind; crossed the tracks and walked more slowly now toward their lodging place.

"That's not right," Acel said, "going down there without money and letting them yell at you. I feel like a Peeping Tom."

"What's the difference?"

"I heard a girl say one time that a down-and-out man became a bum and a woman turned whore."

"I don't feel sorry for them. They don't have no con science and they'll break up a man's home."

"I just don't know myself. I've quit thinking about it. I used to know a girl pretty well. I was kind of sweet on her, and that's what she's doing now. She didn't say so, but I could read between the lines, and I know good and well that is what she is doing. A man out of work doesn't have any business thinking about any kind of women. I lived with this girl awhile up in New York before she started it."

"Women are just born thataway," Cook said. "I don't have any use for them."

The white linens of the man approaching glistened. The girl with him clung to his arm with both hands and looked up into his face and smiled. Her face was soft and fresh and clean. Acel and Cook stepped into the street to give them passageway. Perfume lingered in their wake. Acel twisted his head and looked after them.

". . . . The first thing on the menu always sells best," Cook went on. "If you have something you want to get rid of, just put it first on the menu and it'll sell every time. That guy must mean business, or he wouldn't be telling me to come back."

"I got a hunch you're going to get that job," Acel said. "I hope you do and get me a job. I wouldn't mind learning how to hash."

26: ACE'S FOUR VAGABONDS

Lying on the cot of his cell-like room, Acel stretched his arms and flattened his palms on the crumbling calcimine of the room's walls. It was that narrow, all right. Above the foot of the cot was a small, screened window looking on the scabby walls of an adjoining building. In the courtyard below the window, that kid next door was practicing on his clarinet.

Acel looked at the soot-sprinkled bowl and pitcher

on the washstand. The stand was covered with *Times-Picayunes*. I got the blues this morning. I'm feeling that way, and there is no reason for it, because nothing is different from what it was last night, and I was feeling pretty good then. My room rent is paid, and I got a few dollars, and there's no reason for it.

The clarinet squawked on the fourth note of the attempted scale.

No, I don't have a good reason for feeling blue this morning. The government is going to spend one hundred thousand dollars here this winter to set up free shelters and stabilize transients. That is a lot of money, and there ought to be some jobs. Thirty-dollar-a-month jobs. They are going to have to have some workers to register these bums and ask them questions. I could do that.

An ant crawled on the grey blanket, and Acel flicked it off with his middle finger and thumb.

It might not be a bad idea to look up that Mr. Jessup, the man, the papers said, who was head of the relief organization that was going to spend the money. That man will have to hire somebody. Not everybody is going to try and get jobs in a flop house, and I might get one. I believe I'll write him a letter. I could tell him that I'm pretty familiar with the way they run flop houses over this country and ought to be a help to him. *Dear Mr. Jessup: I see in the papers where you have been named director of the relief work for transients here this winter and it has occurred to me that I might be of some service to you in establishing these places. I am familiar with these shelters all over the country and know the various systems. I know the type of men you intend to help and I should be of some assistance in handling them. I have been having a pretty hard time and . . . .*

No, it wouldn't do to tell him in the letter that I'm down and out, because they're not going to hire regular bums. They can get them for nothing, and they know it. He won't have to know anything except that I've been in college and look all right and am intelligent. I can look pretty good in that tweed, and he can talk to me and know that I can do that kind of work easy . . . .

I am a college man. Salary is no object. I realize you do not have much money to spend for salaries and for that reason I will be satisfied with a modest wage . . . .

Should I tell him thirty bucks? He'll think I'm pretty cheap if I say that, though. They may be planning, on paying more than that, too. One thing is certain, he is going to have to hire men, because a man that has been secretary of a merchants' association isn't going to know much about bums, and he needs somebody that is familiar with them. I believe I'll say sixty dollars. No, I won't say anything. I'll just leave that up to him . . . .

I can take a conscientious interest in these men and assure you that I will work hard to make your welfare work here a success . . . .

That wouldn't be bad, a place to stay and thirty bucks a month. I'd feel like going around and getting acquainted with the musicians in this town then. If I stay in this town long enough, I'll run into a playing job. That's been my trouble, changing towns and not just keeping ding-donging at some of these bands. I could get me a horn if I got this job and get up a lip and sit in now and then with some of these bands and get acquainted, and the first thing I would have a job. I can't think about getting a horn, though, the first month. I ought to get an overcoat of some kind. I could get along without an overcoat down in this country, though.

The clarinet screeched on the sixth note.

I'd kind of like a job in a flop house registering transients. I could stay clean, and by spring I'd have some money saved. I wonder if there are many musicians on the road. There is Wayne and Lou. If four or five showed up around that shelter, we could organize us an orchestra. Say, that's an idea. If we had a sax and a piano, Wayne and Lou and I could have a band. That's an idea. I could call ourselves *The Vagabonds . . . . Ace's Four Vagabonds*. That would be a good name. Maybe I should tell Jessup about that in this letter. That would make him sit up and take notice. *Ace's Vagabonds*. I can tell him all that, though, when I see him in person. But, by god, he ought to go for that.

It is my plan to call on you in a few days and I hope this letter will serve as an introduction . . . .

Acel got up and got the limp tailor-made out of the breast pocket of his shirt on the foot of the bed and after lighting it lay back down.

Now I'm getting ideas that will get a man somewhere. Ace's Four Vagabonds. I've been fooling around long enough and not thinking. I have to get women out of my mind and get down to business. An orchestra in a flop house that way could get publicity. We could get on the radio in no time at all. They would write us up in the papers: *Ace's Vagabonds, a novelty orchestra, made its debut over Station KLRN here last night. The band*

*featured melodies and songs of hobo camps and trails.
One of the songs, "The Flop House Blues," was written
by its director, Acel E. Stecker. The orchestra is to be
booked for stage appearances . . . .*

Now I'm having good ideas. Wayne can play
baritone, and Lou plays bass and doubles on the banjo.
Lou's got a pretty good voice, too, and he and I can do
some duets. I'll look up some hobo songs with good
harmony.

*I will await your reply hopefully and now I beg to
remain, very respectfully, Acel E. Stecker.*

Acel got up and, putting on trousers and undershirt
and shoes, went out onto the gallery to get the socks he
had hung out. Mom, the woman who ran the rooming
house, and the Baroness were in the courtyard below.
The two old women were poking in a heap of cans and
flower pots. Mom saw Acel and beckoned.

"Wait till I put on a shirt," Acel said.

Mom smiled as Acel approached. "Now you said you
wanted to meet a real live baroness, here's your chance,
young man. Baroness, this is one of my boys. He's a
musical young man."

"How do you do?" the Baroness said. The powder on
the stiff black silk bosom looked like flour, and it lay, too,
a scaly crust, on her wrinkled throat underneath the high
lace collar. "I love geraniums," the Baroness said. She
exhibited the flower. "I just love these. Do you know
where I could get some more, my boy?"

"I could look around for you, Baroness," Acel said.
Mom indicated the pile of cans and pots. "We were looking for a pot to plant this geranium in."

"Maybe I can find you one." Acel bent down and began picking up and examining pots.

Mom was a smaller and more shriveled woman than the Baroness, though she was younger. She moved in sparrow-like hops. It was said that she had once been a wealthy woman and a society belle. She had never married. She and the Baroness had known each other in their youth, and now the Baroness, it was said, was dependent on Mom.

"If you want to do something for the Baroness," Mom said, "you can go get some dirt. I think that pot there will do. I saw some earth down on the corner where they are fixing up that sewer. Take that pot and fill it up, and then you can take it up to the Baroness' room. She would like for you to visit her awhile, wouldn't you, Baroness?"

"I just love geraniums," the Baroness said. "In France I had millions of them. Oh, millions." She looked at Acel and shook her head sadly. "But no more, my boy, no more."

The Baroness occupied the choice, front bedroom of Mom's Place. It was a linoleum-floored room with a white iron bed covered with a rose-colored cotton counterpane. There was a washstand with a marble top, and a huge brown wardrobe, and a brown dresser on which stood an oil lamp.

The Baroness was seated in a rocker with a cloth-bound scrapbook in her hands when Acel entered with the filled pot. "Now where do you want me to put this, Baroness?"

"Are you a gardener, my boy?"

"I'm afraid I'm not."

"Just put it out on the gallery, then. Mom will fix it for me."

The Baroness showed Acel the scrapbook. It contained a number of big, slick photographs, and these the old woman handed to Acel one at a time.

"I was in the moving pictures once, you know," she said. She was in these pictures, all right. Here she was a lady-in-waiting to the star queen, and here in a ballroom and here at a banquet table. She looked like royalty, all right. She looked as regal as the actors and actresses.

"Here I am, see? I was acting in this picture, just a little part, you know, but I was really employed as a technical adviser. Oh, it was such hard work. I was at the studio all day, and at nights I was so exhausted. I had been in Hawaii, and when I arrived in Los Angeles they called me up and asked me to be what they call a technical adviser. Oh, it was such hard work. Fifty dollars a week they paid me. I did not like it at all, it was such hard work."

"You look about twenty years old here." Acel tapped the picture.

"That is what everyone says. Now everyone says I look so much younger than Mom, but do you know that I am seven years older than she? Now don't you tell her I said that, because it makes her very angry when anyone says that."

"You sure look young, all right."

"I hope you understand me. Some people do not understand me so well, though until three years ago, until I moved here from California, I taught expression. I taught a bunch of young men once in Hawaii. I lived in Europe so long, you know, but I was born right here in this country. I was such a little thing when I went to Europe. Oh, it was so long ago. It was a wonderful little town and the most beautiful château that my husband took me to. The Baron, you know. But I have nothing now, my boy, nothing."

Acel eased a little down in the chair.

The old woman brought out a sheet of paper from the scrapbook. "Would you like to see this that is written about me? . . . It was written by the dearest little girl who took expression from me. She was a typist, you know, worked in an office, I think it was, and she wrote this about my life. My wedding, rather. She was a dear little thing. I understand that some magazine would pay a lot of money for this. I told her about the wedding, and she wrote it up, and I would like for some magazine to pay me for it."

Acel took the sheet of paper. It was typewritten and single-spaced: "Not so many years ago in Europe occurred a wedding of great importance. It joined two distinguished families, one on this continent and one of the Old World. Just a little slip of a girl left her American home and journeyed across the deep sea to be united in holy bonds of matrimony with a member of one of Europe's most distinguished royal families. The little girl—"

Acel read it all and then handed it back to her. "This is very interesting, Baroness. Very interesting."

"Oh, it was a wonderful wedding. The horns went ta-ra-ta-ta." The Baroness cupped her hands to her mouth.

"The horns went ta-ra-ta-ta, like that. And there were so many flowers. Oh, they were so beautiful. My husband was so handsome. That is his picture there on the wall. Oh, it was wonderful. The horns went ta-ra-ta-ta."

Acel got up and went over and looked at the photograph in the round frame on the wall. It was of a young man in military uniform, standing stiffly with his hand resting on the back of a carved chair.

"In Paris we had our own box at the opera. Thousands we had then, oh, thousands. I could have my friends, and, oh, I could give away so much." She shook her head and fixed her eyes on Acel. "But I have nothing now, my boy, nothing."

Acel sat down again.

"Do you know of a magazine that would buy this article? The little girl said that there would be many magazines that would pay money for it. Oh, it was a wonderful wedding. Do you know of a magazine?"

"Not one that I can think of right off."

"Oh, it was marvelous. The horns went ta-ra-ta-ta, like that."

Acel cleared his throat. "How come you to lose your money?"

"The war, my boy. We had everything, our own box in the opera, and I gave away thousands to my servants. We had wine. Oh, so much wine. But I have nothing now, my boy, nothing."

"I guess it must be pretty hard to have had a lot of money and then lose it all."

"What is that? Sometimes I do not hear so well. Oh, it was a wonderful wedding."

"I say it must be pretty hard to lose everything."

"Oh, you have no idea. And the people in this world are becoming so cruel. When I was a little girl, the people were kind to one another and helped each other, but the world has changed. These politicians are the cause of it all. These Republicans and Democrats. My boy, don't ever have anything to do with men like them."

"I guess monarchies are about as good as anything," Acel said. "I used to be interested in things like that, but what I'm interested in right now is an orchestra I'm planning on organizing."

"Oh, you have no idea. I have a little money, but it is nothing. I get fifteen dollars a month from some property I have in Florida, but do not tell anyone that now. Every month when I get my money I buy avocados. I love avocados. I bought two lots in California for fifteen hundred dollars apiece, and you know they told me that they would be worth five thousand dollars, but I have only been offered one thousand for the both of them."

"Yes, you sure look young in that picture there, Baroness."

"It was taken eight years ago. That is what everyone says. Do you know about these advertisements endorsing face powders? You know, I would do that now. I am not proud any more, my boy. I need money. Do you know how to go about that? I would not mind."

"I'm afraid I don't, Baroness."

"I need money, my boy."

"It must be pretty hard, all right, to have had a lot and then lose it all."

"Oh, we had so much. He's been dead so long now.

We had so much wine. Mom likes whisky, but I do not care for whisky. In Europe my husband had cellars of wine. Oh, we had so much. The cellars were just filled with wines and brandies and champagne. But I have nothing now, my boy, nothing. Not even a little wine."

Acel shifted in his chair. "I guess I ought to be going, Baroness." He got up.

"I love gin, though. Do you know where I could get a little gin, my boy?"

27: LOU AND WAYNE

Lou was twenty-four and the older of the two brothers. He walked loosely, his chin down, and shot quick glances at passers-by. Wayne, twenty, was larger in build, a smooth-muscled giant with the clear complexion of a child. The eyes of women lingered on Wayne.

The brothers dressed alike, corduroy trousers and faded, neckless jersey sweaters which clung tightly and outlined their big chest muscles. They were musicians and for two years trouped with carnival bands, but the last show got six weeks behind with their pay and they quit. In New Orleans they had been soliciting shoe-repair work for an Italian shoemaker for twenty-five per cent commission.

"I hate the houses where the niggers come to the door and say the lady of the house isn't in," Lou said. "I feel like telling them to go to hell, I want the lady of the house, not them."

"That was a nigger gave us all the shoes Monday," Wayne said. "Four dollars' worth, that was. I guess you remember that."

"One place out of about a million. What I think we ought to do is get out of this town and go to California. That is the place for all of us. I promise you two that I'll hit every bakery between here and L. A."

Acel shook his head. "No, I keep telling you two that got a deal on here that's liable to bring us all three some thing I want to let that letter soak in a little, and then I'll go up and see him. You two stick around now, and if I get in with these people I can fix you up. We can pick up a sax and a piano, maybe, and have a pretty good outfit. There are possibilities to this idea of mine."

Lou stared across the park toward the Pointalba Building moodily. "There's nothing in this town. You don't have a horn, Ace, even if that guy gave you a job, and ours are in Chicago."

"I'm not worrying about a horn. If I get in with these people I can get a horn soon enough, all right."

The sun blazed blindingly beyond the statue of General Jackson and above the Cabildo. A man in his shirt sleeves on the next bench peeled a peach. A woman in an over-washed, bile-green dress and wrinkled hose went by.

Lou got up. "I guess you two could eat, all right, if I went and got something off a bakery."

Wayne grinned. "Sure, go get us something to eat."

Lou looked at Acel. "That's the way with him. He won't bum nothing himself, but it's okay for me to do it."

"He's your kid brother," Acel said. "You got to look out after him."

"I notice both of you always eat what I bum, but I don't see y'all bumming around."

"You're the best bum," Acel said. "We admit it, don't we, Wayne?"

"Get me some cream puffs," Wayne said.

"I'll take jelly doughnuts," Acel said.

"You goddamned guys give me a pain," Lou said. He turned and stalked around the park path and disappeared on Chartres Street.

"That bud of yours is a funny guy," Acel said.

Wayne nodded. "Uh huh."

"I was afraid he was going to get us in a jam this morning with that copper. You can't afford to jaw with cops like that when you're on the bum. It's a wonder he didn't run us in."

"He hates cops to beat hell. Ever since that time up in Kentucky he sure don't like them."

"What happened up in Kentucky?"

"Some cops gave him a dirty deal up there. Constables, I mean. It was the time he came down to see me when I was visiting an uncle of ours on his farm. He'd been playing in a little old dance band back home and had him about sixty bucks saved up, and he came down to see me."

A young couple went by looking straight ahead. The fellow had a box camera.

"How did he run into constables?" Acel said.

"They were looking for a gangster to show up in that town from Indianapolis, and Lou looked like him and he was from Indianapolis, and so they put him in the calaboose. They took his money off of him and used most of it up telephoning long-distance and sending telegrams. They found out the next morning he wasn't the one and let him loose, but they had spent his money, most of it, and scared him to boot, and it sure made him sore. You ought to hear him tell about it."

"I'll be damned."

"And I'd already gone home, because I didn't know he was coming, and old Lou had to catch a freight train out of there to get home."

"Can you beat that!"

Lou came around the walk carrying a loaf of French bread like a club. He pitched it suddenly, and Wayne caught it. "I guess they think a man can live on bread," Lou said. "I hit four places, and that's all I got, the damned cheap skates."

"Did you ask them to let you work?" Acel said.

"Not me. I been hooked too much that way. You remember that guy in Charlotte, don't you, Wayne?"

Wayne nodded. "Tell old Ace about that."

"We run into a smart guy up in Charlotte last spring when we quit that show. I saw him gettin' out of a new Ford, and I went over and hit him up. He tells me he'll give me two bits if I change his spare. I started in taking the spare off, see? And, then I says, 'Which one of these wheels do you want me to put this on?' and he says, 'Any of them.' I says, 'Don't none of these need changing?' and he says, 'Naw, I just believe a man oughta earn the money he gets even if he has to just pile rocks from one pile to another.' I let that spare drop then and I told him to go to hell."

"What did he do then?" Acel said.

"He turned white as a sheet and then just went on in the restaurant."

Acel laughed. "It's a wonder he didn't call a cop."

"He didn't have the guts to do anything, did he, Wayne?"

Wayne broke the twisted loaf in three hunks. "Uh huh."

"That's a good-looking suit you got on there, Ace," Wayne said. "I wish I had a good front like that."

"I got this when I was working on that boat up in New York. A man should keep a good front, all right. I'll need this tomorrow when I see that fellow Jessup. I didn't shave this morning, because that razor blade of mine is just about good for one more decent shave, and I want to look like something when I see him tomorrow."

"I wish I had seaman's papers like you," Wayne said. "I've always wanted to go to South America."

"A college boy with a letter to a shipping master has a better chance of getting out than an A.B.," Acel said. "When things pick up, though, a ship ought to be pretty easy to get. When times are good they can't get seamen in this country. That's what they tell me. They got to get a bunch of foreigners to run American ships."

Wayne scraped off some dried mud on the cuffs of his trousers with his fingernail. "I've always wanted to go to South America."

Acel stood up and shoved his hands deep into his pockets. "You can't ever tell. Something good might come out of me seeing this Jessup. They're going to need some help, all right."

"With a good front like you got on you, you might get something," Wayne said. "I'm going to get me a suit if I have to start paying it out fifty cents a week. We ought to be out now trying to get some shoe work, Lou."

"This town isn't no good," Lou said. "Listen, you guys, we can ride the T.P. outa here to Fort Worth and then catch it out there clear to El Paso. That's a run for you, from Fort Worth to El Paso. It makes passenger time."

"I've made that trip," Acel said

"Or we could ride the I.C. outa here up to Memphis and cut across Arkansas if we're not in a hurry," Lou said. "That's a state I never been in. I been all around, but I never have made Arkansas, and I wouldn't mind doing it just to say I had."

"What do you keep talking about leaving for?" Acel said. "This town isn't so bad. It's the cheapest town in the country."

"Show me what's good about it!"

"You know yourself now, Lou, that when you got out in California you'd stick there a couple of months and then you'd wanta start for someplace else. Just about New Orleans, too. That's the trouble with us fellows, we're always wanting to go on and not sticking in one place long enough to run into something. I've decided I'm going to get back into the music racket if I have to get religion and join a Salvation Army band. You ought to be pumping a bass again, Lou, and making some licks on that banjo. There's nothing to this runnin' around, I'm tellin' you."

"No, I don't think we ought to go to Cal," Wayne said. "If we went anywhere we ought to go back up to Chicago. Sis said she'd stake us to some money if we came up there. I'd like to get a new suit. I'm tired of wearing these damned corduroys."

"Well, I'm not going home," Lou said. "There's nothing in that little old town, and the old man has all he can feed without the rest of us sticking our feet under the table, too."

"I don't want to go home, either, but there's nothing for us in Cal, and we could get a few dollars in Chicago from Sis."

"You two just stick around here for a while," Acel said. "There's nothing to this moving just to be moving."

Lou tried to spit across the walk. "I hear the bulls are gettin' pretty hostile around Memphis."

28: HOBO SPECIAL

The ice cream soda, Acel thought, would be a good investment. He had not spent anything for breakfast, and he needed something on his stomach before he went up to see Mr. Jessup. There was nutrition in chocolate ice cream, and five cents was cheap enough. But he was not hungry. That was it. But the soda would make him feel more fresh, and he needed to feel fresh when he approached Mr. Jessup.

It made him feel brighter, all right. But he had

chumped off, paying that blonde cashier, and bought tailor-mades. If he had quit at the soda and bought Bull Durham it would have been all right, but he had chumped off and spent twenty cents. I can't hold onto money, that's all there is to it. And I don't even have that soap yet. Well, I can just keep on using laundry soap. A man who'll chump off like I do doesn't deserve anything else but laundry soap to shave with.

The offices of the Transient Relief Director in the tall building had a bare, just-moved-in look. There was a woman typing at a desk just inside the door, and she told Acel the man at the desk in the corner was Mr. Jessup, but that he was busy now and Acel could sit down and wait.

Acel sat on the bench against the wall near the door. Mr. Jessup was talking to a young man, a fellow with a Roman nose and horn-rimmed glasses. The young fellow's head went up and down as Mr. Jessup talked. Mr. Jessup was a middle-aged man with a grey face. The lapels of his coat were decorated with civic club buttons.

"I am taking it for granted, of course, that you are coming with us?" Mr. Jessup said.

"Oh, sure, sure, sure." The head of the young man went up and down. "Yessiree."

"You think you can line things up all right?"

"Oh, sure, sure, sure. Yessiree."

There was another worker in the office besides the woman, a man with white hair and of Mr. Jessup's age. He had been dusting a typewriter, and now he put the cloth down and studied the table on which the machine rested speculatively. "Can I help you, Frank?" Mr. Jessup called.

"I think I'll move this table a bit," White Hair said.

Mr. Jessup got up and so did the young man and the woman typist, and they went over and all of them moved the table.

Returning to his desk, Mr. Jessup paused before Acel.

"Did you want to see me?"

"Yessir." Acel stood up. "I wrote you a letter. I am Acel Stecker. I suppose you read it, all right?"

"I am glad to know you. I am very, very busy this morning. What was it, now, you wanted? I don't believe I recall the letter."

"I wrote you a letter. It was about a job."

"Oh, I see. Then you want to see that man right over there. The gentleman there. He handles our employment. Go right over there, he's your man."

White Hair paused in the ribbon running with Acel's approach. "It's a little hard to tell you about it, because I tried to explain to Mr. Jessup in a letter, and of course you know nothing about the letter. I'd like to have a job in one of these transient houses you are going to put up here. I'm pretty familiar with that work, and I thought you might be going to put on housemen."

White Hair yanked out the top drawer of his desk and from a broad pad tore off a blue form on which was printed at the top: *The State of Louisiana.*

"Fill that out," White Hair said. He returned to the ribbon running.

Acel studied the question form. There were a lot of questions, and one of them asked how long the applicant had been a resident of Louisiana.

Acel returned to White Hair. "Does this mean you have to have a poll-tax receipt before you can work in a flop house?"

"Not only that, but you must have two poll-tax receipts and also be a legal resident of this parish as well."

"That lets me out," Acel said. He placed the blue form on White Hair's desk and turned and walked out.

The sun was hot on Canal Street, and Acel took off his coat and loosened his tie and collar. There's no use of cussing about it. There's no use of doing anything. Forget it . . . . forget it . . . . forget it . . . .

The two brothers, Lou and Wayne, sat up on the park grass eagerly.

Acel spread his hands emptily. "Nothing."

"Did you see him?" Wayne said.

"Yeah, I saw him. It's all over, finished." He brought out the pack of cigarettes. "Have one, you two."

"Where did you get those tailor-mades?" Lou said. "I chumped off. Go ahead and take one."

"What did that guy say?" Wayne said.

"You got to have a poll tax and be a voter and things like that. I'm always making a mess of things. All the time. I'll swear, that's all I can do, is make a complete mess of everything I do."

"The sons of bitches," Lou said. "They got a hundred thousand bucks, and all the bums will get is some mush with weevils in it and a damned cot full of bugs."

"All I'm good for is to make a mess out of things. You guys oughten to be running around with me. I'm telling you, I'll make a mess out of things for you. I make a mess out of things for myself and for anybody that has anything to do with me."

"What I'd like to do is join these Communists," Lou said.

"When are these Communists going to do something, Ace? How do you get in with that bunch, anyway?"

"It won't do you no good," Acel said.

"I wish somebody would start something," Lou said.

"We were talking to a fellow just before you got here," Wayne said. "He just got out of the can. They vagged him last night in Lafayette Square, and he was going to leave this afternoon on the S.P. He sure did have it in for this town, didn't he, Lou?"

The heels of a passing girl in a white spring coat clicked on the walk. "I wouldn't mind taking that girl out yonder," Acel said.

"The engineer stops for the bums on that S.P. train outa Gretna every morning," Lou said. "They call it the Hobo Special. They say they stop to let everybody on."

"We're not riding any trains west out of here," Wayne said. "That I.C. hot shot that goes out of here about five o'clock in the morning is a Hobo Special, too."

Lou pinched off his cigarette and put the snipe in his pocket. "We could make it to Chicago in three days. Memphis is the only big town we got to get through."

"I wouldn't mind going to Chicago myself," Wayne said.

"How in the hell are we going to pass away the time in this damned town between now and in the morning?" Acel said.

29: CHICAGO

Between the shores of Michigan Avenue spectators the military band came like a golden-crested wave. The silver slides of trombones glistened in tearing smears. French horns, the melody-drowning drums, clarinets, trumpets passed.

Acel smiled. The band passed, and in a few moments its melody ended in shrill of trumpets. The feet of the following marchers, carrying N.R.A. signs, scraped harshly on the pavement. "I'm about ready to check out," Acel said.

"How about y'all?"

They squeezed through the bank of spectators and emerged in a clear area on the sidewalk in front of a men's furnishing store.

"I hope this N.R.A. gets over," Acel said. "Maybe we'll all have jobs pretty soon."

Wayne went over and looked in the show window and then beckoned.

"C'mere, you guys. This isn't bad, is it? Fourteen ninety-five is all, too."

They looked at the suit. It was a blue suit with white pin stripes.

Lou nudged Acel. "That's something I wouldn't play. Cymbals. If I had to rap them things I wouldn't play in a band."

"If I didn't look so much like a tramp, I'd go around to where Sis works and get that money there," Wayne said. "I hate to go up to the house tonight, because that old man of hers might be there."

"If I ever get a job I'm going to see to it that she quits that guy," Lou said. "He don't want her helping her own brothers. She's working and making her own money, and I don't see that he's got any kick coming."

"He'll be at the union meeting tonight," Wayne said. "I told Sis not to even let him know we were in town. You're going out there with us tonight, Ace. Sis is a swell girl. She won't care how you look or who you are."

"I'll just let you two go."

They walked on up the street and after a while turned into Grant Park. The parkscape stretched in a green, street-grooved shaft to end in the shining masonry of the Field Museum.

They dropped on the grass and began rolling cigarettes. "I been thinking about that army band," Acel said. "I wouldn't mind being in a band like that. They don't have such a bad time."

"It'll be a cold day in hell when I join the army," Lou said. "We was in the National Guard one summer," Wayne said. "That's why we joined the carnival, to keep from going the next summer. If you're out of the state, see? you don't have to go."

"I see you in the army, Ace," Lou said. "You'd get a bellyful of it pretty quick taking orders around. I'll bet a man couldn't get in it, though. There was a couple of fellows in the show with us that tried it, and they told them that the army was full up with musicians."

"Aw, I was just thinking about it," Acel said.

The sky over the lake was like frozen bluing water. Wayne pointed, and pretty soon they saw the airplane, too, and nodded.

"If I had a horn and you guys got yours, we could fire us a little German band," Acel said. "Bass, baritone, and trumpet. You could get some strings for that banjo, Lou, and we could work us up a few songs. I saw some of those bands in New York in the spring, and they looked to me like they were picking up quite a few nickels. Liquor is bringing them back."

"I wonder how much they pick up a day," Wayne said.

"More than we're picking up," Lou said.

"I watched them last spring around over on the East Side in New York. They play little German tunes and 'Good Old Summertime' and 'Sidewalks of New York' and tunes like that. I'll betcha we could start picking up a few dollars a day like that."

"They just pass the hat around, uh?" Wayne said.

"Listen, you guys," Lou said. "I'm not going to be the only one passing the hat, see?"

"What I want to do is start making some money before it gets cold," Acel said. "It's going to be winter here the first thing you know, and we're going to be S.O.L."

"We can go to California," Lou said.

"I wonder how much you could get a horn for," Wayne said.

"I don't know," Acel said. "You can get them for nothing now, almost."

"I'll bet you wouldn't play in a band like that,"

Wayne said.

"Shoot, I'd start out in the morning with you guys."

"I'm going to keep five bucks out of this money Sis gives us for a suit," Wayne said, "but I don't care what you guys do with the rest. Why don't you get you a horn, Ace, and we'll start this thing up?"

A tall, long-waisted man in striped work trousers and a soiled white shirt that billowed over his belt approached them.

"Here comes old One Eye," Wayne said.

One Eye had on new tan shoes. "Which one of you guys got a smoke on you?" he said.

Wayne handed him up the tobacco sack. One Eye rolled the cigarette and then seated himself. He had a grey glass eye. "How about a match, one of you?" he said.

Wayne turned and spat between his teeth with an upward jerk of his head. Acel handed One Eye a match.

One Eye pulled out a bottle from his bosom and began scraping off its transparent covering with his fingernail. It was labeled: *Rubbing Alcohol.* He unscrewed the blue cap and extended the bottle, but the three younger men shook their heads. One Eye tilted the bottle to his mouth, and the fluid rushed in foamy beads through the bottle's neck.

"I don't see how you drink that stuff," Wayne said.

"It's better than jake." One Eye screwed the cap back on and put the bottle back in his bosom.

"What was you doing to that old man over in that car on the avenue?" Acel said. "Puttin' the bing on him?"

"Yeah. Did you see me? I scared the hell out of that old man. I told him, by god, I hadn't eaten in two days and I had to have some money to eat on. He forked over a half-buck."

"You got the bowels, all right," Acel said.

"That's what it takes to get by on in this world, pal. If you don't ask for it, you don't get it. I'll bum the hell out of 'em."

"I'd rather work for mine," Acel said.

"I got a pal that's got the right idea," One Eye said. "He ain't nobody's fool, that guy ain't. He says the guys that stay in these flop houses and work all day for ninety cents a week are scabs. Dirty scabs. Bum it, that's what I say. Bum 'em until the people know something is wrong with this damned country. That's the way they can fix this country up until it amounts to something."

"You sound like an I.W.W.," Acel said.

"What do you know about the I.W.W.?" One Eye said.

"One of those I Want Work guys."

"That's what you know about it, uh? That's what guys like you know about it."

"I probably know a helluva lot more about it than you do."

"Ho, you're a smart guy." One Eye brought out the bottle and took another drink. The lids around the glass eye were fiery. "Lot you know about it. Where's your card?"

"You think you have to have a card to know about it?"

"Ho, you're a smart guy. Know all about it. When the revolution comes, smart guys like you are liable to know a helluva lot more about it." One Eye made a slitting gesture with his forefinger across his throat. "Like that."

"Old Booger Red himself," Acel said.

One Eye got up. "Smart guys." He stood there for a moment and then turned and walked away. His shirt tail was out.

"I'll bet he's as strong as an ox," Wayne said.

"If I couldn't whip a derail like him I'd kiss anything you say," Lou said. "These Reds are a bunch of dopes."

"He's all smoked up," Acel said. "He's too radical."

30: ".... GOOD OLD SUMMERTIME"

Acel Stecker leaned against the lamppost, pitching the mouthpiece of the cornet up and down on the palm of his hand. Lou and Wayne were under the Elevated waiting for the traffic to clear to join him.

"If we pick up two more bucks today I'll ask Suzanne to go to a movie with me tonight, Acel thought. She'll go, all right. I can tell that she will go with me, all right. I got to take her to a show or something though the first night. A man has to have money when he starts out with a girl. It'll be all right to be broke some later on, but going with a girl the first time or two you got to have a little money.

Suzanne has been around. Girls in cafés have been around, but Suzanne isn't but nineteen, and she hasn't been around much. You could tell that in her eyes. Corinne's eyes got hard at times, but she was older, and she had been around a whole lot. She had been around too much, and you could tell it in a girl's eyes. I'll say to Suzanne tonight: "Would you like to go with me to a movie tonight when you get off, Suzanne?"

Wayne stepped up onto the sidewalk. "We going to make a stand here, Ace?"

"No, not here. I thought we'd take a turn around that corner yonder and play the backs of some of those apartments This is a good time of day."

Lou dragged up. He pushed the banjo back on his shoulder and lifted the bass horn and, pressing the spit valve, blew into the mouthpiece. The saliva in the instrument made a gurgling sound.

"A drunken guy jerked loose with four bits over there," Lou said. "1 like to dropped dead."

"We're doing pretty good today," Acel said.

A man smoking a pipe stopped and looked at them and smiled. The clerk in the delicatessen peered through the window.

They moved on up the street, Wayne and Acel walking abreast and Lou behind.

The taxi driver waiting for the green light leaned out of his cab window: "Hey, how about a tune, boys?"

Acel and Wayne smiled and saluted and shook their heads. "Go on and peddle your moonshine," Lou shouted.

"I wish we were working toward Madison instead of this-away," Wayne said. "I'd like to put this two bucks I got in on that suit while I got it."

"Listen, Ace," Lou said. "Let's make Jim's Place again tonight. That's a good bunch around there. I wouldn't mind gettin' drunk again tonight myself."

"And puke all night like you did the last time,"

Wayne said.

The girl in the short fur jacket and mesh hose smiled as she passed. Wayne turned and looked after her.

"There you go," Acel said, "gettin' your mind off your business. You got female trouble, that's what's the matter with you."

"She wasn't looking at me, she was looking at you," Wayne said.

"Women don't look at me no more since I been running around with you two punks. You're the sheik, Wayne."

"You're the one that's got female trouble. How about Suzanne? When you going to take that girl out, anyway? You're the one that's got female trouble."

They turned into the rear courtyard of the apartment building, into a canyon six stories high. Two children came up out of the basement steps and watched. A poodle on a leash jumped up and started barking. A woman with a towel around her head and a cloth in her hand stood at an opened window on the second floor and looked. Acel lifted his cap to her, and the woman smiled.

A window on the left raised, and a man in a smoking jacket leaned out, with his hands on the sill. He turned and then held a child up to the window.

Acel lifted his cornet. "'Good Old,'" he said, "and put the pecks in, Wayne."

After that they played *"There'll Be A Hot Time,"* and now there were a dozen figures in the windows.

Lou set his bass horn down and loosened his banjo. He and Acel sang "Down by the Old Mill Stream." Coins wrapped in brown sack paper and newspaper dropped into the courtyards from the windows, and Wayne went around and picked them up.

"'Sweet Adeline,'" the man in the smoking jacket called down.

They sang that, and then Lou picked up his bass and pushed his banjo back and they moved out of the court-yard.

"That bastard in that jacket just gave us a dime," Wayne said.

"Did that woman with that towel around her head pitch anything down?" Acel said.

"A quarter."

"I figured she would."

One Eye was standing in front of the cigar store on the corner. There was a man with him, a short man with a Hitler mustache and checkered trousers and blue coat.

"I thought that was you," One Eye said. His good eye was as glassy as the other with drink. "Ho, strike us up a tune."

"'The International,'" Hitler Mustache said.

"That's it," One Eye said. "'International.' We'll give you a nickel."

"Go to hell," Acel said.

One Eye lurched out and grasped Acel's arm. Acel jerked away, and the cornet fell from under his arm and clattered with a tinny sound on the sidewalk.

"You goddam fool," Acel said. He struck at One Eye's face with his fists, struck at it again . . . . again . . . .

A circle was growing around them. One Eye clutched Acel and clung, and Acel struggled to extricate himself and strike with his fists. One Eye dragged him down and lay on top of Acel. People crowded closer, their feet in the faces of the fighters. One Eye lay on Acel's chest, his chin digging into Acel's flesh. Acel hit at his ear . . . .

The circle widened suddenly, and then the policeman was yanking at One Eye's collar. One Eye clung tighter, and then the officer struck One Eye on the back with his stick . . . .

The policeman stood between One Eye and Acel on the curb, waiting for the wagon. One Eye's nose was bleeding.

He held one hand over his glass eye.

"Where are you going to take this fellow?" Lou asked the officer. "We want to testify for him. That one-eyed guy there started it every bit. We were just walking along, and he started it every bit."

"You got my horn all right, haven't you, Lou?" Acel said.

"I got it, Officer. I'm telling you that we were just walking along here, and that guy started it."

The police wagon smelled of disinfectant, like a jail. Acel sat forward on the bench, and One Eye back. They did not look at one another.

This blood I got on me is off of him. I'm not bleeding nowhere. I don't remember him hittin' me a time. Aw, Christ, I would get into something like this. I have the hardest luck of any man in this country. I never did see anything like it. I'll swear . . . .

One Eye gagged and then began to vomit on the floor.

31: *"THE INTERNATIONAL"*

The Judge on the high bench was a fat, youngish man
with long black hair brushed back across his temples and
with a shaved, red neck. Sometimes he would lean
forward, his broad, cleft chin resting in his left hand, and
when he straightened he ran his hand through his hair.

From time to time the clerk read names, and one of
the shabby men on the long bench with Acel and One Eye
would get up and stand before the judge, and then in a
few minutes they would cross the room and sit on a
bench on the other side.

If I could just have shaved this morning I wouldn't
look so much like a tramp, Acel thought. I'm going to
shake when I stand up there. I'm going to have court
fright. If I could have just shaved, then I wouldn't mind
it. *I'm not guilty, your honor. If you will permit me, your
honor, I will tell you just how it happened, and then if
the court believes I am guilty I will take my punishment.*

I'll get it in the neck, though. Thirty days, and I
might just as well get ready for it. I expect to get it, all
right, and if I do get out of it with less than that I'll have
something to feel good about. Thirty days? It'll be cold
when I come out and me without an overcoat, and I'll
have this six bucks I got spent by the time I get out. Lou
and Wayne will head for California as sure as hell. Well, I
can go to California as soon as I get out. I'll hang onto

this six bucks and have something to start out on.

The judge will know I am no ordinary bum when I address him. He will know that by the language I use. *Your honor, my companions are here in the courtroom now, and they will testify that we were just walking along there, minding our own business, and this man steps out and starts trouble.* The judge will know by the language I use that I am no ordinary bum in court for fighting on the street . . . .

The clerk called "Acel Stecker."

One Eye followed Acel to stand before the bar. He had a handkerchief tied across his bad eye. The policeman was there, too, his cheeks round and puffed like shined apples.

One Eye said he was guilty, and then the clerk motioned with his thumb and One Eye went over and sat on the bench on the other side.

Acel's eyes shimmied in their sockets. He looked at the judge and struggled to keep his eyes steady. "I'm not guilty, your honor."

The policeman spoke with jerks of his head. "They tied up traffic around that corner for fifteen or twenty minutes, and it took me quite a while to clear it up. They were both fighting. This fellow here is a street musician, and they got into a fight over what they were going to play."

The judge jerked a hair out of his nose and then looked down at Acel.

"I'll tell you, Judge, just how it happened. The fellows that play with me are here in the court, too, and they can tell you just what I tell you. We got a little, and we been trying to make a living by playing around on the streets, and we were coming by this corner and that man over there steps out with another fellow and asks us to play 'The International,' and we—"

"The what?"

"The Communist song."

"I see. Go on."

"I told him we wouldn't do it, and we were going on, and then he jumped out and jerked my horn out of my hands, and it fell on the sidewalk, and the first thing I was protecting myself. We don't make very much, and I can't afford to buy new horns, and so we started fighting. I didn't want to fight, but he grabbed me and I couldn't do anything else but protect myself."

"How old are you?"

"Twenty-six."

"What kind of a band is this you have?"

"It's what you call a little German band, but one of the boys plays banjo and we do some singing. We're just trying to make a living."

"Why wouldn't you play 'The International'?"

"That tune? We don't play tunes like that."

The judge straightened in his swivel chair, looked around over the courtroom, and then leaned forward again. "I do not excuse street fighting. It is dangerous to the safety of innocent passers-by and a public nuisance and menace. However, there is something significant in this case, and I wonder if you realize its significance, too. But I am sure that you do. The fact that you refused to play the hymn or the song, or whatever it is, of a corrupt foreign country is significant and a patriotic gesture to me that deserves consideration."

Acel struggled to control the shimmying of his eyes. The judge raised his voice:

"Communism is an organized effort to overthrow the democratic governments of this world. 'The Star-Spangled Banner' stands for liberty and justice and freedom, but that song stands for the interbreeding of Negroes and whites and Mongolians and Hindus, and it stirs up riots and bloodshed and sabotage and civil war. It means the destruction of courts meting out justice and trials by jury and would set up a dictatorship of the unintelligent classes and crush the skilled worker and the professional man and the man who appreciates the finer things of life. I am going to let you go this time."

"Thank you, judge."

The clerk read another name.

Lou and Wayne were waiting in the corridor outside the courtroom. "Boy, you sure made a speech," Wayne said. "Boy, you sure did tell it to him. Boy, that was good."

"Y'all didn't say anything to Suzanne about me getting in jail, did you?"

"No, sir," Wayne said.

"Let's get the hell out of this place," Acel said.

The man in the double-breasted suit with the handkerchief in his breast pocket who had leaned against the bar beside the judge halted them. "How long you boys had this band?" he said.

"About two months now, I guess," Acel said.

"You just play American tunes? Is that the idea?"

Acel nodded. "What are you, a reporter?"

"Yes. I'm planning on doing a little feature about you boys. I'd like to get your pictures, with your horns and things. Can you get to your horns right away?"

"Aw, don't put nothing in the paper about this," Acel said.

"Why not? I've got a photographer coming, and we'll shoot you around here some place. What I want to do, though, is put you boys onto something. I'm in charge of a program for a veterans' smoker Friday night, and I want you boys on it. I'll see to it that your pickings are good. You ought to pick up fifty bucks or so in a bunch like that. You fellows wait here now until I go back in here and get a few names."

They looked at the closed doors of the courtroom through which the reporter had gone. "I don't guess that guy is horsin' us, is he, Ace?" Lou said.

"He was a reporter, all right. Say, we'll look hot in a picture, won't we? That's pretty good."

"I'd like to see that fifty bucks he was talking about," Wayne said. "I wonder if he was bulling."

"He's not bullin'," Acel said. "Listen, you guys, we got a name from now on, see? The Three Americans. We got to get up some war songs, Lou. 'Over There' and 'Tipperary' and stuff like that, see? Break your necks when this reporter comes back. He'll get us in the papers, and that's publicity. If we play at this smoker, I know damn well we can get some more jobs. That reminds me, we got to get up a dirty song or two. A mademoiselle song or two. I got some ideas, by god."

THIEVES LIKE US

TO

MY COUSIN and MY WIFE

BECAUSE THERE I WAS WITH AN EMPTY GUN

AND YOU, ROY, SUPPLIED THE AMMUNITION

AND YOU, ANNE, DIRECTED MY AIM

"Men do not despise a thief, if he steal to satisfy his soul when he is hungry; but if he be found, he shall restore sevenfold; he shall give all the substance of his house."

–Proverbs of Solomon

Chapter 1

There was no doubt about it this time: over yonder behind the rise of scrub-oak, the automobile had left the highway and was laboring in low gear over the rutted road to where they waited. Like a saliva-wettened finger scorching across a hot iron, Bowie's insides spitted. He looked at Chicamaw.

Chicamaw's eyes were fixed up the weed-grown road, his thick-soled, convict shoes quiet on the rain-sprinkled earth that he had scarred with pacing. "That's him," he said.

Bowie looked behind him, across the creek's ridge of trees and over the field where the blades of the young corn glimmered like knives in the late-afternoon sun. Above the whitewashed walls of Alcatona Penitentiary reared the red-painted water tank, the big cottonwood tree of the Upper Yard and the guards' towers.

The car was coming on. The jew's-harp twanging of the grasshoppers in the broomweeds seemed to heighten. I can rib myself up to do anything, Bowie thought. Anything. Every day in that place over there is wasted.

The car's springs creaked nearer. Bowie looked at Chicamaw again. "You're not planning on going someplace, are you?"

Chicamaw did not move his head. "I'm just waitin' to
see a horse about a feller," he said.

The taxicab bumped around the hill and wallowed
toward them. Bowie squinted to see better. The figure in
the backseat had on a straw hat. It was old T-Dub
though. Come on, you cotton-headed old soldier!

The driver was that Kid that had been peddling
marihuana to some of the boys. Jasbo they called him.

The cab stopped a few feet away and Bowie and
Chicamaw moved toward it.

"Hello, Bowie," Jasbo said.

Bowie did not look at him. "Hi," he said.

T-Dub sat there with a big, paper-wrapped bundle
across his knees. The yellow brightness of the new hat
made his blond hair look like dry corn-silk.

"Well, what we waitin' on?" Chicamaw said. He
opened the door.

T-Dub handed Chicamaw the bundle and then
reached inside his blouse and pulled the gun. He scraped
the barrel against the driver's cheek. "This is a stick-up,
Jasbo," he said.

"Godamighty, Man," Jasbo said. His head quivered
on his neck.

Chicamaw ripped at the bundle strings and slapped
at the paper. It contained blue denim overalls and white
cotton shins. He began stripping himself of his cotton-
sacking prison clothing. Bowie and T-Dub began changing too.

Jasbo said: "Bowie, now you know me. You tell these
Boys I'm all right."

"You just do what you're told," Bowie said.

"All you gotta do is tell me," Jasbo said.

Their clothing changed, Chicamaw pushed Jasbo over and under the wheel and Bowie and T-Dub got in the back. They turned and went back up the road. On the highway, the wind began beating the speeding car like a hundred fly-swatters.

There was a car under the shed of the filling station on the right. A man in coveralls stood beside the red pump twisting the handle.

"Don't you let me see you throwing no winks, Jasbo," T-Dub said, "or I'll beat your ears down."

"I'll put my head 'tween my legs if you say so," Jasbo said.

They passed the filling station and Bowie looked back. The man was still twisting the pump handle. The empty highway behind looked like a stretching rubber band.

Bowie looked at the revolver in T-Dub's thick grasp. It was a silver-plated gun with a pearl handle. This old soldier knows what he is doing, Bowie thought. "Any rumbles in town?" he said.

T-Dub shook his head.

The highway still stretched emptily. They're finding out things back there now in the Warden's Office, Bowie thought. The Colonel's bowels are gettin' in an uproar now. Get out the stripes for that bunch of no-goods, he is saying. That's what you get for treatin' them like white men. No more baseball and passes to go fishing for that Bowie Bowers and Elmo Mobley. That T. W. Masefeld is not going to work in this prison commissary any more.

Get out the dogs and the shotguns and the .30—30's and run them sons of bitches down . . . .

A car shot up over the rise; hurtled toward them. It passed with a swooshing sound. Cars coming this way don't mean nothing, Bowie thought. No more than them crows flying over yonder. T-Dub shifted the revolver to his left hand, wiped his palm on his thigh and regrasped the gun. Old T-Dub knows what he is doing.

The tendons of Chicamaw's lean neck played into two bony knots behind each ear. That Chicamaw knows what he is doing too. A man won't get in with two boys like this just every day. No more Time for any of them. They had shook on it.

The explosion was like the highway had snapped. The escaping air of the right back tire wailed. The car began to bump. On the left was a sign post: *Alcatona . . . . 14 miles.* It was right in the middle of thirteen, Bowie thought. Old unlucky *thirteen.*

They bumped across the wooden bridge and moved up the dirt side road. When they were out of sight of the highway, Chicamaw stopped. The casing looked like it had been chopped with an ax. The spare was no good either.

Dusk was smoking out the ebbing glow on the horizon. Crickets in the roadside grass sounded like wind in loose telephone wires. Old unlucky *thirteen* is getting us uptight, Bowie thought. Hundred and twenty-two miles to Keota and Chicamaw's cousin, Dee Mobley and our Hole and *thirteen* riding our sore backs.

Chicamaw yanked at the barbed wire of the fence with the pliers and then came back with a strand. He lashed Jasbo to the steering wheel.

They moved now across the field of growing cotton toward the farmhouse light. "This gentleman up here might have a car with some tires on it," T-Dub said.

The earth of the field was soft and the tough stalks whipped their legs. In the distance, back toward the Prison, there was the sound of baying dogs and Bowie stopped. "Man, listen to them dogs," he said. Chicamaw and T-Dub halted. It was a vibrant, sonorous sound like the musical notes of a deep reed instrument.

"Hell, them's possum hounds," Chicamaw said.

They walked faster. The cottonwood stumps squatted in the field like headless toads. The farmhouse light glowed nearer, a fierce orange. T-Dub broke into a lope and Chicamaw and Bowie followed.

The woman with the baby in her arms led T-Dub and Bowie back to the lamp-lighted kitchen and the little man at the table half turned in his chair, a raw, bitten onion in his left hand, and looked up at them, at the gun in T-Dub's hand.

"We need that car out there of yours, Mister," T-Dub said. "Come on up."

Little Man turned and put the onion on the table. There were fried eggs and yellow corn bread on the plate. He got up and pushed the chair against the table.

"Where's them keys, Mama?" he said.

The skin about Mama's mouth was twitching and her lower lip looked like it was going to melt on her chin.

"I don't know," she said. The baby in her arms began to whimper.

Little Man found the keys in his pocket.

T-Dub looked at Mama. "Lady, if you like this gentleman here and want to see him again and I think you do,
you just don't open your mouth after we leave."

"Yessir," Mama said. She began jogging the baby up
and down. It began to cry.

Dust was as thick as silk on the car's body and there
were chicken droppings on the hood and fenders. Little
Man got in front with Chicamaw. "I haven't had this car
out in more than a month," he said.

The highway paralleled the high embankment of the
Katy railroad now. Bowie watched the rising speedometer needle: *forty-five* . . . . fifty. Stomp it, Chicamaw.
Two pairs of nines riding our backs now. That kid Jasbo
is squawking back yonder now all over the country.
Ninety-nine years for highway robbery. Another pair for
kidnapping.

The lights of the little highway town ahead spread
with their approach and then scattered like flushed prey
as they entered its limits. Under the filling station sheds,
swirling insects clouded the naked bulbs. The stores were
closed; the depot dark. No Laws jumping us here, Bowie
thought. No Square-Johns with shotguns. He turned
toward T-Dub. "How many miles you think we done?"

"Twenty," T-Dub said.

"My woman has been pretty sick," Little Man said.
"Been awful torn up lately."

Chicamaw's head went up and down.

Awful sick or scared, Bowie thought. District 'Cuter
shouting that all over the Court House won't sound so
good, boys. Stomp it, Chicamaw. Fog right up this line.
Hour and forty minutes like this and we'll be cooling off

with Real People. That Dee Mobley was Real People. Him and Chicamaw had thieved together when they were kids. Chicamaw had been saving this Hole for eight years.

"Hasn't been well since the baby," Little Man said.

The motor coughed, spluttered. Chicamaw yanked out the choke button. The motor fired again, missed; the cylinders pumped with furious emptiness. Loose lugs rasped on the slowing wheels.

"Get her off the highway," T-Dub said. "Goose her. Gentlemen, this wins the fur-lined bathtub."

Bowie, T-Dub and Little Man pushed, their feet clopping on the pavement like horses. At last they reached the crossroads and they pushed the car up over the hump and out of sight of the highway.

Chicamaw started tying Little Man. T-Dub struggled, breathing like he had asthma. "I've had plenty of tough teaty in my day, but this is the toughest. I might as well turn this .38 on me and do it up right."

A car was coming; its headlights glowed above the hump. It sped on, its sound diminishing like the roll of a muffled drum.

"Let's get moving," Chicamaw said.

They crossed the highway, crawled through the fence and waded the hip-deep grass of the railroad right-of-way. They climbed the embankment and got down on the railroad bed.

"We could flag a car and throw down on them," Chicamaw said.

"To hell with them hot cars," T-Dub said. "I'll walk it."

"We can do it by just keeping right down these ties,"

Chicamaw said.

"Like goddamned hoboes," T-Dub said.

The moon hung in the heavens like a shred of finger-nail. There was only the sound of their feet crunching in the gravel Chicamaw led.

The rails began to murmur. It was a train behind them. After a while, the locomotive's light showed, tiny as a lightning bug. It began to swell.

They climbed up the cut's side, clutching at the grass, and on top lay down. The earth began trembling as if the cut's sides were going to cave in and carry them under the wheels. The pounding wheels of the freight-train thundered and crashed and after a long time, the twin red lights of the caboose passed.

"I wouldn't of minded holding that down for a while," T Dub said.

"Why didn't you holler for them to stop, Bowie?" Chicamaw said.

"I didn't want to make them mad at us," Bowie said.

The nail in the heel of Bowie's right shoe was digging now into the flesh. To hell with it, he thought. Bad start is a good ending, boys. You can't throw snake-eyes all day. Boxcars won't jump up in your face every throw. There's a natural for us up this road.

~§~

Bowie came out of his sleep with T-Dub's voice, deep as a cistern's echo and Chicamaw's muffled rattle still strok-ing his ears. His feet felt like the toenails had been drawn out and the bits ground in his heels. The sun was piercing the plum thicket like ice picks, and when Bowie turned on his back he placed his forearm over his eyes.

"I cased that bank in Zelton four times," T-Dub said. "It was a bird's nest on the ground, but every time something came up. Maybe this time will be different."

"I'm ready for a piece of it myself," Chicamaw said.

"I tell you one thing," T-Dub said. "When I rob my next bank it will be my twenty-eighth."

"I hope it's twenty-nine in a couple of weeks."

Bowie's insides quivered. I can rib myself up to do anything, he thought.

"These kids trying to rob these banks are just ding-bats," T-Dub said. "They'll charge a bank with a filling-station across the street and a telephone office above and a hardware store next door."

"You got to watch them upstairs offices across the street from a bank too," Chicamaw said. "There's lawyers and doctors and people with shotguns just waiting for a bank to be robbed."

"I'm not going to fool with any of these clodhopper town banks," Chicamaw said. "You got to work just as hard for a thousand out of one of them as you do in a good one for fifty."

"Pick you a bank that's a depository for the county and city and you're going to find a set-up," T-Dub said. "That's why I say it don't hurt to case a bank for a week before you charge it."

Five thousand dollars and I'm backing off, Bowie thought. Five thousand salted away and I'm going back to Alky. I've done so much Time that I can do a couple of

more on my ear. Go back there and grin at them from ear
to ear. I can twist that Warden around my little finger.
He's all right, though. He'll close them books on me and
my record will be clean in a couple of years. Then I'll buy
me a mouthpiece for a couple o' thousand that's got
friends in the Capital and you'll see me coming out of
that Alky squared up and with a stake.

The best way to case the Inside of a bank, T-Dub
said, was by going in and cashing twenty-dollar bills. In
Florida he had opened up an account in a bank just to
big-eye it good.

Bowie sat up.

"The Country Boy is up," Chicamaw said. His teeth
were as white as the pearl of a gun butt.

There were tiny lights in T-Dub's eyes, gray as .30—
30 bullets. "What do you want for supper, Bowie? Plums
or fried chicken?"

Bowie looked at a ripened plum on the stem above
his head. "I'll take plums," he said.

Chicamaw had his trousers rolled to his knees and
now he was pinching into his hair-matted legs.

"What the hell are you doing?" Bowie said.

"Red bugs," Chicamaw said.

Bowie looked at his blood-crusted feet; at the curled
toes and grass-filled wrinkles of his shoes. Just one more
night of walking though. Just a half a night. He lay back
down.

Chicamaw was talking now about a bank he robbed
in Kansas. "I knew I hadn't sacked up no more than two
thousand out of that nigger-head and I just happened to
pick up that cash slip. You know that one they put in

every night to show how much cash they got on hand? . . .
Well, it didn't jibe with what I had so I went back up to
that Dutchman and I says to him: 'Friend, have I got
everything around here?' He says: 'You got every bit of it.'
I says: 'Is your cash receipt slip usually right?' He says:
'Why, yes.' I says: 'Well, I haven't got but two thousand
here and this slip shows four thousand eight hundred
and sixty-two dollars. Now cough it up.' That guy began
swearing up and down so I just put the twitch to him. His
eyes turned as red as any red you ever did see."

Bowie sat back up. "What's a twitch?" he said.

"Don't worry, you'll see one pretty soon. When I
work I always carry myself one. Get you a piece of
window cord and make a little stick with a hole in it and
fix a loop and just put that around a man's head and give
it a twist and he's gonna think his brains are coming out
his ears. Anyway, this Dutchman hollers calf rope and he
shows me the bottom drawer of a desk there. Sure
enough, right there in it was four little packs of the
prettiest *five hundred-* and *one hundred-dollar* bills you
ever saw."

A gust of wind combed the thicket and bent the
stretch of high Johnston grass that separated them from
the railroad. Bowie lay back.

"You know what that banker would have done if you
hadn't of got onto that slip," T-Dub said. "He'd of
squawked that he had been robbed of it all just the same
There's more of these bankers than you can shake a stick
at that's got it stacked around over their banks and just
praying every day to be robbed."

"Sure," Chicamaw said.

"They're thieves just like us," T-Dub said.

Bowie flecked an ant off the back of his hand. I'm not going to get in this too deep, gentlemen. You going to see this white child backing off when he's got five thousand.

The feet of T-Dub and Chicamaw scraped in sudden violence and Bowie jerked up like a jackknife. He looked toward the two. They were looking into the Johnston grass. T-Dub had the gun in his hand.

Bowie watched. Something was moving in that grass yonder all right. It wasn't wind either. He picked up his shoes. The grass parted again!

Chicamaw led the way, plunging through the thicket like a football half-back; T-Dub behind and Bowie following barefooted and carrying his shoes. They did not stop running until they reached the woods Then they stopped and looked back toward the thicket.

"What did y'all see?" Bowie said. "Jesus Christ."

"Something was in that grass," Chicamaw said.

"If there wasn't I left a damned good three-dollar hat over there, T Dub said "I can see your socks hanging from here, Bowie."

"I thought all the Laws in the county were in that grass the way y'all tore out," Bowie said.

"I'll bet it was a hog or something," T-Dub said. "Turkey or something. I'll bet any amount you guys want to name."

"If you think it's just a hog why don't you just trot back over there and get that hat?" Chicamaw said.

"Ah, I want to go bare-headed anyway. Like these jelly beans."

Bowie sat down and began putting on his shoes. His feet were bleeding again.

"Think you going to make it, Bowie?" T-Dub said.

"The way I come across over here looks like I could run it," Bowie said.

Chapter 2

That rain-blurred sprinkle of lights yonder was Keota. Before the rain commenced, Bowie had heard sounds of the town, but now there was only the smacking of the wind-driven rain against the shocks of old wheat around him and its clatter on the stubbled earth. He had been alone now more than two hours and it must be getting along toward three or four o'clock. In the black depths underneath those lights yonder, T-Dub and Chicamaw were looking for Dee Mobley's place. When they found Chicamaw's cousin, they were coming back after him. Three flashes of the headlamps, if they got Dee's car, would be the signal.

Bowie reached down now and pressed his numb feet. They felt like stumps. A man on stumps couldn't do much good if he was jumped and that is why he had stayed here to wait.

The thunder in the east rumbled nearer and then cracked above him in a jagged prong of lightning. The flash bared the sodden stretch to the sagging fence and road.

I won't be hearing any more from my people, Bowie thought. Mama. Aunt Pearl. Cousin Tom. Goodbye to you people. The first thing the Law does is look up the people a man has been writing to and watch them places.

Goodbye, Mama. There's one thing about you. Whatever I ever did was all right with you. This is the only way. Maybe you'll be getting an envelope with three or four hundred dollars in it pretty soon and then you can go off and get that pellagra cured up. Get away from that husband you got for a while.

So long, Cousin Tom. Thanks for them letters and cigarettes. But all the cheering in the world don't help you none, Pal, when you're in a place like that back yonder. You know every day what is going to happen the next.

Aunt Pearl, you're a fine woman, but all the Christian Scientist stuff in the world don't help you none if you haven't got the money to buy a lawyer. And to get a good one you got to have good money.

Approaching car lights bobbed on the road and Bowie got up. The laboring machine plowed the mud of the road right on past. Bowie lowered himself back to the ground.

Them boys will be back here. Takes time to locate a man when you don't know where he lives. Let him stay out here? Them boys weren't made that way. It was getting doggone late though. There wasn't a dozen lights in the town now.

Lightning slashed the swirling heavens. Maybe a man saw something like that when they kicked the switch off on you in the Chair, Bowie thought. It didn't seem like no nine years since that morning when his lawyer came and told him they weren't going to burn him. Maybe though he had died back there in the Chair? This was just his Spirit out here in this rain? In this old world, anything happened. Maybe I'm like a cat with nine lives. I done lost one of them back there in that Alky Chair. Eight more to go . . . . Look here, Bowie, old boy, snap out of it. You're going to go ding-batty out here. Another car was coming. It sounded like a Model-T; had one twitching feeble light.

Bowie moved toward the fence in a half crouch. The car was a Ford pick-up, its body boards thumping and rattling. That light on it was either just going off and on or signaling. What was it doing? He checked the shout in his throat. The car went on, the sound of its straining motor dying in the night.

He sat now at the side of the road. It couldn't be very long until daybreak. Well, I can't sit out here up into the day. Them boys must have got a rumble over there. They might be in trouble this very minute. They wouldn't leave me out here though. Not them boys. We've had our heads together too long on this business. Take old T-Dub. Him knocking down in that Commissary every day so they would have a stake. A man didn't start out with money that come that hard with two fellows and not intend to go through with it. Not any four hundred and twenty-five dollars. And planning as far ahead as they had? Cooling off at Dee's and then going on down into Texas and getting hold of T-Dub's sister-in-law and getting her to get them a furnished house. No sir, that boy just wasn't made that way. And Chicamaw? Them white teeth.

The rain slapped his face and crawled on his numb feet. *But I can't stay out here forever. If they ain't here by daybreak, I've just got to go on in. I can't help it. I'm going in.*

~§~

The harnessed mules plowed the road's muck toward Bowie, pulling a wagon with a tarpaulin as gray and soggy as the morning. The driver, his drooping straw sombrero bowed against the drizzle, slopped along at the wagon's side. His overalls were rolled to his calves and hunks of mud leaped from his moving shoes. Now the sombrero raised.

"Good morning, Friend," Bowie said.

Sombrero shifted the wad of tobacco in his jaws. "Mornin'," he said.

Bowie pointed at his shoes. "Mind if I hang on the back of your wagon into town? My feet have plumb played out on me."

Sombrero nodded toward the wagon's rear. "Climb up in it if you want to."

Bowie went around and climbed through the canvas flap and into the wagon. The smell of alfalfa was dry and clean. He saw now the woman and the little boy. They sat on quilt-covered straw against the seat.

"Your man said I could pile in here, Lady?"

The woman nodded.

Bowie leaned back against the sides, stretched his feet in guarded relaxation. The wagon's movement was soothing and its clean dryness began to sponge him like a dry chamois skin. He closed his eyes.

"Who's that man, Ma?"

Bowie opened his eyes, looked at the child and grinned, "You don't mind me riding with you, do you, Son?"

The boy burrowed his face against his mother's bosom and she patted him. "He's a friend of your pappy's, honey."

The hoofs of the mules began clopping and Bowie asked the woman: "We in town?"

The woman nodded. "On the Square."

Bowie edged feet forward to the wagon's end, parted the flap and slid out. The pavement was like a cushion of pins.

In the center of the Square was the Court House, a two-story sandstone building with big basement signs: *Whites . . . . Colored.* One- and two-story buildings fenced the Square: *Greenberg's Dry Goods Store . . . . Keota State Bank . . . . Rexall Drug Store . . . . Hamburger's 5 & 10¢.*

The rain had stopped and the sun looked like a circle of wet, yellow paper. Bowie walked across the Court House lawn toward the dry goods store on the corner.

The clerk leaned against the doorway with his arms folded across his chest and when Bowie neared he pushed with his shoulder blades and stood erect.

"Yessir?" he said.

"I got ten bucks, Pardner," Bowie said, "and I got to have a pair of pants and a shirt and socks and shoes and some short-handled drawers."

"We'll see," Pardner said.

Bowie followed him back into the gloom and deeper into the smell of damp wool and bolted goods and floor sweep. Pardner turned on a fly-specked bulb above a table of khaki work pants.

In dry clothing now, Bowie sat on a bench while Pardner laced the new shoes on his feet. "You don't know a feller around here by the name of Tobey or Hobby or something like that, do you?" he asked.

Pardner cocked his head. "Don't believe I do."

"I used to know a feller up in Tulsy who settled down here. Been in this town a pretty good while I understand. Mobby or something like that."

"What does he look like?"

Bowie described Chicamaw. "Oh, he's sort of an Indian looking feller. Come up to about my shoulders. Black eyes and pretty skinny."

Pardner shook his head.

"He was working in a filling station up in Tulsy."

"Well, there's a fellow named Mobley out on the Dallas highway that's got a little store and station out there."

"It wasn't Mobley, I'm sure of that."

"Did he have a girl named Keechie, little Indian-looking girl?"

"No. It don't matter. I didn't know him so well."

The new shoes made his feet feel like they were not even sore. It was good to walk. The sun was blotting the puddles and making the dry stretches of the highway glare. He passed the lumber yard with its fence of shredded show posters, the closed cotton gin, the tourist camp:

Kozy Komfort Kamp.

That was the place yonder all right. That station right yonder with the orange-colored pump. A man sat under the shed in a tilted chair. Back of the station was a smokehouse-looking structure and then woods. Farther up the highway, on the left side, was another station.

Bowie went up under the shed toward the man in the tilted chair. "How you do, Friend?" Bowie said.

"Howdy," the man said. He had a heavy face, rough as oak bark and long, black sideburns touched with wiry gray. The black cotton shirt had white buttons.

"Got a cold soda?" Bowie said.

The man got up and lifted the lid of the ice-box Bowie reached in and picked up a bottle.

Bowie saw now the girl standing behind the screened doorway of the store. She was dark and small and her high pointed breasts stretched the blue cotton of the polo shirt.

Bowie looked at the man. "I wonder if I could see you private a minute?"

The man looked toward the girl and she went away.

"You're Dee Mobley, aren't you?"

"That's me."

"You haven't had a couple of visitors lately?" Mobley looked at Bowie's shoes. "You got on some new shoes there, haven't you? Feet been hurting?"

"You doggone whistling. I just got these uptown."

"New pants too?"

Bowie grinned.

"Where in the hell," Mobley said, "have *you* been?"

"Waiting for that Chicamaw and that T-Dub Masefeld."

"I went after you last night myself," Mobley said "Raining cats and nigger babies."

"In a Model-T truck?"

"That was me."

"Well, I'll be— Can you beat that. And I just sat out there and let you go by."

Mobley made a thumbing motion toward the filling station up the highway. Two figures in uniform coveralls sat on a bench under its shed. "Them Square-Johns up yonder are always big-eyeing this way so you just go on past like you were hitchhiking and then cut back through the woods. The boys are in that bunk of mine right back of this place."

Bowie dog-trotted through the woods toward the filling station. He could see the place that Dee called his bunk. It had a corrugated iron roof and the limbs of a big pecan tree shaded it, He crawled through the fence and went to the bunk's door and knocked. The springs of a bed inside creaked a little. He knocked again. There was no answer. "Chicamaw," he called.

Feet thumped on the floor inside, stomped toward the door. T-Dub's face was framed in the parted door. "For Christ's sake, come in," he said.

Chicamaw lay on the iron bed in his underwear. "We thought maybe you had gone back to Alky."

"I just been swimming that's all," Bowie said. "And thinking I was a lone wolf."

"I was going to go back out there tonight myself," Chicamaw said.

T-Dub pointed at the bare wooden table. On it was a

bowl of pork and beans, a hunk of yellow cheese and a broken loaf of bread. "You want to glom?"

"Man, I'll say."

"We didn't get holed up here until five o'clock this morning," Chicamaw said. "I was going to go back after you tonight. I don't see how Dee missed you."

"It was my fault," Bowie said. He poured beans on a hunk of the bread and pressed it into a sandwich. He took a bite and chewed and grinned.

Chapter 3

Up until a year ago, Dee Mobley had been bootlegging corn whisky, but the new Sheriff in Keota had it in for him, he said. He squatted now against the wall of the bunk, his breath as strong as rubbing-alcohol fumes, a finger-rolled cigarette wagging on his lower lip. "The Sheriff likes these druggist boys here," Dee said. "They're doing all the booze business here now."

"Them Laws and druggists are thieves just like us," T-Dub said. He drew his hand across his sweat-beaded forehead and his fingers made a clicking sound as he slung it on the floor. "It's getting so a man has to have a gun to make a piece of money."

The afternoon sun was packing heat into the low-ceilinged, crowded room. Chicamaw sat on an upturned bucket filing on the barrels of the .12—gauge shotgun with a hacksaw. Bowie lay on the bed, a wet towel across his face.

The druggists were fixing up the cheap trade with jake and orange peel and hair tonics, Dee said, and the Indians were buying their canned heat at the five & ten. Doctors were getting the good business with prescripttions.

Dee said he had been running the grocery and filling station since fall. His daughter Keechie helped him. She stayed up in town with his sister Mara, and he stayed in the Bunk here at nights.

"That girl of yours sure mean-eyed me this morning when she brought that grub out here," T-Dub said. "I don't think she likes us around here worth a doggone."

"She don't have much to do with nobody," Dee said.

Bowie took the towel off his face so he could see Dee.

"She'll take care of you while I'm up in Tulsy," Dee said. "Just you boys don't go around in front of the station and be careful about lights at night."

T-Dub counted out three hundred and twenty-five dollars and gave it to Dee. This was to buy a second-hand car in Tulsa, cover ten dollars for the shotgun and twenty-five for Dee's trouble.

"I might be able to make it back by tomorrow night," Dee said. "But if I see I'm going to get in here after daylight I'll just wait until the next night."

"We'd like to shell out of here about eight o'clock at night," T-Dub said.

"We don't forget our friends, Dee," Chicamaw said. "You do the best you can for us and when we get in some real money, you're liable to see a piece of it."

After Dee left, T-Dub said they had only ninety-five dollars left. It had to take them to Texas and pay a month's rent on a furnished house.

Chicamaw put the shotgun down and went over and picked up a road map on the bed.

T-Dub said the best way to leave a Hole was early in the evening when the traffic was heaviest. Stay off the main highways as much as you could and follow timbered country. Keep a couple of five-gallon cans filled with gasoline and circle cities like Dallas and Fort Worth where the Laws had them scout cars and radios.

The wheels of a truck ground in the gravel of the station's driveway and they listened. Bottles rattled. "Soda-pop truck," Bowie said.

"I can run these roads all day and night through," T-Dub said. "Just keep your car clean and not let it look like it was being run hard and everybody stay shaved up and looking like you were just a fellow about town. I can count it on my hand the times I been jumped on the road."

"Just give me one man driving and me sitting in the back with a .30—30 and I can hold off any carload of Laws that ever took out after anybody," Chicamaw said.

"You can do it with a nigger-shooter," T-Dub said. "I don't see where these fellows they call G-men, them Big Shots, get that stuff about thieves not having no guts. I don't see how they get that."

"Me neither," Bowie said. "They don't do anything unless they got ten carloads and when they jump anybody they use about fourteen hundred rounds of ammunition."

"Laws never did worry me," T-Dub said. "It's the fellers you thought were your friends that beats you. And a woman mad at you. They are what beat you."

"Liquor too," Bowie said. "Some guys have to be stewed to the gills before they can work. Me, I want my head clear when I start out."

"Whiss will do it all right," T-Dub said. "But a woman mad at you can get you in a rank quicker than anything. Yessir, the Laws would be up tight if it wasn't for sore women and snitches."

"They're full of rabbit all right, them Laws," Chicamaw said.

"I wouldn't trust Jesus Christ," Bowie said.

"Listen to old Country Boy," Chicamaw said.

"Even if I saw Jesus Christ walking right in this place I wouldn't trust him," Bowie said.

The heat was getting more intense. It stuffed Bowie's nostrils and seared high up in his nose. He took the towel and soaked it again in the bucket of water.

Chicamaw started taking off his overalls.

"You ought not to do that," Bowie said. "No tellin' when that girl might come out here."

Chicamaw resnapped the overall straps.

"I'd sure like to let that sister-in-law of mine know I'm coming," T-Dub said. "But that's a good way to get a rumble. Writing letters. We'll just go on to MacMasters and I'll get her on the phone."

Chicamaw looked up from the road map. "It's three hundred and twenty-five miles from here. That country is sure bald out in there. Nothing but oil wells and mesquite trees."

"Plenty of roads though," T-Dub said. "Man, I was raised in that West Texas country."

"I guess you know that sister-in-law of yours pretty good?" Chicamaw said.

"She's Real People," T-Dub said. "A woman that has stuck by that bud of mine like she has isn't going to turn down a chance to make some money. That bud of mine can be sprung out of Texas with a couple of thousand. He's just doing five years. On a two-for-one job now. And that woman of his is going to do all she can."

"Zelton is forty miles from MacMasters," Chicamaw said. "That's where we going to get the house, uh?"

"There's mighty nice banks in both of those towns, but Zelton, I think, takes my eye first."

Chicamaw folded the map. "I know a mouthpiece in MacMasters," he said. "Name Hawkins. Archibald J. Hawkins. Old Windy we called him. Him and me were holed up together in Mexico for a year. There's one old boy that sure beat the Law."

"What did he do?" Bowie said.

"He was a county treasurer right there in Mac-Masters and he sacked himself up twenty or twenty-five thousand just knocking down every month and then things started gettin' hot and he rabbited to Mexico."

"Unlatched a vault?" Bowie asked.

"Oh, no. Just knocking down. He bought all the County's stuff, see. Gravel and machinery and things like that. He would make out a voucher for five loads of gravel when he had bought only one and then go down, to the bank and cash it and pocket the other four. He was in Mexico for fourteen years. All the witnesses died or forgot and then he went back just as big as you please. And on top of that took the bar examination and is practicing law right there now."

"Them politicians are thieves just like us," T-Dub said. "Only they got more sense and use their damned tongues instead of a gun."

"If you ever need a mouthpiece," Chicamaw said, "Old Windy wouldn't be bad."

"I'm not needing any more lawyers myself," T-Dub said. "The way I figure is that when they get me again I won't be in any shape for a lawyer or anything else in this world to do me any good."

"That's me," Bowie said. "I mean to get me out of any new trouble."

"Well, the way I figure it," Chicamaw said, "is that two and two make five and if at first you don't suck seed, keep on sucking 'til you do suck seed."

"Aw, you damned Indian," Bowie said.

~§~

The voice of the girl, Keechie, made Bowie's veins distend and there was a velvety, fluttering sensation in his spine. She was squatting over there now by the Bunk's kerosene heater, the brown flannel of her skirt stretched tight across her bottom, showing T-Dub how to keep the wick from smoking. T-Dub had tried to boil coffee on it this morning and had only succeeded in filling everybody's noses full of soot and blacking the underwear Bowie had washed.

"Just wipe it off with a match like this," Keechie said.

"That's one thing old T-Dub don't know nothing about," Chicamaw said.

Keechie got up, holding her blackened hands out. Bowe snatched the towel off the bed post and held it toward her. "It's pretty dirty," he said.

Keechie took the towel. "Thank you."

"That big Country Boy is some gallant, ain't he, Keechie?" Chicamaw said.

Bowie's ears felt like the velvet was being pressed against them now. "Don't pay no attention to that ignoramus," he said.

"Were you raised in the country?" Keechie said.

Bowie shook his head. "Don't pay no attention to them two."

"He's just hard-headed, Miss Keechie," T-Dub said. "That's all."

"Soft-headed," Chicamaw said.

"His head looks all right to me," Keechie said.

Bowie tried hard not to swallow. "All right, you guys, that's enough."

Keechie pointed at the bed. On it was a filled paper sack and two folded newspapers. "There's some canned soup in that sack and you can heat it on that stove now." She turned toward the door.

"Thanks for the grub and papers, Miss Keechie," T-Dub said.

Bowie looked at her, the black hair, cut like a boy's; the short, strong neck and compact shoulders. "Sure thank you," he said.

"Forget it," Keechie said. She went out the door.

"That little girl don't think any too much of us, I'm here to tell you," T-Dub said. He went over to the bed and picked up a newspaper.

"She's all right," Chicamaw said. "Just stuck up."

"She acts like a little soldier to me," Bowie said.

"Old Dee just lets her do him anyway," Chicamaw said. "He won't never go on a real toot around here anymore. If he wants to get boiled, he'll go clear up to Muskogee. That man's got a right to drink though. Wife leaving him like she did."

"Keechie's mother?" Bowie said.

"She run off with some damned guy. Running a medicine show."

"That little girl hasn't got no business around a bunch of criminals like us," Bowie said.

"Man, lookee here," T-Dub said. He had the Oklahoma City newspaper spread out on the bed and was tapping the left top column. "Just lookee here."

Bowie went over and he and Chicamaw looked:

ALCATONA, Okla., Sept. 15— The escape of three life-term prisoners who kidnaped a taxicab driver and a farmer in their desperate flight was announced here tonight by Warden Everett Gaylord of the State Penitentiary. Combined forces of prison, County and City officers were looking for the trio. The fugitives are:

Elmo (Three-Toed) Mobley, 35, bank robbery; T. W. (Tommy Gun) Masefeld, 4, bank robbery; and Bowie A. Bowers, 27, murder.

"Pulling that toe stuff again on me," Chicamaw said. "All right, you Sons of bitches."

Mobley and Bowers, Warden Gaylord disclosed, took advantage of permits allowing them to go fishing on prison property and Masefeld of a pass to town. All prison property and Masefeld of a pass to town. All three were privileged trusties.

Jed Miracle, 21, Alcatona taxi driver, was bound in his own taxi which the fugitives abandoned after a tire blew out. E. T. Waters, a farmer living at the edge of Akota, twelve miles south of here, gave descriptions of three men who commandeered his car at the point of a gun. After traveling with the trio for more than an hour, the fuel of the car was exhausted and Waters was tied and abandoned in his own car like Miracle.

The desperate trio are believed to be headed for the hills of Eastern Oklahoma where so many criminals have found refuge in the past few years.

Bowers, youngest of the escaped men, was serving a life sentence that had been commuted from the death penalty. He was convicted in the murder of a storekeeper in Selpa County when he was 18 years old. The killing took place during an attempted robbery. He was a member of the prison baseball team.

All of the men had good prison records, Warden Gaylord said. Masefeld had charge of the prison commissary, selling cigarettes and candies to the inmates. He had been in the prison six years. Mobley, also a member of the prison ball team, had served five years of a 99 year sentence from Larval County.

Miracle, the cab driver, described tonight how he was lured to the creek a mile from the prison by Masefeld and forced at the point of a gun to surrender his cab and accompany them.

"Masefeld told me in town he wanted to take some sandwiches and soda pop) out to some friends of his who were fishing," Miracle declared. "I had done that plenty of times for some of the trusty boys and I did not think am thing about it. When we reached the place, Masefield jabbed the gun in my back and said he would kill me if I did not obey him," Miracle asserted.

"A tire blew out," Miracle went on, "and the extra was down too, so they tied me up and went on across a cotton field toward the highway. I managed to work myself loose and drove the car back to town."

The shouts of Waters, the farmer kidnaped by the men, attracted coon hunters who freed him. He declared the men treated him courteously.

"That toe stuff," Chicamaw said.

"It tickles me," T-Dub said, "about this Tommy Gun they're putting on me. I never did have but one machine-gun in my life and I never did even try it out. I'll take an automatic pump gun any old day."

"It's not a very long piece about us though, is it?" Chicamaw said.

"Brother, I wish it was just two lines," Bowie said.

"Nothing at all you mean," T-Dub said. "Papers can raise more heat than anything. These Laws work like hell to get their names in the papers."

~§~

They lolled on the ground in front of the Bunk, unrecognizable bundles in the darkness, only their slapping and blowing at mosquitoes interrupting the quiet. This was the second night they had waited on Dee Mobley. The lights of the station had not been turned on this evening. Everything was set to take off. Chicamaw had the shotgun sawed off so he could carry it underneath the old lumber-jacket Dee had given him. Keechie had two five-gallon cans of gasoline filled up in front of the station, two sacks of groceries and three cotton-picking sacks.

"I just hope it's not the car that's holding him up," T-Dub said. "I'll be damned if I start out in a wreck."

"He's probably drinking a little," Chicamaw said.

Bowie got up and stretched. "I wish he had picked some other time to drink if that's it." He walked over to the edge of the tree's inky shadow and stood there, looking at the back of the station. Then he came back and stood above Chicamaw and T-Dub. They were quiet again.

Bowie moved up the side of the station and peered around under the shed. He saw the figure sitting in the chair by the ice-box and his shoes rasped in the gravel with his start.

"My goodness," he said. "I didn't know that was you."

"That's all right," Keechie said.

He cleared his throat, "I didn't know anybody was around here."

"That's all right."

He looked at the Model-T pick-up parked just off the driveway. "I was thinking though that I hadn't heard it leave."

"No," Keechie said.

Bowie moved toward her.

"Sit down if you want to," Keechie said.

He lowered himself to the bottom of the doorway. There was a car under the shed of the brightly lighted filling station up the highway. Two men were standing beside it and watching the attendant fill the tank. "I don't know what could be holding that Daddy of yours," he said.

"I have an idea. If it had to be done I should have done it."

Bowie shook his head. "We don't have any business around here anyway."

The lights of a car popped around the curve from town, sprayed the highway with luminous foam. Bowie strained back against the door screen. The car passed.

"I read it in the paper about you," Keechie said.

Bowie's head went up and down.

"I guess you thought you had to leave?"

"I didn't see any use of doing any more Time. It wasn't getting me anywhere. All that was keeping me in there was money."

Keechie shook her head. "You won't get anywhere like this. Not with company like that back yonder."

"I don't know," Bowie said. "What will be, will be."

"That Chicamaw wouldn't be anything else if he could."

"I think you got them boys down wrong now. You take old T-Dub. He's got him a little farm picked out already up in Kentucky. He wants to settle down."

"That Chicamaw Mobley has never liked anything but trouble all his life."

Bowie grinned. "He's a little wild all right."

The car under the shed of the other filling station drove away. The attendant went back and sat on the bench.

"If I wasn't so hot I'd like to have me a filling station," Bowie said. "Now what I would like to have is a tourist camp."

"That would be too slow for you," Keechie said. "You want to live your life fast."

"You got me down wrong, Keechie. You'd see me following a one-eyed mule and a Georgia walking stock if I had to and what's more, like it. If I could."

Keechie took a pack of cigarettes from her polo shirt pocket, pushed up one and offered it to Bowie. When he touched her hand, the velvety glow stiffened his blood. The lighted cigarette trembled between his fingers.

"How come you to ever get in trouble?" Keechie said.

"I never was in but one."

"That one."

"You mean the Chair?"

"Yes."

"Just some fellows on the carnival I was traveling with said they knew how to make some money and I just sort of went along to see how it was done. I wanted to get some money so I could go up to Colorado and join another show. Them boys had a safe picked out and I just went along."

"You were on a carnival?"

"I went on it when I was fourteen, Just rousta-boutin'."

"Did you run away from home?"

"I just left. Year after Dad died."

"Your Dad is dead?"

"Killed. Man killed him."

Shoes crunched at the side of the station and Bowie's head jerked. It was Chicamaw. "I wondered what had become of you."

"Just talking," Bowie said.

"Don't let me bother you." Chicamaw went on back.

Keechie flipped the cigarette toward the pick-up and Bowie watched its glow on the dark ground.

"Did you shoot that man in Selpa?" Keechie said.

"It was me or him," Bowie said. "He was coming around the car after me with a gun."

The chair under Keechie creaked a little as she moved.

"If I had run like the others I wouldn't be this way now. The guy that knew all about robbing safes was the first one to run. The Big Shot."

Keechie took another cigarette.

"You smoke a lot," he said.

"I don't want it." She broke it in her hand.

"I know a man can't last Out Here long. But I'm not going to try and last. I'm going to back off and it isn't go-

ing to try and last. I'm going to back off and it isn't going
to be long. I can still square myself up."

"No," Keechie said. "You can't beat it this way."

"Deep down in me I know I can't, but I myself says I
can."

Another car was coming around the curve. Suddenly,
its lights were flooding the shed under which they sat.
Neither moved.

It was a coupé and Dee. He got out of the car awk-
wardly. He was drunk all right. "Hadtufftime," he said.

Bowie went back and told Chicamaw and T-Dub.
"You think it's too late to start tonight?" he said.

"Hell, no," Chicamaw said. He and T-Dub went in
the Bunk.

The motor of the Model-T around in front fired and
Bowie started moving fast toward the shed. When he got
around there the pick-up was already on the highway. He
watched it go, listening to the sound of the motor perish-
ing in the darkness.

T-Dub and Chicamaw were piling things in the car.

"Where's them cotton-picking sacks?" T-Dub said.

"I got them," Bowie said. He went over to the chair
where she had been sitting and picked up the sacks.

"Hadtufftime," Dee said. "Tufftime."

They drove off. Shortly the wind was whipping the
sacks on the fenders and insects swirled in the lamp
beams and splattered on the windshield.

Chapter 4

The two five-gallon cans rattled emptily in the coupé's rear and the red level of the gasoline gauge was below the half mark, but Fort Worth and Dallas were behind now, given the run-around without a rumble. One hundred and forty miles out this straight stretch and they would be in MacMasters. Bowie was driving.

On this side of MacMasters, at an old, abandoned wildcat well that T-Dub had described, Bowie and Chicamaw were getting out and T-Dub was going on in to contact his sister-in-law. Just as soon as he got a house, he would come back and get them.

They talked about houses now. When they had about five places, T-Dub said, and all had good hotel lobby fronts, he would say they had a real set-up. He wanted a house in Zelton and another one in Gusherton. Then one in that resort town, Clear Waters, and one in Lothian and Twin Montes. These towns were within a radius of two hundred miles and not more than an hour's driving apart. A house in each of them would give you a Hole that you could be cooling off in within an hour after a bank was sacked.

Always get places with double garages, T-Dub said, and keep the cars out of sight. And never let the neighbors see more than one man at a time. And don't let anybody ever do any questioning. If there was any questioning, you do it yourself. Now up here in Zelton and Gusherton, they could be lease buyers or promoters as soon as they got good fronts.

"We're cotton pickers tonight and look it," Chicamaw said. "How much cotton can you pick a day, Country Boy?"

"Oh, a pound if I worked real hard," Bowie said. He looked at the fuel mark. It was getting damned low.

"And another thing," T-Dub said. "Always give the landlady the best of the deal. Keep her satisfied."

"I had me a landlady down in Florida," Chicamaw said, "and I want you to know that there was one woman that could drink me under the table. There wasn't anything that woman wouldn't do. And just when everything was going smooth with us, they got me."

T-Dub started telling about a house he had in Colorado. The damnedest, smallest thing got him in a rank there, this right arm almost shot off and a big Law with a double-barreled shotgun jamming it in his eyes and him standing there and not even able to lift his arms. The thing he had done though was going off and staying a couple of weeks and not telling the milkman. That bastard got scared over a couple of dollars and he went to the woman that owned the house. She went over to the house and saw it all locked up and she just went in. She got an eyeful. He had that damned machine gun in that house and a bunch of shells. She goes to the Law and they show her a bunch of pictures and sure enough she picks him out. The Laws sit around that house and here he comes back. They would have killed him if it hadn't been for a woman on the porch of a house across the street. She got to shouting and screaming and telling the Laws to stop or they would have killed him. He had them black eyes where that big yellow bastard poked him with that shotgun for a month and a half.

"We sure got to stop and gas up pretty soon," Bowie said.

"That state of Colorado though," T-Dub said. "You ain't never going to get me back in it. They were going to try and put the Chair on me up there. I was praying for Oklahoma to come and get me. They had me positively identified in that state anyway. This Colorado cuter was after me right now and I just figured that I had been unlucky enough to draw him and I wasn't going to be lucky enough to beat the Chair. There was a little old auditor that used to come around to us boys in them death cells and talk. Kind of wanted to write pieces for the magazines or something. I got to feeling him out and finally I just showed him a *five-hundred* dollar bill. I had carried that in the sole of my shoe for six months. He tumbles and brings me a .25 automatic and some tape too just like I asked. I taped that right between my legs and Man, I was set. I had made up my mind that if they went ahead and started putting that Chair on me I was going to kill everybody around me that was man enough to die."

"They didn't even try you up there though, did they?" Chicamaw said.

"Naw. That's how come me to be back in Alky. Oklahoma finally come and got me. A little old jailer up here in the Panhandle took that gun off of me. I'd been trying to get rid of it for two weeks."

The highway turned in a banking curve and then down the highway they could see the scattered lights of a small, sleeping town. "We got to gas up here," Bowie said.

Everything was closed in the town. Small globes burned in the rears of the stores, over the sacks of grain, the cans of oil and tire tubes in the filling stations and the showcases in the hardware store.

"Looks like we going to have to wake somebody up," T-Dub said.

"We can just unlatch one ourselves," Chicamaw said.

Bowie drove under the shed of the filling station across the street from the Hardware Store. It was dark under the shed, but in the office a light burned. He got out and went up to the door. On the desk lay a man, suspenders down and his head on a rolled coat. There was an empty scabbard on his left hip.

"Hell, wake him up," Chicamaw said.

Bowie rattled the door and the man stirred, raised up and began to work his mouth like his jaws were sore. That old boy is a Law all right, Bowie thought.

Old Boy came out. He had a pistol in the scabbard now. "What do you boys want?" he said.

"Little gasoline, Pardner," T-Dub said.

Old Boy scratched his head. The hair looked like rope frazzle. "How much?"

"Fill it up," T-Dub said.

Old Boy moved toward the coupé; looked inside of it. T-Dub stepped toward him, brought the barrel of the revolver up into Old Boys back like he was driving an uppercut. "Unlatch that pump, you nosy old belch before

I beat your ears down good and proper."

Old Boy looked like he was trying to spit acid off the end of his tongue. Chicamaw snatched the six-shooter out of his scabbard. "And do it right now," T-Dub said.

"For God's sakes, boys," Old Boy said. "Take it easy now. I got a wife and four kids, boys. For God's sakes now. I'm an old man."

"You going to unlatch that pump?"

"For God's sakes, boys." Old Boy brought out the rattling ring of keys.

The car was serviced now and T-Dub told Old Boy to get in the car.

"We might just as well unlatch that hardware store over there while we're here and got him," Chicamaw said.

T-Dub drove with Old Boy sitting beside him; Chicamaw and Bowie stood on the running boards. They stopped in front of the Hardware Store.

Chicamaw pried at the door with the tire tool and when the lock burst, it sounded like all four tires on the coupé had blown out.

Bowie pushed back the glass door of the gun-case and began piling the weapons in his arms like sticks of wood. Chicamaw was filling the cotton sack with shells and cartridges.

The town was still undisturbed as they left it.

Behind the high signboard, twenty miles from the town, Chicamaw bound Old Boy, pulling his arms behind a post and twisting wire around the thumbs.

"You can holler somebody down in the morning," Bowie said.

"That's all right, boys. Perfectly all right. You boys

are all right."

The white center line of the black asphalt was running under them again like a spout of gray water.

"I'll swear," Chicamaw said. He was looking at the six-shooter he had taken off Old Boy. It was an old frontier model, a .38 on a .45 frame. "I wish you could see this."

"What is it?" T-Dub said. "Hell, I'm driving."

There were six notches on the cedar butt of the revolver.

"I didn't know we were doing business with a bad man," T-Dub said.

"Nigger killer," Chicamaw said. "That's how he got these on here. That town was full of niggers back there."

"I ought to have stuffed it down his throat," T-Dub said.

"I got fed up on him right now. Started big-eyeing this car."

"He was trying to pull a smartie all right," Bowie said.

"That back there might heat us up a little," T-Dub said. "This car here now, but I believe these cotton sacks cover it pretty well. He never saw no license on this car you can tell the world. We got to get some duplicate plates though pretty soon. You can buy all them you want for a dollar apiece. We ought to get a dozen sets."

"Naw, that old boy back there couldn't tell you whether this was a truck or a Packard," Bowie said. "Squawking the way he was."

Day began to break, with a haze like cigarette smoke in a closed room and the barbed wire and cedar posts of the fences and the low, twisted mesquite trees began to take form. Bowie rubbed the bristle on his chin. "You know I haven't washed my teeth since we left Alky," he said.

~§~

The wildcat-well spot was a good place to hole up for a day or so all right. It was three miles from the Zelton Highway, a gully-scarred mesquite-clumped distance. The weed-grown road beside it was as rough as a cog wheel. It went on North, T-Dub said, beyond those cedar-timbered hills yonder and connected with a lateral road that tied up with the Gusherton Highway.

The mesquites were thick and made, a fence for the clearing on which the old derrick rose. Its timbers were as gray as an old mop; away from it a little piece lay a huge wooden bullwheel with rusty bolts.

Not even possum hunters ever came to this spot, T-Dub had said. He had holed up here three days once after he sacked a bank.

This afternoon, the second that T-Dub had been away from them, Bowie sat on a spread cotton-picking sack, trying the action again of his .12—gauge pump gun. He and Chicamaw had drawn straws for this Baby. It had a pistol grip and a ventilated rib. But the rib was coming off and about four inches of the barrel just as soon as Bowie got hold of a hack saw.

Near the edge of the sack lay more of the guns they had gotten in the Hardware Store, the polished were two

.12—gauge shotguns, a .30—30 rifle stocks and barrels glittering in the afternoon sun. There and a .30—06. There was a .22 pump rifle.

Chicamaw patted the scarred stock of the shotgun he had sawed off at Dee's. "I'll still take old Betsy," he said. "All you have to do with her is point her in a general direction." He was drinking. He had found a half-gallon of whisky in the back of the coupé that Dee Mobley must have left.

"This baby here has got a trigger pull and action like a watch," Bowie said. He brought the gun to his shoulder and drew bead on the pulley at the top of the derrick. "Boy, oh boy," he said. "What I could do to a covey of quail."

Chicamaw picked up the fruit jar and started unscrewing the cap. He extended it toward Bowie.

"I'll pass this time."

Chicamaw drank and then shuddered and clenched his teeth.

"Now when I get a pistol on me I'll be willing to call it a deal," Bowie said. "There's an army store in Gusherton," T-Dub said, "and I might be able to pick me up one there."

"We got us enough guns now to start us a little war all right," Chicamaw said.

Bowie squinted down the sights of the gun.

"I'll take a .30—30 myself," Chicamaw said. "I can cut capers with them little gentlemen. I know one thing though you can shoot a man through the pratt with one and it won't bring him down. I saw it happen. I did it. Me and a couple of boys were running out of Wichita and a carload of Laws jumped us. That old wreck we were in wouldn't do forty. So I just told these boys to let me out at that bridge and I'd stop them gentlemen.

"I got out and here they come. I cracked down and them Laws started flushing out of that car like it was going to explode. One of them weighed around two hundred pounds easy and I popped him while he was running across a field. He just kept going. He didn't drop until he got in the timber."

"He finally dropped though, uh?"

"He told me about it himself later. He come up to Alky. He knew who did it. Laughed about it. Thanked me for not killing him. I could have killed him all right."

"I don't care about being jumped myself," Bowie said. "I'd just as soon they stay away from me."

"The Laws never got me in a rank but twice in my life. The first time was in this State and I was just a snotty-nose punk. I'd been unlatching so many safes that I'll swear I begin to think it was on the level."

"They got me all right in this State once. I done four years down here on one of these prison farms, boy."

"Man, I hear they're tough. These prison farms?"

"You heard right." Chicamaw started taking the cap off the jar again. "It's not everybody that beats them farms."

Bowie placed the shotgun on the ground and picked up the .22 rifle. "I always wanted one of these little guns when I was a kid," he said.

"That time they got me in Florida," Chicamaw said, "and sent me back to Oklahoma was just my fault. That landlady I was going with and me just got a little reckless;

I wish I knew where that woman was. She wasn't no spring chicken, but I'll take her to anything you could ever show me."

"How come them to ever get you down there?"

"I had a run-in with a Jew down there in a gambling place. I was drunk. I don't mind telling you. This Jew didn't want to play stud poker. He had to play draw or nothing. I called him a Christ-killer and a few other things and he said he wasn't going to take it. I told him he'd take it or else. He started out of that place and I decided I'd better frisk him. I caught him and throwed down on him. He didn't have a gun on though. I was smart enough to get out myself because you know they're hard on you in that State for showing a gun, but I got too smart and went back there the next Sunday and there was more Laws on me than I thought there was in Miami."

"A man sure ought to stay sober Out Here," Bowie said.

"What are you trying to do, preach to me?"

"Course not, Chicamaw."

Chicamaw took another drink.

"There I was down there in Florida with twelve thousand dollars and a woman that was the stuff. That woman just wouldn't leave that town with me. Where I wanted to go with that stake was Mexico. Hole up down there like I did after beating them here in this State. If she had just gone with me."

"How is that Mexico business?" Bowie said.

"I done a year down there. It's just like any place else though. If you haven't got no money it's no good."

"I don't imagine I'd like it down, there. Some of them greasers might try to kick you around like fellows do them up here and I wouldn't stand for that."

"If you got the pesos to throw, you can get by down there. But you can't make no money down there and when my four hundred dollars went I had to get out."

"I don't savvy their lingo either and gettin' across that border would bother me."

"I never had to show a passport all the time I was down there and besides, you can buy one. Fifty pesos will get you anything you want in that Chili country. Them Laws down there are all hoss thieves."

"You savvy that lingo of theirs?"

"*Seguro.*"

"Rattle me off something."

"*En Mexico hay muchas señoritas con culas muy bonitas,*" Chicamaw said.

"You're another one. What did you say?"

"I said there was a lot of pretty gals in that country with prettier behinds."

"You look kind of like a Spick anyway. That's why you got by so good and then rattling off that stuff that way."

Chicamaw drank again. "I stayed on an old hacienda down there that was run by an old boy that used to be a thief himself. One of them revolution thieves. There was three more white guys on the place, all of us cooling off for something up here. I told you about Old Windy Hawkins."

"Who were the other two?"

"Banker from New Mexico and then the one we called

Tangle Eyes. He was a deputy sheriff right out this line here close to El Paso."

"What did he do?"

"Killed a couple of farm boys. He just wasn't smart enough to make it. You remember when they had them big placards plastered up all over this state offering five thousand dollars reward for dead bank bandits?"

"Man, I was in Alky so long that I never knew nothing 'bout Out Here."

"They were doing it all right. This Tangle Eyes just planted a couple of old boys in front of a bank and let them have it. He just wasn't foxy enough."

"They don't still have that five-thousand dollar stuff in this State, do they?"

"Christ, no. The bankers had to stop it before they got everybody killed. The Laws were planting more people than there was bank robbers."

Spilled liquor wet the lines in Chicamaw's face, ran over his Adam's apple and down his neck. He put the bottle down and wiped his face on his shoulder. "You're in a good tough state, Boy. You didn't see that in the paper the other day. 'Bout five men dropping dead from heat prostration on that Bingham Prison farm. Heat, my hind foot. I know what killed them."

"I'm backing out of this just as soon as I get a little salted away," Bowie said. "I been intending to tell you boys."

Chicamaw lifted his left arm demonstratively and held his right hand up. "It's pretty tough when a man will take a hatchet and whack his arm off like this!"

"God damn, do they do that?"

"I saw four boys chop themselves in one week. One would whack the other and then that one would come down on the other one."

Bowie felt like his eyes were wired together.

"Them boys wanted to get off that farm pretty bad to do that, didn't they? And they just didn't want to get out of work. That's what they tell you in the Capital and them prison bosses say. There ain't a man in this State prison system that couldn't do the work they got. It's the way they work you and what they do to you."

"It don't sound good to me."

"Say it's cotton-picking time. All right. Maybe the cotton is five miles from the bunk house. Well, the building tenders rout you out at daybreak. Them are the little snitches that are doing a couple of years for busting a two-bit grocery and they give them saps and dirks and let them run over you. Anyway, they get you out and then the next thing you are going out in that field. Don't think you walk that five miles. You run it. Just as fast as that farm boss wants to lope his horse. And you do that back and forth three times a day. And if you fall out, it's spurs then and the bat or a barrel that night."

"That sure don't sound good to me."

"I've had them drop by me and they were as dead as doornails. And one of them Bosses sitting up there on a horse with a double-barreled shotgun and he can't even read or and saying: 'Old Thing, ain't you going to get up?'"

"Man," Bowie said.

"Yeah, they call you Old Thing. And if they get it in for you, you're not going to last. They'll say 'Reach down there, Old Thing, and pick up that piece of grass.' If you're not foxy and don't see that shotgun laying there in that grass, your pratt is mud because they want to go back and say you were trying to get to a gun."

"That sure don't sound worth a damn to me."

"I've heard that farm sound like a slaughter pen. Men squealing and begging like hogs. You don't last on that farm if you're any man at all. Unless you beat it. Then you either come off there a whining rat or still a man."

"I couldn't stand them doing me that way," Bowie said.

The dreggy contents of the fruit jar jostled as Chicamaw shook it around. He drank.

"No, I couldn't take that kind of stuff at all," Bowie said.

"Boy. I'm going up this road a long ways," Chicamaw said. "Plenty of people are going to know it. I ain't going to kill nobody. They're just going to kill themselves."

Bowie watched Chicamaw drain the jar. Now I know why he ain't got no toes on that right foot, he thought.

Chapter 5

They had a furnished house in Zelton now all right, but they were as broke as bums. In MacMasters yesterday too, T-Dub had almost had a rumble and then he came over here and almost the same thing happened. While he was getting the coupé gassed up in MacMasters, a car of Laws drove right up alongside of him, with guns sticking out all over. It just turned out that the Laws were looking for a couple of fellows that had made a Hole in the jail in the next town, Then in this town he draws up at a *Stop* sign and right there, looking him straight in the face, is a Law he has known since he was a kid. But that Law must not have recognized him.

"Naw, he didn't recognize you," Bowie said. He was lying on the cretonne-covered iron cot of the living room. "You could have told it the way he acted right there."

"It's not anything to feel good about anyway," T-Dub said.

"We got a good Hole up in this joint though," Bowie said.

"Hell, seventy-five dollars is a lot of money for a dump like this," Chicamaw said. He sat slumped in the rocking chair by the empty fireplace. His eyes were red-veined from yesterday's drinking.

"Things are always high in these oil towns," Bowie said. "This is a pretty good place when you take every-thing into consideration."

It was a five-room corner house, three blocks off Main Street. On the corner back of them was a machine shop, grinding day and night. Across the street was a fenced-in lot piled with drilling materials. On the oppo-site corner was a church tabernacle and across from it a two-story, barn-looking building that was a lodging house for oilfield workers. Moving cars kept sand and dust sifting through the window screens all the time and there was nearly always somebody walking on the street.

Right now, the three of them were waiting on Mattie, T-Dub's sister-in-law. She had gone up to the hamburger stand on the corner to get sandwiches and a milk bottle full of hot coffee. She was using her own money to feed them.

"I'm fed up on running around in these overalls like a damned Hoosier too," T-Dub said. "Now, Bowie, you look more like an oilfield guy in them khaki pants."

"I feel more like a hungry man than anything else," Bowie said.

"Quit crying, T-Dub," Chicamaw said. "I can get us some eatin' money from Old Windy over in MacMasters. I can give Mattie a note and it will be good for fifty bucks."

"Fifty dollars, won't do us no good," T-Dub said. "It's going to take a couple of thousand. I'll be doggoned if I'm going to charge this bank here halfcocked. We need cars and a bunch of stuff."

"It takes money to make money all right," Bowie said.

"You know that little town we come through this morning," T-Dub said. "Morehead? The one that's got the bandstand in the middle of the street?"

"Yeah," Bowie said.

"There's a bank there that I robbed when I was a kid. Sawed me off a bar and crawled through and got fourteen dollars in pennies. I used to live in that little town."

Bowie grinned.

"What are you grinning about?" T-Dub said.

"You crawling through them bars and sacking up them pennies."

"I was a cutter then. I was getting me some bicycle money. It was the day after Christmas."

"What were you saying about Morehead?" Chicamaw said.

"I've got half a mind to charge that bank there. I just got a hunch. That bank will go for four or five thousand."

"And it might go for five hundred," Chicamaw said. "I swore one time that I never would fool with them two-bit banks again."

"Beggars can't be choosers. What do you think about it, Bowie?"

"Anything suits me. Whatever y'all say."

"Don't get me wrong, T-Dub," Chicamaw said. "If you boys want to charge a filling station I'm with you."

"When you hear me talking about banks you're not listening to me talk about my first one," T-Dub said.

The footsteps on the porch were like a man's and they listened. It was Mattie though. T-Dub went to the door and she came in. She was a big woman with hips like sacks oats; the lines in her face were like the veins in dried corn blades. She had a grease-slotted sack in her hand. "I thought they never were going to get these damned things cooked," she said.

"What's the matter, Mattie?" T-Dub said.

"Nothing." She put the sack on the fireplace shelf. Her toes knotted the leather of the loose black pumps. "I'm going to be checking it to you boys though in just a few minutes. I got to get back to my job."

"I sure hate to see you having to work as hard as you do, Mattie," T-Dub said. "I sure don't know what we would have done without you."

Bowie nodded.

"This is a cash on the barrel-head proposition to me," Mattie said. "I need some money."

"You're going to get it, girl," T-Dub said.

After Mattie left they started eating the hamburgers and T-Dub told them about her. She worked in a sandwich shop for a dollar a day. Showed you what a woman would do when she liked a man. His brother had been in two years and she had never missed a week without sending him money. One woman in ten thousand. He was going to see to it that she got hold of a good piece of money so she could buy a lawyer and spring that bud of his. He was going to stake them to a tourist camp too. Wasn't going to be any more need of that brother of his having to be a thief.

"This is not getting that Morehead business settled," Chicamaw said.

"I'm just waiting on you two," T-Dub said. "We can sack them gentlemen up right tomorrow. Rabbit that seven miles through MacMasters and then cool off at that wildcat. When it gets dark, come right back through that town, right on over here and tomorrow night I don't think we'll be setting here quite as busted."

"Call your shot, Bowie," Chicamaw said.

"I'm in," Bowie said. "I'm ready."

"It's settled," T-Dub said.

Chicamaw said some boys liked to rob a bank before it opened and others around ten-thirty in the morning and two o'clock, but any old time suited him.

T-Dub said that the bank in Morehead didn't have

more than three or four working in it and they wouldn't have to count on handling more than the same number of customers if any at all. This bank here in this town though would be a man-sized job. Four men would be the best number to charge a bank like it. One man holding the car down outside and seeing to it that nobody came out; one holding down the lobby and keeping everybody in and the other two working the vault and cages and seeing to it that nobody kicked off any switches.

Bowie was lying on the cot again. I can rib myself up to do anything, he thought.

"Time you split money four ways though you haven't got enough to go around," Chicamaw said.

"Three is plenty."

"I'm just telling you," T-Dub said. "These won't be the first banks I ever charged."

"I didn't mean anything," Chicamaw said.

"He didn't mean nothing," Bowie said. He sat up and looked at the hearth, but the cigarette stubs on it were too short to snipe.

"The Outside man has the hardest job," T-Dub said. "Some of these dingbats think the guy in the car has the snap. But he's the man that gets the rumbles first. The Inside is a snap. I never saw a banker yet that wouldn't fork over as soon as you throwed down on him. You can always figure that a man that's got sense enough to work in a bank has sense enough to act like a little man when you throw down on him."

"I've had to high-pressure a few of them," Chicamaw said.

"Only Hoosiers kill," T-Dub said.

"I don't believe you have to kill them," Bowie said.

"Them bankers will tell you to help yourself. It's insured. It's them billionaires up in New York that lose it. Them capitalists."

"I hope that Morehead bank will go for a nice piece," Bowie said.

"We'll get cigarette money anyway," Chicamaw said.

"Nossir, I've never robbed anybody in my life that couldn't afford to lose it," T-Dub said. "You couldn't hire me to rob a filling station or hamburger joint."

"I don't believe in that either," Bowie said. "Them boys in them filling stations don't make but two or three dollars a day and if they're robbed, they got to make it up. I'd just as soon beg as do that."

"I know one thing," Chicamaw said. "I'm going to be wearing me a fifteen-dollar Stetson and a sixty-dollar suit here pretty soon or it might be a black suit with some silk plush around me, but I'm sure not going to be wearing no overalls."

T-Dub went back to the kitchen and returned with three broom-straws. "The short man works the Outside," he said.

Bowie drew the short straw.

The others slept now. Bowie lay in the living room's darkness, his elbow on the windowsill, his fingers scratching the screen. Five thousand, gentlemen, and I'm backing off.

The bed in the middle room creaked and Bowie listened. He smiled. That Indian, he thought.

Voices sounded in the yard outside and Bowie sat up, his hand extended toward the pump gun beside the cot. It was two men with dinner-pails cutting across the yard; going back to the machine-shop. Bowie lay back.

The next time I see that Little Soldier, he thought, I'll be driving a brand-new auto job and looking pretty good in a gray suit and red polka-dot tie and a flannel shirt with pearl buttons. I'll say to her: "I'm looking for that little girl that gave me a big lecture here a couple of years ago." She would look plenty surprised. He'd get a smile out of her though.

Who was that snoring? That old soldier. I got to be doing a little of that myself. One . . . . two . . . . three . . . . four . . . . five . . . . six . . . .

Chapter 6

With its four blocks of filling stations and lunchrooms on the north side of the widened highway and then the intersecting, one-block main Street, the town of Morehead had a business district shaped like a funnel. The funnel's mouth was corroded with low buildings of stone and wooden fronts. With Bowie driving the coupé, the three moved up it now toward the frame bandstand at the end of the block. It was ten-thirty o'clock.

The Farmers State Bank stood on the left corner near the bandstand. It was a one-story structure with two cement columns and barred windows. "There's our meat," Chicamaw said. T-Dub touched his forehead in a mock salute. "We'll be in to see you in a few minutes, gentlemen. Don't be impatient."

Bowie made a U turn around the bandstand and drove, motor idling, past the bank, the Pressing Shop with its window display of bolted goods, the patent-medicine display of the Drug Store and then cut in to park diagonally in front of the Variety Store. In the Variety Store windows were women's underwear. To the left of it was a Meat Market and then a Grocery. Two farmer-looking men sat on cakes of salt lick in front of the Grocery. A youth in a red sweater with an *M* on it came out of the Pressing Shop and got in a truck.

T-Dub and then Chicamaw got out of the coupé. Chicamaw turned around, winked. "Ten dollars, the Sox beat the Giants this afternoon?" he said.

Bowie grinned. "Called."

The two moved up the street, the sagging seat of T-Dub's overalls wrinkling and Chicamaw's head bobbing on his long neck. They turned and entered the bank.

The bubble in Bowie's stomach broke and sprayed; he put the car in reverse, backed out and then moved down the street toward the highway.

The woman in the sedan ahead stopped parallel in front of the Post Office and Bowie turned out and passed her. That's the way I'll be parking in front of that bank in a minute, he thought. There were two men in broad-brimmed hats and boots standing on the corner in front of the Dry Goods Store. They did not look up. A dog, its ribs bulging, trotted across the street in front of Bowie toward the depot.

There was a crated plow on the station's loading platform.

Bowie turned the second corner, passing the Lumber Yard. One block this way now and then another turn and he would be at the Bank again. That dream again last night? His Dad. He could hardly remember what his Dad looked like and yet he was as clear as himself in these dreams. Always the same thing happening. Him in that pool hall with his Dad and that other man getting ready to hit his Dad with the cue; him hollering and his Dad not hearing; him trying to shoot the gun and kill the man and the pistol breaking into pieces in his hand.

Bowie turned the last corner. Maybe that dream meant bad luck coming? If he counted to *thirteen* now with his fingers crossed, it would break the bad luck, *One . . . . two . . . . three . . . . four. . . .*

Bowie stopped in front of the bank . . . . twelve . . . . *thirteen* . . . . pulled the sawed-off shotgun up a little higher between his knees. Come on, Pals. Come on, you Old Soldier. Come on, you Indian. We got tall tracks to make . . . .

There were two more men standing now in front of the Grocery, one smoking a pipe with a curved stem. The pipe-smoker turned and looked up the street toward the Bank. All right, Square-John, that's a good way to get your eyes full and get in trouble. The man turned back.

T-Dub came out of the bank, the front of his overalls bulging. Chicamaw following, two cigar boxes under his left arm. Bowie looked up and down the street, across to the other side. Nobody big-eyeing or smelling anything yet.

They got in the car and Bowie gunned the motor; Chicamaw slammed the door. The two men sitting on the salt cakes stood up and the others turned and looked.

Bowie swerved onto the highway, the left wheels groaning; the approaching oil truck stopped with a jerk.

The driver shouted. Bowie pressed the accelerator harder; the *City Limits* dropped behind. The boy driving a cow with a stick turned his head and watched them go by.

"Anything behind us yet?" Bowie said.

"Naw," Chicamaw said. "Them guys are not going to get out of that Vault for a half-hour. They don't know the Civil War is over yet back there in that town."

T-Dub looked back. "Clear as a whistle."

"Y'all do any good?" Bowie said.

"I think so," T-Dub said. He pulled a revolver from inside his overalls. "I picked me up a brand new Colt .45 here anyway. I'll will you that pearl-handled job, Bowie. Did you see me get it out of that till, Chicamaw?"

"Yeah, I saw you."

"Sacked up something else though, didn't you?" Bowie said.

"It went for three or four thousand, I think," T-Dub said.

Chicamaw turned back. "Naw, they don't know yet what it's all about back there."

A car zoomed over the rise ahead, hurtled toward them. It had a California license.

"Four thousand isn't bad, is it?" Bowie said.

"I don't say we got that much," T-Dub said.

"Man, you didn't expect us to stop and count it before we come out of there, did you?" Chicamaw said.

Bowie laughed.

The skyline of Zelton showed now: the fourteen-story hotel, the standpipe, the college buildings on the hill.

"We're going to be holed up before they get out of that vault," T-Dub said. "Makes me half decide to go on to the house, but I want to save that place. We'll just go on to that wildcat."

Bowie turned the coupé off the highway and onto a dirt road this side of Zelton. They passed the Filtration Plant, the City Mule Barns, and then Bowie turned back East and presently they were on a paved, residential street. They crossed the town and cut back onto the highway by the Airport.

As they neared the turn-in to the old oil derrick, a car ahead of them approached and Bowie slowed. It was a big sedan with a Negro driving and a man in the back seat smoking a cigar. After it was out of sight, Bowie turned the coupé onto the derrick road.

Chicamaw climbed the ladder of the derrick and started a lookout toward the highway. Bowie spread the big cotton-picking sack on the ground and T-Dub dumped the contents of the small canvas bag on it. The pile of currency, in rubber-banded packs of hundreds and twenties and tens and fives and ones, was as big as the crown of a cowboy Stetson. The two cigar boxes were spilling silver.

Chicamaw whistled and they looked up. "What's that stuff you boys are playing with down there?" he said.

"For Christ's sake," T-Dub said.

"Nose-wipin' paper, you damned Indian," Bowie said. "And there's ten bucks of it you'll never see. Them Giants have the Sox in a hole by now."

"Another ten says you're a liar."

"Accepted."

"Voices carry out here," T-Dub said. "You guys do your talking after while."

"Let's pipe down, Chicamaw," Bowie said.

T-Dub took four hundred and twenty-five dollars from the pile and snapped a rubber band around it. This represented the amount he had started out with and he put it in his shirt pocket. Bowie took a ten-dollar bill, "I'll take out six for Chicamaw," he said. "That's what he had."

Three piles of currency grew as T-Dub dealt out the bills like playing cards. Finally, it was divided and there was one thousand and twenty-five dollars apiece. The silver, it was decided, would just be left in the boxes and they would use it for general expenses like gasoline and beer and cigarettes. There were three or four hundred dollars of it.

Chicamaw descended the ladder and joined them.

"I just started telling Bowie here about that old banker back there," T-Dub said. "That old boy like to have never got it in his head that it was a stick-up."

"Never did put up his hands, did he?" Chicamaw said.

T-Dub laughed. "He never did. He was sitting at a desk there, Bowie, when we went in, just pecking away at an old Oliver typewriter and I had to almost kick the chair out from under him. 'Whatthehell?' he says. 'Whatdoyouthinkthis is?' I had to yank him up and knee him back into the Vault. I think we had the place half sacked before he ever caught on."

"All them others acted like little men," Chicamaw said. "They couldn't get in that Vault quick enough."

"No customers?" Bowie said.

"One," T-Dub said. "Didn't you take a sack off him, Chicamaw?"

"Yeah," said Chicamaw. "I got thirty or forty dollars here I think." He pulled a small money sack out of his hip pocket. "Naw, I don't have no kick coming about that little Bank, but we could have sacked up that Bank in Zelton just as easy. And had ten or twelve apiece. Isn't that right, T-Dub?"

"We'll get to them gentlemen," T-Dub said.

Long ranges of clouds, thick as beaten egg-whites, moved in the afternoon sky. Through the rifts, the dome was as clear as bluing water. The only sounds were the thrumming cars over on the highway and they would stop and listen to them pass. When they talked now, it was in quiet voices.

As soon as it got dark, it was decided, they would return to Zelton and then Bowie could take the coupé out to the edge of the town and burn it. Chicamaw would get a bus and go to El Paso and come back in a couple of days with two fast, light cars and some extra license plates. T-Dub would go over to MacMasters, get Mattie to rent a car and they would get at least two more houses. One in Gusherton and one in Clear Waters.

"We ought to have a sure-enough set-up here in two or three more days," Bowie said.

"Might be that kid sister of Mattie's will go along with me and her to get them houses," T-Dub said. "You know, boys, I hadn't seen that little girl since she was in diapers. Cute as a bug now. I want you two to meet her."

"What I'd like to have right now is something to eat," Chicamaw said. "You guys realize we haven't eaten nothing since them hamburgers last night."

"Funny, I'm not hungry," Bowie said. "What I could take on is a good tailor-made cigarette."

"I remember the last time I was cooling off in the country like this we had us a radio and we were getting a ballgame," T-Dub said. "Chicamaw, maybe you'd better get radios put on them cars. Sure help pass the time when you're out like this."

Chapter 7

Bundle-laden Zelton people jostled and tripped and cut, around Bowie in this Saturday-night shopping spree. He was downtown tonight just to stay away from that furnished house. Three nights now he had stayed in it alone and it was getting on his nerves. He had stayed in all morning and afternoon thinking that surely the boys would show up today, but Chicamaw was still somewhere out toward El Paso and T-Dub was, rustling houses.

Tonight, Bowie had planned on going to a picture show, but there was nothing on at the two theaters except shoot-em-up cowboy stuff. Rain on that kind of show, he thought.

In front of the Drug Store with the window display of Kodaks and photographs he paused now. There was a picture of a young couple with a baby; a hunter standing beside a car on the running board of which was an antlered deer; a bathing suit girl in a canoe. Bowie peered closer. The gun in the hunter's hand was a .415 Winchester and the deer had six points.

Bowie went on. That Keechie Mobley would make a good picture, I'll bet.

Shaded lights behind the plate glass flushed the colors of the women's things; the silk blouses, dresses, hose, under-things. Now in a little town like she had to live in, Keechie never saw a bunch of pretty things like this.

In the panel mirror of the Department Store entryway, Bowie looked at his reflection: the iron-gray suit, the broad-brimmed hat, the white handkerchief in his breast pocket. His right hip pocket bulged a little with the .38 T-Dub had given him. Just as soon as I get around to it, I'm going to get a holster and strap and wear it under my arm. Then I won't notice it any more than my hat. I look pretty good though. What was it old T-Dub said about him: "That Bowie looks more like a Law than he does a thief." And Chicamaw: "Like a country boy come to town." That Indian.

Bowie turned and went back up the street, past the 5 & 10, J. C. Penney's, and on the corner, The Guaranty State Bank. He turned it and then was on Front Street a dim-lighted thoroughfare of small cafes and dollar-hotels. On the other side of the street was Texas & Pacific Railroad lawn with its mulberry trees, the depot and the freight offices and platforms.

A Negro in a porter's cap and white jacket sat on a stool in front of the hotel doorway. On the white globe above his head were the lighted letters: *Okeh Rooms.*

"Looking for a nice lady friend tonight, Boss?" the porter said.

"Hell no, you black bastard," Bowie said.

In front of the *New York Café*, on the corner, a policeman stood talking to a bareheaded man who had one foot on the bumper of an automobile at the curb. Bowie walked past them. You got the advantage of Laws all right. You can them, but they can't tell you. And the detectives and deputy sheriffs out here might just as well have uniforms, you can tell them so easy. All of them in cowboy boots and white hats and black suits and shoe-string ties. And say that flatfoot back there recognized him when he went past? All right, all that Law had was a pistol. And didn't he have one on too? One thing though, he had to get out in the country pretty soon and practice up with this .38. Get used to it.

Bowie turned toward the railroad lawn, going to the furnished house.

There were two new-looking automobiles in the driveway of the house and Bowie checked the impulse to break into a lope. That Indian is back just as sure as the dickens, he thought. The cars were Ford V-8's. One a black job with a trunk and the other was gun-metal colored, both sedans. It was T-Dub who let Bowie in. He had on a new blue-serge suit and tan shoes.

"Chicamaw come in?" Bowie said.

T-Dub thumbed toward the sound of rushing water in the bathroom. "Taking a bath and gettin' drunk as a Lord. I think he bought up all the tequila in Juarez."

"I begin to think you two had fell in somewhere," Bowie said. "How long you been here?"

"I got here a little after dark and he was here then." T-Dub went over and lay down on the cot. There was a pile of scattered newspapers beside it.

"I guess you read about Morehead," Bowie said. "Wasn't that a joke? Got one number right in that license. *Three.* And calling it a green coupé and the only thing green about that old Chevy was the stripe around it."

"Them newspapers never get nothing right. You been casing this bank here any?"

"Every morning since y'all been gone. I went down yesterday morning before daybreak and I been inside of it three times. That Vault kicks off either at nine or maybe before because it's open when the doors open."

Who goes in first?"

"Nigger. The porter. Around six o'clock. It's a bird's-nest on the ground to go in with him. And the nearest Law is up at the Depot right at that time watching that passenger come in."

"Don't sound half bad."

"How you been doing, T-Dub?"

"We got them houses all right. She went with us on both trips. Lula. That's Mattie's kid sister. I told you about her though."

"Gusherton and Clear Waters?"

"Yep. That Clear Waters place looks like a million-aire's dump. Lula sure liked it."

"Them cars out there look like old Chicamaw has been doing his stuff. That was a job to tow that gun-metal job all the way in here."

T-Dub sat up. "You know I'd just as soon charge this bank here Monday as not. What do you say?"

"Tomorrow would suit me if it wasn't Sunday."

"I'm going to see the girls tomorrow," T-Dub said.

Chicamaw came out of the bathroom and into the living room. He had on silk shorts and undershirt and his hair dripped water. The big veins of his biceps and forearms looked like pale earthworms.

"If it's not the old Country Boy himself?" he said.

"Hi, Chicamaw."

"Been teaching Sunday-school over in that tabernacle while we were gone?"

"I been asking for a job down at this nice little bank they got in this town."

"Old Bowie," Chicamaw said. "Believe anything anybody tells him." He looked at T-Dub and winked.

"Anybody except you," Bowie said.

Chicamaw laughed and his bare feet slapped the floor back toward the bedroom.

T-Dub picked up the newspaper again and Bowie went over and sat down in the rocker and lit a cigarette. The flung newspaper rattled on the pile. "Every time I pick up a paper I see that damned little Squirt's name," T-Dub said. "If I ever run across him you going to see a guy get the damnedest behind-kicking a man ever got."

"Who's that, T-Dub?"

"Newspaper guy. He gave me the dirty end of the stick one time. I tried to make a Hole in this prison in this State one time and it went haywire and this Squirt comes to me and wants me to tell him all about it so he can write a big story for the magazine. Couple of the boys had gotten killed and I was shot right through the fleshy part here of my hip and it was all a mess. Everybody knew all about it anyway and this Squirt said if I would tell him the straight of it he would get it printed and split the money with me. I didn't even have cigarette money so I told him. You should have seen the way it come out in that magazine. I was the Big Shot, see. And I sent them two boys over that got killed first because I figured the guards would use up all their ammunition and then me and the other boy still down at the bottom of the ladder would have a clear way. Anybody knows that the Chair boys get the first break and that's why they went over first. Hell, I didn't go on up because the damned ladder had broke. One of them joint ladders you know. Then that Squirt getting it put in the magazine like that."

"Don't guess he ever sent you any money?"

T-Dub looked up and sneered.

Chicamaw came back in with a bottle of tequila in his hand. He had on brown tweed trousers with pleats, a blue shirt and yellow tie. He offered the bottle and Bowie shook his head.

"For Christ's sake, come on and be human," he said.

Bowie took a drink.

"I ran into a pooloo in a sandwich stand close to Pecos that we knew up in Alky," Chicamaw said. "You guys remember that kid we called Satchel Pratt?"

Bowie and T-Dub nodded.

"He knew me right off and crawled all over that car and got to telling me how he knew where there was a good piece of money."

"Tin safe somewhere with thirty dollars in it," T-Dub said.

"I played him along. Told him I'd shove on and be

back to the number he gave me right after dark and we would go and get together on that job he had."

"I remember that kid," Bowie said. "He played a banjo pretty good."

"I brought you something, boy from the city," Chicamaw said. "I run into some good Colt .45's out there and you can throw that .38 job of yours away."

"Man, I'm glad to hear that."

"You got to promise me that you won't sleep with it under your pillow though."

"Now what's the joke?" Bowie said.

Chicamaw looked at T-Dub and winked. "All right," he said and pointed his finger at Bowie. "I'll bet that's the way you been sleeping at nights?"

"Yes."

Chicamaw looked at T-Dub and then back at Bowie. "That's just what I thought. Look here, man. Always sleep with your gun under the cover by your side. Then if anybody walks in on you, you got as much of a throw-down on them as they got on you. Just let 'em have it. But you sure can't do any reaching up and behind you . . . . like *this*."

"I never thought of that before," Bowie said. "I'm sure glad you told me, Chicamaw."

T-Dub stood up. "What do you say we start talking about this bank here? Bowie is ready to go Monday, Chicamaw."

"You don't have to ask me if I'm ready. I'm always ready." He lifted the bottle and there was a gurgling sound.

"Boys, it's going to be my thirtieth," T-Dub said.

Chapter 8

Last night, T-Dub had drawn the short straw, but because he knew more about the Inside of a bank, it was decided Chicamaw would drive the black V-8 and Bowie would go Inside with T-Dub. They had gotten out of bed at four o'clock this morning, driven out to the Derrick Hole and left the gun-metal sedan. Now it was six o'clock and they sat parked in front of the Sears, Roebuck Company store next to the Guaranty State Banks. The empty street looked as wide as a river.

"If Bowie and me are not out of there by nine o'clock," T-Dub said, "you better be coming in after us, Chicamaw."

Chicamaw lifted his head in a laughing gesture.

Somewhere the sound of a street-sweeping machine whirred and threshed. Away down the street, in front of the Cafe, a man came out and got in a car. The slamming door echoed in the canyon of buildings. The car vanished.

"Here it comes, Boys," Bowie said. He pointed up the street. A Negro in a gray rope sweater was approaching. Bowie and T-Dub got out of the car and stood beside it.

The Negro was a middle-aged man with sideburns like steel wool. He stood there at the bank door, selecting a key on the ring. He inserted the key and grasped the knob.

"We're going in with you, Shine," T-Dub said. Bowie pressed the gun's barrel firmly against the rope sweater and they went into the bank's clean, early-morning gloom. Bowie squatted down and looked under the slit of the drawn blind. Chicamaw was driving off.

The Negro breathed like he had been running, his wrists sticking rigidly out of the frayed sweater cuffs. "I doesn't quite understand this," he said.

"Don't bother yourself, Shine," T-Dub said. "You're liable to wake up with somebody patting you in the face with a spade if you do."

Bowie started tying the Negro's thumbs behind him with capper wire. "Mistah, I been porterin' heah fawh twenty yeahs. You can ask anybody in Zeltan. Everybady heah knaws ald Ted. Right heah in this bank fawh twenty yeahs. When they had the old building. Yassah, I been—"

"That's enough, Shine," T-Dub said. "Now you'd like to be able to go to church again next Sunday, wouldn't you?"

"Yassah,"

"Then you just answer the questions I'm going to ask you."

"Yassah. I never lied to nobody in mah life. You can ask anybody in Zeltan about me."

The clock over the front door indicated 6:30. On both sides of the gray tile floor at the front of the bank were brown railings and inside of these were clean desks with lettered stands: *President* . . . . *Vice-President* . . . . *Vice-President* . . . . The bronze cages fenced the passageway of glass-topped tables back to the Vault. It was a big, broad door of aluminum and black colors. To the right was a passageway that led to the side-entrance door.

"What time does that big vault back there unlatch, Shine?" T-Dub said.

"Cap'n, that something I doesn't know about. Some of the big basses don't even know that. Mistah Berger knows about it."

"What time does he came down?"

"He's the first one. Li'l before eight."

Bowie moved around. Through the slits of the Venetian blind at the side-entrance door he saw the closed, steel doors of the freight depot. An oil truck went past.

The clock clicked: 7:00.

More automobiles were sounding on the streets outside now. A switch engine whistled and then the intersection railroad signal began to dang. The exhaust of a bus popped, fluttered. Bowie read the hand-lettered football schedule on the wire stand by the front door.

The knob of the front door turned and the man smelling of hair tonic and shaving lotion came in. He was short and had a belly as round as the sides of a mare in foal.

"Mister Berger?" T-Dub said. He had an open packet knife in his left hand.

The man stood there, his left hand extended in a paralyzed, door-closing movement. His head went up and dawn.

"Mister Berger, this is a stick-up, and if you want to stay a healthy man, and I think you do, you'll just co-operate."

"I see," Mister Berger said.

It was 7:15.

The heavy doors of the freight depot creaked and groaned. Boxcars bumped in the railroad yards. Automobile horns sounded.

7:45.

Through the blind slats of the side door, Bowie saw the black flannel coat, the silk-clad ankles of a woman. He turned and T-Dub, standing in front of the Vault with Mister Berger and Shine, nodded. Bowie opened the door.

The woman gasped like she had been pricked with a pin and Bowie put his hand over her mouth. She became limp in his arms. "Take it easy now, Lady," Bowie said. "Nobody is going to hurt you."

"Be calm, Miss Biggerstaff," Mister Berger said. "These men are not desperadoes."

"I never kill anybody," T-Dub said, "if they just do what I tell them to."

8:30.

Bowie peered through the blind slats. The black V-8 was parked there now, Chicamaw's head down over a spread newspaper on the steering wheel. A match worked in his mouth. That Indian.

Mister Berger and T-Dub were inside the Vault now. A cage door clicked and rattled. Bowie's toes squirmed in his shoes. Sack it, T-Dub. Dump it in. Just a minute, Chicamaw . . . .

Mister Berger came out; then T-Dub with the bulging laundry sack slung across his back.

"Ready?" T-Dub said.

"Ready," Bowie said.

"We're going to take you folks with us," T-Dub said.

"There's a Ford just out that door there and you go out there and get in it and don't let me see any of you looking at anybody 'cause if you do you're liable to get somebody killed."

There were two men in striped overalls working on the loading platform across the street, but they did not stop. Mister Berger and Miss Biggerstaff and Shine got in the back; then Bowie. He told Shine to lay on the floor. T-Dub got in front with Chicamaw.

They moved off. The young fellow parking the coupé stared. He had on a tan suit and horn-rimmed glasses.

T-Dub turned around. "You know him?"

"One of the boys in the bank," Mister Berger said.

The speed indicator rose: past the Candy Factory.... Produce Company . . . . Cotton Compress . . . . Nigger Town . . . . A farmer, high upon the cotton wagon, saluted. Chicamaw waved back.

They crossed the railroad tracks and then sped up the straight, dirt road toward the picket of telephone poles that marked the highway. Miss Biggerstaff looked at Bowie. "What are you going to do with us?"

"Don't worry, Lady."

"I have done everything in the world I could, Men," Mister Berger said.

T-Dub turned around. "You folks just sit steady now. You have done all right and everything is okeh now."

Bowie could see the grinning lines on Chicamaw's cheek. He smiled too. The speedometer needle vibrated on 80. Miss Biggerstaff shivered as if she were cold.

~§~

Holding to the top rung of the derrick ladder, Bowie saw the car leave the highway, its aluminum glittering like signal mirrors, and come onto this road. He whistled and below, T-Dub and Chicamaw picked up the corners of the spread cotton-picking sack with its piles of currency.

But the car was only turning around. Bowie whistled again and shook his head violently. The canvas was spread again.

Over in the black sedan, Mister Berger, Miss Biggerstaff and Shine sat, the feet of the men bound in copper wire. For three hours now, T-Dub had been dealing the bills and still he was wetting his fingers and going on. That's the prettiest sight I ever saw, Bowie thought. Bar none. He shifted his arm through the rung and grasped his belt. Bar none.

Chicamaw relieved Bowie on the lookout.

T-Dub grinned as Bowie approached. "Nossir, Bowie, that wasn't my first bank, but I never saw one go sweeter."

"I never saw a prettier sight than looking down here from up there," Bowie said.

Over in the black car, the glass rattled and Bowie saw Miss Biggerstaff rapping. "Go see what they want," T-Dub said. Bowie came back. "It's the Lady. I think she wants to go to the bathroom. I think that's what she wants."

"She won't rabbit. Let her out."

"That Berger over there told me we got ten thousand dollars in securities here that's not worth anything to us and mean a lot to him."

"He's a damned liar. There's sixty thousand dollars' worth here, but he can have them back. They're no good to us."

At last the money was counted and divided. There was twenty-two thousand six hundred and seventy-five dollars apiece.

In the dusk, Chicamaw and Bowie tied Mister Berger and Shine to mesquites. Then Chicamaw went on up the road, out of sight, and presently they heard the motor of the gun-metal firing. It moved toward the hills and the Gusherton Highway.

Bowie drove the black car and T-Dub sat in the back with Miss Biggerstaff. "We're just going to take you up here a couple of miles, Lady," T-Dub said, "if and then you can walk back and untie that gentleman friend of yours."

On the Gusherton Highway, Bowie and T-Dub got in the the gun-metal with Chicamaw and left the flaming black car behind.

~§~

The house in the resort town of Clear Waters was an eight-room Spanish stucco with a patio, a three-car garage and big, sparrow-filled poplar trees in the parkways. It was a corner place and across from it was a four-story apartment house.

Bowie sat in the living room now, soaking in its richness. There was a radio and a secretary and brocaded coverings on the divan and chairs. The lights on the rough plaster of the walls were shaped like candlesticks. Confession and Movie magazines littered the floor and the ashtrays were full of cigarette butts stained with lipstick. From the kitchen, where Mattie and Lula and T-Dub were cooking, came the smell of ham and eggs.

Chicamaw came in, his hair plastered and smelling of perfumed oil and indicated the room with a roll of his head. "Pretty good for some old boys that didn't have a pot or a window to throw it out three weeks ago, eh, Big Boy?"

"Pretty nice," Bowie said.

"You tied up with some fast company, didn't you, Boy?"

"I'll say."

Lula came in with T-Dub following. She was tall and had on a cotton housedress and blue anklets. Her shaved legs had scratches on them and there was the tattoo of a red heart on the back of her left hand.

"Don't think Lula and me would make a team," T-Dub said. They sat on the divan and T-Dub put his arm around her waist and began fingering the cloth over her stomach. "Last time I saw this little outfit she was just about up to my knees and now look at her."

"He's nuts," Lula said.

"I think you got him going, Lula," Bowie said.

Lula slapped T-Dub's hand away and reached in his coat pocket and brought out a package of cigarettes. She extended them toward Bowie and then Chicamaw. They shook their heads.

T-Dub held a match for her. "Yessir, this little girl is going to put a tattoo on her for me pretty soon." He winked at Bowie and then Chicamaw. "And it ain't going to be on her hand."

The smoke gushed from Lula's nostrils and she flecked the cigarette toward the ashtray. "I wouldn't be so sure about that now, Mister," she said. "And if I'm going up to that drug store before our midnight supper, you better be giving me a few nickels and let me get started."

Mattie came in. She had a dish towel tied over the black silk dress, like an apron. "You boys come and get it. Was that Lula leaving, T-Dub?"

"We ought to wait until she gets back 'fore we eat," T-Dub said.

"Come on," Mattie said.

Their knives and forks scraped and slashed the eggs and ham. "I don't wonder that bud of mine isn't working his head off to get out with cooking like this, Mattie," T-Dub said.

"It's not cooking that's going to get him out," Mattie said.

Lula thrust the newspaper toward T-pub. "It's all over the front page," she said. "All over it."

T-Dub pushed plates aside and spread the newspaper, and Chicamaw and Bowie bent over him.

ZELTON, Sept. 28.— In one of the boldest bank holdups in West Texas history, three armed bandits this morning robbed the Guaranty State Bank here, kidnaped A. T. Berger, vice-president, his secretary, Miss Alma Biggerstaff, and escaped with what bank officials estimated at more than $100,000 in cash and securities.

Berger and Miss Biggerstaff with Ted Phillips, negro bank porter, also kidnaped by the trio, were picked up by passing motorists, 21 miles east of here at 8 o'clock tonight. Miss Biggerstaff was in, a hysterical condition from the day of terror and imprisonment.

Working with the precision of master criminals, the robbers entered the bank before the doors opened this morning. Arriving bank employees, unable to get into the bank at 8 o'clock, sounded the alarm. William Pleasant, bank bookkeeper, saw a black, crowded sedan leave the bank's side entrance as he was getting ready to park, but did not realize its, full significance until later.

Today's holdup followed within less than a week the $3,000 robbery of the Farmers State Bank at Morehead, adjoining community. Local authorities believe both crimes were committed by the same band.

One of the bandits, Police Chief Robert Blakely announced here tonight, has been positively identified as an escaped Oklahoma convict.

"Oh, oh," T-Dub said. "They got me identified."

"I don't care which one they got identified," Chicamaw said, "they ain't going to have to guess long to know who was with you."

The food in Bowie's stomach felt like it was expanding.

A posse of more than two hundred police officers and citizens combed the country around here throughout the day in a fruitless search. At a called meeting this morning of the Chamber of Commerce, directors authorized the posting of a $100 reward for the capture, dead or alive, of any member of the gang.

"Now what did we do, boys?" Chicamaw said.

L. E. Sellers, a farmer living four miles east of town, reported that a loaded car passed him shortly after 8 o'clock this morning, traveling East at a high rate of speed.

The bandits were described as being well-dressed men around 30 years of age.

"If it had not been for the bravery of Mr. Berger," Miss Biggerstaff declared, "I am afraid we would not be alive to tell our stories. They threatened our lives almost every minute. Mister Berger talked to them coolly."

The two bank robberies in this vicinity this past week mark the first time in four years that a bank has been robbed in this section. The last one was at Stockton, 40 miles southwest of here, by the famous Trawler gang. Trawler was hanged by an enraged mob at Stockton last December after he killed a jailer in a desperate attempt to escape.

T-Dub pushed the newspaper aside. "Well, boys, that's the situation."

"They sure did put it all over the front page, didn't they?" Lula said.

"The next time, Sweetheart," T-Dub said, "you bring us some good news."

"Christ, let's finish eating," Chicamaw said.

Bowie lay on the ivory-inlaid bed, under the smooth sheet and silken comfort, in the feminine, mirror-paneled room where the perfume of powders and toilet waters still lingered. That blows me up, he thought. Yessir, that sure blows me up on going back to Alky.

Up in the living room, Lula giggled and then there was T-Dub's rumbling laugh. The Mexican orchestra of the Border radio station was playing *La Golondrina*, a background of guitars strumming plaintively.

Bowie moved and the .45 was cold against his naked thigh. Yessir, that sure blows me up. But what are you gripin' about, Man? You got twenty-two thousand dollars right under this bed.

Chapter 9

On the afternoon of their third day in the Clear Waters Stucco, Chicamaw became staggering drunk and bumped around the house, his shirt tail hanging, and demanding who in the hell had hid his tequila. Mattie and Lula threatened to leave and T-Dub became white-faced. Bowie finally got Chicamaw into the back bedroom. "Come on now, Chicamaw," he said, "and sleep a while. It'll be good for you."

"I'm not sleepy," Chicamaw said. "I'm drunk. I don't

mind telling you I'm drunk. They ain't but two things I like to do and that's love and drink and there ain't enough women here to go around so I'm drinking. What do you think I left Alky for?"

"Don't talk so loud, Chicamaw."

"What do you think I left Alky for? To drink chicory coffee and look at art magazines?"

"Take it easy now, Pal."

"All right, old boy, old boy, old boy."

"You're scaring them girls."

"Let old Battle Axe leave."

"Snap out of it, Chicamaw."

"Old Country Boy is telling me what to do. You're just a big old farm boy, Bowie, but goddamit, you got something and I don't mind telling you, I can't figure it out. Let's you and me shell out of this place, Bowie. Go up to Oklahoma. Let's get us a bus and go to Dallas and get us a Packard and throw us a good one. You're going to Oklahoma with me, aren't you, Pal?"

"We ought to cool off here a few more days. There's still some heat out there."

"You going to Oklahoma, with me, aren't you, Pal?"

"We'll talk about that later. What you want to do now is get yourself some sleep. You got to snap out of it, man. That real estate man was in here this morning taking an Inventory and he big-eyed around plenty and that man that come up to the front door and said he was a census taker might just be nosying. There might be a little war around this place before you know it."

"You going to Oklahoma with me, aren't you, Pal?"

"We'll talk about that after you sleep a while. That

and going to Mexico."

"Come on now, Bowie, wouldn't you like to go up to Oklahoma and see that little cousin of mine?"

"She's not interested in seeing me."

"That home town of mine is just forty miles from there and I want to see my folks, Bowie. I got to see them."

"I'd like to see Dee get three, maybe four hundred dollars."

Chicamaw compressed his lips and closed his eyes and there was a whistling in his nostrils as he breathed. Bowe watched him for a little while and then bent down to unlace his shoe. Chicamaw's eyes opened. "You know why I want to go to Oklahoma?"

"Sure, boy. See your Old Man and Old Lady. And you want me to go along and stand on the corner with that pump gun of mine and see to it that nobody comes nosing around."

"That ain't all."

"You want to say hello to your folks."

"My folks know what I want and I got to take them the money to do it with. Them folks of mine haven't got a pot or a window to throw it out and I got to get them some money. Bowie, they ain't going to catch me floating around in no tank in them doctor schools if they ever get me. That's what they do to you if you can't pay the undertaker. They'll throw you in one of them tanks and carve on you."

"You must be drunk, boy, to talk that way."

"I want to be planted right. Goddamit, I'll give them every cent of it and I want to be planted right."

"I'll go get you a cold towel."

"Don't you leave me, boy."

T-Dub came in. His shaven face had a pink blush now and his hair was as white and soft as a baby's brush from the vinegar washing Lula had given it. He touched his forehead in a salute. "Feeling better, Chicamaw?"

"Who hid that tequila, T-Dub?"

"Man, I don't know where it is."

"Tell that Battle Axe to rout it up."

"You're drunk, man, but you better start quieting down," T-Dub said.

"Old Foxy T-Dub," Chicamaw said. "Old Foxy."

Mattie came in, holding out a magazine. "Maybe this will sober him up some," she said.

It was a True Detective magazine and on the opened page were all their pictures: Oklahoma Fugitives. $100 Reward.

Bowie brushed back. "He don't care about seeing that thing. Go burn that damned thing up."

T-Dub and Mattie left.

"Bowie, you going to Oklahoma with me?"

"If you'll go to sleep now I'll go. I don't mean that, boy. I'll go with you anyway."

"Then I'll go to Mexico with you, Bowie."

"That sure suits me."

Bowie lowered himself to the edge of the bed and after a little while, Chicamaw slept.

Bowie went up to the living room and there were Mattie and Lula standing at the door, dressed up and bags around them. T-Dub was pale again. "The girls are going down to the Penitentiary to see my bud," he said.

"I'm going to take them to the depot."

Bowie nodded.

"Your friend decided to quiet down?" Mattie said. The short fur jacket looked like she had another bag under it.

"He's all right," Bowie said. "I was telling them that there's not a finer boy when he's sober," T-Dub said.

"He's all right," Bowie said.

"I hope we see you again soon, Bowie," Lula said. There was lipstick salve on her chin.

"Goodbye," Bowie said. After T-Dub and the girls left, Bowie went back to the bedroom and looked at Chicamaw. He was snoring and had his mouth open. It was growing dark and Bowie stepped over and raised the blind a little. Then he sat down on the bench in front of the vanity.

I'll go on up there with him, he thought. There's nothing else for me to do and there's gettin' to be too many women around this joint. I'm ready to go to Mexico right now myself. If these boys want to rob that bank at Gusherton I'll help them, but I'm ready to clear out of this myself.

The breathing sounds in Chicamaw's throat sounded like air escaping from a flabby tire.

Mexico? Deer and wild turkey and cougars and bears even. A .414 Winchester would be the best for deer. A bear? Now that's something I'll have to do some figuring on when I get down there. Christ. If I was in Mexico with a .22 I would be satisfied. And just rabbits to hunt. Let me down there, man, and I'll run them rabbits down on foot.

The front door sounded and Bowie went up to the living room. It was T-Dub. He went over and sat down on the divan and began flecking at bits of cigarette ash on the blue serge of his broad thighs. "I hated to see that little girl go," he said.

"You'll see her again," Bowie said.

"That Chicamaw back there has got it down all wrong," T-Dub said. "You can't make women a money-on-the-barrel-head proposition. Love 'em and leave 'em. It don't work when you meet somebody decent. He's nuts though."

"This business is no good for a girl," Bowie said. "That's what he means."

"Where would we have been if it hadn't been for Mattie?"

"I know it. It's a proposition."

T-Dub said that if Bowie and Chicamaw went to Oklahoma, he might go down to Houston and try and get Lula to go off with him on a little trip to Galveston or New Orleans. Mattie would come back and keep their houses held lawn. He had given her two thousand dollars to buy a car and have something to run around on.

Bowie said he and Chicamaw would come in and do their part on that two thousand.

In the distance, a siren sounded and they looked at each other and listened. The sound grew nearer and then they heard the bells of the fire engine clanging and they relaxed.

"But I been thinking, Bowie, and you're not going to get three together like us again nor a set-up like we got now. In couple of months if we just stay foxy we can, have fifty thousand apiece and then will be the time to back off for keeps."

"If we're going to charge that bank at Gusherton I'm in favor of doing it and gettin' it over with."

T-Dub shook his head. "These banks out here are looking for trouble now. Look at what happened to those two kids day before yesterday. Trying to work right in our heat."

"You kill somebody though like they did and your heat really gets hot."

"They were Hoosiers."

Bowie began cleaning his fingernails with a split match.

"What I want to do," T-Dub said, "is get me about fifty thousand salted away and invest it in one of the Big Syndicates and get it paid back to me two or three hundred dollars a month. I'd like to find me a doctor that's a thief like us and get him to saw off these fingerprints and I'd grow a beard about a foot long and rear back up in them Kentucky hills on that little farm and let the mistletoe hang on my coat tail for the rest of the world."

"I hate to stay cooped up like this in a house," Bowie said. "I'm like a mule though—I never know what I do want."

"You got to put up with things I don't care how you make your money. And you take a chance in anything. Take them aviators. I got a cousin that's in the army and he was writing my bud and telling him how he was soloing around up there. I'll bet that kid don't last as long as I do."

"I know I'm in this a lot deeper than I planned to be. I'm going to be like that Indian back there I guess. Go up this road as long as I can. Win, lose or draw."

"I made my mistake when I was a kid," T-Dub said. He lifted his leg and looked at the polished toe of the shoe critically. "But a kid can't see things. I should have made a lawyer or run a store or run for office and robbed people with my brain instead of a gun. But I never was cut out to work for any two or three dollars a day and have to kiss somebody's behind to get that."

"I don't guess I could have done anything else except what I have," Bowie said. "What will be, will be."

A little after midnight, Chicamaw's feet padded in the hallway and then he came into the lighted room, rubbing his nose and twisting his face. "Got a cigarette, anybody?" he said.

Bowie gave him a cigarette. Chicamaw went over and sat on the divan by T-Dub. The cigarette trembled in his, hand and he began rubbing his ankles together and finally he reached down and scratched the left one. "What time is it gettin' to be?" he said.

"After twelve," Bowie said.

"What have I been doing around here?" Chicamaw said. "I feel like hell."

"You just been guzzling a little," T-Dub said. "The girls left."

"Did they?"

"They went down to see my bud."

Chicamaw scratched his other ankle and then his elbow.

"Bowie and me have been talking business," T-Dub

said. "If you boys are going to Oklahoma, what do you say
we let things rock for about a month and all of us meet up
again in that house in Gusherton, say, November
fifteenth?"

The cigarette fell out of Chicamaw's hand and he
grunted as he picked it up. "Suits me."

"I'm in," Bowie said.

"November fifteenth in Gusher-ton then," T-Dub
said. "Boys, if we sack them up over there it will be my
thirty-first."

Chapter 10

It was cold this morning and the fallen leaves of the
poplar trees rustled and clattered on the sidewalk in the
wind. Bowie carried Chicamaw's black Gladstone and his
own brown strapped bag out to the gun-metal and put
them in the back seat. In Dallas I'm going to buy myself
an overcoat. Pretty good to know you got the old mazuma
in your pockets to buy yourself a coat and anything else
you might need. And I sure got it on me. Seven thousand
in that bag; ten thousand in this coat pocket and these
two pants pockets. And three thousand in silver in the
trunk of this car.

Chicamaw came out with the guns in a blanket and
then T-Dub with a black Gladstone. T-Dub's collar was
turned up around his throat and he moved like his bones
were on hinges. He said it was rheumatism.

"All you need is a good dose of Lula," Chicamaw said.

At the Sante Fe depot downtown, T-Dub got out, saluted and grinned and went on in. He was going to Houston.

On the road to Dallas, Bowie and Chicamaw talked about how they were going to do things there. They would register in at the biggest hotel, Bowie as *A. J. Peabody* and Chicamaw as *Frank Masters*, baseball players from Denver, Colorado. They would stay there all day, Chicamaw getting his car, and right after dark take out for Oklahoma.

"You better not go too strong on one of those big cars," Bowie said. "Get one of them big jobs and everybody will be big-eyeing you."

"That shows you what you know about it, boy. If I could get me a green Packard with red wheels and a calliope whistle I'd do it. Then they big-eye the car instead of you."

"After we give this car to Dee I think I'll get me another V-8," Bowie said.

The quiet of the thick-carpeted hotel room—814— was that of a bathroom and Bowie, alone now, soaked in it. A hotel is just about the safest place for a man, he thought. Say one of these hotel clerks thought he saw something? Well, he wouldn't be in any too big a hurry to call a bunch of laws in.

People staying in hotels wouldn't appreciate a little war busting in their faces. Then it was pretty hard for a man to get in a rank as long as he was throwing money. People taking your money just didn't run off and squawk.

Men just weren't made that way. He took a sheaf of currency from his inside coat pocket and dropped it on the blue counterpane. "And, Brother, I got it to throw."

After bathing and shaving, Bowie went down and sat in the lobby. Everybody around him had on pressed suits and shined shoes and watch chains across their vests. They're not the kind of fellows that big-eye you, Bowie thought. It's these Hoosiers in these little filling stations that don't have anything else to do but chew tobacco and look in them damned detective magazines.

After a little while, he went to the street and started looking in the shop windows. In a mirror he studied his hat and decided that the brim was too broad. Too much like a cowboy. He went in the Department Store oil the corner, and besides the new hat he bought a double-breasted blue overcoat, two handbags and a powder-blue suit with a belted back. I'll show that Indian a fancy thing or two in duds myself.

In the Jewelry Store, he bought an open-faced watch and chain and then a lady's wrist watch with six diamonds on the band. That Little Soldier will open her eyes when I hand her this.

It was noon when he returned to 814 and Chicamaw had not showed up.

He tried on the Powder-blue, but it was just too much of a go-to-hell suit for him. That Little Soldier would give him the laugh if he turned up in it. What am I ribbing myself up about that girl for? I'm just going to fool around here and make a donkey out of myself. That girl has other things to think about besides a damned thief like you, Man.

Now was the time, he decided, to send some money to Mama. Five of these one-hundred dollar bills with one of these pieces of hotel stationery around them and one of them envelopes. I wouldn't mind sending her five thousand if it wasn't for that no-good husband she's got. He'll get every damned bit of it. Now if it was that second husband she had it would be okeh. He was a pretty good fellow. Dumb, but I wouldn't mind helping him.

Old Jim and Red up there in Alky could sure stand a few bucks. Jim sure liked his sweet milk and them charging twenty cents a quart up there in that Prison when you could buy it in town for a nickel. And old Red wouldn't smoke nothing but tailor-mades. I'll get to you boys. I'll stop in one of these post offices pretty soon and send you boys a hundred apiece. I've got to do some stopping in some of these towns pretty soon and get some of these dollar bills changed into twenties. Got enough of them things to pack a washtub. I'll just start shoving them through these bank windows, twenty and thirty at a time, and pretty soon I'll get rid of them.

Bowie pulled off his shoes and lay on the bed. 814. Oh, oh. *Eight* plus *one* plus four equals *thirteen*. Aw, there's nothing to that. That's carrying it too far.

Mexico? Man, money will go a long ways down there. Three of them pesos for a dollar. Twenty thousand? Jesus Christ. That would be forty-five thousand pesos even after he took out for a car and the other expenses he would have while he stayed up here. Now if I go on through with it at Gusherton? Jesus Christ. I'll be a damned rich man . . . .

Bowie woke up with Chicamaw standing above him.

"I thought I was going to have to pop my pistol to get you up. Man, you'd be a pushover." He smelled of liquor.

"What time is it?"

"If we're going to get out of here right after dark we better be gettin' in the saddle."

Bowie had the delicate, spraying feeling in his belly.

When Chicamaw, up there ahead of him in the new Auburn, held out his hand, Bowie slowed and then turned in to park alongside of him at the sandwich stand. It was a neon-lighted place with beer signs and a lettered board of sandwich prices. When the uniformed girl came out, Chicamaw said he wanted twelve bottles of beer to carry. After the girl went back into the stand, Chicamaw pointed up the street toward the filling station on the left corner with the *Gas . . . . 13¢* sign. "I run in that very station up there once and there was an old boy in there that sure big-eyed me. He had a wooden leg, I remember. I noticed him, see, out of the corner of my eye and finally he says to me: 'Boy, it ain't none of my business, but I know you.' I says to him: 'Brother, you just think you know me.' He says: 'You're Elmo Mobley as sure as hell, but after you leave here, I never have seen nobody that even looked like you.'"

"He really knew you, did he?"

"Sure he did. But I never did let on, see. He says to me: 'Boy, I just wish you had got this bank here 'fore it went busted and took my wad. I'd rather for a poor boy like you to have it than them goddamned bankers. Both of them bankers are out of prison now and still living swell on what they stole from me and about four or five hundred more folks here.'"

"I'll be doggoned. He was Real People."

"I gave him a ten and told him to keep the change."

"You run into Real People once in a while all right."

The girl returned with the bottles of beer in a sack and Chicamaw put them in his car. He said to Bowie: "If you're in such a big hurry, I'll just let you set the pace out of this town and I'm telling you, boy, you better stomp it or I'm liable to run over you."

"Okeh," Bowie said.

Bowie moved out the boulevard toward the Oklahoma Highway, the rear-vision mirror of his car reflecting the following lights of Chicamaw's automobile. I'm going to be in Keota in an hour and a half. This buggy is going to get stomped. He felt of the small-hard bulge in his left vest pocket. Yes, the watch was still there. He pressed the accelerator harder.

The one-lamped car approached on the intersecting street ahead from the right, but there was a Stop Sign there and Bowie stepped back on the gas. The other car lunged right on across the Stop Sign and Bowie stomped brake and clutch, swerved, but the One-Lamp hit and then a bucket was shoved down over Bowie's head and tons of shattering glass were burying him. He thought: *This is liable to get me in trouble . . . .*

Thrown from the sprung door of his car, Bowie rose from the parquet grass, feeling like the figure in a slow-motion picture. He was on his feet now, a terrific weight on his back. Yonder was his car; the radiator caved in against a broken lamppost and behind it was an old coupé, somebody inside of it groaning, its one lamp still burning.

Human forms moved like shadows about Bowie now. "Are you hurt, Friend?" a Shadow said. "No," Bowie said. He moved toward his car, dragging the weight that was like a plow. I got to get that stuff . . . . *I got to get that stuff . . . .*

It was a woman in the wrecked coupé: "Oh, my God. Oh, my God. Oh, my God . . . ."

Bowie reached his car, grasped at the handle with hands that felt like they had gone to sleep. He staggered with the push. "Get on over in my car, you damned boob," Chicamaw said.

Somewhere now there was a sound like a thousand trucks straining up a high hill in first gear. Them's not trucks, Man, Bowie thought. Sirens. His fingers groped at the emptiness of his right hip. Gun gone. That's the kind of luck I have, gentlemen. He moved across the street, through the working Shadows, dragging the Plow, toward Chicamaw's car.

He climbed into the front seat and then thrown bags were thumping in the rear. To hell with the rest, Chicamaw, boy. Come on. Everybody and his dog is coming . . . .

The flashlight was like a blowtorch in Bowie's face. The voice behind it said, "What's your hurry, buddy?"

"I'm in no hurry, Bowie said.

"I'm taking him to a doctor, Officer," Chicamaw said. Another bag thumped in the back. "He's bunged up pretty bad."

"I'm pretty bad bunged up," Bowie said. The flashlight clicked off and then he saw Officer, the bulging chin that was like a licked hog's knuckles. Another form in a black hat was with him.

"Where you from?" Officer said.

"Denver," Chicamaw said. "You fellows come on to the hospital, by God, if you want to ask questions."

"There's a woman over there hurt and from what I hear you were traveling too fast," Officer said. "You get out of that car and come on with me. And you too, Buddy."

"Not this time, Friend," Chicamaw said.

Second Officer said: "Listen here, Bub, you going to get in jail yourself here 'fore you know it."

"Not this time, Friend . . . ." Shoes scraped and then the hoofs of a thousand horses were thundering on a tin roof above Bowie's head. Guns! Bowie reached toward the panel pocket: *This is liable to get me killed.*

Like a cut radio, the noise ended. Then Chicamaw was getting under the wheel; the motor roared like an airplane taking off and Shadows scattered in the street, ahead of them like cotton-tail rabbits.

The car sliced the highway wind with the sound of simmering water. Chicamaw pressed the panel button and the illuminated speedometer, to Bowie, glowed through a mist. Chicamaw tapped and the instrument board was dark again.

"You're bleeding like a stuck pig," he said.

"I'm all right."

"You better snap out of it."

"It was a Little War."

"They were men enough to start it. Let 'em be men enough, to take it."

"It was an old one-light Jalope that got me. Come right out and got me good."

"I'm going to dump you at Dee's. There's plenty of heat behind us and I'm going to let you out and get on up the road and burn this car."

"It was a Little War. That old Jalope."

"You're not hurt bad, are you? You're bleeding like a stuck pig."

"I'm all right."

They whipped around the red tail-light of another car; then the twin glow of another.

I'm just sick at my stomach, Bowie thought. That's all. Why I used to get sick just from standing up when Mama was cuttin' my hair. Her name was Peabody then. No, that was the first man. It was Vines, the carpenter one, then. See, Chicamaw, that shows you I have snapped and my mind is clear. Vines was his name. Pain seized Bowie's back with the grip of a twisted monkey-wrench and his belly muscles became as rigid as a wash board.

"What the hell?" Chicamaw said.

"I'm all right."

~§~

Chicamaw ran the car under the darkened shed of Dee. Mobley's filling station, got out and vanished behind it. Just let me lay down for an hour, Bowie thought, and then I'll feel just as good as ever.

Chicamaw came back with Dee and when Bowie got out, his legs felt like cooked macaroni and he sunk to his knees. "Ain't that funny?" he said. They carried him back to the Bunk.

"I put everything under the bed here," Chicamaw said.

"Thanks, Chicamaw," Bowie said.

The motor of Chicamaw's car roared and he was gone and then Dee Mobley gave Bowie a drink of whisky. It clawed his mouth and throat like fingernails.

Dee kept sitting down and getting up and moving around the room. Finally, he said: "You're not hurt bad, are you?"

"No," Bowie said.

"You see any use of me staying here?" Bowie shook his head. "Not a bit, Dee."

"I don't know what kind of trouble you boys got in," Dee said, "but I don't see any use of me hanging around your heat. You're welcome to this place though, and if it wasn't for the fact that I'd be losing money I'd just as soon close it up and put a sign out there on the front door and go up to Tulsy. I could put plenty of grub in here and water and you could stay here as long as you wanted."

"Don't worry about the money."

"I got to worry about it, Bowie."

Bowie gave Dee ten fifty-dollar bills. "You better let your folks know to stay away from here."

"Nobody comes around here except Keechie and I'll give her some of this money and she can visit up in Muskogee or somewhere."

"You better do that."

The scraping branches of the pecan tree against the Bunk's tin roof sounded like cat claws on a screen. I could be a lot worse off, Bowie, old boy, and don't you think different. I could be laying back yonder. You doggone whistling. I still got the money. The silver is gone, but to hell with that. That old Jalope. 814. That was it. *Eight plus one plus four equals thirteen.* There you are; that was it. And if it hadn't been for that Chicamaw?

Chapter 11

Dawn oozed through the cracks of the closed Bunk door, the veins of the drawn window-blind, and pressed with leaden heaviness on Bowie's frozen soreness. The suit of winter underwear, Dee Mobley's, hung on the post of the bed like a scab. I will get up in a minute, Bowie thought and light that stove. I'm chilled and that's what is wrong with me.

He touched his loosened front teeth with his tongue and heard them creak in their sockets. A car droned around the curve, thundered past the filling station and faded with the sound of a covey of quail in flight.

I'm going to get up. *One for the money, two for the show.* Now when I say *four to go,* I will get up. But what's the use of gettin' up? I've got all day. One for the money . . . . Chicamaw won't be gone more than two days. He might show up right tonight. *One for the money . . . .*

This might not really be happening, him lying here in this place and getting ready to get up. This was just his Spirit? His Real Self was back up that road. No, that was his Spirit, too. His Real Self had got the Chair. I'm like a cat with nine lives. That's it. One of them in the Chair and one of them back yonder. Seven left. I'm going to go ding-batty if I keep lying here. *One for the money!* . . . A car was coming under the shed of this filling station. Bowie sat up, his right hand reaching for the floor. Man, you don't even have a gun . . . .

The knob turned and then the unarmed figure in the red sweater was standing there. It was Keechie. Bowie's face felt like it was encased in a cellophane mask and if he breathed his skin would crackle.

She closed the door and came toward him. "What's the matter with you?"

He breathed. "Accident."

She stood beside the bed. "What's the matter?"

He touched his mouth. "I guess you see my lips now. They're busted up pretty bad."

"Anything broke?"

He shook his head.

"Shot?"

"Just sprung my back a little."

She went over to the kerosene stove and then a match popped and the igniting wick sputtered. Bowie lowered himself back to the pillow. The pan of water rattled on top of the heater.

Two lines creased Keechie's face from her cheekbones to the corners of her thin, dry lips. Her eyes were the color of powdered burnt sugar. "Hungry?" she said.

He shook his head. "Your Dad said you were going up to Muskogee or some place."

"Uh huh."

"I guess he left all right."

"Yes."

"I guess you better be careful about staying here, Keechie. I've been in a little trouble."

"You look like it."

The hot, wet towel melted the brittle casing on his face, softened his lips. Her fingers touched his face and he wanted to lick them. Just let her stay a little while. Just a little while . . . .

"I got money," he said. "On me and in that brown bag under the bed. Nineteen thousand dollars."

She straightened, cupping the towel in her hands, looked at him.

"I don't know why I said that."

"I'm glad you have it if that's what you want."

"That wasn't what I wanted to say. What I wanted to say was I don't guess it's best for you to be here."

"You need help."

"I just thought that I had this money and maybe you would like to take a trip or go someplace. All girls like to go places."

"I don't know what other girls like to do."

"Now I didn't mean anything by that, Keechie. Now don't get me down wrong."

"I would do this for a dog," Keechie said. "If you will turn over and pull your shirt up I will put some liniment on your back"

She left at noon, but she was coming back. It would be after dark and she would bring plasters and cigarettes and something for him to gargle. She would leave the model-T and walk back out, telling her Aunt Mara that she was leaving town. She would sleep in the filling station at nights.

Bowie rested on the bed, his back and head propped against a quilt and pillow. It's all right, he thought. I've had more than my share of bad luck and I know it's going to be all right for two or three days.

The cotton underwear on the bed looked like the skin of a dead rabbit. Bowie got up, picked the rusty file from the window sill and scraped the garment to the floor. Then he kicked it under the bed.

Chapter 12

Their spoons tinkled in the peanut-butter glasses of soft-boiled eggs and crumbled crackers. Keechie sat on the edge at the foot of the bed, the golden glow of the oil heater's jagged crown caressing her face.

"It's about time you started eatin' something," Bowie said. "I never heard of anybody not eatin' any more than you do and not gettin' any more sleep. Just two or three hours a night. I never heard of it."

"I've gone three nights without sleeping and it doesn't bother me at all. I've done it all my life."

"You've fallen off some too since I saw you last and you better start sleepin' and eatin' more, young lady. Now me, I've got to have my eight and nine and ten hours Now me, I've got to have my eight and nine and ten hours at night or I'm just blowed up."

Their spoons scraped in the emptied glasses and they laughed.

"Don't you ever want to leave this town, Keechie?" Bowie said.

"Yes." She got up and took the glass out of his hand; placed it with her own on the table. Then she came back and sat down. She talked. Her voice was as soft as the reflection on the heater's dull brass.

Once, she said, an old couple drove into the filling station and she got acquainted with them. The man was paralyzed and they were touring the country for his health. They dropped her postcards and talked about her coming to live with them and she would like to have gone, but then the cards stopped and finally one day she got a card from the woman saying the old man was dead.

"It makes it pretty hard on a girl when she doesn't have . . . ."

"Have what?"

"A Mama."

Keechie shook her head. "It depends on the mother."

"I don't know what I would have done without mine. Never has bawled me out for a thing."

"My Aunt says my Mother is the reason why my Father drinks and goes on like he does, but that doesn't have a thing to do with it. He is no good and perhaps she was, but I can't see that she is any better."

Outside, there was a sound like the sirens in Texaco City and Bowie stiffened and the skin on his chin and throat stretched.

"What's the matter?" Keechie said. She got up.

It was only wind in the telephone wires over on the

highway. "Nothing," Bowie said.

"Your back?"

He shook his head. "This old world is some old world, ain't it, Keechie?"

"Yes."

"Who's your fellow, Keechie?"

"Why do you ask that?"

"I just thought I would ask."

"Why?"

"It isn't any of my business. Most girls have fellows and I was just asking."

"I don't know what most girls have."

"I don't believe you like menfolk, do you, Keechie?"

"They are as good as the women I have seen."

"I believe you are kind of down on people."

"I don't know."

"And you never have had a fellow?"

"No."

"Even just to go to church with or something like that?"

"No. Why, do you think I should have?"

"Why, no. I was just asking. That's your own business."

"I never did see any use of it." Keechie reached over him and picked up the pack of cigarettes on the windowsill. The breasts under the polo shirt stirred.

"I'll take one too," Bowie said. "You know I don't know what could have happened to that Chicamaw. I guess he is seeing his folks."

"You will get along a lot better if he stays away from you."

"Aw, Keechie, you just got that cousin of yours down wrong."

"I'm not kin to anybody."

"You're a Little Soldier, that's what you are."

"Why do you call me that?"

"Because you are. Isn't it all right?"

"Yes."

She went over to the table and picked up the granite coffee pot and looked inside of it. She put it down and then picked it back up.

"Keechie."

She turned, the coffee pot in her hand.

"You know I have been wanting to give you something ever since I been here and I'd like to give it to you now."

"What is it?"

"A little old watch."

She returned the pot to the table.

"Do you want it?"

"Do you want to give it to me?"

"Yes."

"Yes, I want it."

Chapter 13

On the fourth night, Chicamaw came, his eyes like a dog sick with distemper, his face the color of ham rind. Bowie's head quivered on his neck and he called, but Keechie left the Bunk without speaking to Chicamaw.

"You look like you been making it all right," Chicamaw said.

"I been all right."

"Well, I haven't been doing so well. I've throwed every cent I got."

"I'll swear, Chicamaw. What's been the trouble?"

Chicamaw said he had throwed it in a Tulsa hotel gambling. He did have a new car though and some guns. A tommy gun too. By god, he had a Big Papa out there now and he was as ready as anybody to start a Little War.

"You didn't see your folks?"

Chicamaw shook his head and began plucking at a hair in his nostril. "I didn't want to go around them as hot as I was, Bowie."

"Well, you're not broke, Chicamaw. I still got it see, and you're we come to what you need."

"Sure makes me anxious to get back with T-Dub in Gusherton and get me another piece of money. You going to feel like getting up in a few days and running these roads again?"

"I guess I could go right now."

"No, I wouldn't ask you to go now. If you'll let me have five thousand I'll go on over and see the folks. Make it six thousand. Will you do that?"

"Christ, yes, man."

"Can you beat me throwing that much though, Bowie? You know I'm a damned good poker player. They just took me to a cleaning. When I get to thinking about it, damned if I don't believe there was something crooked about it."

"Them big gamblers are thieves. You better stay away from them, boy."

"I guess you been reading the papers all right?"

"I haven't seen anything."

"Is that so?"

"I been just laying right here. You mean Texaco City?"

"Man, we're hot."

"Them Laws?"

"We're hotter than gun barrels, boy."

There was a scratching sound and Bowie looked toward the closed door expectantly, but it did not open. It was the pecan tree touching the Bunk.

Chicamaw left the Bunk and returned quickly. Bowie had the brown bag on the bed and was taking money from it. Chicamaw put the two .45's on the bed.

"Sure glad to see them guns," Bowie said.

"Thanks for this loan," Chicamaw said. "You know I been thinking about you, Bowie. You don't throw your money away and you don't get drunk. You're just a big old country boy, Bowie, but by God, I believe you're going to make it. You got something and I just can't figure it out."

"It didn't do me no good in Texaco City."

"Well, I guess I'll be shoving off, Bowie. Now if I get jumped and can't get back here in a couple of days or you have to rabbit from here, I'll see you in Gusherton. We sure can't let old T-Dub down."

"You be careful, Chicamaw. Go a little easier on the whiss, boy."

"Then if I don't see you here in a couple of days I'll see you in Gusherton?"

"What is it them Mexicans say when it's okeh?" Bowie said.

"'*Sta bien*," Chicamaw said.

"'*Sta bien*," Bowie said. "Man, I sure do want to get down there in that chili country some of these days. A man can't live like this always, Chicamaw. You know that."

"We'll make it down there, boy. Don't you worry."

Chapter 14

In the early mornings, when shadows crawled in a gray gloom and Bowie lay alone in the Bunk, he thought of First Officer, his hog-knuckle chin; the smothering bucket and shattering glass; the Chair, Spirits, Cats. The branches of the pecan tree scratched the roof a hundred times and Keechie was never coming, he thought. For God's sake, man, snap. But at last she did come and then all that screwy Spirit stuff got out of his damned head.

In this evening's twilight, the polished peanut-butter glasses glowed with the delicacy of a blue flame. Bowie watched Keechie: the flipping cloth in her hands was like a blowing skirt and he seized her bare, strong fingers with his gaze. She had paint on her mouth tonight, but looking at her lips was like spying on her unclad through a keyhole.

She straightened the drying cloth on the back of the chair and then picked up the kerosene can. "I'd better fill up your heater for tonight," she said.

"You ought to put a coat on," he said.

While she was gone, he planned what he would do in the morning when he woke up. He would not read the Sunday newspaper she had gotten him until in the morning. And then he would only look at the funny pages and the comics.

Keechie returned, and after filling the stove she came to the bed. "I hope you get a good night's rest."

He played with the point of his shirt collar. "I hate to see you go."

"Do you?"

"I guess I've kinda got the blues tonight."

"I have done about everything I could around here, but I'm in no hurry. If you want me to stay."

"Just a little while if you ain't in no hurry."

She lowered herself to the edge of the bed and crossed her legs. The sound of the tree now was like a gentle rain.

"I don't like to look behind," he said. "I try to just think of maybe the good things that will happen ahead. But I guess I know what is going to happen."

"No, you don't, Bowie. The things that you are afraid of most never happen. I'm a lot older than you in a lot of ways."

"I never have seen nothing like you before, Keechie. I know now what makes a fellow get him a little missus and swing a dinner pail."

"You mean that?"

"Yes."

She moved and he reached out and said, "Don't go."

"I'm not."

"My ears are ringing," he said.

She bent toward him and touched his face. He seized her then, brought her toward him. "Don't you go. Don't you go."

"I'm not, Bowie."

Strength swelled within him. I can snap her little body in my hands. I can break her little body in my grip. Her tight lips yielded until there was only softness and then her breath became as naked as her body . . . .

~§~

Frying bacon spluttered in the skillet on top of the oil heater and then it popped and Keechie jerked back and turned and smiled at Bowie.

"You better be careful, Little Girl," he said. She sure did look different. Where did he ever get the idea that she wasn't pretty? Those lines in her face. Where were they? And that little mouth was as soft and pretty.

"Wonder if you would take time out and come over here and give your Daddy a kiss?" he said.

She came over, the fork in her hand and bent down. "There's nothing sick about you," she said.

He kissed her. "I feel like a million bucks. I been thinking about getting up and running a half-mile before I eat."

"You just stay there. How do you want your eggs?"

"Any old way."

"How do you want them?"

"Any old way, honey. Over easy I guess. And hand me that newspaper over there while you don't have anything else to do."

She handed him the newspaper and he pointed at the three pale prongs of sunlight that lay on the splintered floor near the window. "Look, I believe the sun is going to shine today."

"I noticed the stars last night and I thought then that it might be clear today."

He began turning the pages and then he saw the thing that seized his eyes like a fishhook:

TEXACO CITY, Texas, Oct. 6— Fingerprints found on the steering wheel of the wrecked, new automobile which the fugitive slayers of Plainclothesmen Vic Redford and Jake Hadman abandoned here last week, may lead to the identity of the killers, Chief of Detectives Musser revealed here, today. The chief said his department was basing its hopes on this and also a revolver found nearby.

Redford and Hadman, veteran peace officers, were ruthlessly slain in a gun battle on Ector Boulevard while investigating an automobile crash. A woman received minor injuries in the collision.

"Are you very hungry this morning?" Keechie said.

The white of the paper glimmered like heat on the highway and Bowie jerked his eyes away. "I didn't understand what you said?"

"What's the matter, Bowie?"

"Nothing. Not a thing. I was just reading here."

"What are you reading?"

"Just something here."

Six suspects arrested here in connection with the case have been released. Two are still being questioned.

The abandoned automobile of the killers was purchased in El Paso, Texas, it was reported. Witnesses of the battle say that three and possibly four men were in the car that sped away after the shooting. One witness declared he saw a woman in the outlaw machine.

A police benefit here last night for the widows of the two slain officers netted $320.

Bowie took the warm plate the warm plate with its eggs and bacon from Keechie's hand and put it on his lap. After a little while, he stuck the fork into the egg's yellow.

"What's the matter, Bowie?" She sat on the bed's edge, with a plate on her knees.

"I don't want to hold nothing back from you, Keechie. I'm pretty deep in this business. I'm a lot deeper in it than I was when I was here before. I want you to know that."

"What is it?"

"I had some trouble back up the road. Two Laws killed."

Keechie placed her plate on the floor.

"You can see that I'm in it pretty deep now."

"Did you do it?"

"Them Laws?"

"Yes."

Bowie's head went up and down.

"You did not. You can't tell me that. I know who did it. Chicamaw. You can't conceal anything from me." She clutched his trouser cuff. "He did it."

"It don't make any difference who did it. And you got Chiamaw down all wrong. I wouldn't be sittin' here now if it wasn't for him."

"You did not do it, Bowie."

"I wouldn't tell you nothing but the straight. I got it on my back and there's no gettin' around it."

Keechie got up and the plate on the floor rattled and broke. She looked down at it and for a moment her mouth twisted as if she were going to cry.

Bowie held up his plate. "Don't mind that. We can split this."

Keechie picked up the plate fragments and the spilled food. On the table was Bowie's untouched food.

"I'll just tell you the straight of it, Keechie. I'm not sorry. I'm not sorry for anything I ever did in this world. That when I was just a punk kid and they put the Chair on me don't count. But I'm not sorry for a one of these banks. The only regret I got is that I didn't get one hundred thousand instead of ten. I'm just a black sheep and there's no gettin' round it."

"The only black about you is your Hair," Keechie said.

"You're a Little Soldier, Keechie. You're a Little Soldier from them toenails of yours up to your hair, but you can't get mixed up with me."

Keechie's face twisted like he had driven his fist into it. He grasped her arm. "Keechie, what's the matter?"

She shook her head.

He pulled her to him. "What's the matter, honey?"

"Didn't you mean that last night?"

"Mean what?"

"Bowie. You know what you said."

"Honey, I can't think of everything right now. What was it, honey? You come on now and tell me."

"You said you wished you had me."

"Sure I do. Godamighty, honey."

"What do you mean then? Getting too mixed up with you?"

"Don't you see how it is? When a man has them Laws after him and it's all in the papers they'll shoot you and ask questions afterwards. They'd just as soon shoot a woman down with him as not."

"Is that what you mean?"

"You see now, don't you, honey?"

"Does anybody else have any strings on you, Bowie? Anybody else?" She pulled away from his grasp.

"What do you mean?"

"Is there anybody else? A woman?"

"Oh, no, honey. Lord, no."

"I just wanted to know."

"How come you to ask a thing like that?"

"I'm in this pretty deep and I just wanted to know."

Bowie lay back against the pillow. "Keechie, come and lie down beside me a little while."

She got on the bed beside him.

"You like me, Keechie?"

"Yes."

"A whole lot?"

"Yes."

"Hundred bushels full?"

"Yes."

"Thousand bushels full?"

"Yes."

"A hundred thousand million trillion gillion bushels full?"

"Yes."

"Keechie, I love you." Her finger nails dug into the flesh of his throat.

~§~

There were sounds in the filling station and Keechie got out of bed and went, across the darkened room to the door; Bowie following, in his underwear, a .45 in his right hand. Keechie peered through the cautiously opened crack of the door. After a long time she closed the door easily and Bowie stepped back. "It's my Aunt. Stealing some groceries."

Neither was sleepy now. They lay in bed, both their heads on the one pillow. "You know I been thinking, Keechie. This business of me staying here can't go on. I been here eight days now and Dee is going to be coming back pretty soon and this just can't go on now."

"Do you have anything in mind?"

"How would you like to go somewhere with me?"

"You want me to go?"

"You know doggone well I want you to go."

"What do you have in mind?"

"I'd like to get in a big city, Keechie. I mean like New Orleans or Louisville. Old T-Dub was always talking about them towns. In them big cities, people don't big-eye you so much and if you keep your nose clean, you can last as long as you want to."

"I guess so."

"I just don't know what's happened to that Chic-amaw. That Indian can take care of himself though. He's probably gettin' everything fixed up at his folks."

"We don't have to go around any of them, do we? Mister Masefeld and them?"

"No sir, honey. Not you. I should say not."

"I've been thinking some too, Bowie, and what I have had on my mind is what some people that used to live next door to my Aunt told me. Mister Carpenter and his wife and they had a girl my age named Agnes. Mister Carpenter had tuberculosis and they moved away down in Texas almost to the border in the Guadaloupe Hills. Agnes wrote and told me about it. They lived away out in the hills and wouldn't go to town for two months at a time and Agnes said that the only people they ever saw were some Mexican sheepherders and then a few sick people like Mister Carpenter. People chasing the cure, Agnes said they were."

"Close to Mexico, uh?"

"Bowie, I don't see why we couldn't go to a place like that and just live to ourselves and pretty soon people would forget all about Bowie Bowers and then finally there would just be the real Bowie Bowers."

"You know I hadn't thought of that. Them little towns, though, Keechie, are bad. Everybody wants to know your business."

"We won't be in a town. We'll be away out and don't have to see anybody."

"You know I sure hadn't thought of that."

"That's where I would like to go."

"Man, we got the money to do it. Right here under this bed and in my breeches and coat yonder."

"I think that would be the best and just stay away from everybody you ever knew."

"How you and me going to get out of this place, Keechie? No car or nothing?"

"We can manage."

"Any trains stop here at night?"

"Two o'clock to Tulsy."

"We could get that train, by golly. You could walk about a half-block ahead of me and get a couple of tickets and I'll be hanging around and every once in a while we'll give each other a wink and then we'll sit in separate seats on the train and . . . ."

"We'll sit together on the train."

"Sure, we can sit together on the train and then we'll get in Tulsy and I'll buy us a new V-8 and then we'll scat down to this Guadaloupe Hills country. Where is that place, Keechie?"

"I've looked at it on the map a hundred times. When Agnes was writing me I wanted to go down there. There's deer and wild turkey and squirrels and everything else, Agnes said."

"Man, I could knock me off a deer. I'll get me a .30-30 or a .415 Winchester and you and me will eat venison, kiddo. You just let me down there, Keechie, and I won't even need no gun. Just give me a rock."

"If we go down there, either you or me will supposed to be lunger, you know, with t.b. Maybe both of us had better be. Now in renting a cabin or something we'll have to let on."

"I'll look the best t.b. in the world."

"That's the thing for us to do. And you just forget everybody you ever knew."

"You'll have to get you some clothes in Tulsy, honey. How about a fur coat? To set that watch off I gave you?"

"We'll think about that later."

"I'll buy you a whole windowful of clothes. You can get anything you want. All you got to do is name it."

"We can't look like no millionaires. We're going to be sick people."

"Ah, you can get a few things. How you like them riding boots and pants, Keechie? Aw, I don't know though whether I'd like to see you in pants or not. You just get dresses. And plenty of them silk doodads. We'll get a couple of thermos jugs and keep them filled with soda pop and get some blankets and sun glasses and an extra can or two of gasoline and we'll split the breeze."

"When do you think we should go?"

"What time is it now?"

"It must be twelve."

"We can make it. Two hours. Let's get in the saddle, honey."

"Tonight, Bowie?"

"You doggone whistling. And honey we got the money to do it on too. Twenty thousand good old bucks. I mean fourteen. That's a lot of money, Keechie. You can say what you want to about money, Keechie, but by God, it talks."

"I guess so," Keechie said. "Well, let's start dressing."

Chapter 15

Mesquite trees persisted even into this foothills country, but the plains were far behind now. There were Spanish oaks and cedars and in the late afternoon this way the sage grass had a lavender flush. Away ahead, in the distance, a long range of sharp hills embroidered the horizon. Above the range, the sky was streaked with white, rigid panels as if the rain had crystallized and awaited a crack of lightening to unleash.

Keechie was driving and Bowie sat low in the seat, his hands deep in his pockets. She drove like Chicamaw, her left hand on the crossbar and the other on the wheel; took the curves like they weren't there. In the holster under Bowie's left arm was a .45 and in the panel pocket another. There were four blankets in the back, a thermos jug of coffee, a sack of sandwiches, four cartons of tailor-made cigarettes. And Keechie had on hose that cost two dollars and shoes that cost ten and that military craven-ette coat. It was her own fault that she didn't get the fur, but she looked like a Little Soldier in that coat and he had to hand it to her. And the way she had that little brown hat cocked over her eye . . . .

Down the road, beyond the Curve sign, the cement disappeared around the stone-studded bank; straight ahead, low, white barriers and space and blue sky. What if they just kept going straight and into that space and sky? They would keep going like a plane right over the valley. But cars don't fly. What if they did go off? It would just mean that he and Keechie had drawn the poor cards. But what if they made it? It would mean Luck was riding with them for a long time to come . . . .

The wheels of the machine sung tenaciously on the curve and now they were on a long straight-away again. They ain't nothing going to stop us, Little Soldier.

"Light me a cigarette, Bowie."

"Yes, ma'am."

The dairy barn was white with green trimming and over its roof, white and black pigeons circled. On the porch of the house lay a big dog, its paws dangling over the edge. They passed an old sedan, its slender wheels wobbling, the top tattered and in pennants.

"Them old Jalopes," Bowie said. "They cause more accidents than anything else on the road. It's no crime to be poor, Keechie, but there ought to be law against letting cars like that out on the highways."

They passed a Schoolhouse, two filling stations and on the porch of the General Store sat two men bent over a checker board. The black lettering on the highway board read: *San Antonio . . . 186.*

Down this highway, thirty miles more and then they would turn west on a dirt road. Out that road one hundred miles and they would be in them little hill towns, Antelope Center, Arbuckle. There they would start house-hunting.

On the left was a cemetery, with a half-dozen low tombstones and then an unpainted, box house. Farther down, at the wooden gate, two cows with swollen bags waited.

"You know anything about cows, Bowie? Do they ever have twins?"

"You got me there."

"I was just wondering."

"It looks like to me they could though. With that woman up in Canada doing what she did, it looks like to me a cow could do it."

"Those cows back there made me think of it."

"That woman up there in Canada, Keechie. That shows you nothing is impossible in this old world, doesn't it?"

"It sure does."

"And I was thinking back there. What is it you say we

are doing? *Chasing the cure.* Well, what if we really did have t.b.? Well, I don't know but what I'd rather be a lot hotter than I am now than have something like that riding me. Don't you kind of feel that way about it?"

"I should say I do."

~§~

Bowie chose the big filling station with its stucco front and Keechie turned the car up the curving driveway. There was another car under the shed, a woman at the wheel, but it drove off as they stopped. The next time we gas up, Bowie thought, we'll be having us a home to go to. Just fifty miles more now and they would be in the town of Arbuckle.

The filling station attendant in the leather jacket said: "Yessir?"

"Fill 'er up and I got a couple of cans."

Keechie entered the Restroom door and Bowie went over to the Coca Cola box and lifted the lid. The exhausts of stopping motorcycles popped and he turned. The two cops were coming right in here.

The Cops came toward the Coca Cola box and Bowie moved over. The tall cop was as brown as saddle leather and the short one had chapped, scaling lips. They had on gray uniforms and black Sam Browne belts. Their pistols were pearl-handled.

"What kind you want?" Tall Cop said.

"Coke," Short Cop said.

Their lips made drinking sounds on the mouths of the

bottles.

"Got you a new one there, haven't you?" Tall Cop said.

"Yeah," Bowie said. "Them jobs over there can outrun it in reverse though, can't they?"

"They'll outrun that car all right."

"I guess them motorcycles there will outrun just about anything that gets on these roads, won't they?"

"Don't you think it, Mister," Short Cop said. "There's plenty of them out there I don't go after."

"You can tie them up in traffic sometimes," Tall Cop said.

"Ninety is about all I want to push that cycle over there of mine," Short Cop said, "and if anybody has anything that will do better than that I just check it to them."

Keechie came around the corner, stopped and then started smoothing the dress about her hips. Bowie winked and she went on to the car and got under the wheel.

"That all, Sir?" the Attendant said.

Bowie paid him.

They drove off and Bowie turned and reached toward the back seat. Tall Cop and Short Cop were sitting on top of the Coca Cola box.

"You didn't bat an eye, you doggone little dickens. Not an eye."

"What were you talking to them about?"

"Damned if I know."

"It looked like to me you were trying to make friends."

"They didn't know me from Adam's off ox, Keechie. Why, they're that way all over the country. How they going to know you? Look at a picture. Well, what's that?"

"I would stay away from them."

"Man, when they drove in that station though, I says to myself: 'Here's where a Little War starts.'"

"You better look behind."

Bowie looked back. The ribbon was clean. "Not a thing, honey. Nossir, you didn't bat an eye."

"I think maybe I had better start carrying that pistol in the pocket there, Bowie."

"Not that big gun, honey. That thing would jump clean out of your hands. I'll get you a little gun one of these days pretty soon though. Every woman ought to have a gun. I'm going to get you one. There's always some sonofabitch ready to get smart with a woman."

"I'm not afraid of that gun."

"Did you ever shoot a .45?"

"No, but I have a real strong grip. I could out crack any of the girls in school on pecans. You remember that game. I won all the time."

"Yeah, I remember that game. What did we call it?"

"Hully gull."

"That's it. Yessir, Keechie, it just goes to show you how a man don't have to jump from his shadow. I'll bet I could go right up to the Law over here in this town of Arbuckle and ask him if he knew of a furnished house and I'll bet he wouldn't know me from Adam's off ox."

"I will do the asking about the houses. I will go to the real estate office and do the asking."

"You going to tell them we're lungers?"

"That is what we are down here for now, Bowie, and you want to remember it."

Bowie made a coughing sound and slapped his chest. "The bug is gettin' me down. How's it doing you, Little Lunger?"

"You'll make it, old Foot-in-the-Grave."

~§~

There were no furnished houses in the little town of Arbuckle or near it, the Real Estate Woman told Keechie, but over at Antelope Center, she said, forty miles farther West, the cottages of an old Sanitarium were being remodeled for tourists and sick people and deer hunters. Bowie and Keechie went to Antelope Center.

It was almost noon when they left the graveled highway, two miles west of Antelope Center, turned through an arched gate and started climbing the narrow, high-centered road. Through the cedars and frost browned oaks, on the side of the Hill, stood a big gray building.

"Looks like a jail," Bowie said.

"It won't hurt to look," Keechie said.

The closed building was the old hospital, its cement the color of dead broomweed. Through the dust-filmed windows there were stacks of bare beds and piles of mattresses. Back of it and east, rows of small stucco cottages fenced it like a carpenter's tri-square. The cottages had glassed-in rooms and stone chimneys and there were lettered boards over the entrances: *Come Inn . . . . Suits*

Us . . . . Journeys Inn . . . . Bella Vista.

The man raking the weeds in front of the corner cottage in the V of the Square stopped, leaned on the handle and looked at their car. When Keechie got out, he dropped the rake and came toward them.

The man had on a khaki army shirt and a white cloth belt held his slick, blue serge trousers. He was middle-aged and his teeth were broken and tobacco-stained. Yes, he had some cottages. He was the caretaker out here. He had just fixed up another cottage and it was twelve dollars and fifty cents a month and that included water and electricity. It was the last house at that end. Now he lived in that house on the corner, and below him a School Teacher batched and next to him an Auto Salesman with his wife and two children, They were the only ones that lived out here now, but he hadn't got around to fixing up any more cottage. They were fine people, the folks that lived out here.

"You want to look at it, honey?" Keechie said.

"Yeah, I'd just as soon."

"You take that School Teacher feller yonder," the Caretaker said, "he got him a hot plate from Sears, Roebuck and he's just batching fine."

Bowie got out of the car.

The Caretaker thrust out his hand. "Lambert is my name, young man. Old Bill Lambert. Traveled out of San Antonio for thirty-five years, leather goods, saddles, grips and harness. Had a lung collapse on me here a year ago and this air up here, Son, is fine. What's your business, Son?"

Bowie removed his hand from the other's grip. "I'm

a sick man right now. Used to play ball."

"Son, you come to the right place. Not a healthier place in the United States than right in here. Ball Player, uh? Well, we got a School Teacher and two Salesmen and now we got a Ball Player. Now that Salesman feller over yonder used to be worth a right smart lot of money. Owned his own business right yonder in Antelope and just went busted like any of us can do. His wife didn't like it much out here at first, her being used to gas and fancy things, but now she just likes it fine. Your missus will like it too."

"Pretty quiet out here, I guess?" Bowie said.

"You won't get lonesome. Now that Salesman has got him a radio and everybody out here is fine people."

"Used to be a lot of people out here, I guess?"

"I don't know all the history of this place. Now all this was built right after the War, I think, and then it petered out and then for a while it was a sort of tourist camp and I might just as well tell you folks because I'm not the kind to hold nothing back. This place got a pretty bad reputation with the folks in Antelope because here a couple of years back some bootleggers got out and people come out here and throwed wild parties. But that's not any more, son. Your wife will be just as safe here as any place in the world now."

"He has to stay awful quiet," Keechie said. "Let's go look at the place."

Bill Lambert walked, ahead on the narrow sidewalk in front of the closed cottages, talking, spitting. "Now it's nothing swell, you know, but I'll fix it up just like you want it. There's one thing, I want to put you in some

linoleum in the kitchen and if you ever have company
and need an extra cot, why just let me know."

He stopped in front of the last cottage—*Welcome
Inn*—and opened the scraping screen and inserted the
key in the lock. The wooden floors inside creaked under
their feet. In this front room there were a blackened,
empty stone fireplace and an iron army cot covered with
a yellowed counterpane. There were two hide-bottomed
rocking chairs and a rickety breakfast table. In the
windowed sleeping-room there was a broad iron bed, a
huge dresser with a smoky mirror and two straight
dining room chairs. The kitchen had a three-burner,
grease-caked oil stove, a sink and an enamel-topped
table. The bath had a shower and the toilet seat was split
and part of it lay on the cement floor.

"Some strong lye soap and a mop and whitewash
would help a lot around here," Keechie said. "Don't you
think so, honey?"

Bowie grinned. "Don't you think the price though
will about keep us busted?"

"Now, let tell I tell you, Mister . . . ." Bill Lambert
said, "What did you say your name was, Son?"

"Vines. V-i-n-e-s."

"Well, I tell you now, Mister Vines. It's just the best I
can do. A bunch of millionaires own this out here and
you know how they are. I been trying my best to fix these
places up here and get some money to do it with because
people just want things a little nicer for the money, but I
tell you, it's just like gettin' blood out of a turnip to get
something from one of these millionaires. Now you take
Mister Philpott over there, he's the Salesman, and they've

fixed that place up over there just as pretty as a picture."

"There is a lot to do around here all right," Keechie said.

"I'll tell you what I'll do," Bill Lambert said. "I don't want to rush you folks, but if you decide to take it I'll throw in a half-cord of wood for nothing and tack that linoleum down the first thing this afternoon right after dinner."

"We must stay awfully quiet," Keechie said.

"Don't you worry about that, Mizzis Vines. Now you take here last month, it was the night of September fifteenth, there was a couple come out here and I thought I smelled liquor, but I didn't want to cause no trouble and I let them have the place although they just wanted it for two or three days. Well, before the night was over she was running around tight in this house here, without anything on and kicking up as high at them trees and the blinds up to the ceiling and so I just politely told them we didn't want that going on around here. Now, Son, you want your wife protected and that is just the way I do out here. This is a place for respectable people and any time anybody runs around here kicking . . . ."

"That's all right, Mister Lambert," Bowie said

"Just one more thing now, Mister Vines, and then I'll let you go. Now you take Mizzis Philpott over there. One day she goes off and while she's gone her oil stove burns over and I busts in there and saves the whole place. They were mighty appreciative of that."

"I'm very satisfied," Bowie said.

"If we ever catch you in this house, you had better be putting out a fire," Keechie said.

Lambert laughed. "All right, Lady. All right. Now then I'll just leave you two together and let you decide."

Alone, Bowie and Keechie walked in the rooms. "Think it will do, Keechie?"

"I'm crazy about it."

"If I ever catch old Filthy MacNasty peepin' around here, I'll kick his hind-end clear off," Bowie said.

"He's harmless. Bowie, this is just the thing."

Bowie walked in the sleeping-room, Keechie following. "Some of them big, red Indian blankets would sure look pretty in here," he said. "And we'll get us a big radio to sit in yonder."

"I can go to town this afternoon and I'll buy enough groceries to last us three months," Keechie said.

"I forgot to ask old Filthy if there was really some deer around here," Bowie said.

Keechie sat on the edge of the bed and moved up and down on it experimentally. "Good springs and mattress, Bowie."

"I'm sold on it myself," Bowie said. "Go on out and pay Filthy a couple of months' rent and tell him I'll tack the damned linoleum down."

Chapter 16

There was one hundred dollars' worth of bright-colored blankets on the big red bed and the cot now, a radio that was as big as the fireplace in the living room, two automatic shotguns and a rifle on the mantel and Keechie had a cigarette case with a diamond in it. They had done a lot in four weeks. Old Filthy never did snoop around anymore and just once had somebody come, Mrs. Philpott, the Saleman's wife, to borrow some sugar. Out here they never did see anybody except that little Philpott boy, Alvin, and then he was away down in the woods back of their place with a .22 rifle and that Spitz dog of his, Spots.

Bowie sat in front of the radio this evening, smoking the curved-stem pipe that Keechie liked, and thought how everything was looking pretty good. In that food-packed kitchen, Keechie was frying Irish potatoes the way he liked them, crisp and brown.

I don't care nothing about it myself, Bowie thought, but we can start taking in some picture shows down there in that town pretty soon. Girls like to get out and go places. And that Law down there? I got him spotted and he ain't never going to get close to me.

In the darkened living room, the flames of the fireplace logs splashed on the ceiling and walls. Had he brought in the wood tonight? Yes. What time was it? *Seven-thirty.* Christ, that Mexican orchestra Keechie liked was on. Bowie switched the dial. This was the station all right, but now they were talking about them damned constipation crystals.

If they were jumped now and had to rabbit, this radio and everything would have to be left behind. Well, I'm no damned soda skeet making ten dollars a week. I'll buy another one. Five hundred-dollar one and two hundred dollars' worth of blankets and if we go busted I know where I can get plenty more.

He placed another log on the fire and sat back down. The prongs of light shadow-boxed now on the walls, hooking and jabbing frenziedly. The orchestra was playing and Bowie got up and went back to the kitchen. Keechie was standing in front of the oven with a cloth in her hand.

"Hear that piece?"

Keechie nodded. *"La Golondrina."*

"Always makes me kind of sad somehow. Makes me think of them boys."

"Why?"

"I don't know. I been thinking about Chicamaw though, Keechie. I don't know whether I did that boy right or not up there in Keota, Keechie. He might have been expecting me to wait for him there and I didn't leave him no note or nothing."

"How were you going to leave him a note?"

"I don't know."

"Well, quit worrying about it then."

"I was just thinking about them."

"You have somebody else to worry about now."

"We just all started out together and you can't keep from thinking about things like that."

Bowie went back to the living room and sat down. The fire had lowered and its glow filtered the darkness like a luminous screen. A cowboy singer was yodeling now about the prairie.

I do have to meet them boys in Gusherton, Bowie thought. They never did let me down and I sure can't go back on them. Why, they would just wait and wait and wait on me and I wouldn't let them do that. She will understand. You will understand, won't you, honey?

The cowboy was singing *Nobody's Darling but Mine:*

> Goodbye, Goodbye, Little Darling,
> I'm leaving this Old World behind.
> Oh promise me that you will never
> Be Nobody's Darling, but Mine . . . .

Bowie cut the Voice off. I wish we could get more newspaper news over this and not that Mussolini and Africa and Congress and stuff like that. No news is good news though. If anything had happened to them boys, we would have heard about it.

Keechie called him. On the enameled table there were black-eyed peas, corn bread, fried potatoes, pineapple preserves and black coffee.

After supper, Bowie took the galvanized-iron tub of hot water off the stove and carried it into the living room and lowered it to the floor in the hearth's glow. Keechie was going to take a bath.

He spread the bath mat and towels on the hearth around the tub and then looked around the room. The blinds were pulled close all right.

Standing, her naked thighs and legs glinted through the tub's rising vapors. She's sure filling out, Bowie thought. Now she raised her left arm and the soaped, dripping cloth in her right hand moved toward the shadowed pit. "I didn't know you were such a hairy little thing," he said.

Her arm came down. "Do you think I should shave?"

"I should say not. I like it. Don't you ever do it."

"I won't then. As long as I have you."

The whipping, drying towel covered and revealed and Bowie felt the heat of her burnished body glow in his eyes. He got up and picked up the white flannel pajamas off the radio. They smelled of clean soap. He handed them to her.

"Are you going to wash your feet tonight?" she said.

"Not tonight, honey. I washed them last night."

They lay under the warm, soft blankets flow and Keechie's fingers played in the flannel over his chest. Outside, on the narrow cement walk, wind-kicked leaves scraped and scurried. In the daytime, he had watched the leaves leave the oak and they had twisted and spiraled to the ground like birds shot with an air gun.

She lay quietly now and he said softly: "Keechie?"

She half raised. "What is it, Bowie? Did you call me?"

"I thought you were asleep."

She peered at him hard. "What is it?"

"Nothing, honey. I didn't go to wake you up."

"What is it, Bowie?"

Distant, tiny, taut wires trilled in Bowie's ears. "I just been thinking."

"About what?"

"Just about things in general. Got to thinking about some of the boys up there in Alky. They come in there, Keechie, bragging about the women they got outside waiting for them and after a little while they hush up and there's nothing more heard about it."

"I don't know anything about that."

"It doesn't make any difference, I don't suppose. I don't care what kind of a man you take. A doctor or a big college professor or any kind of a man and let him die and pretty soon his wife will be out running around with somebody else. These widows are just about as bad as any kind of a woman."

"I don't know about women like that."

"Some of these women bury a man and in no time at all pick right up with another. There's women, Keechie, that will take up with a dozen men in their lives. Just one right in after another."

"Those women didn't love."

"Well, I don't know about that now, Keechie. They are bound to have been pretty crazy about them and maybe they didn't love all of them, but they loved some of them."

"A woman just loves once."

"What makes a woman live with one man a while and then with another one and then just run around with four or five more?"

"They just don't love."

"They must like it, Keechie, or they wouldn't do it."

"I don't know why other women do things. Maybe they are just looking and can't find anybody and then I guess some of them marry for a living."

"It just looks like to me that every woman will do it."

"I don't know what other women do."

"Now what would you do, Keechie, if I got in a little trouble somewhere and you and me might not be able to see each other again?"

Keechie did not say anything. The tiny wires were as

loud as crickets now and they swarmed in Bowie's ears.
"Didn't you hear me?"

"There wouldn't be anything for me after you were
gone. There is no use to think about that."

"Keechie, look at all these other women. Maybe they
don't the first year and maybe they go two or three or
four years, but pretty soon you see them lettin' some man
slobber all over them."

Keechie was quiet.

"Now what do you have to say to that, Keechie?"

"I guess a woman is kind of like a dog, Bowie. You
take a good dog now and if his master dies that dog won't
take food from anybody and he'll bite anybody that tries
to pet him and if he goes on, he'll rustle his own food and
a lot of times he will just die too."

"You know that's right?"

"A bad dog will eat out of anybody's hands and take
things from anybody."

"That's those big thoroughbred dogs that cost a pile
of money that do that I guess. Them are real dogs."

"Maybe they do. I never did see, I don't guess, a real
thoroughbred. The dog I am thinking about was there in
Keota. I don't know what he was. Nobody else I don't
guess. Old Man Humphrey owned him and after he died I
felt so sorry for that dog. But he wouldn't have anything
to do with anybody and he wouldn't eat or drink and then
he just died too."

"I'll be doggone, Keechie. You know that's right. It
just goes to show you. You know, honey, you are the
smartest little old thing I ever did see."

"I'm not smart."

"You're a Little Soldier, that's what you are."

"You go to sleep now."

The ringing in Bowie's ears faded far, far away and his eyes grew heavy and he closed them . . . .

Chapter 17

The back yard of *Welcome Inn* had the width of an alley and then a fence of barbed wire and beyond that was ranch land, sage-grass and broomweed; far reaching woods of green, pollen-blowing cedars and gray-trunked scrub-oaks. In it, long-horned, white-faced cattle grazed and sometimes one would come to their fence and nose in the rusty iron drum of burned cans and garbage. Once, Keechie had seen a doe and she called Bowie, but when he got to the back door, it was gone. Away to the south, beyond the woods, the Hills embossed the sky in a great, crawling circle. This evening, the sinking sun had flushed the horizon to a pretty pink like Keechie's underthings.

They sat now on the back steps of the cottage, Keechie in the coat of Bowie's gray suit. She was funny that way, always wearing something of his and even sleeping at nights in one of his shirts and be had paid fifteen dollars for that negligee and boudoir slippers.

Keechie pointed now and in the woods they saw the Philpott boy, Alvin, and the dog.

"I been kind of wanting to get out there with that kid some evening," Bowie said. "I never have seen him bringing back anything."

"He's having a good time though," Keechie said.

"Guess I just got too much else to think about." He tapped the bowl of his pipe on his palm and then slung the charred tobacco with a finger-spreading movement and wiped his hand across his thigh. The lining of his mouth felt thin and his tongue needle-pointed. I'll tell her after we go in, he thought. Only four days now and I got to be in Gusherton. That's all there is to it.

"Alvin yonder made me think of the little girl who used to live down on the corner from my Aunt. She died."

"Huh," Bowie said.

"She was awfully pretty. She used to say pieces in the church and her Mama fixed her up so pretty. It liked to have killed her Mama and I guess it was the reason that her Father went crazy. He was crazy before that, I would say though. He was a printer and he saved gold pieces. Every bit of money he saved he would go to the bank and get gold pieces. Go up in the, front room at nights and sit at a table and count it and look at it. His wife told him that it was going to bring bad luck."

"And then the kid died?"

"And it took every bit of the gold he had saved to pay for the funeral."

Bowie started filling his pipe. "Chicamaw was telling me about that lawyer friend of his he knew down in Mexico. Hawkins. That lawyer didn't believe in this heaven or hell stuff and said that the only way a man lived on was through his children. That was as far as this After-Life business went."

"Is that why you would like to have children?"

He looked at her. "Why, I never said nothing about having children."

"I know it."

"Why, would you like to have a baby?"

"Someday, maybe."

"Someday is right."

She stood up on the step and pulled the coat about her throat. "I'm satisfied now."

The match snapped and he flipped it and felt in his pocket for another. "No, a baby wouldn't have very much business with us."

"Well, if it couldn't be with us, I'd rather for it to be just you and me."

It was getting dark. The storm-broken limb yonder on the big oak-tree was twisted about the trunk like a petrified snake.

Bowie got up, knocking the unlighted tobacco out on the heel of his shoe. "I been thinking about the boys, Keechie. I guess I'll have to see them in a few days."

"Why?"

"A little business. I promised them I would meet them on the fifteenth of this month."

"Why?"

"Just business. I'll just be gone a couple of back here before you know it."

"What are you planning on?"

"I just promised them, Keechie. That's all."

"What are you planning on doing?"

"Now I want you to understand, Keechie, that I'm not looking for trouble any more. I'm going up there, but I don't have anything in mind except just not let them boys wait days and be and depend on me. We got a bank picked there all right, but I'm not planning on robbing it."

Keechie turned and grasped the doorknob. "I'm going with you," she said. Then she went in the house.

He stood there alone. Up at the end of the row of cottages there was the sound of ax splitting wood. After a little while, he went in the house.

She lay on the bed in the darkness of the sleeping-room and he went over and sat on its edge. "No, you are not, Keechie," he said.

She did not say anything. She got up and went to the kitchen and he listened to the sound of water running in a glass. Presently, she came back.

"I said you weren't going," he said.

"I heard you."

"Well, quit running around when I'm talking to you."

She sat down on the bed beside him.

"Being in my heat is bad enough and you're certainly not going to get around three of us. I made up my mind about that a long time ago."

"All right, Bowie."

"Now let's get this straight. What do you mean all right?"

"I mean it will be all right."

"How are you going to be feeling when I come back?"

"All right."

"You are going to be here, aren't you?"

"Yes."

"And it is all right?"

Keechie got up and took his coat off, folded it and laid it on the bed rail. "You are keeping your promise and when you get up there you are going to let them know you are through with all that kind of business?"

"After Gusherton, I'm through."

"You know that I expect that, Bowie?"

"I sure do."

"All right then."

Keechie went into the kitchen and Bowie heard the wick of the oil stove sputter and then the rattle of the kettle on the flames. He lay down on the bed. After a little while the water in the kettle began to simmer. It sounded like a whimpering baby.

Chapter 18

The front door of the Gusherton house parted and there was the smell of cold bacon and raw onion and then in the crack of light was Lula's water-color face. The door opened farther and Bowie went in and now he was shaking T-Dub's rocklike hand.

"Where's Chicamaw?" Bowie said.

T-Dub nodded toward the rear of the house. "Sleeping one off."

"For God's sake don't wake him up," Lula said. She had on a green velvet dinner gown that reached her ankles, and was adjusting a gold earring in her lobe. "I will absolutely leave."

"He sure has been guzzlin' it, Bowie," T-Dub said. "I don't know what's going to become of that boy."

"He's sleeping, is he?" Bowie said.

"Don't you wake him up now," Lula said.

Bowie lowered himself to the studio couch, balancing his hat on his close-pressed knees. T-Dub looked tired: like the morning they had walked the railroad ties all night. "Take his hat, Lula," he said. "Boy, you act like you just dropped in to say hello."

"I've been traveling pretty long and fast today," Bowie said. He watched Lula carry the hat and place it on the table by the door under the mirror.

"Where you been keeping yourself, Bowie?"

"Down south of here. Say, Chicamaw has been drinking a whole lot?"

"Oh, Christ, man. He brought an old bat in here last night that I'll swear to God he must have picked up in Nigger Town. Right in this house with Lula here."

"She was as drunk as he was and of all the goings-on," Lula said. "I told T. W. there that if you weren't here by nine o'clock tonight I was packing up and going to the hotel."

"She was too drunk to notice anything," T-Dub said. "That was one thing and as soon as he passed out I took her out and dumped her."

Lula had the other earring adjusted now and she smiled at Bowie. "We have something to show you and if you will just sit there I'll bring it right back."

"Okeh," Bowie said.

Lula disappeared in the back. "She has been pretty-ing up for two hours just because you were coming, I think," T-Dub said.

"How you been gettin' along, T-Dub?"

"Just gettin' by. Chicamaw had to go over day before yesterday to MacMasters and get fifty dollars off that lawyer friend of his to buy us gasoline and something to eat."

"You don't mean you have throwed all that, do you?"

"I got a family on my back, Bowie. I sunk twelve thousand dollars in a tourist camp over in MacMasters for that bud of mine and Mattie."

"How is he?"

"We've had hard luck about him. The parole board turned him down. I think that next year, though, he'll make it."

"That's too bad. I guess old Mattie is still up in the air."

"Me and Lula have been having a pretty good time too. In that New Orleans. Money will just naturally get away from you fast down there."

"Chicamaw been with you?"

T-Dub shook his head, "I thought he was with you all the time and then I figured too that he wasn't. But I haven't seen him. He showed up here three nights ago it was. Drinking jake."

"I'll swear. I wish he would ease up on that drinking a little."

Lula came in. She had a roll of parchment-looking paper tied in a red ribbon and she looked at T-Dub now. "Do you want me to show it to him?"

T-Dub was grinning and his head went up and down.

Lula, smelling of fresh perfume, bent toward Bowie,

unrolling the parchment and then spread it on his knees. It was a Marriage License.

"Did you two go and get hitched?"

T-Dub's head was still going up and down.

"Why, you got your right name on here, T-Dub," Bowie said.

"Just turned the initials around. W. T. Masefeld."

"That sure floors me," Bowie said. He handed the license back up to Lula.

"How are you and that little Oklahoma girl getting along?" T-Dub said.

Bowie's eyes quivered. "Who is that?"

"What's her name? Keechie. Keechie Mobley?"

"What do you know about her?"

"You remember, Bowie. I met her when we were all up there at Dee's place. I didn't know though that you two had teamed up until I begin to see that stuff in the papers."

Bowie's Adam's apple ached like it had been hit and he could not swallow. "What stuff is that?"

"Haven't you been seeing any of it?"

Bowie shook his head.

"I read something just last Sunday I think it was," Lula said. "Had her picture."

"Picture?" Bowie said.

"Why, hell, Bowie, I thought you knew all about that. That Dee Mobley up there claims you kidnaped her and I told Lula here that all that guy had done was yellowed up. Some Law got to pumping him and he just about let out that kind of a squawk, I told Lula here that that was the way it was. I knew damned well you wouldn't kidnap anybody. I mean a girl like that."

"And it's in the papers?" Bowie said.

"The last one was just last Sunday," Lula said. "It was a picture of her, I know, that she had taken when she was going to high school."

"Huh," Bowie said.

"It will die down, Bowie. I wouldn't let it worry me."

"It don't worry me."

Lula went over and sat crosswise on T-Dub's legs; he spread them and she lay against him and put her arm around his neck, the Marriage License roll in her left hand.

That means you and me have come to the parting of the ways, Little Soldier, Bowie thought. You can't be running with me no more.

T-Dub and Lula made a smacking sound as they kissed.

You can go on back up to Oklahoma and get everything squared up, Bowie thought. Let them think, what they want. You have some money now, Little Soldier, and you can tell that old man of yours to go straight to Burning Hell.

"You go on back and pretty up some more, Sugar," T-Dub said. "Bowie and me want to talk a little business."

"Don't you go and get a headache now," Lula said.

I'd like to see some Law bother you while I'm gone, Bowie thought. Lay just one finger on you. I'll take care of myself, Brother Law, but you lay one finger on that girl and goddamn you, I'll get a machinegun and hunt *you* down!

Lula disappeared in the back of the house.

"This bank here is a bird's-nest on the ground," T-Dub said. "And it will go for fifty thousand or not a dime."

"I can use money," Bowie said. "A man never knows when he's going to need money and plenty of it in this business."

"You're not going to get three boys like us together every day," T-Dub said. "That is the way I look at it."

"And Chicamaw has been feeling pretty low?"

"Bowie, I think he would charge that bank tomorrow by himself if you and me both backed out."

"Well, he won't have to do it by himself."

~§~

They robbed the First National Bank of Gusherton at *10:01* o'clock the following morning, Chicamaw looking like a man with galloping consumption and driving Bowie's car; T-Dub complaining of rheumatism. There were no rumbles and at *10:15* they were switching cars, setting a match to Bowie's machine, and at *10:30* Chicamaw drove T-Dub's car, T-Dub and Bowie crouched in the back, into the garage of their house at the edge of the city. Chicamaw went on in the house and fifteen minutes later T-Dub and then, after another interval, Bowie.

The bank went for only seventeen thousand dollars.

At noon, T-Dub fried bacon and eggs and made toast, but only Chicamaw ate. Bowie drank coffee.

That afternoon there was a football game on the radio and Bowie lost ten dollars to Chicamaw.

"You guys give me the jitters," Chicamaw said. "Why don't you say something?"

"You need a drink," T-Dub said.

"I need something to taper off on and just as soon as it gets dark I'm going to town and get it."

A little before dusk a car entered the driveway and they picked up guns, but it was only some damned bastard turning around to go back to town.

At dusk, T-Dub said he was going up to the first Drug Store and give Lula a ring at the Red Bonnet Hotel. "I might just go on down and pick her up and we'll shell out for New Orleans right tonight. You want to go down with me, either one of you?"

"I do," Chicamaw said.

"If you boys are going, I think I'll just go with you too," Bowie said. "You can just drop me off at the bus station. I got some business to attend to and I want to get it over with."

Chicamaw had his hat on his head. "Why don't you hang around with us some, Bowie? I believe you're getting stuck up or something."

"I'll see you boys pretty soon."

"You want to watch yourself on these busses," T-Dub said.

"When I get down the line a couple of hundred miles I'll hop off and get me a car," Bowie said.

T-Dub named the night club on Bourbon Street in New Orleans and said he and Lula would be in it the night of December first.

"Okeh," Bowie said, "I guess you'll be there too, Chicamaw?"

"If I don't stump my toe," Chicamaw said.

~§~

The child in the shrunken coat slid off the Waiting Room bench, stood there, the drawers leg hanging, her hands behind her, looking at Bowie. He winked again. The child approached and when she got close, she thrust out her hand, palm up, fingers stretched.

"Oh, you want a nickel?" Bowie said.

The mother got up, a woman in a faded red coat with a cheap fur collar, and came toward them with her hands outstretched. "Is she bothering you?" she said.

"I should say not. Where are you going, Little Lady?"

"Grandpa's," Little Lady said. She extended the other hand now. "Why of all things, honey," the woman said.

Bowie placed the quarter on the child's palm and the fingers closed about it. "How about you sittin' up here by me a little while?" Bowie said. He patted the bench. The child looked at the coin and then up at her mother. The woman helped her up on the bench.

The hard heels of the Policeman scraped on the tile floor toward the ticket window and he talked for a moment with the clerk there and then turned and moved back toward the door. At the door, he stepped back and then aside and two girls in fur coats, carrying weekend bags entered, a man in a tweed topcoat following. The Policeman went on out and the girls and the tweed-coated man stood at the ticket window now.

Bowie carried Little Lady in his arms, and inside the crowded bus a bald-headed man in the third seat got up and gave Bowie and the Mother his seat.

The woman talked. The skin in the hollows of her eyes had the coloring of tobacco-stained cigarette paper. She said her husband was a barber and couldn't find work and she was going now to her father until things got better. The child was just getting over a bad cold.

Little Lady slept on Bowie's lap, and now he shifted her a little so her head would not touch the hardness of the gun under his arm. The mother said she was hoping her husband had work by Christmas.

The fingernails of Little Lady's limp fingers were black-rimmed and looked like paper. Keechie's nails were always clean and rounded short and pretty; not long and sharp like Lula's. The night before he left she had trimmed his toenails. All right now, Big Boy, don't start that stuff . . . . Now this woman here was having a tough time. She could stand a little piece of money and here he was with almost six thousand dollars on him.

The Mother was silent now, her head pressed back against the seat, eyes closed. Pasteboard showed through the paint of the purse on her lap.

What if he slipped a twenty in that purse? If he picked up that purse and she grabbed out and started yelling? It would win the fur-lined bathtub. It would bring him luck to get some money in that purse though. If he got five twenty-dollar bills in that purse and she didn't wake up it would break any jinx that was waiting up this road here. If be counted to thirteen and got five twenties in that purse there wouldn't anything stop him on this trip.

The woman was snoring now, the money in her purse.

A little after daybreak, Little Lady and her Mother left the bus and at eight o'clock, in San Angelo, Bowie got off and at ten o'clock he was driving south in the new automobile.

The clouds above the lowering sun looked like a picture of sea waves in the moonlight. A tiny flame was burning in Bowie's stomach. I've got to eat something. I haven't had anything to eat since . . . . Jesus Christ . . . . I haven't eaten since day before yesterday. I'll be dog-goned. I'm going to fool around and starve myself to death. Thinking about other things and here I am starving myself to death.

The sign read: *EATS*. Bowie drove into the broad parkway and stopped close to the screened door of the roadside lunch stand, a low frame structure plastered with tin beer signs.

Bowie went in. There were a Counter and five stools and a playing electric gramophone by a slot machine. A man in a white apron came from the back through the arched door and moved up inside the counter. The face of a woman peered through the kitchen slot.

"Soft boil me two and coffee," Bowie said. He straddled the first stool.

The man had a double chin, lumpy and soft-looking like the belly of a frog.

The gramophone was playing *El Rancho Grande*. Next to the cash register, held by the bottle of catsup and white mustard jar, was a folded newspaper. Bowie reached toward the newspaper and then brought his hand back. To hell with them damned newspapers.

The music ended and the machine made a clicking sound and was still. Frog Chin moved around the cash register and presently the coin slot jingled and then the machine was playing again: *El Rancho Grande.*

Bowie stirred the soft-boiled eggs and then broke crackers and dropped the crumbs into the glass. He got the salt and pepper and then picked up the newspaper. It was a San Antonio paper. He took a bite and then spread the front page:

GUSHERTON, Texas, Nov. 16— One bandit was dead here tonight, another wounded and the wife-accomplice of the slain desperado was in jail as a vengeful aftermath of the bold, $17,000 holdup of the First National Bank here this morning.

The dead bandit is T. W. (Tommy Gun) Masefeld, escaped Oklahoma convict and sought for two months in connection with a half-dozen bank robberies in West Texas. He was shot to death by officers as he sat in a car parked in front of the Red Bonnet Hotel. His companion, Limo (Three-Toed) Mobley, badly wounded, was in the hospital here under heavy guard.

Bowie A. Bowers, fast-triggered killer and leader of the bank bandit gang, had still eluded late tonight the combing search of a posse that numbered more than 300 peace officers and outraged citizens.

Mrs. Lula Masefeld, reputed wife of the slain bandit, was captured a few minutes after the shooting and lodged in jail.

The downtown gun battle terrorized scores of pedestrians and sent motorists scurrying for safety. The officers beat their quarry to the draw and neither bandit was able to fire.

Ten thousand dollars of the First National Bank loot was recovered in the bullet-riddled automobile. Credit for the heavy blow against the gang was being given tonight to Hotel Detective Chris Lawton. It was he who secured the tip that resulted in the laying of a trap for the bandit gang.

"What's the matter," Frog Chin said, "aren't them eggs all right?"

"Sure," Bowie said. He dipped the spoon into the glass.

At least three men and possibly two women participated in the sensational robbery here. Two bandits, identified as Bowie Bowers and Masefeld, entered the bank at 10 o'clock, forced a half-dozen bank workers and officials and a dozen customers into the vault at the points of six-shooters, rifled the safe and tills and escaped in the waiting car of confederates. Witnesses who saw the bandit machine speed away declared there was a woman in it.

Bowers, who escaped from the Oklahoma Penitentiary while serving a life term for murder, is wanted in connection with the murders of two Texaco City peace officers and a half-dozen bank robberies in Oklahoma, Kansas and Texas. Phantom-like, he has been seen traveling about the country in high-speed motor cars with a woman companion, said by Oklahoma authorities to be Keechie Mobley, cousin of the bandit wounded and captured here tonight.

"Those eggs done enough for you?"

"Fine," Bowie said. He took a bite and the food was like the man's phlegm in his mouth.

A woman is believed to have figured in Bowers' escape in Texaco City just as authorities here believe his disappearance here was abetted by a woman.

Mobley was suffering from wounds in the head and chest, but attending physicians declared he had a fighting chance to live. If he survives, however, he faces the electric chair. District Attorney Herbert Morton announced here tonight that he would ask the supreme penalty in the event Mobley went to trial.

"I loved Tommy more than anything in the world," pretty 19-year-old Lula Masefeld sobbed in her jail cell tonight. "He was the best thing in the world to . . . ."

Bowie folded the newspaper and placed it back behind the bottle and jar. Then he got up and reached in his pocket before the cash register.

"It is getting so that you can't please anybody these days," Frog Chin said.

"I just wasn't hungry," Bowie said.

As he walked toward the car, his feet felt like clumps of prickly pear.

Chapter 19

The green-shaded lamp in the kitchen of *Welcome Inn* was burning, their signal that there had been no rumbles while he was gone, and now he closed the car door quietly and the leaves on the walk crackled under his moving shoes. He lifted on the knob so the door would not scrape and went in. Pale coals studded the mound of dark ashes in the fireplace and then he saw Keechie sitting on the end of the cot by the shadowy radio.

"I'm back," he said and he had the feeling that no sound had left his mouth and the words were melting in his hollow stomach. He strained: "I saw the light burning. You remembered all right."

"I did not know whether you were coming back or not," Keechie said.

He went over and stood on the hearth, clasping his hands behind him. Water dripped in the kitchen sink. "How has everything been?"

"All right."

The motor of a speeding car way over on the highway beat like a tom-tom.

"You want me to turn that light off in the kitchen?" Bowie said.

"If you want to."

"It doesn't matter. It really doesn't make any difference to me."

"I don't see that it makes any difference whether you

came back here or not."

The heat at the base of his skull ignited and a film-like smoke, burned his eyes. "Oh, you mean about me, I guess?"

"Yes."

"Everything has happened pretty fast," he said. "Before you could say Jack Robinson, everything happened. You know about it?"

"Yes."

"About you?"

"Yes."

He moved toward her. "Doggone it, Keechie. I didn't mean for you to get mixed up in a business like this."

"Don't you worry about me."

He stopped.

"I will have to learn to take care of myself."

"All that old money is yours, Keechie. It will take care of you. Just don't go back around that . . . . that old man of yours."

"I am not going back there. Don't worry about that."

"You will have to go back there, I guess. But don't you worry about that business. Them goddamned ding-bats can't put nothing on you, nothing in this God's world."

"When did you start thinking about me?"

"Thinking about you?"

"You surely didn't think about me when you were gone?"

"Didn't think about you while I was gone?"

Keechie stood up. "You lied to me. *Lied.*"

"Why, Keechie." He moved toward her. "Why, you

don't understand, Keechie."

"Don't you touch me." Her fists were clenched. "You took them. It was me or them and you knew it and you took them."

He lowered his hands. "I don't like to talk about them boys."

"They don't mean anything to me. They never did. You knew that. All right, you and me are through."

She was going toward the door now and he saw that she had on the cravenette coat and there were her to bags on the floor. "Where are you going?" he said.

"What does it matter to you?"

He reached her, bent and grasped the wrist of the hand reaching for the bag. She wrenched from him. "I told you not to touch me."

"You wait a minute," he said.

She stood there, making breathing sounds like her nostrils were stopped.

"You want to leave this way?" he said.

"Absolutely."

"Sore like this?"

"Whatever you want to call it."

His groin felt like it was emptying.

"Is that all?" Keechie said.

"You wait a minute."

"You won't stop me."

"No, I won't stop you, but you just wait a minute."

She stood there and now he turned and went over to the fireplace and looked at the smothering coals. He went into the kitchen and came back with crumpled papers and kindling and he scattered the ashes and placed them on the coals. The papers blazed and then he arranged sticks of wood on the flames.

"You don't have any business leaving this time of night," he said. "If anybody is going to leave this house, it's me."

"I'm not staying here."

"All right. Now I'm going to get it straight after a while. If you just have to go, all right. Now I'm going out this door here, and I'm going to be gone on a long walk and if nothing will do you, but you have to go, there's a car out there and the keys are in it and you know, where the money is."

"I don't want anything of yours."

"Don't be a damned fool." The knob grated with his wrench and he went out the door.

A bulbous crescent hung heavily in the bottom of the moon's slate-colored disk. Wind gushed in the trees with the sound of a distant river and the tops of the cedars, silhouetted against the cobalt and starlit heavens, whipped and threshed like tiny Christmas trees in a storm. He walked now on the gray wood-cutters' road that twisted and slashed deep into the woods.

This is what you wanted, isn't it, Big Boy? It had to stop some time and what's the difference how it happened? You just keep going down this road and walk, by God, until these damned legs of yours come off. *Keechie in front of the oil heater in the Bunk, floor dust tatting the hem of her skirt.* All right now, don't start that stuff.

The wind's chill crawled under his trouser cuffs and down the neck of his collar and he turned up his lapels. I have plenty of things to do. Nothing in this old world will do you anymore good, T-Dub, but, Chicamaw, you got a friend. Don't you think different for a minute, boy. You're just as liable as not to be running these roads again with me pretty soon and it's not going to be any year from now.

His shadow glided on the road beside him, stubby and slender. *Keechie picking cigarette butts off the floor to make him a smoke with a cigarette paper she had found.* Now lay off that, stuff, goddamit. What difference does it make how it happened, just so it happened? Okeh. Okeh. Okeh. *Okeh!*

The broken tree stump yonder with its two short, outflung limbs looked like a man. Bowie pressed his hand against the gun's butt in the holster under his arm. Hell, I don't need a gun with one Law. Brave men. Heroes. Fifty of them to get one Thief, hundred, two hundred, three hundred. Big Shots. Heroes.

A plummeting meteor fragment streaked the heavens like the spark of a shaken log, vanished. That means you're gone, Little Soldier. That means you have left.

He left the woods now, moved across the clearing toward *Welcome Inn,* in a dawning mist that blew like sifted ashes.

The car stood where he, had left it. Christ, girl, you didn't leave this place walking? Now you didn't do *that.* Why, girl, you're liable to get in trouble . . . . Smoke was coming from the chimney.

She sat in front of the burning logs, smoking a cigarette, her coat off. "I couldn't leave," she said.

His neck was rigid, fixed; he could not move it.

"I couldn't leave," she repeated.

"I noticed the car out there," he said.

"There wasn't anything for me Out There," she said. "Nothing. *Nothing!*"

Bowie placed his hand on her shoulder, patted. "You ought to turn in."

"I guess so."

"That is what I would do."

After a little while, Keechie got up and moved toward the sleeping-room and he followed; stood in the doorway and watched her lie down on the bed. Then he went over and sat on the edge.

"I didn't want to leave you," Keechie said.

His head went up and down.

"You wouldn't have let me go, would you, Bowie?"

"No."

"Even if I had wanted to?"

"You would have made me stay?"

"Yes."

"I help you, don't I, Bowie?"

"Yes."

"A whole, whole lot?"

"Yes."

Keechie closed her eyes and presently she sucked in a deep breath through her mouth and nose, jerked convulsively and he placed his hands on her. She jerked again, easier though, and now her mouth was closed and she slept. Bowie took the gun out of his holster and placed it just under the edge of the bed, loosened his tie, unbuttoned his collar. Then he lay down beside her.

Chapter 20

Keechie said it looked like Santa Claus would have to come this year in a boat instead of a sleigh. It had rained for six days. In the daytime, the rain-shrouded woods and hills were merged with the sky and their cottage stood on a tiny island. They went to bed at night with the rain caressing their roof and awoke in the morning with it still beating a gentle, broken rhythm.

It was getting close to five o'clock this afternoon and any time now Alvin Philpott, the little boy, would be showing up with the San Antonio newspaper. Bowie had made a deal with him four weeks before, fifty cents a week, and every afternoon now, as Alvin came home from school, he brought a paper. They were going to get the boy something for Christmas. That was only four days off now.

"How would you like to have a little eggnog for Christmas?" Keechie said. She stood there in the kitchen doorway, a sweet potato in one hand, a peeling knife in the other.

Bowie placed Keechie's polished oxford on the floor and picked up the other one. "Did you ever drink any of that?"

Keechie shook her head. "Maybe I did when I was little, I don't know. I just saw a recipe in the paper and I think nearly everybody drinks it around Christmas time. The eggs in it are good for you."

"If it's just the same to you," Bowie said, "we'll just get a quart of whisky and drink it straight. But no eggnogs for me. I got sick as a horse on it once and I swore to God in heaven that if I ever got over it, I would never drink no more eggnog no more."

Keechie laughed and went back into the kitchen. They were going to have pork chops and candied sweet potatoes with marshmallows for supper.

Bowie rubbed the brown polish into Keechie's shoe. We'll do something Christmas all right, he thought. It won't be just like any other day. He had that Christmas present to his Mama off his mind flow. One thousand dollars. He and Keechie had driven yesterday to San Antonio and mailed the envelope. There was one thing, though, he had to do pretty soon and that was get some money to that lawyer friend of Chicamaw's in MacMasters. Archibald J. Hawkins. He and Keechie would have to go back to San Antonio and attend to that. Two thousand dollars in an envelope to a lawyer? The guy might be dead and somebody else would get it? The thing to do was go in some bank in San Antonio and get a draft and send it to Hawkins. Lawyers knew better than to go south with a thief's money. That one in Tulsa had found that out. Now he could send Chicamaw a postal order for one hundred dollars. In the Christmas rush in them banks and post-offices in San Antonio, nobody would big-eye Keechie or him.

The screen rattled and Bowie got up and went to the door. It was Alvin. Water dripped from the boy's nose and he pulled the dry newspaper from underneath his soggy coat.

"You going to get wet, boy, if you ain't careful," Bowie said.

"It don't bother me," Alvin said.

After Alvin left, Bowie went back to the kitchen. "I know now what we will get that kid," he said. "A rain-coat."

"That will be better than a shotgun," Keechie said.

There was nothing in the newspapers. There was enough in there day before yesterday, Bowie thought. Chicamaw was going to trial February fourth. That lawyer Hawkins sure had to have some money pretty soon because they would sure put the Chair on Chicamaw if he didn't get some money.

After supper, Keechie and Bowie played checkers. It was raining harder now, wind whistling in the window-screens and water splashing in the puddles under the eaves.

Bowie stacked the checkers in the box with the sliding top. "You know I been thinking, Keechie, about what you said the other day about it being easier for a woman to disguise than a man. I believe it's easier for a man when you get to thinking about it. A man can grow a beard and wear glasses and get his hair cut different."

"He can't use powder and paint though."

"He sure can. He can dress up like a woman and get by with it."

"I'd like to see you dressed up like a woman."

"Not me."

"And I'm not going to dress up like a man."

"I know it," Bowie said. "But you know, Keechie, there's men in this world though that go around all the time dressed up like women. They're no good."

"There was a woman in Keota that smoked cigars and acted just like a man," Keechie said.

"Them people are no good, Keechie. Absolutely. They're no good."

"There are more no-good people in this world than there are good ones," Keechie said, "A blind man can see that."

"Up there in Alky, Keechie, you never saw the like. You would never have thought so many no-good people could be gotten up all together at one time. That was one of the reasons why I just couldn't stand it there any longer. I don't know though, but what it's just about the same Out Here."

The window-screens whined and Bowie listened. Then he put his finger in his ear and jiggled it. "Yessir, Keechie, I think you hit the nail on the head when you said that the only way to beat this game was just go off and pull the Hole in after you. Not have a single friend."

"You can't trust anybody, Bowie."

"I've always said that, honey. Hell, I wouldn't trust Jesus Christ if he come right in this door right in this door right this minute."

"You just have to depend on yourself in this world and nobody else," Keechie said.

Bowie got up and placed the box of checkers and the board on the mantel. He turned, placed his elbows on the mantel's edge and pushed his stomach out away from the heat. "But you know, Keechie, you never will see three boys like us together again. I think about that Chicamaw up there in that jail pulling through by himself and I'll bet he doesn't even have cigarette money."

"Nobody but a lawyer can help him now."

"I know it. That's what I have been thinking about. I'll bet that boy is beginning to think that he doesn't have a friend in this world."

"There is nothing you can do about it. Unless you want to get him some money."

"That will do it, Keechie. It will do it nine times out of ten in this world. That's what I have to do. Get him a lawyer lined up. And a good one."

"You don't have to go anywhere around him though?"

"What are you talking about? I should say not. No, all I have to do is to get some mazuma to a good lawyer and that will be all there is to it."

Keechie got up and went over to the wood box. She carried the stick to the fireplace and said: "Move over a little, Bowie."

Sparks popped under the dropped wood and Keechie stood there watching the flames lengthen.

"Don't that rain sound good, Bowie?"

"What did you say, Keechie?"

"I said don't you like to hear that rain on the house?"

"Uh huh. I sure do. You bet I do."

"I like it," Keechie said.

The floor planks creaked as Bowie began moving about. "I should have brought in more wood today," he said. "I guess this rain is just going to keep on forever."

~§~

On Christmas Eve morning, icicles hung from the eaves, but the day was breaking clear. The sun was going to shine. Bowie and Keechie lay in bed, talking now about how Alvin was going to act when they gave him the raincoat this afternoon. They had bought the raincoat in Antelope Center yesterday and also a half-dozen, handkerchiefs that they were going to give Alvin to give to Filthy MacNasty.

"If we're going to go to San Antonio this morning and get back here by four o'clock, we got to be gettin' up and going," Bowie said. "We're not going to get any business done much less seeing a show at this rate."

"Well, I don't see nothing holding you down in this bed, Booie-Wooie," Keechie said.

"You usually get up before I do, don't you? What's got hold of your legs this morning? Can't you take them icicles this morning?"

"Sure. I was just waiting to see you show what a he-man you are. Why don't you get up and start the fire this morning?"

"Who, me?"

"I hope it's you and not somebody else I'm talking to."

"By God, I hope so too. Now let me see. All I got to do is just get up and sort of walk in there to that fireplace. All right, you win, Keechie-Weechie." Bowie swept back the covers, got out, tucked the blankets back under

Keechie and trotted, barefooted, into the cold living room.

In the kitchen, Bowie saw the flooded floor and then the burst pipe of the shower in the bathroom.

"I will go and get Filthy and tell him to phone a plumber," Keechie said.

"No, you just stay here," Bowie said. "I'll go."

It was ten o'clock when the rattling, banging Ford pick-up with the vise stopped in front of the cottage. Bowie the mop in his hand, stood at the window and watched the plumber get out. The man had a head shaped like an Irish potato and an unlit cigar stub in the corner of his mouth.

"You the folks that are having a little trouble out here?" Plumber said.

Bowie thumbed toward the back. "Bathroom."

Plumber looked at Keechie standing by the bed.

"In the bathroom," Bowie said.

Plumber's smile was soggy. The cigar stub darkened against his draining face. "We been swamped," he said. "Freeze. Bathroom?"

Bowie pointed.

Plumber moved across the living room and into the, hallway toward the bath.

Bowie turned and looked at Keechie.

Keechie framed the question with soundless, lips: What do you think?

Bowie's head went up and down.

Plumber came out of the hallway walking briskly toward the door. "Tools," he said.

They watched him through the window. He got in the

pick-up, started the motor and then the machine moved off with a violent jerk.

Bowie pointed at Keechie's coat. "Get on out and start our car."

Mud-thickened water geysered from the puddles at the Gate and splattered on their windshield. Bowie pressed the wiper button and then turned onto the highway. The road extended ahead, gray and slick as phlegm; gravel rattled under the fenders.

"Light me a cigarette," Bowie said.

Keechie looked in the panel pocket. "We don't have a one, Bowie, not a one."

"Can you beat that?"

"We will get some."

"Can you beat that? Now that's what I call luck for you. You mean to say there's not a one there?"

"We will get some, Bowie."

"Now that's what I call luck."

Thunder rolled. It was like the hills around them had been undermined and were bumping around.

"I'm sure fed up on rain," Bowie said. "I'm sure fed up on it."

"Where are we going, Bowie?"

"MacMasters."

"MacMasters?"

"I'm going to see a lawyer there."

"MacMasters," Keechie repeated.

The highway stretched on like a long ribbon of wet funeral cloth; the rain-drunk weeds of the right-of-way rushing behind.

"Alvin won't get his raincoat," Keechie said. "It was

laying there on the radio."

Bowie cleared his throat, "I been thinking. It's a good thing we gassed up yesterday and got them cans filled. What if we were just starting out with a couple of gallons like we had yesterday morning? By golly, we sure got some gas in this buggy."

"We're lucky," Keechie said.

Chapter 21

The house of J. Archibald Hawkins, the lawyer, was a straight, two-story house with a porch of warped planks and next to the First Christian Church. In the furniture-stuffed Front Room, there was a roll-desk, its top stacked with law books of tan and red cloth; a piano with two hymn-books on the rack and framed portraits on the shawl-scarfed top. The worn places in the carpet looked like burlap sacking and on the square of cracked linoleum by the broad, sliding door a gas-stove ejected long, curling flames.

When Hawkins smiled, his eyes became wrinkled pockets and his cheeks looked like balls wrapped in cellophane. His Sister, who lived with him, had, gone to Amarillo to see her son and it had looked like he was going to spend Christmas night alone. "It appears though," he said, "that I have some pretty distinguished company."

Bowie, sitting there on the claw-carved leather divan,

grinned, and Keechie looked down and covered the strip of house dress over her legs with the coat's skirt.

"Now about Chicamaw again, Judge?" Bowie said.

We will get him fixed up, Hawkins said. He did not practice criminal law himself, he added, but he knew personally the members of the Law Firm in Gusherton who could do something with the case. It would take money though.

"How much?" Bowie said.

Hawkins smiled. "Just about all they decide a man has."

"Around how much?"

"I know this firm will not take a case for less than two thousand."

"Say three thousand?" Bowie said.

Hawkins nodded. "It is a pretty good newspaper case too."

"I'd like to see Chicamaw get some money too. Think you can manage it?"

"I can see him very easily."

"And I'll leave you five hundred for all this trouble."

"I can certainly use it."

Bowie crossed his leg and leaned forward with his elbow on his knee and chin in hand. "You know anything how that happened in Gusherton? Them boys gettin' in trouble, I mean?"

Hawkins nodded. "Yes, I know. That girl. What is her name? Masefeld's wife."

"Good lord," Bowie said. "Sure enough?"

"It was pure simple-mindedness. That hotel detective over there made some advances that were unwelcome to her and, instead of ignoring them, she made a scene, complained to the Manager and said she had a husband and plenty of money. It seems this hotel detective got suspicious then sure enough and plugged in on her telephone. He got the tip that way."

"I'll swear," Bowie said.

"She is going to testify for the State in Chicamaw's trial."

"I'll swear."

Keechie said they had better be going.

Hawkins said that he had a big chicken back there in the oven and it would only take a half-hour for it to warm. Wouldn't they keep an old man company a little on Christmas night?

Bowie looked at Keechie. She consented.

The lawyer talked. There're more millionaires in this country than in any other, he said, and at the same time more robbers and killers. Therein lay significance. Extremes in riches make extremes in crime. As long as a Social System permitted the acquisition of extreme riches, there would be equalizing crime and the Government and all law-enforcement organizations might as well fold their hands and accept it.

"The Rich," Hawkins said, "can't drive their big auto mobile and flaunt bediamonded wives and expect every man just to simply look on admiringly. The sheep will do it and the sheep will even laud it and support it, but at the same time these sheep will feel something that they do not understand and demonstrate it and that is known as so-called glorification of the big criminal,"

"I'm not proud of nothing I ever done," Bowie said.

Money interests fix the punishment for crime in this country, Hawkins said, and consequently there is no moral justice. A bum steals a pair of shoes from another and that is a great crime, but what will happen to the complaining bum at the police station? If that same thief pilfers fifteen cents from the telephone box of a big utility company, he can receive fifteen years, but if he snatches that amount from the cup of a blind beggar, he may get a twenty-dollar fine.

Hawkins' stomach gurgled and Bowie looked down, saw the dried mud on the toe of his shoe and then looked at Keechie's shoes. There was mud on them too.

"Now you take the Stupid Sheep I was talking about a moment ago," Hawkins said, "just like this young fellow that lives right down here in a little two-room apartment across the corner from me. He drives a milk truck for a millionaire creamery man here and he works ten and twelve hours a day and he goes home at night and there is a baby that he has to help his wife with. His wife is sick. Still weak and unable to work from bearing that child. Now you take that boy. Is it strange that he doesn't feel what these newspapers yap about glorification of the criminal?"

"These newspapers never get nothing straight," Bowie said. "They got me working in towns that I have never even been inside of."

"There is nothing like a manhunt and trust the newspapers to make an arena and ballyhoo the Kill. The Romans were not cruel. At least no more cruel than these newspapers that get their readers' tongues hanging out for the Kill. And just here last week the Chamber of

Commerce gave the Creamery Millionaire a silver loving-trophy as being MacMasters' most useful citizen of the year. And the irony of it all is that you take that fourteen dollar-a-week boy that is working for him and put him on a jury and some Prosecutor who wants his name in the newspapers more than anything else will have that boy thinking that red-hot spikes are too mild for a bank robber."

"I get a kick out of robbing banks," Bowie said. "I don't mind admitting it."

Keechie touched the back of Bowie's hand. "It's getting pretty late."

"We'll go in a minute, honey."

"We have some chicken coming up," Hawkins said. "I bet you young folks think I am a long-winded old cuss."

"Go on," Bowie said. "I like to hear you."

"Speaking of crime," Hawkins said. His stomach gurgled. "There was a Consumptive that come down here from Detroit in an old rattletrap here a couple of months ago and he had two little dogs. That is all that man had and he moved in a little shack on the river down here close to town and then that ranchman, who lived across the river and is worth, I guess, fifty thousand dollars, killed those two dogs with a shotgun and there is not a law in this state that will punish that cold-blooded, low-down, degenerate murderer."

"'Fraid he would get a cow bit, I guess?" Bowie said.

"That. But that man shoots dogs down like he would rattlesnakes."

"They caught a fellow in the town I used to live in,"

Keechie said, "throwing weenies with poison in them out to dogs. He was just driving around town doing it."

Bowie looked at her. "You never did tell me about that," he said.

"Prisons are simply pimples on a corrupt world," Hawkins said. "The great criminals, I mean the real enemies of man's welfare and peace and happiness, never go near a prison and the dead ones, out in these cemeteries, have the highest tombstones over their heads. Normal men with abnormal tendencies. Abnormal men with normal tendencies. My God. It is a wonder people do not smell, their minds are so rotten. Excuse me, young lady."

"Them capitalist fellows are thieves like us," Bowie said.

"They rob widows and orphans."

"I do not fool myself one minute," Hawkins said. "I possess that. You take me, Bowers, and that five hundred you have given me. I am going to run for Justice of the Peace this spring. When an old broken-down lawyer gets old, Son, he runs for Justice of the Peace."

"You don't look old," Bowie said.

"Anyway I am going into this next election and I rather think I am going to have that Office. I will get a couple of constables, gun-toters, and these boys will go out and break up Negro dice games, raid petty little homebrew joints in Mexican-town and take in some of these tourists that are exceeding the speed limit by a few miles. We will make good fees. Vultures are all we are."

"I guess a man has to make a living," Bowie said.

"In this system he is forced to be a criminal."

"I never robbed nobody that couldn't stand to lose it," Bowie said.

Hawkins looked at Keechie. "And whatever road a man takes there is always a woman that will follow him."

"If this man here will just get up and start," Keechie said, "I will follow him right now."

"Don't pay no attention to her, Judge," Bowie said.

The gurgling sounded in Hawkins' stomach again.

~§~

The strung, colored lights of this town's Main Street illuminated an empty, quiet thoroughfare. On the Court House lawn, a big, lighted Christmas tree glowed greens and reds and yellows. The sign at the edge of the town read: *New Orleans . . . 590 mi.*

"You think we will be there this time tomorrow night?" Keechie said.

"Uh huh. Keechie, I can just see that Indian's face when them big lawyers start coming in his cell. He's sure going to know he's got a friend Out Here."

"You have done everything you could now."

Bowie turned his head toward her and grinned. "Say, did you hear Old Windy's guts growling?"

"I thought he was never going to stop talking."

"I never heard anything like it," Bowie said. "You could have heard it out in the street."

Chapter 22

Bowie and Keechie had the renting of a furnished house on their minds when they entered New Orleans, but it was late and they were so tired that they looked at an apartment and there were so many nice things about the very first one that they took it. The place—*The Colonial Apartments—was* a remodeled home and as big as an old West Texas court house. On an avenue of palm-fenced homes and big churches, this house was shadowed and darkened by spreading cottonwoods and hackberries, and crêpe myrtles screened the windows.

Mrs. Lufkin was the owner of *The Colonial Apartments.* She was a stout-bosomed woman with dyed black hair and smelled like a brewery. Mrs. Lufkin did not have much to do with the running of the apartments, leaving this to Rebecca, the little Negro woman with gold teeth. From Rebecca, Bowie and Keechie learned about the other occupants of the place: the Professor who taught in the University up the avenue; the Interne and his Nurse-Wife who were at the hospital most of the time; the four girls who lived in the two apartments upstairs and were students in the University. Rebecca said Mrs. Lufkin bought whisky five gallons at a time and she prayed for her every night.

The ceiling of their living room was so high that Keechie could not touch the plastered dome even when Bowie lifted her. There was a wide, high fireplace a log gas-heater. In a few days, when they made that one big shopping tour downtown, they would get a radio to put beside the library table and beaded parlor lamp. And a red-checkered cloth for the kitchen table, Keechie said.

The sleeping-room had a tiled floor and in it were wedged a bed and a clear-mirrored vanity. The kitchen was small too, but it would look a lot better, Bowie said, when that big pantry was filled with stuff to eat. The bathroom was as big as the kitchen and steaming water gushed from the *hot* tap. Now you can get all the baths you want, Bowie said, and when Keechie said she had been thinking about that, Bowie said he did not see how they had put up with it back in those Texas hills.

They would get a telephone put in, they decided, and any time there was drugstore buying or anything like that to do, they would have delivery boys bring it to their door. Rebecca had said that she went to the Grocery every morning and would be glad to get their things too. They would give her a few dollars a week, Bowie said, and that old black gal would break her neck for them. There would not be anybody to see except Rebecca and delivery boys and at nights they could duck in suburban picture shows.

The best thing about it all, Keechie said, was that no one in the world knew where they were. She lettered the slip that Bowie inserted in the slot of the mailbox in the lobby: *Mr. & Mrs. F. T. Haviland.*

When the trial of Chicamaw started back in Gusherton, Bowie waited in the kitchen every afternoon listening for the thump of the thrown newspaper on the back steps. There were three days of the trial and then on the fourth day, Bowie read in the Sunday morning paper of its outcome. Chicamaw had beaten the Chair. He had drawn a pair of nines—ninety-nine years.

Bowie carried the newspaper back to Keechie who was still in bed this Sunday morning. "That boy beat them," Bowie said. "They're not going to kick any Switch off on him. It's right here in the paper, Keechie."

"I'm glad," Keechie said.

"Go ahead and read it, Keechie. Here it is, right here."

"Now you will feel a lot better," Keechie said.

"And don't think he is just sittin' up there in that jail with his brains sittin' too. And he won't have to kill anybody to beat that Pen either. Any day you want to kill somebody, Keechie, you can beat a Pen easy."

"That is none of your worry now."

"Go ahead and read it. I'll stir up some breakfast. How about me cooking it up this morning? How about it?"

"All right."

By ten o'clock, sunlight was knifing through the crêpe myrtle and the raised windows, cutting bright squares on the living room carpet and blue linoleum of the kitchen. This is one day I'm not going to stay cooped up, Bowie thought. We're going to get out. Keechie sat on the vanity bench with a curling iron in her hand. She had on the Chinese wrapper with the yellow and red dragon designs.

"Let's get out of this place today, Keechie, What do you say?"

"Where?"

"Don't make one bit of difference to me. Just so we go."

"Would you like to go walking in that Park up the avenue?"

"You're doggone whistling."

Keechie put the curling iron on the vanity and stood up. "I've always wanted to go through it in the daytime. I'll wear my gray flannel suit."

"I'll strut out in that double-breasted. Say, Little Soldier, you're getting as broad as I don't know what."

Keechie looked down her body, at her hips.

"You're puttin' on plenty," Bowie said.

"Don't you like it?"

"I should say I do. You could get as big as the side of a barn and I'd like it."

"Well. There's no danger of that."

~§~

The lower limbs of the big oak in the Park grew on the ground as if the task of going up was too much. The gray Spanish moss that fringed the boughs, Keechie said, was whiskers and showed how old the trees were. They circled the tree now and moved across the smooth fairway of the golf course, pausing near the fluttering pennant on the green, and then went on toward the lagoon. A couple passed ahead of them, a wire-haired terrier straining on a leash held by the woman. The man bent down now to tie a shoelace and then trotted to catch up.

"If I had a dog I would want one of them big police babies," Bowie said. "They're mean as hell."

Swans glided on the lagoon, the traced water Smoothing behind them. Around the bend of water-dipping willows, a rowboat came, the oars splashing; three girls in it. The swans moved closer to the shore. On the boat were the letters *Nellie*. The girl rowing had on brown slacks and a white sweater. Bowie and Keechie lowered themselves to the grass on the bank's edge and watched the girls and the boat disappear around the bend below.

"What are you thinking about?" Keechie said.

"I had an aunt named Nell," Bowie said. "I was thinking about her."

"Your Daddy's sister?"

Bowie shook his head. "Mama's. We lived with her a while, I mean Grandma's, after my Dad got killed. It's funny that I got to thinking about her."

"What about her?"

"Oh, I don't know. She used to come on Sunday afternoons and bring a big old sack of red-hots and licorice drops and candy like that. You remember that kind of candy, don't you?"

Keechie nodded. She reached out and plucked a bit of grass from the silk of Bowie's socks.

"Makes me think of that boy I was running around with too then," Bowie said. "You know that kid, the last time I heard of him, was a big football player in Oklahoma University and he was just a cutter and a half. We were a pair now. His Dad was the County Treasurer in that town and why he was running around up back alleys and gettin' junk and sellin' it, I don't know. That boy had more devilment in him than anybody I ever did know. We got to going in vacant houses and tearing the plumbing out and selling the brass and lead. I remember one day we made eighty cents. We bought four of them nickel pies apiece. That kid always had money in his pockets. He would steal it out of his Dad's pants at nights."

Keechie plucked a blade of Bermuda grass and began chewing the white root.

"I don't know how come me to ever think of him, but he just knew about everything that was going on in that town. That's how come me to go out to them houses at the edge of town one day. The Red Light district. He said there was women out there who would give kids nickels and dimes if they just went out there and hung around the back door."

The hoofs of running horses sounded and then on the bridle path, on the other side of the lagoon and through the trees, they saw the bright jackets of the women riders.

"I saw her, but I don't think that she knows to this day that it was me. When the old woman in the house started hollering at us to get away, she come to the back door and I saw her."

"Saw who?" Keechie said.

Bowie looked at her. "My Aunt, I thought I told you."

"Oh," Keechie said.

"She didn't recognize me though."

Keechie leaned against Bowie's leg, picked another bit of dead grass and smoothed the silk. The horsewomen were passing yonder again, posting.

"Ain't that a helluva way to ride?" Bowie said. "Bobbing your bottom up and down like that?"

"Uh huh."

Bowie indicated the golf green behind them with a twist of his head. "That's something else I never figured why anybody could get interested in. Batting that little old ball around and puttin' it in holes."

"Some people don't have anything else to do," Keechie said. "It wouldn't bother me though if they stood on their heads if they were having a good time."

"Me neither."

They walked now along the lagoon's bank toward the white dome of the Memorial Bandstand. Bowie stopped and pointed at the rat swimming in the water toward the little island of weeping willows. "I'll bet that rat has him a hole over there," he said.

"I didn't know rats could swim," Keechie said.

"Their kind can. I know one kind that can't do anything but snitch. Them are yellow and have two legs."

"Oh," Keechie said. "Now I get you."

"I can tell you something else about some of these boys that are gettin' in trouble every day," Bowie said. "They like to see their names in the newspapers. Why, Keechie, there's guys that will put on acts and do anything just to get their names big in the newspapers."

"I had just as soon talk about something else," Keechie said.

"Just one more thing, Keechie. Have you been thinking about us not gettin' our names in the paper no more? There hasn't been hardly one thing since that damned plumber flushed us back yonder in them damned old rainy hills."

"Just don't do anything to get your name in the paper," Keechie said. "That is the thing."

"Say we got jumped here, Keechie. Now I know. There isn't a chance just as long as we keep our noses clean like we're doing. But just say we were. Where would you like to go?"

"I don't know."

"You know where I would like to go? Mexico. It takes somebody, though, that knows the ropes to get you across that border and situated good down there. Now you take Chicamaw, he knew the ropes down there from A to Z."

"Well, Chicamaw isn't here and he isn't going to be here."

"I know it. I was just telling you, honey."

The couple coming across the narrow rustic bridge were holding hands, and Bowie and Keechie stepped aside and gave them passageway. The girl had on a white silk dress and the black hair of the fellow grew long and curling down his neck. As they stepped off the bridge, the fellow put his arm around the girl supportingly.

Bowie and Keechie went on. "You can tell by looking at them they're not married," Bowie said.

"How can you tell?"

"I don't know. Just the way he was holding her hand as if she was going to fall off that bridge or something, I guess."

"Clever, aren't you?"

"I notice little things like that."

"Maybe she would have fallen off if he hadn't been helping her. Married or not married. A girl likes that anyway."

Bowie looked at her. "Say, do you want me to hold your hand like that?" He reached toward her. Keechie swept his hand down. "Just keep that to yourself," she said.

"Gollee, honey. What's come over you? What did I do?"

Keechie turned around. "Let's go home."

"Gollee, can you beat that. What have I done?"

Keechie started back and he caught up and walked alongside her again. Near the broad stone arch of the Park's exit, a bunch of boys, their shirt tails flapping, were playing with an indoor ball. Bowie asked Keechie to wait a minute and they stood there and watched the players a little while.

The sunshine was gone now and the air touched their bodies like cold feathers. The avenue would be quiet and then, with the spreading green of the green signal light down the thoroughfare, the gears of the waiting automobiles would grate and crash, and then they came, passing in rushing trains.

"I've been thinking about old T-Dub," Bowie said. "I guess that girl was just dumb. But you know they were like a couple of kids showing me that Marriage License."

"First I had heard about it," Keechie said.

"Didn't I ever tell you about that? Well, they were just

like a couple of kids, dragging that License out and showing it all around."

"I guess it mattered to them."

Bowie looked at Keechie, a loosened curl moved on
her upturned coat collar. "I guess it did," he said. "They
were like a couple of kids."

A streetcar crashed past, its trolley popping, a glued
mass of humanity through its closed windows. At the intersection, Bowie touched Keechie's arm as they stepped
down off the curb.

"Would you marry me, Keechie?"

She looked up at him, then ahead again. "I don't
know whether I would or not."

"Now just what do you mean by that?"

"I can't see what difference some writing on a scrap
of paper makes if that's what you are thinking about."

"I don't either. That's what I have been thinking.
What difference does a piece of red ribbon around some
paper make? Besides, you're married to me already if you
didn't know it."

Keechie looked up at him again. "Where do you get
that?"

"It's the law, Keechie. Honest. If you introduce a
woman three times in public as your wife you're just as
much married as if you had a Justice of the Peace and
nine preachers to do it. Honest. That's the law and you
can't get around it."

"I didn't know that."

"You take you and me now. All right, didn't Filthy
MacNasty get it that way and Mrs. Lufkin up here and
Rebecca and anybody that looks at that mailbox? You

can't get around it."

"I didn't know that."

"You can't get around it," Bowie said. "That's the law."

At the next crossing, he took her arm and held it the rest of the way home.

Chapter 23

For several days now Keechie had not been feeling well and this morning, after she smoked a cigarette, she felt sick at her stomach and had to lie down. Bowie rinsed towels under the cold tap in the kitchen and put them on her forehead.

It was only May, but the damp heat was like a jail cell in July. It clogged the nostrils and sweat streaked Bowie's cheeks from his sideburns. He said it was the heat that was making Keechie feel this way; that and the change of climate. The thing they had better do was go to town and duck in and see a doctor. Keechie said no, she had just been smoking too many cigarettes and everything would be all right in a day or so.

A little before noon, Keechie said sherbet appealed to her, pints and pints of it, orange or pineapple. Bowie said he would walk to the Drug Store and get it because it might take the delivery boy an hour to get here and he wanted her to have it while she was hungry.

On the newspaper rack in front of the Drug Store,

there was a Noon Edition and Bowie picked it up and went on in. The Soda Clerk was at the table of two women and Bowie went on to the fountain, spread the newspaper and began to read the headlines.

Soda Clerk placed his hands, palms down, on the surface at the edge of the spread newspaper and Bowie looked up. "Dollar's worth of orange and pineapple sherbet," he said.

In this headline, the words *Prison Farm* swelled and Bowie began reading underneath it:

BINGHAM, Texas, May 29— Deputy Sheriff Oscar Dunfling of Winkford County arrived here yesterday afternoon after a 650 mile trip with a bench warrant for the custody of Amos Ackerman, inmate of the Bingham Prison Farm, near here, but he was a half-hour too late to get his man alive. Ackerman, serving five years for assault with intent to kill, was shot to death by prison guards at 2:30 o'clock yesterday afternoon when, he made a bold dash for freedom.

Deputy Dunning was planning on returning Ackerman to Winkford County to testify in a scheduled murder trial there.

Ackerman, a trusty and member of a chopping-cotton squad working two miles from the prison buildings, was sent back to get some tools and on the way made his ill-fated break. When he did not show up, a search was instituted and prison dogs led guards to a pile of brush off the farm property. Ignoring the commands to halt, he was slain, prison officials stated.

The effort of Ackerman to escape, farm officials declared, was a lone attempt and not participated in by any other inmates. Extra precautions to prevent escapes were ordered by Farm Captain Fred Stammers today. There are several desperate criminals on the Farm now, including Elmo (Three-Toed) Mobley, bank robber, who arrived here last week from the State Penitentiary.

Outside, the sun stung Bowie's face like a shaving lotion and his knee-bones felt like dry sponges. He walked rapidly.

Water was gushing in the bathroom and Bowie went in there. In the filling tub, Keechie sat, her hair in a knot, water lapping the under-swell of her breasts.

"Feeling better, honey?" Bowie said.

"I'll say," Keechie said. There was the clean smell of soap and Keechie's body. Her long eyelashes clung to the wet skin. "What have you there in your hand?" she said.

"Paper."

The lathering soap in the washrag slowed.

"What's the matter?"

"Nothing. Except they got him on a goddamned farm."

"Chicamaw?"

Keechie turned and looked at the gushing tap and then she bent and twisted it shut.

"You can't imagine what it is to be on one of those farms," Bowie said. "He won't last six months. They don't send you out to them farms unless they want to get rid of you. If you're any kind of a man you won't last, and by God, he's a man."

Keechie placed the soap and cloth on the rack and then pulled the stopper. The draining water began to swish and gurgle.

Bowie took the bathmat off the basin and straightened it on the tile at the side of the tub. "It's cotton-chopping time now and you know what they do to them boys? Run 'em out there like horses and kick 'em with spurs and hit 'em with saps. They drop dead out in them fields, Keechie. Five of them in one day. It was in the papers."

"Well, you can't do anything about it."

Bowie helped her over the tub's rim, put the towel about her shoulders.

"Something could be done about it all right!" he said.

"For instance?"

"I mean if a man wanted to. I could go down there with one man to drive a car and take a machinegun and clean out that whole goddamned farm. Them dirty Laws and newspapers. Calling me a Number One this and a Number One that. I could set them sonsofbitches a real pace. If I wanted to hurt somebody, I wouldn't be sittin' here twiddling my thumbs."

Keechie spread the house dress about her waist and thighs. "You call this twiddling your thumbs?"

"Aw honey, I don't mean you and me. I do tell you, though, one thing about you and me. We got to start getting out of this place here more. Get out and enjoy ourselves for a change. Go down to some of these night clubs in that French Quarter that we're all the time hearing over the radio and do a little drinking and have a good time."

"I think we can go out a little," Keechie said.

"That's what makes you feel bad in the mornings," Bowie said. "Staying cooped up like this all the time. It's not good for anybody."

"I think we can start going out some, but I don't see any use of drinking."

"We can drink beer."

"Beer, I guess, will be all right."

"You have to drink in those places. You couldn't go in one of those places and just sit there. You'd look like a I-don't-know-what."

"I'm going to get my feet dirty if you don't go in there and get my bedroom slippers," Keechie said. "In the bottom left-hand drawer."

Bowie came back with the slippers. They were red felt with black fur. "I just happened to, think. I went out of that Drug Store without paying for that newspaper. I just paid for the sherbet. I'll bet them people over there think I tried to beat them out of it."

~§~

Bowie waited in their paralleled parked car under the shade of the French-balconied Second-Hand Store on Chartres Street. Keechie was up yonder in that big Department Store on Canal getting a dinner gown and sandals and a wrap. They were going to do this stepping out tonight in the right way.

Bowie turned now and looked at the wrapped boxes

on the back seat. There was a white linen suit in the long box and a panama hat in the round one; white oxfords and baby-blue socks in the other. He was going to look like something himself tonight. He had a blue shirt and yellow tie like the combination Chicamaw had had.

The Street on which he waited was the narrowest, craziest one he had ever seen. There were old chairs and stands and vases in front of the Antique Shop that didn't look worth ten cents a dozen and the window yonder was a crazy-quilt of oil paintings. On the corner was a bar: *Vieux Carre Haven.* A man stumbled out of the swinging doors and stood there, swaying uncertainly. He had on a white cotton shirt and faded blue-denim trousers.

If she stays much longer, Bowie thought, I'm going to duck in that bar and get a beer. It takes a woman a lot longer to do things than a man. But he had fooled around and let that girl get down to where she didn't have a thing to wear. She might a well have had a shoe clerk or a flatfoot Law for a man. Not a fellow that had got himself almost thirty thousand dollars over in Texas in a couple of months.

The drunk was coming toward Bowie's car. His shirt was grass-stained and a tattoo showed through the torn sleeve. He grinned loosely: "You got a dime, Mack, for an old boy that sure needs a drink?"

"I'll give you a quarter to get that stinking breath out of my face," Bowie said. He put a half-dollar in the cupped hand. "I just got out of Stir this morning," Stink Breath said. "Thirty days I done."

"I don't give a damn," Bowie said. "Get on."

Stink Breath moved toward the bar, his hands spread

like an exhausted wrestler, disappeared inside. Toward the waterfront, the whistle of a tugboat groaned.

Why couldn't a man get hold of some thief lawyer, Bowie thought, and get him to write out a Bench Warrant? Then get a Sheriffs badge and a big hat. He could go on one of them prison farms, show that and take any man off he wanted to. Them Farm Captains and Bosses couldn't see nothing but Warrant.

A man in a beret and golf knickers stopped now in front of the window of oil paintings, shaded his forehead and pressed against the glass. He scratched his thigh.

It could be done all right, Bowie thought. Just go on that Farm like you owned it and flash your badge and be from one of those far western counties out by El Paso. Deputies and sheriffs were going on them farms every day and gettin' men.

Keechie was coming, stepping around other pedestrians, headed for the car. Bowie pushed out the door. "I begin to think you had fell in somewhere," he said.

"They are going to get the things out by five o'clock," Keechie said. "Sure good to be back here. All those women crowding around give me the creeps."

"Lady, could you spare a dime to a man that hasn't had a bite to eat?" It was Stink Breath, his face framed in the lowered window of the car.

"Get to hell away from here," Bowie said.

"Lady, if you can't spare anything but a nickel."

Bowie pushed the door on his side out with his foot. "Bowie," Keechie called. "Bowie!"

Bowie grasped Stink Breath's collar, kicked him in the seat. The collar ripped in his hands. He kicked again.

"If you don't want to get your head stomped in this sidewalk, you get up this Street, you bastard."

Stink Breath loped up the sidewalk. The man in the beret, the two men that stood now in the Second-Hand Store doorway, were laughing. Bowie grinned. "Bowie, get in here," Keechie said.

Bowie got in the car. "Something ought to be done about stew bums like that," he said.

"You ought to quit making a fool out of yourself," Keechie said.

They moved from the curb. I'll bet he takes his next drink standing up," Bowie said

~§~

Fastened couples churned to the beating music in a center of foaming light, but here among the tables and under the low ceiling, Bowie and Keechie sat in lavender darkness. The Mexican musicians on the palm-screened platform were playing *La Paloma*. Bowie beat on the gray tablecloth with his, index finger. Now Keechie pressed a cigarette in the clay ashtray that was shaped like a sombrero. "You sure like Spanish music, don't you?" she said.

"That's one thing them Chilis can do."

"I like it too."

"I don't see anything to that dancing out there though, do you?"

"I never did care about dancing."

Bowie touched the frosted glass of beer. "Looks silly

to me. Switching your tail around. Look at that gink out there, that four-eyed one, the one with the girl in the blue dress? . . . Don't he think he's a card now?"

Keechie lifted her glass, took a sip of the foamless beer and put it down. "You didn't think that when that Mexican girl was dancing," she said.

"What did I do?"

"You couldn't even find time to light my cigarette."

"I don't remember that. I'm talking about that kind of dancing out there now, honey."

The waiter came and picked up Bowie's emptied glass. His shirt front was a slick gray and the knuckles of his hand looked like a row of English walnuts. "Beer?" he said.

Bowie looked at Keechie. "Want to try something a little stronger? Whisky?"

Keechie shook her head.

"Two more beers," Bowie said. The knuckles moved away.

The orchestra was playing La *Cucaracha* now and the legs the dancing couples were working faster and more heavily beat on the beer glass with the ashtray. "You know, Keechie, I sure wouldn't mind going down to that country Plenty of fellows have gone down there and liked it swell and you couldn't drag them back to this country."

I don't know whether I would like living among a bunch of foreigners or not," Keechie said.

"I tell you a man that knows the ropes of that country. That Judge Hawkins What that man doesn't know about that country isn't on the books"

"That man."

"I've heard you could live down there for a little of nothing. You and me could live like a couple of I-don't-know-whats down there on what we got salted away. In two or three years I'll bet I could get lined up with one of those big mining companies and where would we be then? I don't know but what that is a doggone good idea, Keechie?"

Keechie put her fingers around the glass, but did not pick it up. "It might be all right."

"Now I tell you an old boy that really knows it. Chicamaw. If he was here with us I'd be ready to start out tonight. Put that boy in the back seat of our car with a .30—30 and that Mexican army couldn't stop us from crossing that border. But if anybody knows the ropes, you can make it as easy as falling off a log."

Keechie got up and pulled her wrap off the back of the chair. "Let's go home," she said.

Bowie looked up at her. "Goodness me, honey. Why, I didn't think we was gettin' started good."

"I've had enough of this," Keechie said.

The music stopped. Bowie rose slowly. "Are you feeling bad again?"

"Yes," Keechie said.

Chairs scraped around them as the returning dancers started seating themselves. Bowie beckoned Knuckles.

Chapter 24

Bowie picked up another ink-crusted pen off the table of crumbling blotters and tried the point. This one would write. A revolving door down the darkening corridor of the Post Office made a swishing, jolting sound and Bowie watched. It was a Negro in a porter's uniform, a bundle of papers and letters in his arms. The Negro's shoes crackled on the tile and echoed hollowly in the empty building. Bowie wrote:

> *Dear Mr· Hawkins:*
> *Enclosed here is $200. I want you to get hold for me a Bench Warrant and get a seal and everything on it. Make it out for Elmo T. Mobley on the Bingham Prison Farm. Make it from Becas County and fix it up real proper and everything. Also I want a Sheriff badge.*

A door swished again. The man in the straw hat and seersucker suit dropped the letter in the slot and presently the door bumped and Bowie was alone again.

> *I want you to please have these things*

ready and I may come in on you any time.
So have them ready. Do it as soon as
possible. Remember Xmas night· I am the
same fellow.

       Yours very truly,

                    Xmas Nite.

    P· S· There will be another hundred for
you when the goods are delivered. X. N·

Bowie sealed the envelope, pounded the flap with his closed hand and went over and dropped the letter in the slot.

On the sidewalk outside, he stopped and looked at the fresh, gold painted lettering on the door of his car:

SUNSHINE Co. PRODUCTS
F. T. HAVILAND, AGENT

Around Lee Circle and then out St. Charles Avenue, Bowie drove. Chances are I never will see that Judge, he thought, but that letter will be just in case. I thought of it and I would just keep thinking about it if I didn't get the thing off my chest. This is just kind of like insurance, just looking ahead.

There was somebody in his apartment and Bowie brought his hand back from the knob and listened. Feet approached the door and then it opened. It was Mrs. Lufkin. Smelling of liquor and perfume. "Oh, how do you do, Mister Haviland?"

"All right." Through the doorway he saw Keechie sitting on the couch. She looked all right.

"Pretty warm weather we are having?" Mrs. Lufkin said.

"Too warm," Bowie said. He squeezed past Mrs. Lufkin and went inside.

"Well, goodbye," Mrs. Lufkin said.

"Goodbye," Keechie said.

Bowie closed the door. "What was that old souse doing in here?"

Keechie got up. "She wants us to move."

"Why?"

"It's nothing. She has a chance to rent it to some professor that wants it for a year and she said she knew we weren't permanent."

"You don't think she's smelled something?"

Keechie shook her head. "Oh, no."

"Well, what are we going to do?"

"There isn't anything to do, unless you want to pay her a lot of rent."

"I'll be damned if I do that. I'm ready to get out of this hot dump anyway. I can't see why anybody else would want it.

"There's plenty of places here."

"Sure. It don't worry me."

Keechie lowered herself back to the divan and lay down. "Did you get the sign on the car?"

"You ought to see it, honey. I got that fellow to do it that we saw that afternoon hanging around that Square, the one with the Jesus Christ beard. On both sides. We ought to have thought of that a long time ago."

"I thought you were never coming back."

He went over and sat down on the divan and jiggled the toe of her shoe. "It took him a pretty good while."

"Anything happen?"

"Not a thing."

After the supper of canned soup and crackers, Bowie and Keechie looked at road maps. This one here covered the whole United States and the regions were illustrated with bright-colored sketches: cattle in Texas, oil wells in Oklahoma, shocks of wheat in Kansas.

"Doggoned if I know where to go," Bowie said. "Looks like it would be easy with all this to pick from."

"Well, we don't have to leave New Orleans, you know."

"Oh, I'm fed up on this town, honey. It's just too doggone hot."

Keechie pointed at the Southwest Texas region. "Right in there somewhere is the place we lived."

"That's another place you couldn't drag me," Bowie said.

"Or any place else in Texas," Keechie said.

Bowie tapped the Gulf of Mexico. "You ever seen the ocean, Keechie?"

She shook her head.

"Me neither. I'm almost thirty years old and you know I never have seen the ocean. Can you beat that? Say, how would you like to live on the ocean?"

"Sounds pretty good to me."

Bowie folded the map "We got plenty of time. It never pays to decide a thing too quick. We got a couple of weeks and by then we'll know exactly where we want to light out for."

"Sure," Keechie said.

~§~

Keechie whimpered in her sleep again and this time Bowie sat up and looked at her. In the moonlight that filtered through the crêpe myrtle and screen, he saw her mouth pucker like a child and she whimpered again. A mosquito sang with needle-like vibration in Bowie's ear and he waved his hand over Keechie's head. She was quiet now and he eased back, moving his hand over her head from time to time.

It's malaria, he thought. That's what it is. These goddamned mosquitoes.

Keechie sobbed out. It was a dry, throat-lodging cry. She turned over, her face toward the window and lay quiet. The mosquito sang, and he raised up and fanned furiously.

Back in the kitchen, the clock ticked, smothered now by the rush of a speeding car on the avenue; ticked again. She had bought that clock in Antelope Center and of all things to bring. She bought it the same day she got that big gunny sack of Irish potatoes. They had left it and there wasn't a fourth of them used.

Keechie made sounds now like she was losing her breath and he placed his hand on her shoulder and shook gently: "Keechie, Keechie. What's the matter, honey?"

She raised, her eyes wide open. "What is it?" she said.

"Bowie?"

"You ain't feeling well, honey."

"What is it?"

"Are you hurtin'? Hurtin' any place, honey?"

Keechie let her head back on the pillow. "I'm all right."

"You must have been dreaming, hon. A nightmare or something."

She did not say anything. An automobile horn blared on the avenue, a streetcar was coming.

"You been crying in your sleep, Keechie."

"I had a dream. I guess that was it."

"What was it?"

"Forget it. I'm all right."

The streetcar grated in a stop in front of the house; ground and clicked on.

"Did you think you were falling off something? I've dreamed that. Gun breaking in my hand. I dreamed I couldn't make my Dad hear me a hundred times."

"I dreamed you had gone away," Keechie said.

"It's all right now. Go on and go to sleep. You're going to be worn out in the morning."

"Where did I go?"

"I don't know. You had just gone and I thought I was trying to find you. I couldn't find you."

"Well, there's no danger of me going any place without you."

"You went to town yesterday."

"That's different. I mean off any place. No, honey, it looks like you and me are going up the same road together."

"Up the same road?"

"It sure looks that way."

"Is that the way you want it, Bowie?"

"That's the way I want it, honey, but sometimes I think about you."

"That's the way I want it, Bowie, and you remember it."

Bowie slapped his hands together. "That damned mosquito been bothering you?"

"I hadn't noticed it," Keechie said.

"You sleepy?"

"No, I'm wide awake now."

This streetcar rumbled on past and soon was a distant, fading hum.

"I been trying to figure some place for us to go Bowie said. "It's got me worried."

"There's plenty of places."

"You know, I have just about decided that we got to make Mexico. If only I knew the ins and outs of that damned country. I could kick myself for not pumping some fellows that had been down there. But there's nothing to this, Keechie. I'm not going to really feel good about us until we're plumb out of this country."

"We can go to Mexico."

"If I just knew the ropes about all that border down there and just knew one of them Thief officials down there that Chicamaw was telling me about. Now you take old Hawkins. I don't know but what it would be a good idea to go and see him."

"Not him," Keechie said.

"Why not?"

"There's plenty of other men that know about Mexico."

"Who?"

"I don't know, but there's plenty."

"But who?"

"There's plenty of men that know."

"But who, Keechie? That don't do no good. Just name me somebody that we could go to and he would give us all the lowdown that we got to have? I'm not any plain tourist, you know. I'm not the governor of this state, you know."

"Now don't get smart. What I am telling you is that you don't have any business back there in Texas. Or around anybody that knows you."

Bowie clutched at the air. "I'm going to get up and brain this mosquito in just about two seconds."

There was a little wind and stirred leaves of the crêpe myrtle sighed on the screen.

"Do you really want to go to Mexico, Bowie?"

"It's about all I know to do."

"Do you think Hawkins can really help?"

"I don't know of anybody else. I was just as sure you, would take me up when I mentioned him about that. I even dropped him a line."

"When I was getting that sign put on. That day."

"Yesterday, you mean?"

"Why didn't you tell me?"

"I just didn't. I'm telling you now."

"Did you write about Chicamaw?"

Keechie sat up.

"Now look here, Keechie. Now don't start that, honey, I'm just worried to death." He sat up.

Keechie got off the bed. "You needn't say any more. That's all I want to know."

"Now look here, Keechie. Where you going?"

"What difference does that make?"

"Now look here, Keechie. Now come on, honey."

"Which is it, Bowie? Make up your mind right now. Once and forever. Which is it, Chicamaw or me?"

"It's you. If it wasn't you, I'd been down on that farm long before now and cleaning it from one end to the other gettin' him off. I know now how you feel about it, Keechie. I'm just learning. You been a Little Soldier to me and I'm going to play square with you."

Keechie shivered.

"As long, honey, as I'm any good to you, I'm going to stay with you. I'm telling you straight now, Keechie. I've had things on my mind and I don't mind admitting it to you, but they're all over. That's it, Keechie. The best I know how to tell you."

Keechie lowered herself to the edge of the bed, "Did you really want to see that lawyer about Mexico?"

"When we were talking while ago? . . . Yes, I did. I meant it."

Keechie picked up the edge of the twisted sheet and shook it with a flapping sound out over Bowie. Then she folded it back on her side of the bed and got under it.

"And you think the lawyer is the only one to see?" Keechie said.

"I leave it up to you, Keechie. It's all up to you."

"When do you want to go?"

"I leave that up to you."

"Tomorrow?"

"It suits me."

"The clock was ticking again now in the kitchen. A truck passed on the narrow street by their window and presently there was the sound of milk bottles clattering in a tin rack. The moonlight was gone now and the sleeping-room was dark. Bowie raised up and listened to Keechie's even breathing. She was sleeping sound. He eased back, lay there a moment and then cautiously pulled up his foot and scratched the mosquito bite again.

Chapter 25

The moon had an eye-squinching brightness, radiating six splintered beams, broad as planks. It deepened the dark hollows of Keechie's eyes, shadowed the lines that slashed her face from cheek bones to tight lips. She sat there in their car, parked on the by-road just off the highway, her eyes closed, head resting on the back of the seat.

Bowie, standing on the ground with one foot on the running board, looked again toward the lights of Mac-Masters, as golden as oil lamps in the clear air. They had stopped here a little after sundown, deciding it was best to wait until ten o'clock or so and be sure that Hawkins would be at home.

"You feel any better, honey?" Bowie said.

"I want something ice-cold to drink," Keechie said.

"I know I would feel a lot better if I had a cold soda pop."

"We'll get it when we gas up. The very first thing. I wish now we had stopped back up the road, but there was just so many Square Johns hanging around then."

"I can get along without it."

Bowie moved around the front of the car, got under the wheel. "We can go now," he said. "To hell with this Waiting."

The neon sign on the left, at the city's edge, read: *Alamo Plaza Courts*. It burned in front of a filling station and behind that was a court of white frame cottages. On a bench under the shed of the station sat a man, an old fellow, licking a cone of ice cream. Bowie turned in and the old man rose.

"Fill it up," Bowie said. He went on to the big wooden ice-box.

The spring of the screen door whined and Bowie looked up. The woman coming out was Mattie. She was heavier; gold on her teeth. "Hi you do," She said.

"Okeh," Bowie said. He brought a bottle out of the icy water.

"Passing through?" Mattie said.

Bowie moved his head, indicating the old man holding the hose by the clicking pump.

"Papa," Mattie, said.

"Just passing through," Bowie said.

Mattie looked at Keechie in the car, and Bowie jerked the bottle's cap and started back.

"Who is that?" Keechie said.

"T-Dub's sister-in-law." She took the bottle from his hand "It's cold. She's Real People."

"I'll drink this when we get started."

"Go ahead and drink it, honey. I'll get plenty to carry."

Mattie lifted the ice-box top for Bowie. "How is everything around here?" he said.

"Okeh," Mattie said.

"How's the husband?"

"Still In There."

Bowie ran his hands over the bottles. "That's too bad."

"The cokes are at that end if that's what you are looking for," Mattie said.

"How's my heat around here?" Bowie said.

"You can find better places to run around in."

Papa hung the hose on the rack. "How's your oil?" he said. His voice squeaked like the broken note of a clarinet. "All right," Bowie said. He paid Mattie.

"Take care of yourself," Mattie said.

"Same to you," Bowie said.

The air on the boulevard was cool and clean. Out at the end was Hawkins' house.

"Aren't you going to drink that, honey?" Bowie said.

"Not now."

"What's the matter?"

"I'm afraid it might come up."

"Doggone, sugar."

"I think I had better lie down in the back. If I lie down a little I think I will feel better."

Bowie drew alongside the curbing, stopped, got out and helped Keechie into the back. He took her coat, spread it over her feet, got back under the wheel and drove on.

There were four unoccupied automobiles parked in front of Hawkins' house. The church was dark.

"What are those cars, Bowie?" Keechie said.

"You just lay back down now, honey."

"I feel better. You think it's all right to go up there?"

"I'll be right back now before you can turn around. You just take it easy now."

The porch planks creaked and gave under Bowie's steps and then he knocked on the door. Under the half-raised blind he could see the trousered legs of men seated at a card table.

The door parted and there was a middle-aged woman in a black dress and white-lace collar.

"Judge in?"

"Why, yes. Won't you come in?"

"I'll just wait here."

The woman hesitated. "Who can I tell him?"

"Mister Knight. Mister Knight."

Bowie watched the legs through the window. The card table moved and then feet were coming to the door.

The porch globe showered light. Hawkins was in shirt sleeves, and had a pipe in his right hand. He switched it quickly reached and then the porch was dark again. "Wait a minute," he said. The door closed and Bowie backed down off the porch steps, his fingers grasping the butt of the gun under his arm.

The door opened again and Bowie went back up on the porch and took the extended envelope. It was heavy and he felt the badge's pin. "You busy?" he said.

Hawkins nodded toward the window. "Company," he

whispered.

"I want to get some low down on Mexico."

Hawkins shook his head, "Can't help you there, son. That's the Sheriff in there."

"Okeh," Bowie said.

His heels clicked on the sidewalk toward the car. I promised him another hundred, but to hell with him. He's just a little too busy. I don't need this damned stuff anyway. *Where's Keechie?*

She lay face down in the bottom of the car, her left arm crooked like it was broken. "Keechie," he said. "Keechie." She was limp and heavy. "Keechie, honey. Baby. Keechie." Her teeth were clenched and he couldn't hear her breathing. He straightened her on the seat, got up in front and his hand shook on the knob above the grinding gears.

Papa pushed off the bench and approached.

"Where's a vacant cabin?" Bowie said.

"Just about what kind of a price, do you have in mind, Mister?"

"Any of 'em."

"We got some for a dollar and a half and some for—"

"Where's that woman that was around here?"

"You mean my darter? The girl that was—"

"Where is she?" Bowie started getting out of the car.

The screen's spring rasped and then Mattie came. "I got to have a place," Bowie said.

Mattie went around into the Court and Bowie followed her in the car. At the far, low end she pointed at the corner cabin and Bowie parked in front of it. Mattie went on in and turned on the light.

Bowie lowered Keechie to the bed, straightened the skirt down over her knees. Her face was drained, the lines deeps Mattie stood in the half-opened screen.

"I can't figure it out," Bowie said. He picked up a towel off the foot of the bed and went to the sink and turned on the water. "I can't figure it out. Go get a doctor, Mattie. Go on and get a doctor out here."

He started bathing Keechie's face. "Go on, Mattie. For Christ's sake." Mattie left.

He held, the sopping towel under the running water again, went back and rubbed the back of her neck, pressed it under her collar on her chest. "Come on, Little Soldier. Show your old man you got it in you. You bet you got it in you. You bet you have . . . ."

Her body quivered and then she sucked in with parted lips.

"That's a girl. That's a girl." Her eyes opened and she moved her head front side to side and then suddenly looked at him. "Did you see him?" she said.

"Everything's swell, kiddo. Don't you worry about it one minute. Everything's swell."

"I'm glad." Her mouth twisted and she reached and clutched Bowie's hand. "Something is wrong with me, Bowie. I hate to tell you. I know it."

"Don't worry, honey. The doctor is coming. Don't you worry."

Keechie closed her eyes and Bowie took the dry towel and wiped her face. Then he took off her shoes. "I'm glad," she said. It was toneless, like she was talking in her sleep.

Bowie sat on the stone edge of the fish pond in the

Court's center, watching the Doctor, a little man in a tan suit, through the half-raised blind of the cabin. I ought to have stayed in there. That Doctor's got sick people on his mind and not criminals. That Mattie.

The lights of a car brightened the yard. Papa came around and the car followed him, an old machine with packed running boards. It went on around to the row on the other side.

"I just can't get over it," Bowie said out loud.

The door of the cabin opened, laying a slab of light on the grass, and then Mattie was coming out. Bowie went to her. "What does he say?" he said.

"'There's nothing wrong with her except she's pregnant," Mattie said. "I could have told you that."

"Who said it?"

"He did. Anybody could tell."

Bowie looked at the light from the half-raised blind. "I don't want to get mixed up any farther in this," Mattie said. "You're going to have to go on." Bowie did not answer. He moved toward the cabin, into the smell of licorice and paregoric.

The Doctor had a splotch of moustache over his mouth and sagging eyerims. "That is the only thing to do," he said. "Just keep her quiet and lying on her back and I think she will come out of it fine, but she cannot keep this up. I have given her something and that is going to keep her asleep quite a while. Rest is the thing."

Keechie's breasts were rising and falling in even breathing.

"She sure is sleeping like she is awfully tired," Bowie said.

"That is the best thing," Doctor said. "Now I have put some medicine there on the table there and tomorrow, if she is still in pain, you can give it to her. She is likely to sleep a good while, and if she does awaken she more than likely will go right back to sleep again."

"She sure is sleeping."

"If you need me, call me," Doctor said.

"Sure, Doctor. Don't worry about that."

Bowie sat now on the chair by the sink in the cabin's darkness, watching Kechie's form, listening to her breathing. He got up now and touched her straightened arm, picked it up and put it on her breast; placed it back by her side. Then he left the cabin.

Mattie came out and walked around with him into the deep shadow of the station's side. "That girl can't be moved," Bowie said.

"I don't want anything happening around here," Mattie said. "I've done all I'm going to in this."

"If it's money that's holding you, don't worry about that,"

"I don't want any of your money. All I want you to do is get off this place." The screen sounded and Mattie turned her head and started off.

"Hold it," Bowie said, Mattie stopped. "Now you listen to me," Bowie said, "You're a thief just like me and you ain't going to yellow on me when I'm asking you to lay off. She's not going to be moved, see, and if you or anybody else don't like it, it's just too goddamned bad."

Mattie walked on away.

Keechie had not moved. He lifted the blind, a square of moonlight baring her feet. He pulled the blind back down, took off her hose and placed the sheet over her legs.

The Court was quiet. In Bowie's ears, the cricket-ringing sounds were growing. That yellow Hawkins, he thought. The two-faced sonofabitch.

If only that Indian was here. Them white teeth. Little Soldier, it can't be got around. They got me in a rank now. The whole, lousy, yellow bunch.

Water dripped in the sink and he got up and tightened the tap.

We got to hole-up right pretty soon, girl. There ain't no *ifs* and *ands* about it. I have fooled around long enough.

You got Something Else to think about now, Little Soldier. Old Bowie is not so big in this picture now. But they can't put nothing on you, Keechie. They just can't do it. Don't you let them make you think it for a minute. Don't you let 'em.

The dropped match from his fingers rattled on the floor and he watched her. She did not move and he breathed again. But you're plumb out, honey. You're not going to be waking up until away in tomorrow.

If that Chicamaw was here, Keechie, we could beat them easy. He's the only friend we got in this world. You don't know it, Keechie, but I do, honey. He's the only one in this world that would help us. You and me are going up this road together and we got to find us a Hole and pull it in after us. 'Specially now. You can't run these roads much longer. That Mexico, Keechie. They ain't but one person in this world that can get us down there. Just one.

Somewhere in the night a dog bayed.

Say it worked, Keechie. Say I run that hundred and twenty miles over to that Farm from here, get there by seven o'clock this morning and spring that boy? You would be asleep, honey, and never know a thing about it. I would be back and you'd wake up and that Chicamaw would be with us and then I'd like to see somebody stop us. Honey, we'd be holed up in Mexico two days from now. Deep, Keechie. Pulled in after us.

The dog bayed again.

Well, say it didn't work, Keechie? Say it flopped? All right, Little Soldier, you got Somebody Else to think about now. Old Bowie stepped out don't mean so much. You don't have nobody to beat, Keechie. They can't hang a thing in this world on you. All you have ever done is just kind of run around with me. Say it flopped all right, Keechie? Well, there you are.

Bowie got up and buttoned his coat.

~§~

The high, net-wire fence was broken here by a wooden arch: *Bingham Prison Camp*—and Bowie left the highway and turned his machine through it. Stone-bordered beds of flowers colored the sides of the gray road that led up there to the Buildings. There was the smell of sweetpeas.

There was the Office, a squat, brick building with an empty flagpole and behind it, long, barrack-looking buildings, stone foundations whitewashed, and barns.

A figure in the white sacking of a convict, on his knees and breaking clods around the rose bush with his hands, looked up as Bowie got out of his car. He lowered his head as Bowie passed on toward the Office porch, the two men in khaki uniforms sitting on a bench, cartridge belts around their waists, shotguns beside them.

"How do you do?" Bowie said.

The heads of the Guards moved, "Howdy . . . . Hidy." Bowie indicated the porch-shadowed door. "Captain Stammers in?"

The two nodded.

Bowie entered the smell of disinfectant, looked at the face framed in the top of the high, bookkeeper's desk, a Convict's; moved down the disk's length and stopped before the two men on the bench. The big one was dressed like the men on the porch, the other in blue serge trousers and white shirt. He got up.

"Captain Stammers?" Bowie said.

"That's me," the man said. He had thin black hair, parted in the middle, and held his left arm crooked as if it were in pain. He did not have a gun on. Bowie extended his hand. "I'm Sheriff Haviland, Becos County."

Captain Stammers pumped Bowie's hand. "Glad to know you, Sheriff. What can I do for you?"

The Guard on the bench got up and moved toward the door. "See you after while, Captain," he said.

"I want to see a boy you got on your place here," Bowie said. "Elmo Mobley."

"Yeah, we got him. Let me see now. He's in Boss Herbert's squad today I think. Now what is it we can do for you there?"

"I have a Bench Warrant, but I don't intend to take him." Bowie pulled the paper from his inside coat pocket and handed it to Stammers. "I just wanted to talk to him a little on this trip." The paper crackled as Stammers opened the Warrant:

THE STATE OF TEXAS

To the Honorable *Sheriff A. T. Haviland,*
Sheriff of Becos County, Texas, GREETING:

On this 12 *day of May A.D.* 1935, it appearing to the Court that there is now pending on the docket of this Court, a certain case entitled the STATE of Texas VS. *Elmo T. Mobley,* being our case *No. 754,* wherein said defendant is charged with the offense of murder.
Whereas, said case . . .

"You don't want to take him?" Stammers said. He started folding the paper.

"No, I just want to talk to him."

Stammers went over and picked the gray hat off the hook and turned and touched his left arm. "Neuritis, bad," he said.

"I've heard that it's bad," Bowie said.

On the porch, Stammers said to the three guards: "Watch that telephone, boys."

Bowie moved toward his car and Stammers followed. "We can just go in my car," Bowie said.

"Did you ever hear of anybody that found out anything to help it?" Stammers said.

"It just has to wear off, I hear," Bowie said. Stammers pointed at the dirt road that twisted back of the building and toward the cotton-fields. Bowie moved onto it. The cotton was fresh and green, the earth around it freshly hoed. "Mighty nice stand you got out here, Captain."

"Rain last week," Stammers said. He picked up his left band and placed the elbows on his stomach. "Nice rain last week."

Puffs of dust rose from the chopping hoes of the working convicts yonder, fifteen or twenty men; two men on horses, shotguns in the cradles of their arms, watching. Faces of working men lifted and looked at the car, bent back again.

The horseman with the boots and jagged Spanish spurs approached. He was a heavy man with a billowing waist. There was a pistol on his belt; a rifle in the saddle scabbard.

"Mobley is in that bunch, isn't he?" Stammers said.

Spanish Spurs nodded. "Yessir."

"Bring him over here."

At the head of the squad, a figure raised, listened and then stepped out. He was coming now, the hoe in hand. Spanish Spurs spoke and Chicamaw threw the hoe down.

Chicamaw looked hard and well. He studied Bowie and then Stammers and then Bowie again.

"Get in this car, Mobley," Bowie said. "I want to talk to you a little while, boy. We'll go back up to your office, Captain,"

"Sure,"

Chicamaw sat in the front alongside Bowie; Stammers in the back. They were going now back up the road toward the Buildings. "You didn't stop by State and see the Warden, did you?" Stammers said.

"No, I went to Houston a different way. I'm stopping there on my way back though."

"Well, give the Warden my regards. You didn't go to the Convention this year, did you, Sheriff?"

"No, I didn't," Bowie said.

"You know I was a Sheriff for fourteen years. I'd like to have gone to that Convention this year."

Bowie nudged Chicamaw's thigh, indicated the panel pocket. Chicamaw pulled the ivory knob, grasped the pistol and turned on Stammers. "It's a break, Captain," he said. "Sit there."

"We're going right out through this gate up here, Captain," Bowie said. "Don't you let on to nobody in no way. You understand, don't you?"

"I understand."

The porch was empty. The Convict, working around the rose bush, looked up and then stood. Bowie passed the Office and the chaff of the road began peppering the fenders. He swerved up and onto the highway; opened the throttle wide.

"Well, boys, this is going to cost me," Stammers said.

"Don't let it get you down, Cap," Chicamaw said.

"It seems to me now that I had seen you before, Sheriff, but by God, I still don't know."

"Just forget it, Captain," Bowie said. "I guess you'll find out soon enough. How long do you think it will be before your boys back there figure something is wrong?"

"I wish I knew."

Chicamaw looked deeper in the car pocket, reached in it and explored with his hand.

"What you looking for?" Bowie said.

"Nothing," Chicamaw said.

"This is going to cost me, boys," Stammers said.

"Tell that to the Warden, Cap," Chicamaw said.

"You been treated pretty good on that Farm, boy," Stammers said.

"Pipe down, Chicamaw," Bowie said. "For Christ's sake."

The highway sign read: *MacMasters . . . 6 mi.* At the off-road, Bowie turned and they drove along through the timber. After a half mile, Bowie stopped and they all got out and crawled through the fence, and in the woods Bowie tied Stammers to a tree.

Heat glimmered from the highways cement slabs. "Say they been pretty good to you back there?" Bowie asked.

"They don't use a bat or barrel anymore," Chicamaw said. "Them big political boys stopped all that. They'd still do it, but they're afraid they'll lose them sixty-dollar jobs."

"That's something though."

Chicamaw turned and looked in the back of the car. "You're not going to tell me you didn't bring no pint along, are you?"

Bowie shook his head. "No liquor in this party, Chicamaw. I got some business that needs attending and it takes a clear head."

"I don't believe you're ever going to be human,"

Chicamaw said. "I tell you, man, I don't see how you do it. You get out here and run these roads and pull a thing like that back yonder and beat these Laws right and left, and, by God, Bowie, I don't see how in the hell you do it. You're just a big country boy and just chumpy as hell at times, and yet you do it."

"What did you want to do, stay back yonder?"

"Me? Don't kid yourself. Not with that Texaco City trouble still up in the air. Man, I been thinking any day here they would come. You're the boy they want on that. Them fingerprints of yours sure played hell there. I was pretty foxy in that though. They got you tagged on that, but what they got on me for sure?"

"It's raised a lot of heat all right," Bowie said. "That trouble."

"You seem to beat it all right," Chicamaw said. "You just keep going right on."

"Just luck," Bowie said.

"That's it. Call it that. You're no more a criminal than that damned radiator cap there. And yet you do it. It rips my guts out. You're just a big Sunday-school chump and yet you can pull a thing like that back yonder and run these roads and make me look like thirty cents."

Bowie's head jerked. "You going crazy? What the hell is gettin' the matter with you?"

"It rips my guts out. Take you and on top of that a damned little old girl that was never outside of a filling station and, by God, the papers don't do nothing but print about you all the time. Why, it makes me look like a damned penny slot machine . . . ."

Bowie stopped at the side of the highway.

"What's the matter?" Chicamaw said. "What's this idea?"

Bowie got out of the car and walked around and pulled out Chicamaw's door. "Come on," he said. "You sonofabitch, come on."

"Good God, Bowie. What's got into you?"

"Get out."

Chicamaw got out.

"The only reason I'm not letting you have it right here," Bowie said, "is because there might be some dogs that will do it."

"Listen, Bowie. I want to go see my folks. I ain't never seen 'em, Bowie. Let me get that gun in the car."

"Get."

Chicamaw started running up the road.

A car with a blaring loudspeaker and bannered with lettering about a picture show was the only moving machine on the heat-stilled Square of MacMasters. The music was, *Stars and Stripes Forever*. Bowie turned Off the Square and moved out the highway that led to the Courts. Nossir, God, I never asked nothing from you before. Not a thing in this world. But just let me get up there the rest of the way now. And if it ain't asking too much, keep her still asleep. Just let her wake up and I'll be sittin' there.

The driveway and yard of *Alamo Plaza Courts* were deserted. Bowie drove on down and parked parallel in front of the closed door and lowered blind.

She lay there on the bed, her eyes closed, still breathing, just as he had left her. He looked around. Nothing had been moved. Nothing. Thanks, God.

The afternoon heat pressed against the cabin, making the walls as hot as a dying stove. The roofs tar melted and smelled. Bowie stood above Keechie, flapping the wet towel. The little curls on her forehead trembled under the cooling air. Honey, you got to be waking up pretty soon and eating something. I mean real wide awake.

Dusk seeped into the room now, drying the sweat on Bowie's forehead, stiffening the hairs on his arms. Keechie stirred greater now, and he bent over. Her eyes opened. They were like petals submerged in tiny bowls of unchanged water.

"Bowie?" she said.

"Hello, sleepyhead."

"Bowie?"

"It's about time you were waking up."

"You wouldn't leave me, would you?"

"Me? You don't mean me. I should say not. Don't be silly now waking up."

"Bowie?"

"What, Keechie?"

"I mean it."

"God knows now too, Keechie. I mean it."

Keechie closed her eyes. He touched her. "Listen, Little Soldier, you got to get something inside that stomach of yours. How about a soda pop? Ice-cold to start things off?"

Keechie's head moved up and down on the pillow.

"Now let's see." Bowie stood erect and began rubbing his hands. "Just about what kind, of flavor now would the little lady crave? Strawberry?"

Keechie nodded.

Bowie moved through the gloom to the door, pulled it back. *"Don't let a move out of you,"* the Voice said. It was like the swish of a missing blade. Cat with seven lives, Bowie thought. He whipped out his gun. Steampipes burst in his ears. *Seven.* He swirled in the bell of the roaring loudspeaker on the Square: *Stars and Stripes Forever.* Cat . . . . *seven.* Things were wrinkling, folding gently, like paper dolls in a puff of cigarette smoke. *Strawberry* . . . .

MacMASTERS, Texas; June 21— The crime-blazed trail of the Southwest's phantom desperado, Bowie Bowers, and his gun-packing girl companion, Keechie Mobley, was ended here early tonight in a battle with a sharp-shooting band of Rangers and peace officers who beat, their covered quarry to the draw. The escaped convict, bank robber and quick-triggered killer, and his woman aide were trapped in the cabin of a tourist camp, one mile east of this city, and killed instantly in one burst of machine and rifle fire.

Stirred to a vengeful heat after Bowers' sensational liberation of his old pal, Elmo (Three-Toed) Mobley, from the Bingham Prison Farm early this morning, grim-faced officers swooped down on the camp. After the battle, Bowers law sprawled in the doorway of the cabin, the girl inside on the floor. A gun was clutched in Bowers' hand, another near the hand of Keechie Mobley. Both were bullet-riddled, their deaths instantaneous.

A bag containing almost $10,000 in currency was recovered in the splintered cabin, also a quantity of what officers declared was narcotics.

The killings brought to a dramatic climax a search of more than a year for the desperado and his companion. Wanted in at least four states for murders, bank robberies, filling station holdups, kidnappings of peace officers, Bowers had become one of the Southwest's most feared criminals.

This peaceful, thriving little city was stunned tonight by the news that it had harbored in its environs this pair. Knots of excited people thronged the streets tonight and crowds were viewing the bodies in a local undertaking parlor.

Tall, steel-eyed Ranger Captain Leflett refused to comment at length on the case, declaring that the owners of the tourist camp where the pair was slain, were unaware of the identity of their notorious guests. When he reported to his Chief in the State Capital, he declared simply: "Chief, we have got them."

Elmo Mobley, freed by Bowers earlier in the day when Captain Stammers was kidnaped, was captured by a farmer who became suspicious when he saw Mobley running in the road and then recognized the prison clothing.

Rewards totaling more than $1,000 will be distributed among the twenty picked officers who took part in the slayings.

Supplied a tip before daybreak this morning, local officers began acting quickly. Telephone and telegraph wires hummed to the State Capital and Penitentiary. An airplane brought Ranger Captain Leflett aid four men.

At the State Penitentiary, according to news dispatches received here, Warden Joel Howard admitted to reporters, it is said, that the tip was furnished after a "deal" had been made for the liberation of an inmate in the prison there. "Bowers was a ruthless, cunning criminal," Warden Howard declared, "and we had to exert every resource to bring him down."

True Crime

HENRY the HANGMAN

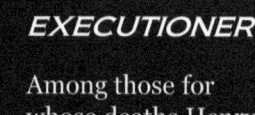

EXECUTIONER

Among those for whose deaths Henry Meyer (above) has received fees, were Kenneth Neu and Mrs. Ada LeBouef (left). Also shown is crack crime reporter Edward Anderson.

Could you kill a man if the law approved and even paid you for it? For years, Henry Meyer, behind his purple mask, was the official executioner of Louisiana. His was the hand that sent thirty-six men and one woman twitching to death at the end of the hangman's rope. Here, from the pen of a master reporter, is a vivid picture of this strange and sinister creature.

By EDWARD ANDERSON

The MACABRE CAREER of HENRY the HANGMAN

THE FLASH CAME that morning of December 15, 1934, from the New Orleans Parish Prison to the city desks of the Crescent City's daily newspapers: Henry Meyer is dying!

City editors bawled and crack reporters clutched copy paper, made sure of pencils and beat it for taxis. *Henry Meyer dying!* (Old Henry who, in his seventy-two years of life had killed one bulldog, one woman and thirty-six men. Old Henry, the hangman.)

The special-assignment newspapermen, straining on the edge of their seats as their cabs raced toward the prison, were well aware of the dramatic situation they had been assigned to chronicle. Vivid in their minds was the last one in which the old hangman had figured. It was not on the gallows, but in a courtroom. It was when the killer, Kenneth Neu, a handsome, cabaret-singing youth, and Henry Meyer met.

Kenneth Neu blackjacked to death in New Orleans, Sunday, September 7, 1934, one Sheffield Clark, prominent hardware man, of Nashville, Tennessee. The killing occurred in a hotel room and followed Neu's demand for money after a casual lobby meeting between the two.

With his victim's car, dressed in his clothing too, Neu was captured with a pretty girl in Jersey City a week later, simply because he did not have a license tag on the car. Neu's conscience drove him to confess not only to Clark's murder but the killing also only a week before and on Sunday, too, of Lawrence Shead, theatre manager. Neu killed him with an electric iron because Shead made immoral advances.

"It's a good thing you caught me," Neu grinned. "I would have killed more."

Several months later Neu waited in the courtroom for the return of a jury which had heard his trial for murder. In the crowd pressing close to the railing was a wizened, old man with shifty, watery eyes. His eyes feasted on Neu. A deputy sheriff saw it and he nudged Neu.

"Who is that?" Neu asked.

"Old Henry, the hangman."

Neu's face lighted. "Oh." He smiled at Henry.

The hangman nodded eagerly and smiled.

Neu indicated the closed jury room with a nod of his

head and made a slitting motion with his index finger across his throat.

Henry nodded. "Yes, yes," he breathed.

And the jury brought in the verdict that resulted in Neu being sentenced to hang. Neu boasted of that meeting with the hangman. So did Meyer. The hangman said: "Me and Neu got to making goo-goo eyes and it made the judge sore."

The days passed. In his cell, Neu sang:

> *"I'm fit as a fiddle and ready to hang,*
> *Don't give a whoop and don't give a bang."*

Over on the corner at the filling station, across the street from the prison, an old man would often pause and look up toward the cell. Perhaps Neu would come to the window and look out. If he did he saw Meyer and they waved and made "goo-goo" eyes. And then Neu would sing:

> *"You're not foolin' me, I know you from A to Z,*
> *"But you're darned good company,*
> *"Oh, you Nasty Man I"*

Of visitors to his cell, Neu always asked: "How's the old hangman?"

Once, a newspaperman told Neu: "The old man is broke. Having a tough time."

"Wish I could help him," Neu said. "Tell him for me that if in any way I can help him this coming year, I'll be very glad to do it."

They told Meyer about it.

"I wish he was hanging tomorrow," Meyer said. "I need some nickels."

It looked though, that December morning of 1934, as if death were going to cheat Old Henry of his ambition to hang Neu. When the newspapermen arrived at the prison they found out that Meyer had fallen writhing on the floor from a heart attack, after he had asked if the execution date had been fixed for Neu.

Internes said:

"The old man got delirious. He kept crying and begging: 'Take them off. Take them off. They're after me!'"

He is being haunted by the ghosts of the men he has hanged, the reporters thought and so they later wrote in their newspapers.

The newspapermen crowded into Room 312 of the prison. It was a gloomy cell with a window, a chair and a small table on which had been placed a piece of toast and a glass of milk.

On the cot lay Henry Meyer. His cheeks were sunken. He was breathing in asthmatic gasps. His hand moved and touched the wrinkled leather of his throat.

"Henry," said Captain Miller (the prison warden) "here's another one of these newspapermen saying you're dying."

The old hangman raised up a little, dull fire coming into his protruding eyes. "That's a damn lie. Do I look like I'm dying?"

"Yeah," a reporter said. Henry's fingers reached out, clutched the toast and he began to nibble on it.

"That looks like I'm dying," he growled. "I'm eatin', ain't I? You tell everybody I ain't dying, you hear? When you're dead you're a dead . . . ."

The reporters left. All of them agreed. He would never hang his "pal" Kenneth Neu. Or anybody else. His heart would not let him. His macabre career was ending.

On his cot, Meyer said grimly: "I'm gonna get up and get the hell out of here today. You see if I don't. I got a job coming up pretty soon."

Neu was to die February 1.

~§~

HENRY MEYER was born over a saloon in Jefferson Parish just across the river from New Orleans, the son of German parents. His father was a huge man. When he died they had to build a special coffin.

At fourteen, Henry was driving a bread wagon and sleeping in the bakery. The baker had a bull dog. The dog got sick and whined. It annoyed Henry and he got up one night and found a rope. He took the dog out, climbed with him up on the sloping roof of the house. Out there he tied one end of the rope around the chimney, made two half hitches around the dog's neck and pushed him off. That was his first hanging. Meyer liked tools and pretty soon he became a carpenter. When he was twenty-eight, he married Tilly Arbo. He worked on construction jobs and for a spell operated a confectionery. A lot of the time he was out of work. He drank a lot of hard liquor. That was the way he lived until November 28, 1919. He was fifty-six years old that year.

Back in 1919, a lone bandit started a series of quick, successful drug store hold-ups in New Orleans that had every druggist in the city watching each customer's entrance with fear. The bandit was dubbed "The Lone Wolf" and he pulled jobs almost nightly—$25, $45 and $100 hauls.

Fifty extra policemen were hired and placed in each drug store of the city.

Jack Connors was one of the policemen and he met the Lone Wolf. In the gun duel that followed, Connors was killed and the Lone Wolf (Louis Berstein) captured.

Berstein was sentenced to die, but as the date neared for his execution, prison officials became panicky. Who was going to hang him? Frank Johnston of Gulfport, Mississippi, and self-described "Human Butcher" who had been doing the hangings in New Orleans for twenty years, was missing. Besides, the prison officials had had trouble enough with Johnston the last time he was in the city on a job.

Andy Ojeda, veteran New Orleans newspaperman, can tell about the trouble the prison officials had with Johnston better than anyone else. Ojeda was almost choked to death by Johnston.

Ojeda's experience with Johnston happened as the date neared for the hanging of Morris Mehojevick, sentenced to die for a criminal attack on an eleven-year-old girl. Johnston arrived in New Orleans, but he indicated right off that he did not care whether he performed the job or not. He kept threatening to leave.

Ojeda wrote a story about Johnston for his paper. It enraged the hangman and the next day the Gulfport man attacked the slight reporter, clutching him by the throat. Deputy sheriffs rescued Ojeda and Johnston was convicted of assault and battery and sentenced to thirty days. Among other things, the prison officials had made sure that the hangman would not leave the prison.

Johnston hung Mehojevick and right after the job, Sheriff Ed Carver of the hangman's home town showed up and took the "Human Butcher" back on a charge of horse theft.

But now had arrived the time for the execution of Berstein. Warden Dick Meredith was worried. Getting a hangman is not an easy job. Who wants to pull a lever that sends a man to his doom?

"I know a man who will do it," James B. Humphrey, New Orleans politician, told Warden Meredith.

"I hope so," the warden said.

Humphrey went to Henry Meyer. The carpenter was working on a job.

"You want a job for a couple of hours?" Humphrey said.

"What kind of a job?"

"Hanging a man."

"What is there in it for me?"

"Seventy-five dollars."

"Sure," Meyer said.

Louis Berstein was Meyer's first job. The next day he showed up on his job late, half drunk and flashing a roll of bills.

"Where did you get that roll?" a fellow worker asked.

"I hung a man."

Meyer was fired.

Tilly, Meyer's wife, never knew about that hanging, or any of the others that followed. She was paralyzed in the legs and rocked all day in a rocker he had bought for her. A little while later she died and Meyer sold the rocker.

In 1921, Phelix Birbiglia and Charles Zelenka, two dance-hall youths in New Orleans, took Bertha Neason, a married woman, out car riding. Bertha was known as the "Million Dollar Doll" around the dance halls because of the diamonds she wore.

The youths took Bertha out the West End Road, around by the Old Spanish Fort, and then up the Turtle Back Road. Birbiglia and Bertha, in the back seat, were caressing and kissing one another. Suddenly, Birbiglia shot her through the breast. He wanted her diamonds.

The two youths were sentenced to die and Meyer was notified. He was happy. This was going to be a two hundred dollar job.

As the date of the execution neared, Charles Zelenka made a sensational move to escape the noose. An ancient French-English law provides that if a woman of spotless reputation will marry a condemned prisoner in the shadow of the gallows, he will go free. Francois Villon, the celebrated French rogue, escaped the noose when a French noblewoman married him. So Zelenka's sweetheart, a seventeen-year-old crippled girl, married him.

Zelenka did not escape. Nor his companion, Birbiglia. Henry Meyer was there in soiled blue denims, dirty suspenders and an old, purple Mardi Gras mask.

Birbiglia went first. He walked firmly toward the gallows. He mounted the steps and stood calmly as the noose was adjusted. Meyer sprung the trap. The knot was deflected in the descent and the youth started clawing at his throat. Witnesses were horrified. On and on he hung there, struggling at the tightening rope. It was forty minutes before the youth expired. Newspapermen shook their heads. This Meyer was a rotten hangman.

Zelenka's death was more merciful. The noose was adjusted with more skill under his ear and his cervical vertebrae was cracked with instantaneous death.

Said Meyer after the hanging:

"They were the scaredest pair I've seen."

On May 8, 1921, a New Orleans garage man and five companions left the city in a high-powered, borrowed automobile for Independence, Louisiana, with the intention of robbing the bank of that little, strawberry town.

Dallas Calmes, a restaurant man whose place of business adjoined the bank, was awakened by his wife who saw a slinking figure in the alley. He got up, went out into the yard and was shot to death.

The six were captured. They were: Natalie Deamore, the garage man; Joe Bocchio, twenty-four, a chauffeur and ex-soldier; Joseph Rini, twenty-five, son of a Chicago barkeeper and ex-sailor; Andrea Lamantia, thirty-one, a barber; Roy Leona, grocery clerk and Joe Giglio, thirty-two, ex-soldier.

They were sentenced to die and twin-gallows were erected at Amite, the county seat of Tanginapahoa Parish, a few miles from Independence. Henry Meyer got the assignment. One hundred dollars a man, six hundred dollars for the whole job.

The whole nation was shocked. Six men dying for the

murder of one. Not Meyer. "I'd hang anybody," he said. "I'd hang my own brother if I had one and he committed a crime."

While Meyer sat in the sheriff's office drinking more and more liquor, two of the condemned men, Roy Leona and Deamore, attempted suicide.

Of the six men, only Joe Rini and Joseph Giglio, showed nerve. The others were carried to the gallows, fainting and half-unconscious. Rini and Giglio mounted the scaffold with firm steps and as Meyer adjusted the hood around Rini, the latter shouted at the witnesses:

"I hope you devils will all be satisfied."

~§~

THE YEARS PASSED and the toll of Henry Meyer mounted. The big muscles in his shoulders loosened more and more and his beaky nose grew sharper. He got drunk whenever he could raise the price.

Austin Boyle, a young reporter for the New Orleans *Item*, was sent out by his city editor to look up Meyer and interview him in his home. Nobody seemed to know where Meyer lived. But at last Boyle got a lead and on Dante Street he found him at home.

The hangman lived alone in two rooms behind a vacant store. It was sparsely furnished. There was an oil lamp, a table, a bench and a walnut double bed.

Meyer did not want to talk this day. At least not about hangings. But he was lonely. He did not want the reporter to go. He said:

"I had rather ride a streetcar than anything. Some

day when I get the money I am going to buy a little car. I am not going to throw my money away after the next job. No more spending it on fellers you thought was your friends. I'm going to hold onto it."

Boyle left the house and a neighbor slipped up to him. "For Christ's sake, don't put it in the paper. People around here don't know he is the hangman. Everybody will move out if you put it in the paper."

On February 2, 1929, arrived the day for the execution of the two principals in Louisiana's most celebrated love murder case. They were Mrs. Ada LeBouef and Dr. Thomas E. Dreher of Morgan City, Louisiana. Illicit lovers, this couple was found guilty of murdering the woman's husband, fixing weights to his body and dumping him in a stream.

It was the first time in the history of the state that, a woman was sentenced to die and what hangman would be willing to send a woman to death?

Henry Meyer would! The Franklin County sheriff came to New Orleans and looked up Meyer.

"How much will you hang Ada LeBouef and Dr. Dreher for?"

"Six hundred and fifty dollars," Meyer said.

"Isn't that steep?" the sheriff said.

"Six hundred flat then. But it's worth more to hang a woman, don't you think?"

Meyer got the job.

~§~

FRANKLIN. LOUISIANA, was the scene of the scheduled hangings. Meyer arrived in town, went promptly to the jail and started drinking. As the hour neared for the execution, he sent out a jailer to get him a mask. The jailer brought back a red bandana handkerchief.

Meyer put on the red hood and waited in the jail hall for Ada LeBouef to pass. When she went down the corridor that led to the gallows, Meyer fell in behind her.

The woman went up on the gallows, supported by Jailer Martel. On it, she begged:

"Don't let me hang there too long. Don't make me suffer any more than I have to. Isn't this a terrible thing? Oh, God, who can do this? This is murder itself."

Meyer tied her dress just below the knees. Then he stood up and placed the hood around her head.

"Don't make that rope too tight," the woman cried.

"Stand up straight," the jailer said.

"I can't," the woman wailed. "I . . . !"

Meyer pulled the lever and the woman hurtled to death.

A reporter, describing Meyer in the New Orleans *Times-Picayune's* account of the hanging, wrote:

"A nervousness was shown by the executioner as he bound the wrists and ankles of the prisoner with sash cord."

Said Meyer later:

"While the preacher was talking, I began tying her legs. I made a loop around her feet and two half hitches around liter legs. I gave her leg a good feel. She had a fine leg on her, but she didn't have her mind on legs then."

It was the LeBouef case that made pathologists re-regard Meyer with some suspicion. Was he a legal "blood lust" killer?

The services of Henry Meyer were in demand all over Louisiana. That is why his toll mounted. Twenty . . . . twenty-five . . . . thirty . . . .

Once he went over to Lake Charles for a job. He was sitting in the sheriff's office when a crowd began gathering outside.

"What's that crowd for?" Henry asked.

"They want to see you," the sheriff said.

"They do, uh?" Meyer got up. "Well, I'll give 'em a good look."

He went out on the balcony of the sheriff's office. The gathering below stared up at him uncertainly. They were a rustic looking bunch, this crowd in straw hats and work shoes. Their horror of the little man was reflected in their eyes.

"I must be a hell of a curiosity to you monkeys," Meyer said. "Take a good look at me so you'll know me the next time."

~§~

IN JANUARY OF 1931, three Chicago gangsters came to New Orleans and stuck up a bank. They were aided by a native criminal. The quartet was captured after they shot five people, one, a grocer, fatally. Meyer hung them all: Ito Jacques, Donald Rylich, George O'Day and Nelson Hart. That was June 1, 1932.

The next highly publicized hanging in which Meyer was to officiate was scheduled May 18, 1933. George Dalleo and John Capaci were to die for the murder of Charles Rabito, young grocery clerk whom they robbed of $900.

Gretna, just across the river from New Orleans, was to be the scene of the execution. Meyer went over early that morning, started greasing the hempen ropes with lard and rubbing lye into them.

The condemned pair were big men, both weighing more than two hundred pounds apiece. Dalleo went first and witnesses fainted. The drop tore the big Italian's head almost off. Meyer worked frantically to do better by Capaci, but it was almost as bad. The blood spurted.

Newspapermen were sickened. There followed editorials and a wave of protest against the hanging of criminals. Why not the chair? Lethal gas? A doctor suggested cyanide in a condemned man's coffee and a politician asked that the guillotine be considered.

The bulbous lower lip of Meyer curled at all this protest. "What's the difference? Chair, knife or rope? They didn't suffer none. If it was left to me, I'd pull their heads off!"

Two bills were introduced in the state legislature doing away with hanging and substituting the electric chair. Meyer got worried. He was broke again and here, if this bill were passed, he never would have a good-paying job again. Not unless he took some precaution. So to W. L. Himes, general manager of the State Penitentiary at Baton Rouge, he wrote:

> *I see in the papers that they may install*
> *electric chair and if you have no one to*
> *handle it I make application for the*
> *position, because I have been handling all*
> *the Execusions for 15 or 18 years and also*
> *whent to different parts of the state. I also*
> *handlet the Ade Labuf Case If you have no*
> *one picket out for the Job I will be Ever so*
> *mutch Oblige if you would let me no as*
> *soon as Possible.*
>
> *Yours truly, Henry Meyer.*

The worries of Henry Meyer were needless, however, because Governor Oscar K. Allen vetoed the bill.

On July 21 of 1933, Willie Walton, a Negro, was hanged, and that made it thirty-seven for Meyer.

On January 2, 1935, prison officials called Kenneth Neu down to the chapel and there, in his blue polo shirt, light trousers and tan slippers, the youth heard the reading of Governor O. K. Allen's death warrant.

"Aw, it's only a piece of paper," Neu said.

~§~

HENRY MEYER, already off his hospital cot, heard the news, tottered out of the prison and made his way home. There he got down his fishing tackle and went to a nearby bayou. He caught a bag of shrimp and these he sent to Neu. Along with a Coca-Cola.

Neu sang:

> "Soon the gallows will be ready
> "And I'll' walk through the little green
>   door.
> "Oh the gallows will be ready
> "With a great big hate in the middle of the
>   floor.
> "Hi diddle diddle, I feel O.K.
> "Fit as a fiddle and ready to hang."

He ate the shrimp and smacked his lips and lingered over the "coke."

Came the eve of the hanging. In his cell, Neu discussed the mechanics of engines with Father Ryan. A telegram came. It was from Barney Rapp, orchestra leader, formerly of the New Orleans resort, Club Forest, and now playing in a Cincinnati hotel. It said: "God bless you. Is there anything I can do."

Neu wired back: "Play 'Blue Moon' and 'Love in Bloom.'"

A little later he heard. Rapp's voice over the radio. "These songs are dedicated to a dear friend in New Orleans."

Over on the filling station corner a thin, aged man with a bony neck paused and looked up at the cell. In his pocket was the commission of a deputy sheriff. He had secured it that day. All hangmen must have commissions.

Neu awoke early on his execution day. He sang in his bath: *Lay My Head Beneath a Rose, June Moon* and *Love in Bloom*. The latter was dedicated to a nameless young woman who met him while he was under the sentence of death and was his greatest love, he said. She was his godmother when he was baptized into the Roman Catholic religion.

He went to Mass and sang the loudest of all. After that he sat in his cell and cheered his visitors.

"It's not the drop that's going to worry me," he said. "It's the sudden stop."

Then came high noon. Neu was going up on the scaffold. When he got on top, he grinned and began jigging. Suddenly, he stopped:

"Where is that fellow?"

"*Umpf,*" a voice said. It was Meyer. He took Neu's hands and began to tie them.

"Thanks for that shrimp and coke," Neu said.

"Umpf," Meyer said. He was in a hurry and he shook out the folds of the hood and began placing it around Neu's head.

"Don't muss my hair," Neu said.

Meyer yanked the noose tight around Neu's throat, stepped back and down the singing killer plunged.

His heart was strong and it took him eighteen minutes to die. It was, technically, a perfect execution.

That afternoon Neu was laid to rest in St. Patrick's No. 3 cemetery. Meyer started drinking.

~§~

AFTER DARK. that evening, Meyer shuffled into the office of the Police Secretary in the Criminal Courts Building. There were court house attaches and newspapermen there. His eyes were drink-blurred. He sat down in a chair.

"It was a good job," he said. "I feel good about it."

The onlookers nodded.

"I want to borrow a few nickels," Meyer said. "I ain't got paid yet."

There was an awkward silence.

"I need a drink," Meyer said.

A man got up and went to the telephone. He got a number and said: "Beer."

Meyer relaxed in his chair. "I'm going home early tonight," he said.

—Real Detective, February 1936

The BLACK CAT *and*
The FOUR WHO HANGED

By GEORGE REYER, SUPERINTENDENT *of* POLICE,
NEW ORLEANS, LA.

As told to EDWARD ANDERSON

SATURDAY NIGHT in New Orleans: wide, famous Canal Street ablaze under the street lamps, the glittering shop windows and traffic straining in the deep, vibrant roar of thousands of moving feet; Decatur, the waterfront and market street of produce smells and roistering bars, blatant and loud-mouthed; the lamp-lighted, old French Quarter with knots of aproned housewives lingering at the corner groceries; fashionable, oak and palm-lined St. Charles Avenue, the thoroughfare of colonial mansions and darkened churches waiting Sabbath.

That Saturday of November 22nd, 1930, I was the new Chief of Police of New Orleans, second in command of all the city's law enforcement organization. But that night I was doing the same thing I had been doing almost every Saturday night since my first detective assignment ten years before—cruising about the city in my car, watching and waiting. More than ever that Saturday night, I felt the responsibility of protecting these hurrying throngs, these busy storekeepers, the city's two dozen branch banks. And New Orleans was busy this night. Money was flowing. It was in the boom days.

That had already been marked by crime. Patrolman William Blumstein, veteran officer, was dead, riddled by the bullets of three escaping Negro holdup men. The case was well in hand though. Several suspects were in jail.

At eight thirty o'clock I called the sergeant's desk at Police Headquarters.

"Everything is okay, Chief," the sergeant reported.

I went back to my car and continued cruising. It was a cold, raw night. Another half hour, I thought, and the banks and stores will close. The danger of holdup's will end. Then I will go home. I did not know that right at that time underworld movements were taking place that within fifteen minutes would throw the city into one of the most sensational nights of its modern crime history and be followed by events that would make the case one of the most dramatic of the South's criminal records.

At nine o'clock, I called the sergeant's desk again:

"That you, Chief? The sergeant shouted excitedly. "Hell is popping at Rocheblave and Iberville Streets. The Canal branch bank there knocked over. Four bandits. Patrolman Alberts is shot. They're shooting up the whole end of town."

I made sure that two of my crack men, Captains John Grosch and James Cripps, were flashed, issued orders for reserves. And then I set out, siren open, for the

Rocheblave-Iberville suburban community. I knew the spot. It was a busy market corner of groceries and meat markets and drug stores and the branch bank.

The community was excited, hysterical and stunned. There was still the smell of gunpowder. Behind the car on the market side of the street was a pool of blood. Here Patrolman Louis C. Alberts had fallen, his stomach full of lead. He had been carried to the hospital.

Witnesses described what had happened:

A few minutes before nine o'clock, a light-colored sedan parked a few feet below the bank's entrance. Three young men got out of it, a fourth remaining at the wheel of the machine. The three moved toward the bank, one taking up a stand at its entrance and two more entering.

Williard J. Drez, the bank manager, inside the teller's cage, looked up. A young man with a sharp, cruel mouth and glinting eyes held a gun on him.

"Stick them up!" the gunman said. His voice had a Southern accent. His companion shoved a briefcase under the window. "Fill that up," he ordered.

Drez began obeying. The other tellers in the cage, John Percy, Edwin Thorn and Maurice Soniat, stared in terror.

"I've got it in my mind to shoot," the Southern-voiced bandit growled. "I've got it in my mind and I'm liable to start any minute."

Drez worked frantically, stuffing currency into the case.

"Don't forget that silver," the bandit warned. "And don't lose any time. I'll kill you if you don't get on faster, I said." . . . . *Spat!* A bullet crashed against the steel of the cage.

Outside, across the street, Patrolman Alberts quit his conversation with Ernest Grunewald of 115 North Rocheblave Street and looked in the direction of the bank. Was that it shot he heard? He frowned and started across the street. The figure in front of the bank lunged toward him. Bewildered, Alberts' hand moved instinctively toward his hip. Then the gun in the hand of the bandit roared. Alberts stiffened, collapsed.

The gunman turned, raced toward the light-colored sedan. The machine was moving even as he hit the running board. The car swerved around the corner.

Out of the bank came the pair with the bulging brief case. In it was more than three thousand dollars in currency and silver. They looked. The car was gone.

Charles Bretchel, of 2905 Bienville Street, a steel worker, was parking his car right at this time. He had seen the policeman fall. He leaped from his car, sped to the side of the fallen officer, seized the dropped gun, and opened fire on the two in front of the bank. His fire was returned. The bandits raced away, turned the Iberville Street corner and dashed toward Tonti.

Salvadore Mancuso, standing in front of his fruit stand, saw two running men approaching, guns in their hand. He picked up his revolver.

"Get back in there," the bandit of the Southern voice yelled and punctuated his command with a shot. Mancuso returned the fire.

The pair fled on, vanishing from the first pursuers into the narrow, dark streets of the French Quarter.

There was by this time a score of officers in that section of the city. Some, off duty, had come in civilian clothes. Storekeepers and citizens kept sounding alarms. Officers followed the hue and cry, here and yonder.

Policeman John Ponsaa, on a motorcycle, came into the district. In his side car was Patrolman Fred Wilson, in civilian clothes. They saw two running figures and Wilson opened fire. They abandoned the motorcycle and started a foot pursuit.

Raymond Rizzo, thirty-eight-year-old grocer at 2235 Iberville, saw the fugitives race by and then the two pursuing officers. He snatched up a .22 caliber pistol and started in behind.

"You better stay out of this," Wilson warned him.

The grocer shook his head and gripped his small revolver tighter.

At Galvez Street, the two fugitives got behind a palm tree, prepared to make a stand. Toward them the two officers and Rizzo ran.

Frank T. Meade, photographer, of 3037 Bienville, saw the battle. The officers, too, got behind trees. The shooting drew a squad of police. There was a burst of machinegun fire. Two figures toppled: Raymond Rizzo, the grocer, and Patrolman Wilson. The grocer cried: "I am shot. I am shot!"

Again the fugitives were on the run. Pansaa, his fellow officer Wilson and the grocer on the ground behind, still hounded their trail.

The two pursued suspects turned into an alley, leaped a fence and vanished. Pansaa went over the fence, too. He crossed the yard, jumped another fence. Right below him was the crouching figure of a man.

Pansaa leveled his gun. "I give up," the panting man cried.

Beside his captive was a .405 caliber pistol and Pansaa picked this up. He shoved his gun in the other's ribs and marched him to the street. There a police car picked them up.

It was this police car, commanded by Captain John Grosch, that I stopped.

"What have you got?" I asked.

"A hot one," Grosch said.

I got in the police car and we started for Headquarters. The captive was a medium-sized youth with a sullen, defiant face. The frisk of his clothing had netted five hundred dollars in currency.

"What's your name, Bud?" I asked.

"Taylor," he said. "Herman Taylor." His voice had a Southern accent. He was from Hartsville, Alabama, he said.

"Well, Taylor, you're in a jam," I said.

Captain Grosch began nodding. "Yep. A jam. A fine bunch of pals you had, Taylor."

"Don't let that worry you," Taylor snapped.

"They certainly took run-out powder on you," Grosch went on.

"They'll look after me."

"Yeah," Grosch scoffed. "Like they looked out for you back yonder. Scrammed while you knocked off a cop."

Taylor stiffened, his eyes widening. "What do you mean?"

"Just what I said," replied Grosch grimly.

"I didn't shoot no cop."

"Maybe you didn't," Grosch said. "Maybe it was one of your pals, but there's fifty people back there ready to swear it was you."

"Honest to God, I didn't shoot no cop."

"Maybe you didn't, but you're going to take the rap for it. You can thank those swell pals of yours for that."

"I didn't kill no cop," Taylor said weakly.

We went into the detective offices of Headquarters. Under the lights, Taylor proved to be an ashen-faced youth of twenty-five. His eyes were bloodshot and his hands trembled. I knew he was weakening. He was undergoing a form of third degree, but it is my conviction that police should use the same methods in dealing with criminals that the criminals uses on their victims.

"Look, Taylor," I said. "Are you going to give us a hand to grab those run-out pals of yours?"

He hesitated. "The rats did pull out and leave me all right."

"Are you going to take it alone?"

"What's your proposition, Chief?" he said.

"There's no proposition. It's all up to you."

"All right," Taylor said.' "I got in New Orleans three nights ago. On a freight train. I was planning on catching a banana boat out of here and going to South America or somewhere. Then I ran into a guy. He said a bank job here would be easy."

"What was his name?"

"Leo. Leo Castelano. I'm not sure though that that is his real name. He had the car and everything and a couple of more pals."

"Where was your hangout?"

"Let me see. Ontario Street."

"Ontario Street?" I repeated. "Taylor, you're lying."

"Nossir, Chief."

"There is no Ontario Street in New Orleans."

"It's by a schoolhouse," Taylor gestured helplessly. "That's where we were to meet after the job and divvy the stuff."

Grosch held up a notebook he had taken from Taylor. "Chief, there's a local telephone number in here. It might lead to something."

I looked at Taylor. "Think you can find that house?"

"Maybe so," Taylor said.

Ordering my men to shoot Taylor if he made the least move to try and escape, I told them to take him out for a ride around the city and see if he could locate the rendezvous.

After their departure, I studied the telephone number. It was a local number all right. I dialed it. A woman's voice answered.

"Who is this?" I asked.

"Ida Lopez."

"Do you know a Herman Taylor, Ida?" I asked.

"No, I don't."

"This is the police, Ida, and I want you to do some tall thinking. Who have you given your telephone number to lately?"

For several moments the wire was quiet and then the woman said: "Ito. Ito Jacques. I gave him my number."

"Who is he?"

"He's been out of town and he just got back."

"Where does he live?"

"I don't know exactly. It's somewhere, though, on Octavia Street."

I clicked up the receiver.

Immediately, I sent out word for Grosch and his men to return with Taylor to Headquarters. Waiting for their return, disturbing reports were coming in. Rizzo, the grocer, was dying. There was hope, however, for the Officers Alberts and Wilson. But the upsetting report was that Rizzo and Wilson were the victims of the gunfire of my own men. Bungling added to unsolved crime! I was sweating.

Grosch came in and said, "Think he's lying, Chief. We looked—"

"Did you go on Octavia?"

"Say, that may be the spot. And there's a school house on Octavia, too!"

Out Octavia Street we drove swiftly. We passed the school. Then Taylor pointed: "That's the place."

It was an old frame house with a second-story attic and shuttered windows. The address was: 1442 St. Claude Avenue. It was at the corner of Octavia and St. Claude.

I went up to the door. A woman met me. She was Daisy Banks, colored, and the landlady.

"Who's staying here?" I asked.

Her head began going up and down excitedly. "I knew there was something wrong. They're upstairs now. I knew it. They came here three days ago. Ito brought them. I was going to ask them to leave. They're white folks."

"How many?"

"Two white men and Ito and the girl."

I began issuing Orders: "Get fifty men here. Surround the house. Shoot anybody that tries to leave it."

Then I started up the stairway to the attic room. It was a narrow, dark stairway, barely wide enough for a man's passage. When I stood before the door of the attic room, I rapped.

"Who's there?" a guarded voice called.

"The Police."

"Go to *hell!*" came the reply, and then the light in the room went out.

The door was a fairly flimsy one, but it did not give with my first lunge. I tried again and this time the lock snapped. The door burst wide. I stood there, gun in hand my flash-light probing. The room seemed deserted.

The windows opening out on the roof of the house were open. I stepped quickly to one. The roof was clear and it was twenty-five feet to the ground!

The light in the room was turned on and there, in a corner, cowered a girl. Her eyes were wide with fright. She could barely speak through her trembling lips.

"Take her on down," I said.

Below, in the street, there were shouts. Squad after squad of officers had been arriving. There were more than fifty men down there now. I went back down the steps into the street.

Fingers were pointing at the top of the house. Behind a chimney crouched a figure. I ordered quiet and then yelled at the man behind the chimney to come down. He only clung there. "Fire!" I ordered.

There was a volley of shots. Corporal Thomas Kieran,

just a few feet away from me, clasped his face. Blood was gushing from his mouth. The figure behind the chimney stood up, reeling. He had been shot. In his hand he weakly waved a white handkerchief. Men went up to bring him down. Corporal Kieran, we found out later, was struck.by a ricocheting bullet of our own fire.

When the officers returned with the wounded captive (he was shot in the thigh), they had another prisoner. He was a light-skinned mulatto. He was found biding under a bundle of soiled clothing in the house.

My rap on the door had made all the men leave the room. Two of them stayed in the house, but a third was seen to jump from the top of the house to the street below. He fled up an alley, but my men captured him, three blocks away, hiding under shrubbery.

Two hours after the holdup of the Rocheblave branch of the Canal Bank we had recovered virtually all of the loot and had four men and a girl in the detective offices at Headquarters. The captives were:

George O'Day, twenty-one, of St. Louis. He was the one shot while hiding behind the chimney. Donald Rylich, twenty-eight, of Chicago, of Serbian descent. It was Rylich who had dropped from the attic window to the street. Ito Jacques, twenty-seven, native Orleanian, a mulatto who called himself a "Creole." Herman Taylor, our first captive, the bandit of the Southern accent. Edna Harte, nineteen, common-law wife of Herman Taylor.

I questioned each one separately. The girl, Edna, a bewildered, cringing figure in her washed-out pink silk dress, velvet coat and darned hose, kept shaking her head. "I don't know anything about it. I didn't know they were going to rob a bank. I love Herman. That is all I know. I loved him and came down here with him. He said if I didn't I would be sorry. We have been here three days. I stayed in the room every day. I didn't know anyone here. Then they came back tonight. They had money. Rylich said: 'I sure bumped me off a cop.' Somebody told me to hand them a paper. I handed them a newspaper and they wrapped some of the money in it. That is all I did to help them.

"I want to go back to Ottawa, Illinois. That's where my mother is. They are in the Salvation Army work. I was in the Army ever since I was a kid. I sang on the street corners and beat a tambourine. It was good, but I only know that now. I started going to the house of a woman who sold beer. There were fellows there and I met Herman. I love him. But I wish I was in Ottawa now. I will walk back there. I will crawl back if you will only let me go?"

~§~

EDNA was placed in a cell. Accessory charges were filed against her.

Donald Rylich, a slender, swarthy man, the lookout and assailant of Patrolman Alberts, kept shaking his head. "It was the black cat," he declared. "That big, black cat. When we were going to the bank, it ran across in front of our car. I said 'It's all off, boys.' O'Day just laughed. I kept on telling them. 'Didn't you see that black cat? Let's pull it some other time.' They all said it was too late to stop. It was the black cat!"

George O'Day, the youngest of the lot, exhibited the coolest nerves:

"Yes, we come here just especially for the job. We been running liquor up in Chi, but we was tired of working for the other feller. What we wanted was a stake to start our own biz and then up shows this high-yaller. He says a bank is a cinch to knock over in this town and he has the car and talks us into coming down here. We gets here and he puts us up in that house and we start getting all set for the job. We tanks up pretty good before we starts out. Corn liquor. We messed things up good."

Ito Jacques trembled and mumbled: "I'm innocent. I didn't even have a gun. I didn't shoot nobody. You can't hold that against me. I was the driver of the car all right, but I didn't shoot nobody."

Three days after the holdup, the little grocer, Raymond Rizzo who had started out with a .22 pistol to aid officers in the capture of Rylich and O'Day, died. All the other wounded were recovering.

Who, killed Raymond Rizzo? This became a problem. Said Patrolman Fred Wilson: "I was felled by submachine gunfire. I saw the flash and then felt the sting."

Only the police had machineguns that night.

There were witnesses who declared that they saw the wife of Rizzo imploring police not to shoot. That her husband was in the line of fire.

Maurice ONeill, head of the Identification Department of the New Orleans Police, started work. The slugs probed from Rizzos body were examined by him, and he declared them to be the lead of a .45 caliber pistol. Patrolman Wilson may have been shot by a machinegun, he announced, but not Rizzo.

~§~

WHEN TAYLOR was captured he had an empty .45.
O'Neill found that the slugs fired from this weapon made
rifling marks that twisted to the left and this was
identical with the slugs that caused Rizzos death. That
settled that.

Immediately, District Attorney Eugene Stanley filed
murder charges against the quartet. For the night of
terror they had caused in New Orleans, he announced, he
would send them to the gallows. The Louisiana law
provides that when a band of persons conspire and agree
to commit a felony and a murder is committed, though it
not be intended, by anyone of the defendants, all are
responsible.

The spectacle of four men facing the noose for the
murder of one was not new in Louisiana. At Amite,
several years previously, six men died on the gallows for
the murder during an attempted bank burglary of a hotel
keeper, Dallas Calmes.

On December 24th, 1931, I became Superintendent
of the New Orleans police, first in command. Over in the
Parish Prison, the three ex-Chicago beer runners and
Jacques awaited trial. Taylor and Rylich were prison
problems. They snarled at guards, showed ill-concealed
rage and finally they were ordered placed in the prison
"dungeon."

The dungeon was on the third floor of the old prison.
Its barred windows were sealed by heavy galvanized iron

and no sunlight entered the cell. Incarcerated in the dungeon on this particular day with Rylich and Taylor was Joseph Smith, awaiting trial for robbery.

A few minutes after five o'clock on the afternoon of January 15th, 1931, a prison porter shouted an alarm. He pointed at three men, one of them running painfully, disappearing up an alley across the street from the prison.

The dungeon was empty. Sunlight streamed into it through a hole, picked out brick by brick, alongside the window. It was just big enough for medium-sized men to squeeze through. The three had crawled, like human flies, from barred window to barred window, down the three stories of the prison to the wall. It was a twenty-five foot drop from the top of the wall, but each had made it. One of them had been injured, however. A trail of blood led across the street.

~§~

A FEW HOURS LATER, E. G. Wooledge of 3510 Calhoun Street, reported that two men had commandeered his car, threw him out and made away with it. We began sending wires to all surrounding cities and towns.

The following day the situation was tense in the Prison. Sheriff George W. Williams fired four deputy sheriffs for laxity of duty. It was the prisoners, however, who were proving a problem. Sheriff Williams feared revolt and I sent him four policemen to stem the threat.

On January 24th, I got a call from Sheriff Albert of Buras, a small community in the Mississippi River delta country, some fifty miles south of New Orleans. Sheriff

Albert said he had a good tip. Would I send him some men?

Four men left for Buras in the fastest police car. There, in the custody of Sheriff Alberts, was Smith. He was badly wounded. Smith said he had shot himself accidentally, and, seeking medical attention, ran into the law. His companions, he said, Rylich and Taylor, were hiding in an abandoned hunter's lodge on an island up the bayou.

In a motorboat, the officers started up, the bayou. A few miles from the described hut, they cut their motor and began rowing. Soon the tiny island appeared—then the outline of the hunter's hut, its roof barely showing above the towering reeds and marsh grass. Quietly, they grounded the boat, advanced toward the darkened hut stealthily. With the shack surrounded, one of the men went to the door. He called.

"What do you want?" a voice called.

"Open up!"

"All right." The door opened and there stood Rylich, his face gaunt, weak with hunger, sleepy eyed. On a pallet, his foot broken, lay Taylor.

~§~

BACK TO NEW ORLEANS came the two escapes. They blamed Smith: "Just 'cause he shot himself like a damned kid and ran away hollering 'Mama' is no sign he should have squealed on us," Taylor said.

"That black cat," Rylich said. "It's still that black cat."

"We planned the break for days," Taylor said. "When

I come to that wall though, I'd liked to have backed out. I thought I was on top of the Woolworth Building. Then I thought, I'm going to hang anyway, and I jumped. I busted my foot. The other fellows had to get the cars. I wasn't any good. They'd get a car and come back and throw me in like a sack. They were pals then."

Two weeks later, the trials of the four started, and within three days they were found guilty of Rizzos murder and sentenced to hang. The girl, Edna Harte, was freed and returned to Illinois.

Then came June 1st, 1932, the day set for the wholesale hanging.

Taylor, the boy from Alabama, the one who had brandished his gun so wildly in the holdup, was now the mildest speaking of all. He acted secretive when visitors came and said he had a device in his mind which would prevent holdups of banks. If his life was spared, he said, it would be given to society. He was regarded as a man losing his mind.

O'Day, freckle-faced and tousle-headed, grinned and talked a "blue streak." A few hours before noon of the hanging day, a guard offered him nerve tonic: "I don't want that stuff," he shook his head. "You need it worse than I do."

Rylich sat on the edge of his bunk, clad only in underwear and a cap. He had given his old clothing to the three Negroes in Death Row, the condemned slayers, incidentally, of Patrolman William Blumstein the officer killed on the same Saturday the quartet pulled their job. Rylich still blamed the black cat.

The hour approached. Henry (Tricksy) Meyer sat in

the Sheriff's office waiting. He was the hangman and all that morning he had greased the four new ropes. It was to be the second biggest day of Meyer's long career as the hangman of New Orleans and Southern Louisiana. He was the hangman in the execution of the six Italians at Amite. Seventy-two years old now, Meyer has hanged thirty-seven men and one woman in his career. The woman was Ada Lebouef, convicted with her paramour, a Louisiana doctor, for the murder of her husband.

In executions, the weak go first and Ito Jacques, the mulatto, was the first to go up. It was a hot, blistering day and the gallows room was stifling. Jacques dropped through the trap as Meyer, hooded in an old Mardi Gras mask, pressed the lever. Next was Taylor, then O'Day and last Rylich. He was the gamest of all, smiling at the sweating spectators as he stood on the trap.

The execution required only seventy minutes, and, technically speaking, was a good job for Henry Meyer, the hangman.

—*True Detective Mysteries, December 1935*

NEW ORLEANS' TWIN TRUNK MURDERS

By ASSISTANT DISTRICT ATTORNEY CONRAD MEYER, JR., of NEW ORLEANS, LOUISIANA

As told to EDWARD ANDERSON

OLD NETTIE PASS, the colored woman, living at the rear of the one-hundred year-old house at 715 Ursuline Street in the old French Quarter of New Orleans, sat in the sunshine of the courtyard that Thursday morning of October 27th, 1927, and wondered why the white folks up there in the front, second-floor apartment were so quiet. Ordinarily, the two pretty young married up there were out on the narrow gallery shaking our bedclothes, or at least the three little children of the household were running around the courtyard or yelling and whooping up and down the long, gloomy areaway that led to the street.

Sunshine bathed the brick-laid courtyard, brightened the green shutters of the windows, the yellow, scrubbed stairway and the high, bolted doors of the apartments. On a line in the courtyard next door some colored clothes fluttered as they dried in the breeze that came off the Mississippi River only two blocks away. It was a characteristic courtyard scene of the *Vieux Carre* (Old Quarter)—a scene that many Southern artists love to paint. Just a few blocks away was old St. Louis Cathedral and The Cabildo, the Spanish prison where the early-day pirates of the Mexican Gulf were hanged.

But Old Nettie, sitting there in front of the one-time slave quarters of the house, kept musing on this morning's strange quiet on the balcony above. Six people lived up there, and there were visitors almost every day.

Up there in that apartment lived Henry Moity, the father of the three children and head of that household. Nettie had not seen him. He was a nice-looking young man, trimly built and meticulously polite to everyone. He painted pictures of beautiful women. That was not the way he made his living though. He painted signs for the lobbies of theaters and up until a few years ago he had had a steady job painting signs in the big brewery over by the river. Everybody said Henry was a first-rate painter and a nice fellow. He drank though sometimes. He was generous then and would come home laden with candies and ice cream for the three children.

Then there was Theresa, Henry's wife. She was a pretty little woman who smiled and laughed a lot. She and Henry were always kissing and hugging. They had been childhood sweethearts back in their hometown, New Iberia, Louisiana, and there they had married.

Theresa was always heavily rouged and wore bright clothes. Some of the neighbors said she neglected the children. She was writing a story about her life, and sometimes she played the piano.

Next of the adults in the household was Leonide, a woman just a little older than Theresa. She also loved rouge and bright clothes. She was the wife of Henry's brother, Joseph. But lately she and Joseph had had a very serious difficulty and they had split up.

Then there were the three children of Henry and Theresa: seven-year-old Theda, six-year-old Gloria, and three-year-old 'Soapsuds', the boy. Sometimes the parents quarreled because Henry did not believe their mother did not look after them well enough. But most of the time they were kissing and going on like they loved each other a lot.

Then there was Joseph Moity, the older brother of Henry and the husband of the other woman Leonide. He lived up there for five months but he moved away after difficulty with his wife. He did not smile very much. Up until a few weeks ago he had been a streetcar conductor, but he lost his job. Things like that did not make a man happy.

Then, too, there was the other fellow who was around the place a lot. His name was Frank Kimmel. He was a sign-painter too, and he and Henry Moity did jobs together. The ex-streetcar conductor, Joseph, did not like Frank Kimmel. Frank Kimmel was one of the reasons why he and his wife, Leonide, had separated.

Down on the street in front of the building in the real estate office, was another man who was thinking

about the Moity's. He was Joe Caruso, the landlord. The
Moity's owed him three weeks back rent. The Moity's had
been pretty good tenants, however, and he was in the
habit of going up and chatting with Theresa once in
awhile.

But on this particular Thursday Old Nettie, there in
the courtyard, continued to look questioningly up at the
silent apartment. For seven months she had been used to
seeing them every day, and now it was as if they all had
vanished.

Up the long passageway from the street came the
sound of steps. Old Nettie waited. A heavy, bland-faced
woman came into the courtyard toward Nettie. She was
Mrs. Alcee Lacamu, a sister of the two Moity brothers.
Mrs. Lacamu was a widow, a seamstress in an overall
factory.

"Did Henry leave any clothes with you for his
children?" Mrs. Lacamu asked.

"Clothes?" Nettie repeated. "No, he didn't leave no
clothes with me for nobody."

"Well, he brought his kids over to my place last night
and they're all naked. Poor me. I have to get some clothes
for them."

Nettie looked up at the silent apartment. So did
Lacamu. But the visitor did not get up to go. She thanked
Nettie and then her steps were heard echoing and dying
away as she walked through the passageway that led to
the street.

Nettie continued to look up at the gallery above. It
was afternoon now and still there had been no sign of
anyone. The children were over at their aunt's, but where

were the two pretty women?

After a little while Nettie got out of her chair and started laboring up the stairway to the balcony. The Moity apartment door was a little ajar. Nettie called, then she pushed door open. All was dark in the front chamber. She called, but again there was no answer. Nettie went in quietly, but she came out screaming.

Two life insurance collectors, Jules Chatelaine, 1009 Kerlerec Street, in an adjoining court yard, turned startled eyes toward the woman.

Nettie was pointing at the door. "Blood!" she cried. "It's all over the floor! Blood!"

The two insurance men hurried to the street and notified the landlord, Joe Caruso. The three of them went up and entered the apartment, but they, too, did not linger. The floor of that front room, the walls even, were splattered with blood!

Outside, in the street, a crowd began to gather. Some seen the terror-stricken face of Nettie and heard the shouts of "blood." A police car, siren screaming, was approaching. Reporters from the newspapers were pushing through the crowd. Already the old house on Ursuline Street was becoming a place of mystery.

Doctor George F. Roeling, one of New Orleans' best known public officials, was the coroner who came that day. With him, too, were Detectives George Grosch and William Vandervoot.

The apartment had four rooms, running from the courtyard to the front street. The investigators entered the rear room. When the light was turned on, the glow of the naked bulb revealed an appalling scene:

The bare wooden floor was streaked and smudged with blood. The bed on the left, its clothing torn and twisted, was saturated with red. Wearing apparel was scattered about. On a dresser stood an empty wine bottle. It was picked up and examined. There were bloody fingerprints on it. Under the bed lay a huge, bloody knife—a machete, a sword-like instrument used in Louisiana to cut sugar cane.

The trail of blood ran from the first room up to the sleeping room on the street front. Detectives bent down and examined the trail. Bare feet had gone back and forth, literally wading in blood.

On the front room bed there was some blood, too. But the bedclothes were little disturbed. An investigator in the bathroom shouted. He had discovered that the tub was blood-smeared. And at its bottom lay human hair, teeth and small bones!

The search went on. Here was a case of painter's brushes. And here, in this front room, a brand new trunk. Its top was raised . . . .

There, quartered and stripped like something on a butcher's block, were the remains of a human body. A woman's. It lay on a pile of baby clothes. It was Theresa, the wife of Henry, the painter.

In the front room officers found another trunk. When the lid was lifted, the body of another female was discovered; it was decapitated, legs severed at thighs and knees; fingers stripped.

It was Leonide, the estranged wife of Joseph, the ex-streetcar conductor.

~§~

OUTSIDE, the crowd learned of the bodies in the trunks; of the monster with the machete. The building on Ursuline Street had become a house of horror. Joe Caruso, the real estate man and landlord, closed his doors.

Coroner Roeling reported that the women had been dead twelve hours.

My chief, District Attorney Eugene Stanley said: "A madman may have killed these two women, but it was a butcher who dismembered their bodies."

Nettie Compass, the woman who discovered the crime said: "I never heard nothing. I saw them women last night. They could have murdered a thousand up there and I wouldn't have heard it."

Newspaper men put Nettie's words to a test. One of them went in one of the horror chambers and closed the door. He yelled. Then he came out and asked the people if they had heard him? They had not. The walls were absolutely sound proof.

Investigators had a list of names within a half hour, people they wanted to question. These included:

(1) Mrs. Alcee Lacamu, the sister of the two Moity boys and the woman who had approached Nettie that morning asking for clothes.

(2) Joseph Moity, the ex-street car conductor and estranged husband of the other dead woman.

(3) Henry Moity, the painter and husband of the other dead woman.

(4) Frank Kimmel, the sign painter who was Henry's assistant.

In the meantime, Coroner Roeling was reconstructing the murders for newspaper reporters whose sweating city editors were pressing them for more and more news of the crime as they rushed extras to the street.

"Theresa Moity struggled for her life," Coroner Roeling said. "She was asleep when attacked, but she probably recognized her assailant. Her beds shows evidence of a terrific struggle. She was struck with some heavy object, a blackjack perhaps. Her jaws were crushed.

"Leonide never knew what struck her. She was hit and fell out of bed. The bed clothing was barely disturbed. All the blood was on the floor."

It did not take investigators long to find Frank Kimmel, the fellow who was in the Moity household a good deal and helped Henry with his painting jobs. He was in the house of detention, incarcerated there the day before on the complaint of Joseph Moity, the ex-streetcar conductor. Kimmel, however was able to establish a satisfactory alibi.

Patrolman Eugene Dakin, whose beat was on Ursuline Street, gave this information:

On the Saturday night preceding the discovery of the bodies, the woman. Theresa, had come to him for help. She said her husband, Henry, was intoxicated and had a gun and was threatening her. Patrolman Dakin accompanied her back to the apartment. Henry was there, drinking. Dakin did not find a gun, however, and after talking to the pair a little while, and smoothing things over, he left.

~§~

OTHER INVESTIGATORS went to the home of Mrs. Alcee Lacamu at 628 Toulouse Street, only a few blocks away.

"Where is Henry Moity, your brother?" the woman asked.

"Henry? . . . I have not seen him since two o'clock this morning. He came then and brought his children. They are here now, the children, and not a stitch to wear. Poor me. I work all day and my daughter, Mary, too, and these children"

"Where is your brother?"

"Joe? . . . .Why he's here. He spent the night here."

Joseph Moity was there. He looked like a man who had had but little sleep lately and he stared at the officers bewilderedly.

Joseph Moity began talking: "Henry was here this morning. Around two o'clock. He came back to where I was sleeping and I got up and started making coffee. He says: 'Joe, our wives are going to leave us.' I wanted to go over to his place then, but we didn't. He was drinking. You go and find Henry. You will see that I am telling you the truth."

"What was this trouble you have been having with your wife, Joe?" the former streetcar conductor was then asked.

"Well, the other night, it was on the nineteenth of this month, she tells me: 'Joe, I don't love you no more, so you take your furniture and babies. Let's separate.' I had been noticing lipstick and stuff like that around that other fellows have been giving her. I took my children to New Iberia and came back here, and I've been living with my sister here ever since. I hope you'll find Henry so you'll know I'm telling the truth."

"These poor little naked children," Mrs. Lacamu shook her head. "Poor me. They won't miss their mother much though. She didn't have much time for them. And me working all the time."

The officers left the Lacamu residence with Joseph Moity in custody. He was cool and calm as he identified the bodies of the two women at the morgue. He was taken to jail where he was held as a material witness, and his bond fixed at ten thousand dollars.

Where was Henry Moity, the painter? Everyone in New Orleans was asking that question the next day. And every police officer in the state of Louisiana was on the lookout for him. The newspapers published photographs of him in the uniform he wore when he was in the American Navy. He was described:

"Dark complexion, dimple in chin. Thirty years old. Weighs around one-hundred and fifty pounds. Has tattoo of nude woman on right arm. Last seen wearing green silk shirt."

Joseph Moity, brother of the hunted man, when questioned in his cell said: "My brother and Theresa were always having trouble. She had been married once and had married my brother before she got her divorce. When we all lived in New Iberia we got along pretty well. Then Theresa started wanting to go to New Orleans. Henry finally took her, and when she got there she started writing my wife, telling her what a good time they could have together. My wife had to come too and then we'd all be there.

"Henry and me never did talk much though about the troubles we were having with our wives. I want to get out of here and make some money to pay for my wife's funeral.

"Henry's gone off and left me to face the music. He must be guilty or he wouldn't have left town. I wouldn't play a trick like that on a dog."

Charles Provenzano, proprietor of a rooming-house at 1024 Conut Street, informed police that a man came to his lodgings early Thursday morning and inquired for a seaman by the name of Gene Akerson. The man seeking Gene Akerson, Provenzano said, was the same one whose picture was in the newspaper—Henry Moity. Provenzano informed the man that he had no man in his lodging house by that name.

Who was Gene Akerson? The police determined to find out. All policemen were ordered to be on the lookout for him.

Patrolman Charles Clifton, policing Lafayette Street Wharf, said that at 10 o'clock Thursday night, a wild-eyed and excited man approached him and asked for information on the Texas & Pacific railroad ferry crossings. The man, Patrolman Clifton said, could have been Henry Moity. "That man either caught the ferry or jumped in the river," he said. "He looked like a man ready to do anything."

Where was Henry Moity? The theory was advanced that he, too, might be dead.

My chief, District Attorney Eugene Stanley, went to the Lacamu residence and questioned six-year-old Theda Moity, the daughter of the missing Henry and the dead Theresa. The little girl and her smaller brother and sister, had been the interest of hundreds of curious New Orleans citizens. They had been showered with gifts of candy and clothing and toys. When questioned, Theda said:

"Daddy took us out and bought us ice cream and candy. He brought us home, and then he said he was going out to look for mama. He put us to bed and then he went out and looked for mama."

"Did you hear anything later, Theda? Were you frightened by anything?"

Theda shook her head. "Papa brought us over here. He could not find mama."

~§~

THE MISSING Henry Moity, police found out, had been a sailor. He had been dishonorably discharged from the navy. There was the possibility then, if he was a fugitive, that he had shipped out on one of the many vessels that leave the port of New Orleans every day. A check was started of all the ships that had departed and their crews.

Bertillon experts studied the fingerprints on the blood-smeared wine bottle found in the same room with Theresa's body. But the prints were so smeared, so indistinct, that the experts shook their heads.

Doctor Roeling, the coroner, had announced that the women had been dead about twelve hours when he examined them that early Thursday afternoon. According to his deduction, Theresa and Leonide were butchered around midnight. Now if the women were slain at midnight, what was Henry Moity doing two hours earlier at the Lafayette Street Wharf inquiring excitedly of Patrolman Clifton about the ferry boats? Of course Patrolman Clifton was not sure they were the same.

And it was after midnight when the man came to the rooming-house of Charles Provenzano inquiring for the seaman, Gene Akerson. Henry Moity brought his children to his sister's home at 2 o'clock in the morning. Were the women already slain then?

There came to police headquarters the report that a stowaway had been found aboard the *S. S. Jersey City*, a freighter, miles out in the Gulf of Mexico. The ship was bound for China. The wireless grew hot between the vessel and New Orleans as a complete description of Henry Moity was sent.

A check of all the little lodging-houses in the old French Quarter was started in the possibility that the missing man could still be in the city.

~§~

THEN OCCURRED the strange thing at the morgue where the mutilated bodies of Theresa and Leonide lay on under-taking slabs under shrouds. Hundreds of morbidly curious had thronged the parlors. On Friday afternoon, the day following the discovery of the bodies, Ted Moorehead, 608 Conti Street, was among the visitors at the morgue. What drew Moorehead's attention was, the actions of another visitor there. This man, a slender, muscular fellow soon had everyone in the morgue alarmed. He had a pencil in his hand and he would go over and lift up an edge of the shroud and then jump back and push spectators toward it:

"What did they look like?" he shouted. "What did they look like?"

Moorehead said, afterward, to reporters: "I thought he was going crazy, he was so excited about the bodies."

The visitor, Moorehead said, had lifted the edge of the shroud time and time again with the pencil and again shouted: "What would you do to a man who did that? What would you do to such a man?"

It was not until that night, however, that Ted Moorehead got his real shock. He picked up a newspaper and there was a picture of the man he had seen in the morgue. It was Henry Moity! Moorehead informed police, and a companion of Moorehead's identified the picture too.

One of the afternoon newspapers came out with screaming headlines: "Did Henry Moity visit the morgue and view the bodies of his wife and sister-in-law? Was he the murderer, the type of fiend whose twisted mentality causes him to mutilate bodies and then return to see the remains?"

Police headquarters assigned an officer after that to stay in the House of Horror every night. If the murderer had that queer mental twist that compelled him to return to the scene of his crime, a policeman, armed to kill, would be waiting for him. Newspaper reporters stayed in the house, too. It was dark and sepulchral in the murder rooms. Huge rats ran about the blood-spattered floor.

In the meantime investigators had discovered in the Ursuline Street apartment, the story of Theresa Moity's life. Written, in a scrawling, juvenile hand on the leaves of a tattered school composition tablet, it was titled, "I Looked for only Good Times," and began:

"I am now a happy one, a mother of three beautiful children, two girls and a little baby boy. My life, as I am writing it, has been one of hardship—cruelty; and romance.

"I was born in a little Southern town, the name I will call it Madon.

"Our family consisted of three daughters and two sons, I being the second child . . . ."

Continuing with her story, Theresa described herself as "Helen Sol." She pictured herself in the little Southern town further and then described her meeting with a "handsome boy" named "Morry." Morry had travelled around the world and Helen loved him and they were married.

Helen and Morry, Theresa wrote, came to the big city—New Orleans. There the gay night life tempted Helen and soon she met a handsome and prosperous older man named "Mr. Levin."

Theresa described how Helen was attracted by Mr. Levin and finally consented to go riding with him one evening in his big, shiny automobile. They went to a secluded nook in a big cabaret and there Helen discovered, Mr. Levin, who had started drinking out of a mysterious bottle, was not the man she had believed him to be. Theresa wrote:

"I finally grew frightened and began to tremble. I tried to get up, but Mr. Levin held me fast and pulled me sitting on his lap. He covered my face, neck and mouth with kisses. Oh, the horror of it all! When I would see his coarse lips near mine I turned in disgust . . . ."

Theresa described further the struggles of her heroine, Helen, and then Helen proved to Mr. Levin she was a good girl. Mr. Levin then promised jewels and fine clothes if she would go with him, but Helen refused. Then Mr. Levin renewed his assaults, and the heroine jumped out of the window. When she opened her eyes again there, above her, was the tender face of Morry, her husband.

In concluding the story, Theresa wrote:

"Then came to my mind why I was suffering for all this because here was an innocent and good man who loved me and I was not worthy of him. God was punishing me."

While authorities were getting this slant on one of the victims, there came from the ship out on the Gulf of Mexico bound for the Orient, a wireless stating that the stowaway aboard did not fit in any way the description of the missing Henry Moity.

At William Bends, a small community near Houma, a town south of New Orleans, there was excitement, however. Into the town had come a hitchhiker and he had put up at the local lodging-house. He looked suspicious, like a fugitive, to the hotel proprietor and when, that night, he observed a sailor's uniform underneath the man's jumper, he slipped out and notified the local officer. In no time a crowd of more than fifty people surrounded the hotel and the man was taken prisoner. In New Orleans, the news of the capture of the seaman at William Bends, was received with elation. Even if the man was not Henry Moity, he could possibly be Gene Akerson. Officers set out post-haste for the little town. From Baton Rouge, Louisiana, came information from J. F. Landry of the Standard Oil Docks there, that two men had approached him on October 30th, three days after the murders in New Orleans, and sought information about shipping out on oil tankers. It was a Negro, however, who was standing nearby, and looking at the two men, who supplied officers with something that convinced them they were on the trail of Moity. The Negro said he saw the tattoo of a naked woman on one man's right arm. The seaman captured at William Bends proved to be a deserter from the *U.S.S. Rochester.* He was turned over to Federal authorities.

Three detectives, including Chief of Detectives Edward Smith, Dan Healey, and Robert Hackett went to Baton Rouge to follow up the trail sounded by the Negro who saw the tattoo. The vigilance of police was increased at Beaumont, Port Arthur, and Houston on the possibility that Moity and his companion were headed for Texas.

From Raceland, Louisiana, in the bayou country forty miles south of New Orleans, came news from William Smith, a plantation Negro. Smith said a man came to the plantation on October 28th, the day after the murders, and asked for a place to stay overnight. The man was traveling afoot and was unshaven and bum-looking in attire. What aroused Smith's suspicions, however, was the incident of the following morning.

Smith gave the man the newspaper; the transient took one look at it, then threw it down and started away, walking fast. The headlines of that newspaper had to do with the New Orleans trunk murders!

New Orleans, lying on the crescent-shaped shore of the Mississippi River, is almost one hundred miles from the Gulf of Mexico. All that country south of New Orleans is mostly swamp and bayou. It is a dismal, trackless country—insect-infested and reptile ridden. To the southwest of New Orleans runs Lafourche Bayou. This is a navigable channel and up and down it ply freight barges and small passenger boats. One of these freight and passenger boats is *The Gem*. From Leesville, near the Gulf, it runs up the bayou to Golden Meadows, Cut Off, and Lockport.

Joseph Barrios, of Cut Off, Louisiana, was the chief engineer on *The Gem*. On October 30th (Sunday) this boat, carrying half a dozen passengers and some cargo, put in at the wharf of Golden Meadows on its trip up the bayou. Chief Engineer Barrios, idling at the rails and watching the loading, noticed a passenger coming aboard. The new passenger was a medium-built, dark-faced man. His clothing was muddy and his beard long.

The Gem shoved off from Golden Meadows and proceeded on up the bayou. The new passenger had stirred the chief engineer's curiosity and he approached him. The other man welcomed conversation and began to talk readily. He was going to New Orleans, he said. He had been on a drunk the night before and his nerves were all shot. Did the engineer know where a man could get a drink?

The engineer did. He gave the shaky passenger a drink of whiskey and they began to talk further. Pretty soon the passenger said he had a pistol he would like to sell. He exhibited it and Barrios bought the revolver for for a dollar and a half. It was worth much more and the chief engineer would have paid for it, for he wanted that gun and wanted it badly.

At Thibordaux, the next landing, Barrios, who was most suspicious of the passenger, got word to Sheriff Shark. He had a suspect aboard. All the engineer asked is that the man be taken off the ship before he was arrested. He didn't want the passengers alarmed. But *The Gem* left on schedule, before Sheriff Shark got to the vessel. The passenger was still aboard.

The next place *The Gem* was scheduled to put in was Cut Off. Sheriff Shark called up Dominick Peret, the deputy sheriff there and said, "Peret, get the man off that boat who got on at Golden Meadows. Get him off and don't alarm the passengers. He may be Henry Moity!"

Deputy Sheriff Peret waited. After hours *The Gem* hove into sight. The seamen were lashing it fast to the dock. Deputy Peret went aboard, like another passenger, and took a place along the rail, beside the man he spotted.

The Cut Off detective has a disarming, unofficial air about him and he struck up a conversation with the other.

"Where you from, friend?" he asked.

"I been working in a shrimp factory down south of here," the man replied.

"Where you going?"

"I'm headed for New Orleans."

They talked about the loading and other passengers and then the deputy asked:

"Are you a family man? Got any children?"

"Three."

The two talked of their families.

Then the deputy asked: "You ever been to sea?"

The other man nodded: "It has been a long time. I was in the Navy."

"Did you ever get any tattoos?"

The other nodded. He did not hesitate. He rolled up his sleeves and exhibited his muscular forearm. On it was a tattoo of a naked woman!

To himself, Deputy Peret said: This is the man. This is Henry Moity!

"I was in a big drunk last night," the man with the tattoo went on. "I wish I had a drink. My nerves are all shot."

"We can get some right over there," the deputy said. "We got time before the ship leaves."

The two left the ship. Once on the landing, Deputy Peret announced: "I'm a deputy-sheriff, fellow, and you are under arrest."

The man with the tattoo turned quickly and stared at his companion. Then he relaxed. "Yes, I'm the man you want," he said. "I'm Henry Moity."

To newspaper men in New Orleans, an hour later, Deputy Peret said: "Henry Moity wanted a drink of whiskey so bad that he walked almost to jail to get it!"

In New Orleans the news of Henry Moity's capture caused demonstrations that amounted to almost a celebration. The newspapers came out with extras. Again hundreds thronged Ursuline Street to view the House of Horror.

A battery of interrogators, including detectives and police officials and members of my own office, the district attorney's office, confronted the manacled Henry Moity upon his arrival in New Orleans. The captive's face was creased and haggard, his eyes streaked with blood. His hands trembled, but these physical manifestations were due more to exposure and drink than the shock of our accusations.

"Yes I knew you were looking for me," he said. "I saw it in the newspaper. I was headed up for here to give myself up when you caught me. I could have killed that chief engineer. I thought about it. I thought about using that pistol on him and then telling the skipper to take me where I wanted to go. But I was coming here to give up—

"I did not kill my wife or sister-in-law. I was there when it happened though. Gene Akerson killed them. He was a friend of mine, a seaman."

Charges of murder were filed against Henry Moity, and as investigators continued to question him he said:

"After the sailor killed them I took the kid over to my sister's and then Joe and me went out and had some coffee. Then I started getting out of town. I caught a ferry and went over to Gretna. Then I highwayed it over to Raceland and stayed at a shanty there that night that a Negro let me in. I saw a paper the next morning, but I didn't read nothing but the headlines. I threw it down and started walking as fast as I could . . . .

"I started highwaying it toward Rockport. I didn't

ask for no rides though. I saw a bunch of cars ahead and they looked to me like they were patrol cars and looking for me. I quit the highway and started running through the weeds. I'd run stooping. I looked back and saw four men coming. I come to a canal and dove in it. I swam to the other side and got out and cut right in through the swamps. That was the hardest work I ever done . . . . going through swamps. I saw snakes, and that night, trying to sleep in a cane patch, the mosquitoes ate on me.

"The next day I went up to the tender of a bridge and asked him for something to eat. He fed me and I offered him a dollar bill, but he wouldn't take it. Then I made it to *The Gem.*

Chained to Detective Harry Gregson, Moity was taken the following afternoon, Monday, October 31st, to the House of Horror. A big crowd thronged the narrow street in front of the Ursuline Street address and struggled to get a glimpse of the accused murderer.

In the first chamber of death in the apartment, Detective Gregson and Moity sat on the bed where the painter's wife was hacked to death five days before. Moity stared at his shoe, at the spot of blood on the floor near it. He looked at Detective Gregson and said, "Move over, will you? My shoe is in blood."

"What do you care?" Detective Gregson replied. "You had your feet in more blood than this the other night."

"I know it," Moity said, "but I was in my bare feet. I could wash it off."

"Tell us the truth now," District Attorney Stanley said. "You have lied long enough. You know you will hang for this, even if you did not actually kill these two women."

"I was mighty drunk when it all happened," Moity said.

"All the fingerprints and foot marks around here have been only yours," Stanley said.

"I can't understand that," Moity said. "Did the Bertillon men look the place over carefully?"

At the direction of the investigators, Moity went from room to room, reenacting the crime as the seaman, Gene Akerson did it. He spoke in a sing-song voice:

"I met Gene that night in the bar and I told him about the trouble I'd been having with my wife. She had to have too many men. There was Jim Ballin (the real name of this man is withheld.) He'd come up and use our bath. I told my wife that had to stop. I had seen them hugging and passing notes. He didn't come up no more.

"Leonide was just as bad. She had to have too many men, too. That afternoon I went home and asked my wife if the kids had been fed? She said no. I offered her some money and told her to go out and get them something to eat. She told me to go do it. I said 'You are not satisfied with one man.'

"I started drinking. I was getting mad. I got some candy and ice cream and took it home. My wife and Leonide were leaving. 'When I get back I'm going to slap you in the face with a ten-dollar bill,' my wife said.

"I gave the kids the candy and ice cream and then I went back to the bar. I was mad then. I was about as mad as I could be. I got the idea of the knife then. Gene was with me. He said 'If you want your wife bumped off, I'll do it.'

"I went and bought the knife. I asked for a meat cleaver, but they didn't have that so I got the cane knife. They gave it to me wrapped in paper. Then the sailor and me went on to the house. We took off our shoes and went up to the place. They were all asleep. The sailor hid under my wife's bed and I went to bed. I turned over after while and the sailor was standing there. I turned my head away put then I looked back. When I saw the sailor strike her with the knife it felt like one thousand needles pricking me."

"Did you point out your wife to the sailor?" District Attorney Stanley asked.

"No, I just showed him the bed."

"How did you plan to get rid of the body?"

"We were going to put the bodies in trunks, rent a car and then dump them out in the river."

"How long did it take the sailor to cut up the bodies?"

"I don't know. I was drunk."

"Did the women recognize you?"

"My sister-in-law didn't. I was standing in the doorway of the room where the children were. I heard the blows, but I did not see it."

After this story of Henry Moity's District Attorney Stanley announced:

"The sailor, Gene Akerson, is a figment of this man's mind. It is a crude attempt of his to escape hanging. There may be a girl with a similar name and Moity may have sought her after the killing, but there is no sailor, and there is no Gene Akerson as described by this murderer."

Doctor Jesse F. Steiner, professor of Sociology at Tulane University, and a famous criminologist, after examining Henry Moity, announced:

"There are no abnormalities in this man's facial features. He seems to be the type that is criminal by passion; that is, through anger, drugs, stimulants, jealousy. Henry Moity is legally sane!"

With rest, a shave, and clean clothing, Henry Moity began to look something like the boyish-faced painter he had been before the killing. He looked younger than thirty. He smiled some and again he was his carefully polite self.

On November 1st, in the afternoon, Henry Moity again faced a battery of interrogators. A shorthand stenographer was there and a dozen police officers and members of the district attorney's office, including myself. Again my chief, District Attorney Stanley, directed the questioning:

"You know what we are here for, Henry?" Stanley began.

"Yes, sir," Moity said.

"We want you to tell of this and from the very beginning."

"Yes, sir . . . . But, sir, there is one favor I want to ask you."

"What is that?"

"After I have finished, and I am going to tell the truth this time, everything, I want you to let me see my brother, Joe."

"I will see to it that you see your brother," Stanley promised.

"All right, sir . . . . I went home that afternoon and my

wife and sister-in-law were going out. I asked my wife why she hadn't cleaned up the children. She told me to do it; that she was leaving me and that there were plenty of other men who wanted her . . . .

"I pointed out to her about the children, but she said she was leaving me anyway . . . .

"That made me mad and I went and bought a bottle of liquor. I began to sip it. I bought some marihuana cigarettes too and began smoking them. I got madder and madder and then I went to the hardware store and got the knife . . . .

"I went home and hid the knife in the bathroom. My wife and sister-in-law came in after a while. I told them. I would buy them something to eat if they wanted it. We went out and I told them to get all they wanted. My wife ate three hamburgers.

"We got back home and all of us went to bed. I lay there and I planned to kill myself. Then I said to, myself, 'I'll get the worst of it that way and she can go on with Jim Ballin.'

"I thought about killing them all the children too. Then I said to myself: 'There is no sense in killing the children. I've lived my life and they have a right to live theirs.'"

"Every once in a while I'd get up and go to the bathroom and take a drink and puff some more of those cigarettes.

"When I was going to the bathroom once, my wife said: 'Why are you so nervous? Why don't you take it easy?'

"'You don't know what, you are doing,' I said. "'I'm

leaving you anyhow,' my wife said. 'Why don't you do like your brother?'

"I went to sleep and then I woke up. I looked over at where my wife lay. It made me more and more mad every time I would think of what was going to happen. It would work on my nerves more and more so I got up and got the knife and laid it on the trunk . . . .

"My wife was snoring. She was sleeping with her neck like this (Henry demonstrated) and I went over and picked up the knife and came back and stood over her bed. I took the measure on the place where I wanted to hit . . . .

"I went to the front room and I got to the right side of the bed where Joe's wife lay. I said to myself: 'You – – –, you're the cause of this; you're just as much to blame as she'. I hit her and she tumbled out of bed and I struck her again.

"I was drunk and I had to lift up my feet to walk . . . .

"I took my wife in the bathroom and cut her up and put her in the trunk. I had no feeling in my hands. Then I cut up Joe's wife and put her in the other trunk. I washed my hands and feet . . . .

"I got the kids up and took them over to my sister's and then Joe and me went out and had some coffee. Then I left town. Now, Sir, can I see my brother, Joe?"

After that confession they took Henry to the cell occupied by his brother. Joseph, the ex-street car conductor, was washing his hands, getting ready to leave the jail, a free man . . . .

"Hello, Joe," Henry said. "You're not sore at me, you?"

"No, I'm not sore," Joe said. "But it was a terrible thing for you to run away and leave me in the lurch like this."

The two brothers then shook hands and in a few minutes Joseph departed. Henry stayed behind. This was to be his cell now. He said he was hungry and asked for pork and beans.

Days passed. In his cell, "a dungeon ridden with rats" a social worker described the prison, Moity passed the time drawing pictures with colored chalk. On the wall of his cell he drew the face of a woman. A reporter viewed it and exclaimed: "Why, that is your wife!"

Moity stepped back and looked at the drawing admiringly. "Yes, it sure is."

Moity welcomed company. He talked freely. Once he begged a newspaper reporter to stay all night with him, complaining of loneliness.

"When my case comes to trial," he said, "I want the same lawyer as in the LeBoeuf case. I knew that druggist, Doctor Dreher. He was a good man. I think I ought to be punished, but I've already been punished a lot by having the sort of wife I had. I don't think I ought to have to die."

~§~

THE CONFESSED KILLER was not without sympathy. Lawyers scored the public for its sympathetic manifestations. The newspapers carried full-page stories of his life; how he and Theresa were school-day sweethearts, and how he carried her books for her.

Old Leon Moity, the seventy-year-old father of Henry, came down from New Iberia to help his son.

"Hello, Dad," Henry said. "I'm in trouble."

"I know you are, Son," Old Moity said. "I've come to help you." Then the father collapsed in the cell.

Joseph Moity, the brother of the man whose unfortunate incarceration and entanglement in the case caused him to receive the sympathy of hundreds, announced:

"I'm through with women. I'm cured."

Said Henry from his cell: "There are plenty of good women in this world."

On February 28th, 1928, the trial of Henry Moity started in New Orleans. I was a member of the prosecuting staff which fought hard to secure the death penalty for him. The jury, however, gave a verdict that enabled him to escape hanging. The prosecution felt that the jury had permitted its emotions to sway them.

Moity is now serving a life sentence at the state prison at Angola, where he is the penitentiary painter.

—True Detective Mysteries, March 1935

DROPPING FROM SIGHT WHILE ON A VISIT TO EL PASO, A FAMOUS NEW MEXICO CATTLEMAN MET A SINISTER FATE.

By EDWARD ANDERSON

The RIDDLE *of the* CATTLE BARON

OLD MAN LYONS ruled the L-C Ranch with indomitable sway. A stern-visaged man with grizzled grey hair, he was New Mexico's most forcible cattle baron. Despite his almost seventy years, he was a dynamic range lord, still grasping power.

In an ox-drawn wagon he had come down from Colorado to the then New Mexico territory in 1872, defying trackless wastes and hostile Indians.

On the Gila river he set up his camp. And from that camp a domain grew. It covered thousands of acres. A lovelorn cowpuncher even though his best girl waited at the other end couldn't have crossed it in two sunrises; a million dollars, American gold, couldn't have bought the privilege of searing any other brand than the L-C (Lyons Cattle) on the stock that fattened in knee-deep range grass.

He loved horses. Sometimes his passion sent him to Cuba where he wagered fortunes on the outcome of the races.

There were no tales of philanthropy about him. His enemies, and he had bitter ones, said he was a range Scrooge, a little man in stature but with a vast appetite for land, cattle and power. Cattle rustlers feared and hated him. He had made it hot for them, prosecuting them vigorously, punishing them without mercy.

The smaller ranchmen did not fare well in the Gila river country. They said it was the Old Man and the "Big Interests" he represented. They were being squeezed out. Lyons was aware of danger. He rode his range with caution. He was alert when he went to town. But he was unafraid. Throughout his life there had been threats, but none had materialized.

In May of 1917 a well set-up man with thinning dark brown hair visited the ranch. Broad-brimmed hat and serviceable boots stamped him as a westerner. His name was R. M. Brown, from Oklahoma, and he had all the appearances of a sharp trader.

The Oklahoman wanted one thousand head of cattle which he intended to ship to his ranch on Red river.

Brown was received at the Lyons ranch with western hospitality. Negotiating for the purchase he was at the ranch and in Silver City, picturesque mining town nearby, for several days.

The Lyons cowpunchers welcomed him. Brown rode the range with them. At nightfall, the men preferred to linger around the smoldering campfire, smoking, chewing, chuckling, singing, talking over the pleasures of last excursions to town. Brown could send shivers down their spines with his yarns of the Indian Territory. At work, Brown exhibited his prowess as a cowhand. He was an expert with a branding iron.

With the deal practically completed, Brown left.

On the night of May 16, 1917, the cattle baron received a call by long distance telephone from El Paso, Texas, colorful border city on the Rio Grande and just across the river from Juarez, Old Mexico. It was Brown. The Oklahoman was ready to close the deal.

A girl telephone operator in El Paso was much annoyed following the conversation. Brown and she had been in heated argument. The telephone toll was thirty-five cents too much. Brown wasn't going to pay it. The operator asked the cigar stand girl in the hotel where Brown placed his call to intervene in her behalf. Brown came across with the thirty-five cents.

Lyons left the ranch the following afternoon. He met a mining engineer acquaintance on the train. They rode into El Paso together.

At the Union Station in El Paso, a stranger to the mining man approached and greeted Lyons.

"Howdy, Lyons," said the stranger.

"Howdy, Brown," replied the cattle baron.

"I've got a car here, Mr. Lyons, and I'll take you up town." The man called Brown ignored the mining man.

"I'll see you in the morning," said Lyons to his train companion. He climbed into a dust-covered, waiting automobile. Nettled, the mining man walked away. A policeman, nearby, observed the rather rude leave-taking and mildly wondered.

Officer and disconcerted engineer watched the machine disappear down San Francisco Street.

On the following morning a little old man, his head battered to a grotesque semblance of its former self, was found dead. The body lay in a sharp ravine in that lonely section of El Paso known as Highland Park. It was Lyons!

In the pockets of the cattle baron's clothing was found only a five-cent piece!

The murder and the mystery that followed became the most talked of in the history of the cattle country. It was food for speculation around the range campfires for days to come; ranchmen talked about it among themselves, in saloons, on the streets, before the immense, open log-burning fireplaces of their homes.

Many days were to pass before the mystery was solved. Thousands of dollars were to be spent in investigations; reputations of powerful and respected cattlemen were to be blackened; gunplay talk was to be plentiful, lynchings were to be threatened and the cattle country was to be in an uproar.

Authorities of two states, Texas and New Mexico, determined to avenge the murder. The wealthy widow hired special detectives from the Pacific coast.

The ill-feeling against the baron was well known. The theory that plain robbery prompted the slaying was discounted immediately.

Sheriff Seth Orndorff of El Paso marshaled investigators.

Near the ravine in which the body was found, Sheriff Orndorff found a whisky case, partly filled with sand. There was blood in the sand. A blood-covered iron bar was also found. It had been tossed in the ravine about one hundred feet from the body. Matted grey hairs were found clustered on the instrument of death.

The hands of the dead man were torn, indicating the struggle he made with his assailants in a vain effort to fight off the death-dealing blows.

The murder was the black deed of cattle rustlers, embittered by the baron's prosecutions? No, said Sheriff Orndorff, shrewder men than cattle rustlers had plotted and executed the death.

The iron bar was identified as a workman's implement used on a downtown building under construction. The sand-filled liquor case had been used to hold Lyons' bloody head, to prevent the fluid from staining the floor of the automobile, Sheriff Orndorff said.

The man Brown? He was suspected immediately. But Brown had vanished as completely as a rebel general following an unsuccessful revolution in the republic just across the Rio Grande. He had checked out the night of the slaying, the hotel register showed.

The governor of New Mexico announced a reward of five hundred dollars for the apprehension and conviction of the slayer. The widow of the baron posted a five thousand dollar reward. Lyons' friends announced an additional four thousand five hundred. There was ten thousand dollars for the solution of the Lyons murder mystery. It was big money and scores of sleuths, professional and otherwise, went zealously to work.

Weeks passed and investigations led to naught. Then came an encouraging tip. A dust-covered machine, answering the description of the mystery car, was being used by two negro soldiers of a military camp near Fort Bliss. The car belonged to a Silver City woman!

The negroes got wind of the sheriff's coming. They appealed to their comrades. The company of seventy-five men promised to see justice done.

The sheriff arrived and demanded the suspects. The two soldiers were surrounded by a mob of other negroes. The sheriff reiterated his demand. The mob was murmuring, threateningly. Guns of the sheriff and two deputies were drawn. The mob hesitated, then pushed two frightened negroes forward.

Feeling was high against the negroes. Immediate trials were urged. And then, surprisingly, Sheriff Orndorff ordered their release!

To appease the clamor of protest that arose, Sheriff Orndorff announced that he had the actual mystery car. The information on the negroes was false. The car the sheriff had in custody had bloodstains. The rug in the *tonneau* was missing, save for strips about the screws that had held it to the floor. Chemists said stains on the strips were blood. Grey hairs were found in the machine also.

The automobile belonged to a rent-a-car company. On the night of May 19, the records of the agency showed, the car was rented by Melton Harrison, prominent and well-to-do Rio Grande Valley ranchman. He had returned it two days later. The agency dealer remembered missing the rug when the car was returned. Harrison had paid for the rug along with the bill for use of the automobile.

Harrison was horrified. He connected with the Lyons murder? The car? Why, he had rented that car many times, before and after the passing of Lyons. He could explain the missing rug.

Sheriff Orndorff hesitated. This was an embarrassing predicament. Harrison was a highly respected citizen, member of one of the pioneer valley families. The evidence, after all, was poor, particularly so for an El Paso county jury, long famed for its leniency in murder cases. The sheriff did not want the enmity of the Harrison family. And he did not wish to do an injustice by making a false accusation. The case was dropped . . . .

~§~

W. G. (WINDY BILL) CLARK was a horse trader. He was a native Texan and proud of it. He chewed tobacco and talked much. His reputation was cloudy. He had been indicted for murder, for theft. He had participated in any number of gunplay incidents and saloon brawls. He emerged from them all, triumphant and with a well-how-do-you-like-that attitude. He was to have a role in the Lyons murder case, a strange one.

In May, 1917, some two weeks before the murder of Lyons, Windy Bill was in the offices of a prominent criminal lawyer in Abilene, Texas. Visiting in the office also was Felix Jones of Fort Worth, a horse trader and cattle buyer. Clark and Jones were more than casual friends. They had met often in cattle dealings, had touched many glasses of American straight over saloon bars and went so far as to exchange the most personal of confidences.

Let Clark tell of that meeting:

"'Will you do a cold-blooded job?' Jones said to me. "'I don't know,' said I. "'There's four thousand dollars in it in fifty-dollar bills,' Jones said.

"I showed interest right now. But Jones wasn't talking much. He just shook his head wise-like. 'See Uncle Ike at Colorado City,' said Jones. We parted."

Clark didn't meet Jones again until May 19. It was in Colorado City. Uncle Ike Monroe was with Jones.

"Well, have you two made a deal?" Jones questioned, eyeing Clark and Uncle Ike, Windy Bill related. "Going to bump off that Snyder banker?"

"Don't believe I want that job, Jones," Windy Bill replied.

"It's easy. I just killed Tom Lyons. Knocked him cold with one lick of the hammer. Put his head in a whisky box. Heard I left five cents on him. Would have taken that if I'd known he had it," Jones chuckled.

Windy Bill was impressed. Jones was exhibiting five hundred and sixty-five dollars in bills. The sixty-five dollars, Jones explained, was taken from Lyons' clothing after the job. The other was money paid him by J. P. Harrison of El Paso, he said. Jones was due fifteen hundred dollars more. Would Clark collect the remainder? It would be worth his while. Jones didn't want to be seen around El Paso—not for a while yet, at least. Clark would think it over.

The following day Sheriff Orndorff left El Paso in haste. He was headed for Abilene. In his pocket was a telegram. It read:

"I know who murdered Tom Lyons.
            W. G. CLARK, Abilene, Texas."

The sheriff found his man. "Yes, I know who killed Lyons," said Clark to the anxious official. Windy Bill was coolly deliberate. His attitude was that of a man who wasn't going to talk readily. He wasn't going to talk, unless . . . . well, he had heard something about ten thousand dollars.

The El Paso sheriff didn't believe Clark was talking through his Stetson. He had an air of confidence that was convincing.

The sheriff excused himself and went to the telegraph office. In an hour he returned and from a wallet took two thousand dollars in bills. Eight thousand dollars more would be forthcoming, providing . . . .

~§~

JONES was trailed to Beaumont, Texas, and arrested. J. P. Harrison and brother Melton, the latter already suspected in the affair because of the car, were arrested also. The horse trader was charged with murder; the cattleman with conspiracy to murder.

Jones was placed in a cell in the county jail at El Paso once occupied by a Mexican ruler, President Victoriana Huerta, a refugee in El Paso following the collapse of his revolution.

"When I show my side of this I will be acquitted," Jones said.

The, Harrison brothers, at first denied bond, later were released on bail of two thousand dollars each. They denied knowing Jones or Clark. It was preposterous, they said. The shock, the humiliation of the accusation broke Melton Harrison. He sickened. He was to die of a broken heart within a year, his friends said.

Here were three men accused. There was the circumstantial evidence of the car and the statement of Windy Bill. Not very promising material for a conviction. The district attorney's office admitted it.

Public sentiment varied. There were those who said the sheriff was on a false trail; that the Harrison brothers and Jones were victims of terrible circumstances, the marks of a cold-blooded falsifier who was bargaining his soul for ten thousand dollars. The sheriff and the prosecuting attorney didn't know whether they had birds in hand or if it was a desert mirage and the birds were in the bush. The sheriff was not idle. He found a telegram and made its contents known. It was signed: "Felix Jones," and read: "Can I draw on you for bank money to buy stock referred to in letter. Note attached. Wire answer."

The telegram had been found in the possession of J. P. Harrison. It was evidence, said the sheriff, that at least Jones and Harrison were acquainted, despite the ranchman's denial.

A hotel clerk looked at Jones in his cell. Jones, the clerk said, was the man who had registered at his hotel on May 16 as "R. M. Brown." There was only one difference. Brown had thinning, dark brown hair. Jones' hair was black!

The negro porter at the hotel was positive Jones and Brown were the same.

"How do you remember Brown?" he was asked.

The porter grinned. "I remembers him because he didn't tip me. No, sir, not a cent."

And the telephone operator who had had an argument with a man named Brown over a thirty-five-cent telephone toll said that the voices of the men were not the same!

Silver City men who said they could remember Brown, the cattle buyer, went to the jail. Jones was lined up in the courtyard along with a dozen or so other prisoners. Most of them, without hesitation, singled him out. He was Brown—except for one thing: the brown hair.

Sheriff Orndorff exhibited a bottle of hair tonic, taken from Jones' cell. The stuff would make a man's hair black, he contended.

Windy Bill was the town's hero. He had solved a big murder case. He admitted he had taken a corresponddence course in detective study. He had money, plenty of it, and more was forthcoming. He packed six guns, legally. The sheriff had authorized the weapon carrying. Bill's life was in danger. There had been threats.

Clark slept at the jail. He didn't go abroad much at night unless accompanied by deputy sheriffs. He went on raiding parties with the officers. On one of them he came near to losing his life.

A deputy was called out to quell a disturbance in a Mexican dance hall on the outskirts of the city. A mean hombre was threatening the clientele. The deputy started out and Bill went along.

The deputy soon quieted the offending disturber. He was ready to go. Bill wanted to linger with the music, the dark-skinned senoritas, and the busy bar. Would the deputy wait until he took a drink? The deputy obliged.

Bill took his drink and then another. Then he wanted to dance. The deputy was accommodating. Bill was getting drunk and noisy. The deputy be-came impatient. He insisted on going.

Clark's reply was the draw. His gun spouted. The bullet passed dangerously between the deputy's legs. The officer, enraged, pulled his own gun. He jammed it into Clark's mid-region and grabbed the drunken man's tie with the other. His trigger finger tightened.

Then he hesitated. If he killed Clark, the state's star witness would be gone. The case against Jones and the Harrison brothers would collapse. It would look like a frame-up. The deputy brought Clark back to town. Windy Bill never accompanied another officer on a raid.

~§~

ONE DAY a newspaper reporter called on Felix Jones at the jail. Jones was sprawling on his cot, idly fingering a ring on his hand.

"Do you know Florence Brown of Dallas?" the reporter asked.

"Don't know her," said Jones, casually.

"You ought to. You've been indicted for her murder," shot the reporter.

Jones leaped from his cot. "What?" he yelled.

The reporter repeated it. A grand jury at Dallas had

just indicted Jones for the brutal murder of Florence Brown, stenographer in a cattle office there. The murder had occurred several years before. The stenographer, young and pretty, had been found beaten to death with a hammer. Her throat had been slashed. One of her fingers was severed, apparently caused when she made efforts to ward off her assailant.

Dallas prosecutors said they had found forged bank documents in possession of Jones, papers once held by the girl. The documents, they said, gave evidence of a gigantic swindling scheme among southwest cattlemen. Jones laughed. He did recall the girl, since her name was mentioned the second time!

This proved a mere incident in the startling developments in the Lyons case. Stranger incidents were to follow.

The trial began February 12, 1918. Ill feeling was evident. Spectators were searched for weapons before being permitted to enter the courtroom. Two Texas Rangers were dispatched from Austin by Governor Ferguson as an added precaution against a possible serious outbreak.

A Fort Worth pawnbroker testified that on April 30, 1917, Felix Jones pawned two pistols and a diamond ring. Three weeks later, the pawnbroker said, the valuables were redeemed. The state introduced this testimony to show that Jones was broke before the murder and able to redeem them immediately afterwards.

A handwriting expert said that the signature on the hotel register in El Paso of "R. M. Brown" was highly similar to that of Felix R. Jones.

And then a peculiar thing happened—Windy Bill, the hero, was kidnaped! His captors were authorities of another county.

Windy Bill was whisked out of town by authorities of Paducah, Texas. The officers exhibited a complaint charging Clark with a murder that had occurred thirteen years before! They hurried Clark out of El Paso by auto, placed him aboard a train at Ysleta, small community down the valley from El Paso, and started toward Paducah.

El Paso authorities heard of the affair with emotions of mingled rage and humiliation. It was difficult to grasp, too. Their star witness!

Then they got busy. They promptly swore out a complaint charging the sheriff of Paducah county, the county attorney and Uncle Ike Monroe of Colorado City, with conspiracy to murder. Clark, the complaint said, was the intended victim. The El Pasoans next called on the Texas Rangers.

That night six Rangers came into El Paso. With them was a sheriff, a county attorney, Uncle Ike Monroe and a smiling, triumphant Windy Bill.

The chagrined and angry Paducah officials immediately filed a one hundred thousand-dollar damage suit against El Paso county authorities. They charged slander, humiliation and insult. The conspiracy charge came to naught, as did the damage suit.

But Windy Bill was back and ready to testify and collect eight thousand dollars. The star witness was his old self again. But he voiced misgivings. "If Jones comes out a free man, I'll have to do it," he said. He patted his gun meaningly.

Clark took the stand.

"You were Jones' friend?" defense counsel, contempt in their tone, asked him.

"I played him for my friend," replied Clark, unabashed.

After nearly a week of trial, in which it was developed that the widow of Lyons was paying the expenses of a score and more of witnesses, the jury retired to deliberate.

Windy Bill, with the trial proceedings indicating a victory for the state and eight thousand dollars in sight, was in high spirits. He talked freely and always had crowds of listeners.

—Detective Tabloid, March 1935

Appendices

Appendix A:
A Miscellany of Biographical Sketches & Criticism

Excerpts from STORY, June 1935:

"[*Hungry Men* is] the significant and thoughtful story of a jobless generation on the move. Men and boys on the bum, roving the waterfronts, roaming the streets, highwaying with bleeding feet. An exciting, challenging book which fascinates with its truth, its power and its hope."

"Edward Anderson, whose short story *The Guy in the Blue Overcoat* (Story, October, 1934) made him eligible to enter the $1,000 prize novel contest conducted by Doubleday, Doran & Co., for the best first novel by a STORY contributor, is the author of the novel *Hungry Men*, which, together with Dorothy McCleary's *Not for Heaven*, was awarded first place in the competition, each novel, in the judge's inability to decide which was best, receiving $1,000. Mr. Anderson is the son of a country printer and was born in Weatherford, Texas, in 1906, of Irish descent with a trace, on his mother's side, of Cherokee Indian. His schooling began in Oklahoma, but he left in his senior year of high school to take a cub reporter's job on a small daily in in Ardmore, after serving an apprenticeship as a printer. He has worked in newspapers for ten years, varied with some experience as a deck boy on a cotton freighter, and turning out prize fight stories for magazines. Married, he now lives in New Orleans."

From *A Southern Harvest*, 1937, edited by Robert Penn Warren:

"BIOGRAPHICAL NOTES EDWARD ANDERSON—
EDWARD ANDERSON was born at Weatherford, Texas, in 1905, of Irish and Indian descent. He has been a printer's apprentice and a reporter on a country newspaper; he was a news editor at the age of twenty, and has been a trombone player in a circus band, a harvest hand in Kansas, and a seaman on cotton freighters to Europe. When twenty-three he started writing fiction, and from 1930 to 1935 he hunted jobs on newspapers, wrote unsalable fiction, handled publicity for political candidates, hoboed all over the United States, and wrote Hungry Men which won one of the two first-novel prizes in the contest sponsored by Story."

From the 1948 Bantam edition of *Your Red Wagon* (aka *Thieves Like Us*):

"*Meet* EDWARD ANDERSON—
"When Edward Anderson's sensational novel of escaped convicts first flashed across the horizon of realistic literature, this is what the critics had to say:
". . . I do not think it too much to say that Edward Anderson is the most exciting new figure to appear in American writing since Hemingway and Faulkner . . ."
—N. L. Rothman, *Saturday Review of Literature*.

". . . an exciting story. Man, woman or child, you'll read it to the bitter end and probably won't forget it so soon. . ." —F. T. Marsh, *New York Herald Tribune.*

". . . Here is a perfect reproduction of a slice of American life . . ." —Harold Strauss, *The New York Times.*

"And who is this Edward Anderson? He once rode the blinds of crack passenger trains, freight manifests and slow locals, in gondolas and cattle cars; slept in welfare flops, ten-cent hotels, parks and darkened churches. And with all this behind him, Anderson then turned his hand to writing and walked off with *Story Magazine's* $1,000 prize for his first novel, *Hungry Men,* later published by Doubleday & Company, Inc." (*Your Red Wagon,* 1948)

Recent reflection upon Edward Anderson's work:

—Richard Rayner, June 2008

"*Thieves Like Us* snaps shut like a trap on its characters, and I'd bet that Nicholas Ray, having filmed it, kept it in mind when he made his more famous picture of youthful disillusion and defiance, "Rebel Without a Cause." Anderson himself never moved on anywhere, artistically, which is our loss because he made fiction that combined fluency of style with potency of form. But he did leave behind these two books, stories from the Depression, yet timeless, testaments to young people roaming the country, hungry and without prospects, sleeping rough or turning to crime. He's a writer who deserves to be rediscovered."

—Morris Dickstein, *Dissent*, Volume 56, Number 3, Summer 2009, pp. 90-96 (Review):

"Just as Hemingway's story "The Killers" taught thirties crime novelists like Dashiell Hammett, James M. Cain, and W.R. Burnett to write lean, tough, suggestive dialogue, other stories like "The Battler," in which Nick Adams is menaced by a punch-drunk old prizefighter-turned-hobo, gave lessons in laconic writing to lower-depths novelists like Edward Anderson . . .

". . . The growth of pulp fiction, especially crime fiction, in the 1930s created an alternate image of American life that was relatively free of the censorship of moralists of both Left and Right, at a time when the "serious" novel assumed a heavy burden of social responsibility. Yet the lower-depths novel, with its indelible portrait of hunger, poverty, rootlessness, and psychological malaise, gave an important though little-recognized flavor to proletarian fiction. At its best it combined the plebeian tradition of Jack London, Maxim Gorky, and Knut Hamsun with the stylistic restraint of Hemingway to give us an important image of depression life, something that strongly resonates with economic dilemmas today."

Appendix B: Lives in Parallel
A Comparison Of Edward Anderson and Jim Thompson

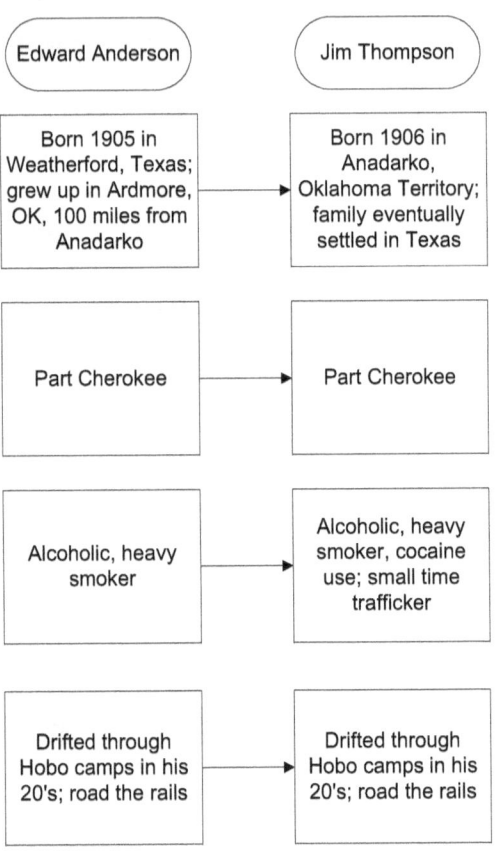

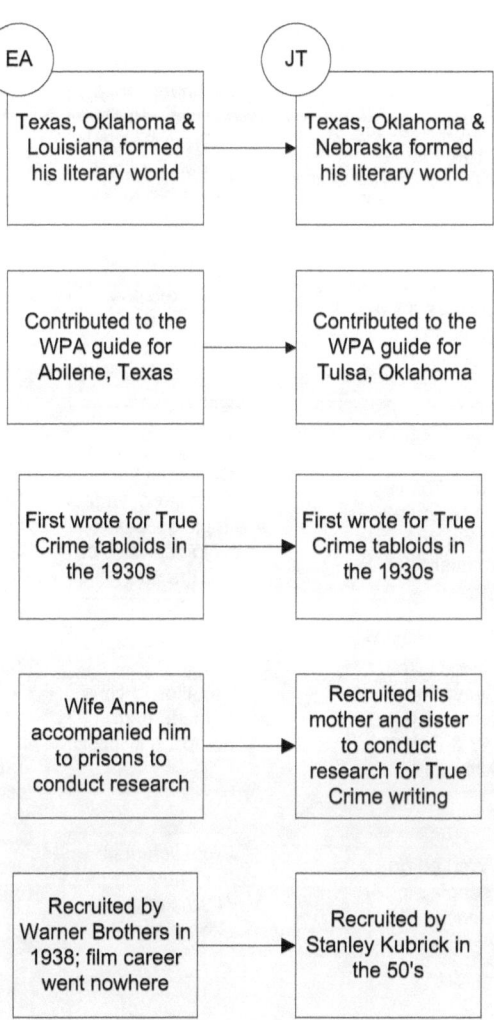

EA

Texas, Oklahoma & Louisiana formed his literary world

JT

Texas, Oklahoma & Nebraska formed his literary world

Contributed to the WPA guide for Abilene, Texas

Contributed to the WPA guide for Tulsa, Oklahoma

First wrote for True Crime tabloids in the 1930s

First wrote for True Crime tabloids in the 1930s

Wife Anne accompanied him to prisons to conduct research

Recruited his mother and sister to conduct research for True Crime writing

Recruited by Warner Brothers in 1938; film career went nowhere

Recruited by Stanley Kubrick in the 50's

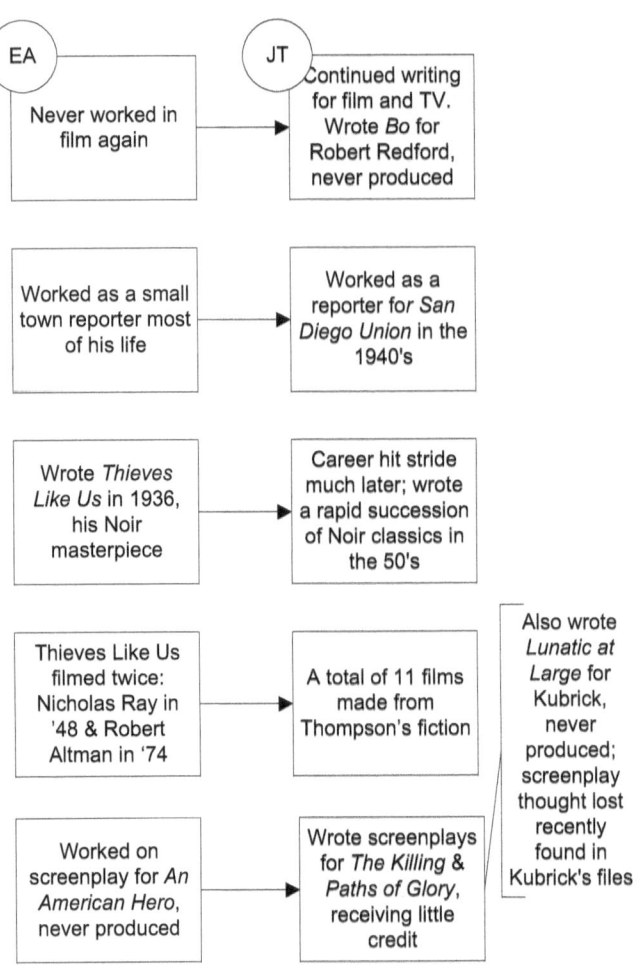

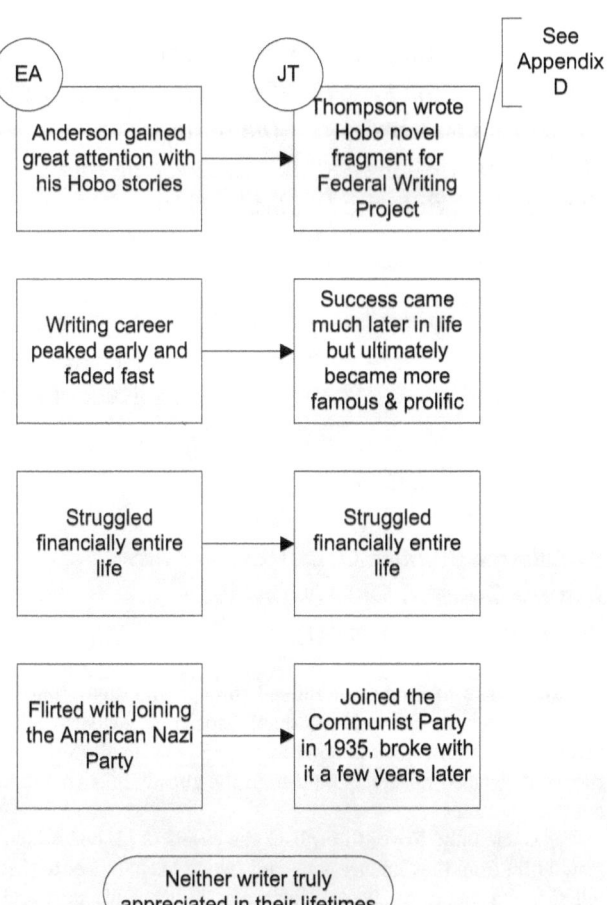

EA

Anderson gained great attention with his Hobo stories

JT

Thompson wrote Hobo novel fragment for Federal Writing Project

See Appendix D

Writing career peaked early and faded fast

Success came much later in life but ultimately became more famous & prolific

Struggled financially entire life

Struggled financially entire life

Flirted with joining the American Nazi Party

Joined the Communist Party in 1935, broke with it a few years later

Neither writer truly appreciated in their lifetimes

Appendix C:
True crime story centered on Anadarko, Oklahoma—
Jim Thompson's birthplace. Note the geographic
references to the Keechi Hills and the town of Chickasha.
Clearly Anderson derived the names of two of his main
characters for Thieves Like Us, *Keechie and Chicamaw*
from these Oklahoma locales.

The CRIMSON
HORROR *of*
KEECHI HILLS

DITCH *of* DOOM

By DEPUTY SHERIFF C. C. RUFF
CADDO COUNTY, OKLAHOMA
As told to JIM THOMPSON

VAGUE WISPS of moonlight filtered through the dust-grimed windows. Shadows fell upon the bed, the shabby sticks of ancient furniture—crept through the dingy rooms in quiet terror, and vanished. In the black-jacks, the wind soughed miserably; and from the ghostly hills an owl hooted his eternal question.

"Uncle Billy" Royce threw back the covers of his bed, which had protected him from the January cold, and swung his bare feet to the floor. He felt for, and found, his boots. Habitually, he wore his shirt and trousers while sleeping. So, with the addition of the boots, he was dressed.

He shot the rusted bolt of the door, and pulled it open. Again, standing on the little porch, he listened. Again, he heard the owl's echoing cry.

That, and other sounds.

The soft shuffle of a spade. Digging. The quiet click of a pick, striking its way through the rocky shale. And—

The grisly crunching of an axe; the terrified pleading of a woman—choking, groaning.

Then—silence!

Uncle Billy shivered in the January wind. He couldn't stand the cold,

The hardships, He didn't rightly know which, himself. Still, in spite of his years, he made an arresting figure. He was thin to the point of emaciation; but he was six feet tall, and stood straight like the Indians who had once roamed these rocky hills.

He grew calmer as the sounds he had heard were not repeated. Finally, he chuckled, his parchment-like jaws shaking silently. Those digging noises were probably the echo of his own day's work; they'd got in his ears that way before, and stayed with him. As for the others well, the wind had a way of teasing and frightening a lonely old man.

A man had to be careful, though; no doubt about that. There was gold on the farm: the buried treasure of the James and Dalton gangs. Jesse and Frank, both, had told him it was there; and they wouldn't lie to a member of their own gang. And, if any further proof were needed, the woman he had called his wife had furnished it.

She had found five thousand dollars. She had left with it, laughing; refusing him any part. Gone away with another man.

Thus Uncle Billy ruminated and his thoughts were bitter. His old eyes strayed out over the barnyard, and came to rest upon the shambling chicken-house. Then, shaking his head in the manner of a man whose memory is not of the best, he went back inside and locked the door . . . .

Morning came to the Keechis.

It was Saturday; but Saturday and every other day was the same to William Royce. He had to dig for his treasure as he had dug daily for the past thirty years. In the aggregate, a good fifth of his hundred and sixty acres were one shovel-scarred battlefield. There were holes in the barn, the chicken-house, the pigpen, along the creek-in every place that a person might look. And still his digging continued.

He ate breakfast hurriedly and stepped out to the porch. A voice hailed him. He stiffened, peered near-sightedly.

A neighboring farmer, one Thomas Taylor, came up the path from the lane.

"Oh, it's you," grunted Uncle Billy. "How are you, Tommy?"

"First rate." Taylor sat down out of the wind and rolled a cigarette. "See all your in-laws out here yesterday evening," he remarked conversationally.

"Yes, the whole durn gang was out," swore the old man. "Clifford, and those two meads."

Clifford was his sixteen-year-old stepson. The Meads were his wife's daughter and son-in-law. Taylor laughed. He had known Uncle Billy for years, and took a good-natured interest in the old man's affairs.

"Where is your wife this morning?" he inquired carelessly. "Inside?"

As he spoke he tried to peer through the window which fronted on the porch. But flour sacks had been hung up there to dry, and he could obtain no hint of the interior.

"No, she ain't inside," said the veteran sourly "She's gone.

"Yes? Where to?"

"None of your—." Uncle Billy halted in the middle of his rude speech. After all, Taylor was his friend even if he was a trifle tactless. "She went away," he said grimly. "Went to New Mexico with a Dutchman, in a big seven-passenger car."

Taylor laughed again, and settled down for a morning's conversation. "You have a pretty hard time with housekeepers, don't you, Uncle Billy? That makes about six that came and went."

"None of them are any good," declared Royce. "Now, you run along, Tommy; I ain't got any more time to talk. I've got work to do."

When Taylor had gone, the old man went about the work of watering and feeding his scanty stocks of chickens and pigs. Then taking pick and shovel he set out for the field.

On his way, he encountered the rusting and dilapidated remains of an ancient touring car. For a moment, although he had passed the car a thousand times, he had difficulty in remembering how it had got there; and he studied its drab lines carefully. Then memory returned. The ancient vehicle had belonged to two young men—tourists—who had camped on the farm one night a few years before.

What had happened to them? Why had they gone away and left their car?

Uncle Billy chuckled.

Every door on the Royce farm bore a sturdy padlock, and only Uncle Billy carried the keys. So, when the tall old man returned to the house for lunch after a fruitless morning of digging, he found the Meads, husband and wife, waiting for him in the yard.

"Where's mother?" asked Mrs. Mead, anxiously.

Uncle Billy told her, briefly and lucidly.

"Why, she didn't tell us she was going," said Mead. "We planned on taking her in town with us. What time she leave?"

"Long about dark. Little while after you left."

"But I can't understand why she would do it," frowned the daughter. "You say she left with a Dutchman? What was his name?"

"Don't know, and don't care!" snapped the old man. "All I know is she's gone, and he had a big seven-passenger car."

"Sure about that, are you?" inquired Mead.

Mrs. Mead put a hand on her husband's arm. The two were not on the friendliest terms with Royce. There had been an argument about some livestock.

Besides this, the daughter knew that her mother was accustomed to taking care of herself. Uncle Billy was past eighty. Her mother was strong, able-bodied, and only a little more than forty years of age.

"Well, Uncle Billy," she smiled, "if you say she's gone we'll take your word for It. But what does she intend to do about Clifford?"

Royce nodded vehemently. "Now, don't you worry about Clifford. Ethel's going to send back for him. The Dutchman' got a big ranch, and he's going to give Clifford a job. Ethel made him agree to that before she'd go. You tell Clifford to come out here and stay with me. His mother will be ready for him in a few days."

No mention of the five thousand dollars in gold she had found. No need to tell them about that.

The Meads drove away, returning to their home in Chickasha.

Clifford Alexander, Mrs. Royce's son by a former marriage, was waiting for them eagerly. When told that he was about to be reunited with his mother, he lost no time in setting out for Uncle Billy's farm. His mother wouldn't leave him there long, he knew. She'd send back after him to come herself, and he'd have to be on hand when she did.

Meanwhile, there were still other persons interested in the unorthodox departure of Lela Ethel Royce.

Uncle Billy had been married first in 1902, and had four daughters by this marriage. About five years before his second marriage, he and his first wife had separated, and she had taken the children. One of the girls died, one was still single, and two of them were married. The first Mrs. Royce made her home with one of these married daughters, Mrs. Reed Norris and her husband, of Norge, Oklahoma—a little town a few miles northeast of Uncle Billy's farm.

The second Mrs. Royce, Lela Ethel Alexander, had kept house for Uncle Billy several months before she married him. And to induce her to marry him the old man had agreed to will her his farm upon his death. And it was well worth inheriting—one hundred and sixty acres of land, with an oil well which produced a royalty of from thirty to sixty dollars per month. Even at a forced sale the farm would bring thousands of dollars.

Sunday afternoon, January 6th, 1935, Clifford Alexander arrived at the farm, and entered the gate. Uncle Billy was seated on the porch, and he displayed more cordiality to his stepson than was his usual wont. Clifford went inside to get a bite to eat, and lie down.

He did neither.

He walked into the kitchen, and found himself looking squarely into the bedroom. He stopped dead in his tracks, transfixed.

"Oh, Uncle Billy," he called. "Ma hasn't come back yet, has she?"

"No she hasn't, son. Don't worry, though. She'll send for you."

Cold terror wormed through the boy's veins. Like a man in a trance he continued to stare into the bedroom, at something which lay there on the bed. Then, slowly, he began to back toward the door. He reached the porch, and stepped off. Uncle Billy peered at him curiously.

"What's the matter, son? You look kind of peaked."

"N-nothing. Nothing's the matter." Still watching the old man, the boy backed away.

"Where are you going, then?" demanded Royce.

"Over to the rock-crusher. I-Iwant to see Mr. Swanson in a minute."

Swanson worked as watchman for a sand and gravel company, which had holdings on an adjoining farm.

Uncle Billy arose. He looked dreadfully tall to the boy.

"Now, see here, Clifford," he began. "You better stay right here. When your mother comes you don't want her chasing all over the country looking for you."

He took a step forward.

Clifford whirled and ran.

At the rock quarry, the frightened boy found his friend Swanson, and told what he had seen in the bedroom. Swanson was alarmed, but he had his job to take care of; so it was not until Monday evening that he came to town to advise me of his suspicions. And since I am regularly employed by the town of Cement, as night watchman, it was Tuesday before I got out to the Royce farm.

The doors were all locked, and no one was there. I sat down to wait.

Dusk came early, and with it, walking wearily through the trees, came Uncle Billy. He walked toward me silently.

"Hello, Uncle Billy," I called.

He said nothing. He acted as if he intended to walk over me or through me. Then, suddenly, when we were almost face to face, he threw his hand out and gripped my shoulder.

"Why—it's Curry!" he exclaimed.

Things like that get a man's nerves. "Yes, it's Curry, all right;' I said.

"But where's your wife?"

"She's gone."

"Where?"

"New Mexico, I think. She left Friday night with a Dutchman."

I was speaking rapidly; if he had no lies made up, I was not going to give him time to think and create them.

"Listen, Uncle Billy," I said. "Clifford saw your wife's hat and coat on the bed, when he was here Sunday. Why didn't she take them with her?"

"How should I know? I wasn't asking her any questions when she left. More than likely she figured on getting some new things when she got to town. This Dutchman had plenty of money."

He spoke without the slightest hesitation, and his eyes met mine, unblinking. I had known him for almost thirty years, and in all that time his word had been as good as his bond. He had had trouble with house-keepers before. They were always getting mad and quitting. I found myself believing the man; I couldn't help but believe him.

"Where did this Dutchman live?" I asked.

"Just a little north of Chickasha. I don't know his name, Curry. Wish

I did. I'd like to help you out."

"All right, Uncle Billy," I said. "I've got to get back to town now, but I'll be out again tomorrow. You stay right here on the place, will you?"

"I sure will," he promised.

I got in my car and stepped on the starter. Once, before turning out into the highway, I looked back. Uncle Billy stood silhouetted against the sky, gazing out over the ghostly Keechis. And I saw that the last rays of the winter sun had left those rocky crags dripping with scarlet . . . .

Returning to Cement, I worked through the night on my regular job as watchman. Wednesday, I started out to check on Uncle Billy's story.

I inquired all around Chickasha, where he had said the Dutchman lived. I went to Tuttle, Amber, Minco—towns northeast of the Royce farm.

But I found no Dutchman; no sign of the missing Mrs. Royce. My way led back by the farm. I drove in. Uncle Billy was gone. Believing that there was nothing to be gained by searching through those hills in the dark, I drove on to Cement. I did not think the old man was hiding out on me; but if he was it would be foolhardy to look for him at night.

At noon of the next day—Thursday—I visited the farm again. Uncle Billy was still gone; but from a passing truck driver I learned that he had driven the old man into Chickasha, Wednesday afternoon. I went back to town, got a search warrant, and returned to the farm, taking two residents of Cement—Sam Kuykendall and C. B. Cook—with me.

The house was still dark, and every door was padlocked.

The shack faced the north, two small rooms setting east and west. On the south, a small combination dining-room and kitchen had been built on. We broke the lock on the north door and entered, tearing the obscuring flour sacks from the windows to let in the light.

At first glance, nothing seemed to be out of the way. Cabinet, stove, and table were in their usual places. I looked into one of the front rooms; as usual it was piled with the accumulated junk and worn out bric-a-brac of thirty years.

From there we examined the bedroom with its two beds. There was nothing to point to the fact that Mrs. Royce had met with foul play.

Turning to enter the kitchen, my gaze was arrested by something I saw on the north wall of that room. Startled, I leaned closer. It was a few tiny clumps of fuzz, glued to the siding by a thin dark streak of what was unmistakably blood. A few feet further along the wall was another of those curious stains; and following them around the room I counted eight in all.

Eight streaks of splattered blood. Eight murderous stokes of an axe or knife. But here was a curious thing. While the blood on the wall was obvious to anyone, the floor was spotless.

I got down on my hands and knees. Tiny grains of grit bit into my palms. That was it. *Sand!* One of the best cleaning agents known. The floor had been scoured with it.

We retraced the spots on the walls; and through them the details of the tragic drama that had been played in that lonesome shack became almost clear as if we had witnessed it.

The murder victim had backed away, terror-stricken eyes on the grisly weapon glittering there in the moonlight. But matching each footstep with his own, the murderer had advanced. One step, two steps, *slash!* Three steps, four steps, *slash!* . . . Backing away, slowly; gasping out unheeded pleas. Six steps, seven steps, nine, ten . . . . Every two steps, like the measured rhythm of a pendulum, the dreadful instrument had swung, and found its mark . . . . Fifteen, sixteen . . . . then, eternity.

At the south door, the stains ended.

We broke it down.

Just below the doorstep was a slight depression, and the earth was loose. But looking along the path which led to the outbuildings, we saw more blood-stains, and we followed them. A few feet from the chicken-house there was a large splotch of blood-stained sand. The body had lain there, temporarily, while the murderer rested. Undoubtedly, the body was nearby, for there were no other such large pools.

Tearing the lock from the rotting door of the chicken-house, we entered. In front of us, the ground was swelling ever so slightly; I would not have noticed it at all, except for one thing: cotton hulls had been scattered over the dirt floor in an attempt to conceal the loose earth. I called Clifford over from Swanson's, and asked him if that was the way the floor should look. He replied that it was not.

I began to dig.

A few turns of my shovel, and the steel struck something that was not earth. I scraped the soil carefully, and uncovered a woman's shoe. And in a minute more I had uncovered the stocking, a leg . . . . And in a minute more had uncovered the nearly nude body of a woman, lying face down. Her fair head grimed now by the dust of days, was horribly mutilated.

Slowly, for the body was beginning to decompose, we turned it over, into a blanket. Clifford began to sob, softly.

There before us was all that remained of Lela Ethel Royce, second wife of Uncle Billy.

I had the body sent to a funeral home in Anadarko, and notified Jim Bond, Sheriff of Grady County at Chickasha, to pick up Uncle Billy. Meanwhile I learned from some men who were working on the road in front of the house that Reed Norris, Uncle Billy's son-in-law, had visited the place the day before. He had driven into the yard and was seen to walk down to the chicken-house, remaining there for several minutes.

Norris, and his mother-in-law, the first Mrs. Royce, were placed under arrest and taken to Anadarko for questioning. One was placed in the city jail, the other in the county jail.

At this juncture, we received word from Chickasha that Uncle Billy had been apprehended. He was picked up in the center of town, on Chickasha Avenue. But while he was armed he offered no resistance. I went to Chickasha and questioned the old man in the private office of Sheriff Bond.

"What became of your wife, Uncle Billy?" demanded.

"She went away with that Dutchman."

"Now, Uncle Billy," I said. "You're in a bad jam, here. We've found your wife buried in the chicken-house. She was killed with an axe. Did you do it? Come, now, tell me the truth."

"No, no, Curry," he replied. "I didn't do it. I don't know a thing about it."

"Tell me the truth, Uncle Billy."

"I already have."

He answered me very steadily, and rationally. Again, if we had not discovered the body, I would have believed him. And in spite of the discovery, I still could not definitely connect him with the crime. Mrs. Royce had been in her prime a fine healthy, vigorous figure of a woman. As for Uncle Billy—well, to look at him you'd think the first puff of wind would blow him over. He was past eighty, too, remember. Supposing that he had the necessary strength to overpower the woman, how could he have managed to carry her body to the grave in the chicken-house? That was a job for a strong man.

"You don't know anything about it, then?" I repeated.

"No, I don't. All I know is that she went away with the Dutchman."

That was his story, and he stuck to it. So, in company with Elmer Finley, Sheriff of Caddo County, Deputy Steve Steverson, and Assistant County Attorney Haskell Pugh, I loaded Uncle Billy into a car and started back to the farm. I figured that if anything would loosen his tongue the sight of his wife's grave would.

The yard of the place was thronged with the curious when we arrived. We drove through the gate, passed the house and stopped in front of the chicken-house. Steverson went in first, followed by Uncle Billy who walked between us. The old man started forward quickly.

"Curry—there is my shovel! Where did you find it?"

I caught hold of him, to prevent him from hurting himself or anyone else, if he were so minded.

"Uncle Billy," I said softly, "why in the world did you do this?"

He made no reply.

I led him out, toward the house, showed him the dried blood. He looked at it like a man in a trance, but remained silent. I allowed him to stand there a minute, then continued the slow march to the house, We passed more traces of blood, and started around to the front door where the lock had been broken. About five feet from the door, he spoke.

"Wait, Curry."

I stopped. "All right, Uncle Billy, I'm waiting."

He sniffled; started to cry.

"I didn't kill her, Curry. I struck her twice with a piece of pipe; once in the house, and once in the yard. We had quarreled. She got a butcher knife and ran me around the table. I hit her with this pipe, and knocked her down, and jumped in the bedroom and shut the door.

"She tried to get in. I opened the door quickly and she fell down. She had got the axe and still had the knife. I ran out over her and she ran me down to the chicken-house. I hit her again, and she didn't get up any more. There was a man standing by me when I looked around and I told him I would give him five dollars to take care of her, and he said he would. I paid him, and that is all I know."

I studied the old man carefully, an inkling of the real solution to the mystery creeping into my mind. Steverson and Pugh had come up and listened to the story.

"Who was this man who helped you?" I said.

"The Dutchman."

"That won't do, Uncle Billy. You've told part of the truth, have to have all of it: Who was the man?"

He hesitated. "All right. I'll tell you. It was Reed Norris, my son-in-law."

"Who else?"

"My first wife. She planned the job, and Reed and I did it."

You will note that he contradicted his first story here, wherein he stated that he was the attacked instead of the attacker. I made no comment on it.

"Why did you do it?" I asked.

"So Reed could move back on the place and take care of me."

"You're still holding out on me, Uncle Billy," I said. "Which one of you used the axe?"

"Well, Reed was in the room with me when I knocked her down with the pipe."

"Where was Reed standing when you knocked her down?"

"Standing right by me with the axe in his hand, but I didn't see him hit her."

Still another story! And all within the space of a few minutes.

We took Uncle Billy into Anadarko and placed him in jail.

As I have said before, Reed Norris and the first Mrs. Royce had been put in separate jails; they had been given no opportunity to get together and arrange concurring stories. But when Pugh, fortified by his talk with Uncle Billy, confronted them with their supposed misdeeds they promptly denied them. Furthermore, while their accounts of their doings on the fatal Friday of the murder disagreed on minor points, told substantially identical and satisfactory stories.

When questioned as to whether he had been on the farm the Wednesday the body was found, Norris at first asserted that he had not been. Then, he changed his mind and declared that he had been there for a few minutes, intending to take Uncle Billy a belated Christmas present. Not finding the old man at home, he went out to let the stock in to water, Uncle Billy having forgotten to do so.

His first hesitation on this point could probably be laid to the fact that he was nervous and excited. A man suddenly put into jail, is often to say definitely just where he has been and what he has done on given days.

Special detectives from the State Department of Investigation furnished proof of the pair's innocence. They went to Norge and made a thorough investigation of Norris' and Mrs. Royce's stories and found them to be absolutely true. They could have had nothing to do with the murder for they were in Norge at the time it happened.

Were they accessories to the act? No, neither before or after. And they had absolutely no motive. One half of the farm—eighty acres had been deeded to one of the Royce girls, several years before; the other half to Mrs. Royce. They had simply permitted the old man to stay on there, splitting the royalty from the oil well with him. Uncle Billy had had no right to will the land to his second wife. The first Mrs. Royce furnished deeds to show that the farm did not belong to him.

Mrs. Royce and Norris were promptly released with an official apology, which, like good citizens, they accepted.

Had Uncle Billy committed the crime alone, then?

He was capable of it. Remember, this was not an ordinary old man, used to an easy chair and house slippers. Uncle Billy had worked hard all his life. For thirty years, without missing a day, he had gone out into the Keechis and dug. Hard, manual labor, that. His appearance was deceiving. He was thin, but wiry. And having handled him, I can testify that this man who might have been eighty or ninety was unusually strong.

The motive?

Insane people do not need motives for their actions.

And Uncle Billy was insane. Waiting there in the Anadarko Jail, he told still another story of the tragedy. But no longer did he talk mildly, with a bold eye. His eyes rolled, and his voice rose to a screech.

"She found money! She found $5,000 buried on the farm, down in the valley just below the barn. When I asked her for part of it she told me that it was hers—that I should have none of it. She wouldn't give me my share, and we fought. I hit her, and she fell down. Then I dragged her into the hole in the hen house and covered her up."

Then he began to babble about the mythical Dutchman.

But was this the only murder the grim Keechis had witnessed? Did the little farm, on whose rocky acres Jesse James had camp, hold further grisly mysteries?

With the discovery of the body in the chicken-house grave, rumors that had lain somnolent for years sprang to life once more. What had become of the two young men who had stopped at the farm overnight; whose car now stood rusting in the barnyard? Where had they gone to?

If they were alive, why was the car still there?

And what of those two women—two of a long series of house-keepers—who had worked for Uncle Billy a few days each, and disappeared. Women, friendless and homeless, without relatives to make inquiry.

Where were they?

Uncle Billy's arrest had received national attention. Few could escape reading of it. Yet days passed, and none of the missing four came forward.

Questioned, the old man declared that each of the four had been back to visit him since their departure. And he was vehement in his denial that he had harmed any of them. But neighbors contradicted his statement.

Not one of the four had ever been back. Or, if they had been, Uncle Billy was the only person who could testify to the fact. No one else had seen them.

Why had the boys left their car? He couldn't say: that had been a long time ago. It was an old car. Maybe they hadn't wanted it any longer. As for the two housekeepers—well, they were fine women. He had liked both of them, and they had liked him.

He wouldn't hurt anyone.

But an oil company scout testified that the old man had shot him in the arm with a rifle. Another man had climbed the fence one day in search of a stout pole to pry his car out of the ditch—and had been marched back to the road at the point of Royce's gun.

How about those two? Uncle Billy scowled. They had been trying to his gold. He had given them what they deserved.

The Sunday following the discovery of the chicken-house grave, a large body of volunteers congregated at the farm to search for the bodies of the missing people. But it was an impossible task which they had set for themselves; a fact which I realized from the outset. Let me explain.

Uncle Billy had been digging on that farm for thirty years, and more. You could scarcely go half a dozen steps without stumbling into some depression he had dug in his search for treasure. Sometimes he had thrown the dirt back into the barren holes; sometimes he had not. But in every place that a person might look—in the sheds, the fields, the pigpen—were the marks of his pick and shovel. There were thousands of possible graves on that farm—figuring each excavation a grave; thousands of places where he had dug for a day, two days, or an hour.

Which of these thousand holes should be investigated? Where should the digging start?

There was only one answer. Unless Uncle Billy admitted the crimes of which he was suspected, and pointed out the unmarked graves) finding them would be practically impossible. True, the searchers did start digging, but when they gradually realized the enormity of their task, they loaded up their tools and departed one by one, until only a few remained.

Then, once again it was dusk; once more the looming Keechis grinned with scarlet. The scattered picks rattled slowly against the rocks, and spades, suddenly gone lazy, clung to the soil as if unseen hands reached up and gripped them. An aching, whining little wind rose out of the south, whispering weird and terrible things . . . .

Terror struck into the limbs of the stragglers. Across the serried and darkening fields they ran, toward the comforting safety of the highway.

If the hills had any secrets they kept them.

And so did Uncle Billy.

At his hearing, he was represented by Attorney H. W. Morgan, of Anadarko, who entered a plea of not guilty for the old man. At the same time, Mr. Morgan entered a plea to the Court for an insanity hearing. This was granted. On January 21st, 1935, a little over two weeks after the murder, he was brought before an insanity board of two Anadarko doctors, presided by County Judge Oris L. Barney.

There followed one of the most unique court procedures in the history of the State.

Under the law, if Uncle Billy was guilty of murder he could not be insane. Likewise, if he was insane he could not be guilty of murder, since the State does not hold the insane responsible for their acts.

But here was the contradiction. The old man's guilt was established; and it was also true, beyond a doubt, that he was insane. What could be done in a case of this kind? Would Royce escape the penalty of his crime?

Not at all. Judge Barney, who is one of the youngest judges in Oklahoma, ordered the murder charges withdrawn. The board then declared the old man insane, and he was duly committed to the State insane asylum at Fort Supply, Oklahoma.

Two weeks after he arrived there, he died.

He was a very old man, Uncle Billy Royce. Eighty or ninety. He couldn't rightly say which himself.

—Master Detective, April 1936

Appendix D: Hobo novel fragment by Jim Thompson.

This piece was written for the Federal Writer's Project. It is the last chapter in a proposed novel entitled Always To Be Blessed. *The novel was never completed, but the fragment garnered quite a bit of interest when it was published in* American Stuff *in 1937, an anthology of Federal Writer's Project prose and verse.*

THE END OF THE BOOK

When he awoke, rain was pattering on the metal roof of the old toolhouse; and a great gray rat was crouched in front of him, its beady eyes and saber teeth less than a foot from his face. He did not move a muscle and the rat remained transfixed. He watched a flea crawl over one of the browless lids, disappear behind a small flat ear, and the rat, as watchful, saw the lice weaving through the filthy forest of hair on his bared chest. Animal and animal eyed each other, expectantly, hopefully.

He had gone to sleep with his head pillowed on one arm-the animal called Lester Cummings. One hand was in the air, hang-ing over his head like the frond of a palm. Now he drew the fingers together into a knot, and dropped the bludgeon squarely on the rat. At the same time he let out a shrill shriek of triumph, adjunct to the blow of the hunter.

The rat screamed also. Terror poured through its tiny brain. Through pain-bright eyes it saw the front foot of the other animal -that strange white, hairless foot-rise again. And helpless to dodge, it felt the impact on spine and skull. Bones cracked and in the shoulder sockets the cartilage gave way: the two front legs flattened against the floor, tangent to the soft gray body. Blood trickled from the glistening black mouth. The pain was gone, now, and the rat moved his head freely, looked with wonder at the legs which should have been upright.

The paws of the other animal scooped him up and held him level with its laughing gray eyes. The mouth laughed, too, and saliva dripped from the corners. He came closer to the mouth, saw it open wider. His head passed through the opening, and he gazed down the concave hall of the throat. An instant only. Suddenly there was no light, no sound. Only something hard and sharp closing upon his neck. He felt his eyes leap from their sockets, his tongue crawl through his teeth. He felt the rush of blood from his jugular, jerked with the sudden energy of his heart. He felt. Then he felt no more. Wiping his mouth on the back of his hand, Lester Cummings crawled to the sagging door, nudged it open with his head, and peered out. The rain was coming down in sheets: curtain after curtain of wavering gauze falling drearily across the cotton rows. He stuck his head out further, lapped the wet boards with his tongue. He stretched out on the platform on his back, and opened his mouth; let the rain beat down his throat.

"I am thirsty. What other way have I of quenching my thirst?"

"You could catch some in a pail. Or a cup."

"Pail? Cup?"

"Of course. Those are the things to drink out of. Don't you remember?"

"I . . . ."

"Think hard."

"I do not want to think. You have been telling me all along that I must not. Now, you want me to."

"But the pail and the cup; surely you do not want them hang-ing in your memory without knowing what they are?"

"I know. I know what they are."

"And yet you lie here in the rain with your mouth open. Come!"

"Oh, God! I can't. I remember other things, now . . . . Annice."

"She is something you can forget. Come. You will get sick and die. I cannot allow that to happen."

"No. I suppose not."

"Good. Get to your feet-where you belong. Wipe the dirt from your face. Your hat inside the door there; fine."

"This is a strange place . . . ."

"Isn't it? It was pure luck that I found you. Row did you happen to come here?"

"I told Mom goodnight and went through the door to my bedroom. There was a train running through the closet and I got on and came down here."

"Ha, ha . . . . I see I shall have to leave you again. But was that all?"

"No; I have forgotten something. You . . . ."

"Never mind. You will have to go home. Mom will be worrying."

"But Mom is in Nebraska and this is Oklahoma."

"So! Perhaps I will stay with you after all . . . . Remember that little bridge you crossed last night just before you got here?"

"No. The train crossed no bridges."

"Oh. . . ."

"I tell you it didn't!"

"Ah, God! It is a pity to leave you, but I cannot help myself."

"What were you going to tell me about the bridge?"

"Quiet! Quiet! You have me so confused that I do not know what I am saying. Like the time—but we were to forget that. The bridge . . . . let's see, there is water under it. You could—ah, that is not right. Or is it? You see what you have done to me. But, listen. I will direct you the best I can . . . ."

Several times on his way through the cotton rows, Lester Cummings turned and looked back through the rain at the tall tower of the derrick. He had a feeling that if he did not look at it frequently it would vanish and he would be left in this dismal limbo of green cotton plants and drifting rain with no point of orientation. Above all was the feeling that he had forgotten something there; that some part of him had remained behind beneath the creaking metal roof of the tool-house. He thought once of going back to search for it; . but, seeing the barbed wire fence before him, he scrambled over it and stood in the road, looking curiously at the bleeding cuts on his hands.

The rain came down in torrents. In the fields the cotton sprang from the washed red soil like long lines of green flame from a flat bed of coals, and the Johnson grass and sunflowers rustled wetly in the wind. Birds huddled beneath the cross-bars of the singing telephone poles; cocks crowed in distant barns. And down the road, slipping from one side to the other on the wet clay, came a family of tenant farmers in their ancient car.

"Get out of the way, yuh crazy idjut!"

He looked at the shaking car calmly, and turned his back on it. The horn rasped angrily; the motor chattered. Indignant yells sounded in his ears. But he kept to the middle of the road, im-pervious to the tumult.

They crept along behind him for a hundred yards, the car and its occupants. Then, with an explosive curse, the raw-boned farmer stopped the motor and clambered over the door. He caught Lester Cummings by the shoulder and whirled him around.

"God dam yuh! Will yuh get outa the road an' let me by? Are yuh deef?"

"This man has snuff dripping from his lips. His son, that slant-jawed stripling with the jack-handle in his hand, would do you harm. And look at those two crones in the back seat, their faces the color of dirty leather beneath their sunbonnets . . . Well?"

"They are in my way . . . ."

"Of course. Reason enough for killing them. Then, look at the snuff and those sunbonnets."

"I thought you had left me."

"I could not see you tormented . . . . snuff, and sunbonnets; people getting in your way."

"What shall I do?"

"There is a knife in your pocket. You can open it with one hand. Quickly. His throat. That will stop the snuff from dripping."

"Paw! Get away from him! That's the . . . . help!"

"Yuh-yuh. I didn't do .... God ...."

"I knew the boy would run. You will not have to worry about him. Take your time now. The women cannot move. Up on the running-board—"

"What is this on my hands?"

"Rain. Even the road is red with it .... The old woman, now, while she is still asleep. And-wait a minute! This looks like Lois."

"It .... it is Lois!"

"I would not be too sure. Remember how you were fooled before. Lift her out of the car. Lay her there on the ground. That dress is rotten; it will tear easily. Now, do you still think it is Lois?"

"I should not be doing this."

"Ah, God! It is Lois. Kneel down by her. Kiss her lips, her breasts, take her into your arms. Hold her against your shoulder. That is good, isn't it? Just to hold her and protect her; let her sleep while you stand guard. All these days, these months, these years, and now you are together again. It was a long time but it is past now. Remember the last day of school when you walked home together? Remember the night you drove your new car around to her house? Remember the lane with the tall elms, the elms dripping diamonds of sunshine from their leaves, the robins teetering on the fence wires, the grass singing in the wind? Ah, God! And the little apartment over the drugstore. The smell of hot coffee on a cold morning. Hands ruffling your hair, probing your ribs, tickling you into wakefulness. Remember the days when you lived for the nights, the nights with Lois asleep on the lounge while you sat at the kitchen table poring over your corre-spondence course in accounting. Remember the kindly gloom of the street light drifting through your window, drawing your strug-gling shadows upon the wall until you laughed at your own antics. And went to sleep. Remember rising on your elbow to look at her; the slow, instinctive opening of her eyes, those serene brown eyes, round and shadowed with love and happiness .... Ah, God! Do not speak! Let me give back what has been taken from you. Her nose is not flat and negroid as you see it,' her hair is not a stringy mass of wool, green with dirt at the roots; her breasts are not brown with sun and rust. She is clean, clean and pure as you re-membered her .... Good, you are smiling; that happy jaunty smile I had almost forgotten. You have pulled your hat over one eye, straightened your shoulders. And you are rising, lifting Lois. with you. You are going back home together. Ah, God! Mom will be glad to see you. A small change in directions, now .... Those men getting out of the car; that fellow in the black hat, settling on one knee, lifting the long barrel of a rifle .... Never mind; you ,cannot get to the bridge, but the ditch leads into the creek; that will do as well. You read this years ago and you remember now. Ten billion years ago you selected the way home, when you should need it; stored it away in your memory

against all time. The map spread out before you, then, spread out with its hills and waterways, its cities and villages, its tall towers and trees and roll-ing plains . . . . The noise! That numbing, grinding pain in your skull! And your hat is gone! Stoop! Pick it up! You cannot go home without your hat. Never mind if you stumble; it will be hours before you strike the water, and you have held on to Lois . . . . Now, as I tell you! Down this ditch to the creek; down the creek to the. Washita; down the Washita to the Red River; down the Red River to the Mississippi; up the Mississippi to the Mis-souri; up the Missouri to . . . ."

"Oh, Mom! Here we are!"

Ridden in a Dodge lately?
Then you're in for a thrill!

"Romance, shooting, and even a bit of grave-robbing."
--New York Times Book Review

THE LONG ESCAPE

David Dodge
Author of
TO CATCH A THIEF & DEATH AND TAXES

BRUIN CRIMEWORKS

INTRODUCTION BY RANDAL S. BRANDT

A beautiful tribute to the beloved Dell Map Books
Other David Dodge titles available—
TO CATCH A THIEF and DEATH AND TAXES

Bruin Books is Branching Out!
Grand Opening in Spring 2013

BRUIN ASYLUM

The finest amenities available:

- Straightjackets
- Bite Restraints
- Mandrake Tea served Daily at 4 PM
- Colorful Hallucinogens
- Helpful Orderlies with *Mommy Issues*
- Scary Stories at Bedtime
- Phantom Screamers

Make your reservations today!

www.ingramcontent.com/pod-product-compliance
Lightning Source LLC
Chambersburg PA
CBHW030839030726
47495CB00005B/1291

9 780988 306219